KINGDOM OF VILLAINS

ELLA FIELDS

Editor: Jenny Sims, Editing4Indies
Formatting: Stacey Blake, Champagne Book Design
Cover design: Sarah Hansen, Okay Creations

For those who forge their own path with empathy,
bravery, and love

ONE

THE DUNGEON WAS SUPPOSED TO BE EMPTY.

Three floors above, the revelry grew in volume. It was always this way after the annual meeting of the two courts, and I'd been counting on the distraction since yesterday. Until this afternoon, the castle had been too tense, everyone on edge and alert as they'd readied for my uncle's return and the inevitable celebration he expected after his travels.

And so I'd waited.

Only to have my plans foiled by some nuisance street thief who'd been caught.

Standing in the shadows, I leaned against the door, weighing my options. The babes squirmed in my arms, tucked within a thick horse blanket. Sadly, there were only three, the rest of the litter dead by the time I'd discovered them during my morning walk yesterday.

Upon finding them, I'd raced back through the forest and into the maze of roses, thorns snatching and ruining my skirts from hurtling over top of a few bushes. I'd ignored the amused glances of the sentinels roaming the grounds and courtyard. And I'd done so again—or perhaps they'd merely ignored me—as I'd returned some minutes later with supplies.

No one had asked any questions, nor did anyone follow me to the forest. Accustomed to my wanderings and curiosities, of which my uncle said I should've long left behind with my youth, they seldom did. Although I knew the grain and water and blankets would help, I also knew they would not be enough. Snow had started to fall, and all too soon, winter would bloom its deathly beauty in full.

The prisoner shifted, and as my eyes adjusted to the near dark, I saw him leaning against the wall, his head hung between his knees.

The two narrow rows of cells often went unused. I'd visited the dungeon enough to know this thief was likely only being held until my uncle had returned from the meeting of the courts to decide his fate. Those caught committing crimes found themselves indebted to the crown, put into service, or executed—depending on the severity.

I looked at the cell across from the prisoner's. The blankets and small bowls of water and grain were thankfully still waiting in the corner. Whoever he was, the guards had apparently been too distracted or hadn't cared to notice much else.

A low growl, similar to a kitten but with more grit, caught the prisoner's attention.

I hushed the babe attempting to nudge its head free of the blanket and looked away when the prisoner's head turned. "Time for bed," I whispered, my steps echoing through the damp expanse of iron and stone and ghosts. The guards would eventually return to check on the male. But there was little else to do unless I hid the narlow infants in my rooms.

Impossible. I could scarcely hide a beetle, courtesy of the castle staff. It was too late to think of another hiding place. I'd have to leave them here overnight and decide what to do with them come morning.

"A visitor?" the prisoner asked, his voice both gruff and rich. "Or a gawker? Which might you be?"

My feet stilled, and my spine locked. The audacity. "None of your business, thief."

"What has convinced you that I'm a thief?"

Lowering to the floor, I carefully set the babes on the ground, catching one when it began to crawl away. "You're in a cell," I said as if he were daft. "So if I were you, I'd be quiet. Unless you wish to start bleating your pleas to the goddess."

Though the words were low, humor drenched each one. "Is that a threat?"

"No wonder you wound up here," I muttered, showing the narlows to the bowls of water and grain. "Utterly stupid." Only two of them were interested, the smaller creature's eyes closing as it curled upon the bedding.

He laughed as he said, "It was a joke, fire-breather."

"Spend more time praying you won't die and less being an idiot."

A snort had me whirling to glare at him. Words fell into fragments over my lips.

Eyes of gold so pure and bright, as if they'd been dipped in gilded honey, narrowed.

It was then that my shock and annoyance faded enough for me to pay attention to his scent. Geranium and oak with an edge of soot.

Boots, pointed and leather, still covered his feet. A dark plum cloak was draped over him like a blanket. His raven, shoulder-length hair shined within the dim light of the sconce above the door I'd entered through next to his cell.

A criminal's hair would not shine.

But it was his features that truly gave me pause. As shadowed as they were, I saw enough. Those eyes, the severity of the sharp lines of his cheeks, and his strong jaw.

A part of me wondered if the luminosity of his gaze made him easier to see in the shadows.

It was my turn to ask, "Who are you?" I had a feeling he was not a thief at all. Not with clothing and a face like that. Not to mention his cultured tone and rotten attitude.

My heartbeat slowed, then grew faster. He wasn't from Callula. The scent and eyes alone confirmed as much.

Rather than answer, the stranger shifted his lupine gaze to my side, to where one of the babes had crawled. Cursing, I carefully grabbed and held it within my cupped hands. "They need their mother," he said. "Her pouch and her milk."

He didn't get to do that—make me feel worse for them than I already did while evading what I'd asked. Leaning against the stone wall, I placed the babe in my lap and reached for the other two. "I asked you a question."

A thick brow rose. "You must be the princess."

"What gave me away?" I said with heaping sarcasm, stroking a finger between the sleepy narlow's membranous, pointed ears. It nuzzled into my touch, fuzzy black hair softening around its pig-like nose.

"One would have to be exceptionally daring or a part of the royal family to bring forbidden creatures into Callula Castle." He paused, then said, "My name is Colvin."

My blood turned a shade colder, my eyes slowly meeting his. "As in *Prince* Colvin?"

Moon above, it couldn't be. That the Unseelie prince would be held prisoner here, or anywhere—

He nodded once.

"But…" I shook my head, more confused than I was afraid. "Why?" Callula and Eldorn had been at peace for many millennia. To capture royalty was an act of war—an act of pure stupidity.

To capture and imprison the Prince of Eldorn was a signed death warrant.

My uncle was cold, insufferably, and naïvely narcissistic, but he was no fool. So what beneath the rotting moon had happened?

"I don't wholly understand it all myself," the prince finally said. "But Mother said I am to behave and remain here until some type of agreement can be forged."

"Regarding what?"

His lips curled, eyes alight as they flicked to mine. "Me."

I swallowed and immediately looked away.

Surely, there was a good reason. Perhaps the Kingdom of Eldorn owed our kingdom a debt, and once it was paid, the prince would be released. I knew little about politics, despite my uncle's insistence I learn as it was indeed my future. But given the peaceful climate the two kingdoms of Gwythorn had maintained for so long, he seldom cared himself unless he had to.

The prince's gaze burned as my mind whirled.

"Why do I feel there's far more to this than you're willing to say?"

"Because you have good instincts," he said, silken and low.

I bristled and shivered, refusing to succumb to the temptation to look at him. Tricksters, all of them, and in such wretchedly wicked ways at that. There was every chance he could lure me into setting him free.

Rumors of the Unseelie prince had reached the farthest corners of Gwythorn. It was said that he would bed no less than two females at once and that even at his young age of twenty and three, he had a revolving harem of lovers.

I had no idea if that were true, though I didn't doubt that the other rumors were. All had been repeated with such zest so often. Rumors that stated he did nothing but hide away for days at a time to fuck, hunt for trespassers in their nightmare-ridden kingdom, and ride with the wild hunt into the mortal lands across the Crystal Sea to conduct trade.

But the most common talk of all when it came to Prince Colvin of Eldorn was his ability to wield a fire so deadly, it could wipe out entire forests.

Perhaps he'd done just that, which was highly illegal, not to mention so deeply immoral that none of our ilk would comprehend, and his mother had been given no choice. The queen had needed to hand him over.

Colvin's mother adored him, my aunt had told me once when I'd dared to ask after overhearing Sylvane and Orla gossiping about him. So much so, she let him do as he wished. Aunt Mirra had a gleam in her eye as she'd said that, making it clear she knew what I got up to in my spare time.

A faint dripping echoed throughout the narrow cells. He knew. This prince knew exactly why he was here. Curiosity scraped talons over my mind, and I couldn't stop myself from asking, "Did you murder someone?"

"Not recently." He said it so quick and firmly that I believed him. Even if I shouldn't have.

"The mother is dead," I said, for something to smother the tense silence that followed. "Not a trace of her left save for blood droplets in the snow. Hunters, most likely." And it was also likely that her hide had already been sold under a market table.

A low curse. "They cannot do that. Narlows are native to Eldorn."

"Perhaps you should have a word with them about roaming too far from home then, Prince." He had to know that anything considered a threat in the wrong territory was fair game, as unfair as it sometimes was. "Besides, it's likely that many of our own creatures meet the same fate. Rules are rules, regardless of whether they are understood."

Silence permeated, and I felt him watching as I folded the horse blanket tight around the nest I'd made. "But you don't understand them, do you, Fia?"

My name wrapped in his voice delivered an unexpected dipping in my stomach. I told myself it was from eating too little dinner as I carefully placed the narlows in their bed. "I understand them just fine." Smirking over at him, I said, "Fine enough to know how to bend them."

His mouth curved, eyes steadfast on mine. They lowered to the bed I'd made a moment later. Heat crept into my cheeks, so I was thankful, even if he might not have seen due to the lack of light. "I'll keep an eye on them."

"I suppose your schedule is very clear." Unwilling to leave them but knowing I would have to before someone checked my rooms for me, I said quietly, "But what can you do if something happens to them?" Whatever his gruesome abilities may be, he couldn't do much trapped behind the thick grate of iron bars.

The prince took his time to answer, his words gentle as if he knew I didn't want to hear them and his promise had been for nothing but false comfort. "Really, there is not much either of us can do. They fight, or they don't."

My eyes filled, and staring down at the narlows, I nodded. It was late, and most would be intoxicated or asleep, so I walked to the stairs that would take me up into the innards of the castle.

"Someone is stationed outside the door atop those stairs at

night," the prince called softly. "They only leave when another comes to replace them."

Back through the forgotten gardens it was then, I decided with a sigh. I would then need to use the kitchen entry and stumble about and feign being drunk should anyone be in there. I'd done so enough times before that I was somewhat of an expert.

The door, heavy and swollen with disuse, opened to ivy-and-moss-carpeted steps hidden deep behind an overgrown hedge. I paused. "Tell a soul about the narlows, and you'll fear more than potential execution, Prince."

Silence.

But just as I was about to close the door, he said with humor lilting his deep tone, "They'll need beef or chicken broth."

TWO

"WHERE BENEATH THE ROTTING MOON HAVE YOU been?"

Shit.

Regin.

Quickly, I tucked the bowl of broth behind the chipped statue of a Pegasus and feigned checking my slipper. "Oh, hello."

"Hello?" he asked, puzzled.

Standing, I brushed my hands over my spotted ivory skirts, which were already marred even though I'd only been awake and dressed for an hour. Typical for me, much to my aunt's and seamstress's dismay, so Regin only scrutinized my face. "Are you well?"

"Since when is greeting you a crime?" I walked past him, unable to meet his teal green eyes. I'd need to lose him then return for the broth. We'd been friends since we could walk. I could trust him, but something told me not to be so quick to trust him with this.

"Since you've never done so." He caught up with me. "Not really. What's wrong with you?"

"Nothing is wrong with me," I said with a forced laugh. "Why are *you* acting so strange?"

He sniffed. "Why do you smell like bad meat?"

Usually, I'd have laughed in earnest. But lately, I'd found myself watching him a little too long, imagining just a little too much for that of a friend. So sarcasm got the better of me. "Why, thank you, Regin. Always an absolute pleasure."

"Wait, Fi." He clasped my hand. "Okay, I'll quit badgering."

I eyed him pointedly, my fingers longing to curl around his. I let them, just slightly.

His teeth flashed, cream brows low. "Right after you tell me where you were last night? I thought we were watching the stable hands jump the fencing again."

It was an incredibly entertaining pastime, given how sloshed all of them liked to get. But I was still a bit annoyed, and I was still needed elsewhere. "We're not kids anymore, Regin."

"Precisely why I was hoping we could find something else to do afterward," he said in a rush, then swallowed. "But you never showed."

Absorbing what I feared and hoped he'd meant, I could only stare. "I... well—"

Tugging me closer, he tucked a strand of hair behind my ear, his roughened fingertip lingering over the arch. "Meet me later?" I blinked, scarcely able to believe this was happening—to understand exactly what *was* happening. He smirked and dragged his finger down my blooming cheek to my jaw, retracting it just shy of my lips. "I'll take that as a yes."

He was walking away before I could remember what words were, let alone say something.

Stunned, I watched him head down the hall toward a hidden exit between two sitting rooms. Since he was the captain of the guard's son, he knew my home as if it were his own. Terror barreled through me at the thought of the memories we'd made within these sandstone walls and the thought of all these years culminating into a fate of something more, or...

One that might ruin a friendship forever.

Then I remembered the broth and raced back to retrieve it.

The princely prisoner was wide awake and watching the narlows scurry and snuffle at the ground of their cell. "I don't think the sleepy one will make it."

My heart stuttered, but I swallowed and clipped, "We'll see," and opened the door I hadn't locked.

The two active babes wasted no time, finding the broth bowl and crawling into it to drink. "You're not supposed to swim in it." Laughing, I plucked them out but gave in when it became clear they would do as they pleased.

The prince was sadly right. The remaining narlow was still curled up in the blankets. "Maybe it just needs to rest and regain some of what it lost to the cold."

"Perhaps it was too much. They dwell in deep caves and huddle with their mother until they outgrow her pouch."

"More blankets then," I fired back, unsure why I was so unwilling to let nature run its course when it was already happening. I picked up the sickly narlow and placed it on the ground before the bowl, the prince's attention like barbed fencing skimming my back.

It was him. His voice. His unexplained presence. His annoyingly smug gaze that never left me.

It was the way I felt somewhat nauseated with just one glimpse or whiff of him. A poison.

He was trying to toy with me somehow, but it wasn't working. Not entirely, courtesy of the iron bars that weakened his strength and, therefore, his powers.

As I feared, the narlow wouldn't eat. Mercifully, Colvin kept his thoughts to himself while I dipped my finger into the bowl and gently placed it on the babe's nose. It sniffed, wriggling in the cup of my hand.

Then curled into my finger.

I dabbed the broth on its tiny mouth, smiling when the babe licked it, then frowned as it went to bite my finger but huddled into my hand instead.

For some minutes, I sat there and stroked its back, willing the rabbit-like tail to twitch and the creature to do something. "Rest, then," I whispered and placed it back in the pouch of blankets.

A little shriek and growl had me removing the other two from the now empty bowl. They squirmed, riddled with renewed energy and covered in broth. One clambered down my arm to the floor in search of more food but found only the grain and water.

"May I?" said the prince, and I'd almost forgotten he was there.

Turning, I pushed to my knees.

He'd extended his hand through the bars.

I stared at it, then at the creature in my hands. Though if he'd intended them harm, he wouldn't have been so appalled by their mother's fate. He wouldn't have told me to bring the broth, which had evidently helped.

Two of them, at least.

Carefully rising to my feet, I carried the narlow to his cell.

Our skin brushed as I placed it in his hand, which was large enough to cover the entire babe when he curled his fingers and brought it to his chest. "I haven't seen a narlow in years."

Brushing my hands over my skirts, I checked on the other babe crawling back into the nest of blankets. "I suppose you've been too busy causing enough mayhem to wind up in a dungeon to notice much."

He ignored my barb. "The western forests are rich with moisture, less dense with our ilk's population, leaving them more confident to breed and burrow." Colvin brought the creature close to his face, trailing a long, thick finger over its fuzzy back when it protested. "This one's a male."

Stunned, I found myself watching him for far too long. The careful brush of his finger over the babe's back and head. The way his cheeks grew sharper when they rose with his laugh as the narlow chewed on the tip of his finger.

A throaty melody, yet as rich as the gold in his eyes, his laughter was unlike any I'd heard before.

His smile waned. He looked over at me, and I noted a drop of dried blood above his upper lip before I quickly turned away. "Did someone come down here this morning?"

"Yes, though only briefly."

I closed my eyes, knowing it was foolish to keep the cubs here any longer. "I'll look for a new place for them. It's a miracle they weren't noticed."

"I veiled them."

I spun back to face him. "How did you do that?"

With a curl of his fingers, shadows crawled from the corners of the ceiling in his cell, swirling in roaming darkness toward his hand.

I blinked, then blinked again. I'd seen many impressive things born from the magic of this land, but this…

I could understand why the Unseelie were often thought of as unnatural and dangerous.

"The iron bars are supposed to stop you from using magic." Though I couldn't deny, no matter how unearthly, that I was grateful they hadn't.

"The shadows are already there, fire-breather. I merely encourage them to move."

I eyed his upper lip. "That is why your nose bled."

A slow nod, his long lashes dipping as he inspected my skirts with a twitch of his lips.

I cared not. He could find me humorous all he wanted. He wouldn't be the first nor the last. "What's it like?" I asked, taking the babe back. "To have powers."

His hand pressed against mine, and I bristled, knowing it was intentional. More of that barely suppressed humor rode along his voice. "Your lot has them, too."

Carrying the narlow to his siblings, I scoffed. "I would hardly call helping flowers and crops grow power."

"I would disagree."

And looking back at him, the earnest stillness of his eyes, I could sense he truly did.

"I cannot even do that." Taking a seat next to the mound of blankets, I cleared my throat and shifted my skirts into my lap. "And that's okay, I suppose, but I wish I could do something. Somehow do more."

I'd spent years trying not to lament my fate. Trying to ignore the odd sense of missing something I'd never known. The envy that would strike when I witnessed my uncle and peers convince vines to grow like giant snakes or turn a hillside of snow into soil at the touch of a finger.

His lips curved. "Like rescue doomed creatures?"

"I don't need magic to help them," I said. "But those of noble blood shouldn't remain holed up in these hills when they could be putting their abilities to use."

"A blessing and a curse," he murmured. "To have so much as a drop of royal blood in your veins."

I stared at him, frowning.

The door at the top of the stairs opened with a groan, and I froze in fear. Colvin clicked his fingers, his eyes wide. "Go," he mouthed.

Jumping to my feet, I ran. The door leading to the gardens mercifully cooperated without too much noise, and I slumped to the bottom step outside. Leaves and dirt gathered in my hands over the stone as I waited and listened.

"Out pretty princeling, and no funny business, or my friend Peldon here might gut you like the monster you are."

Scuffing steps. Creaking. Metal dragging over stone.

"Clean it," hissed Peldon, followed by more scuffing and the sound of sloshing water.

Laughter. Scrubbing. My eyes narrowed as I tried to picture what they were doing. Standing, I pressed my ear against the door, but I didn't hear much else. I waited, every muscle stiff and ready for action. But what could I even do? Reveal myself and potentially the narlows? Make it seem as though I'd been checking in on the prince?

No. I had to trust that Colvin would conceal the cubs and take care of himself. Even so, I lowered back to the step and waited, wincing a little when I heard Colvin curse and more laughter from the guards.

Some minutes later, they left, and I made myself do the same. I was late for needlework with my aunt, which mainly consisted of her eating sweets and gossiping while I pricked my fingers and ruined the garments I was supposed to be creating.

I wasn't sure why such a thing was even necessary. I was a princess with numerous tailors at my disposal.

Aunt Mirra called it "Another tedious family tradition."

Most other males and females in our family lineage could mend and create anything. I'd spent many an hour trapped in the stuffy lesson room wondering if I hadn't any talents because my mother had died while delivering me.

Regin had said that was ludicrous and nothing but a worn-out myth.

Aunt Mirra had made a contemplative face while pointing her smoking stem at me. "You might just be onto something there."

That evening, I laid my book down when a knock sounded on the door. "Princess Fia?" Glenn, the steward, called. "You forgot dinner." He muttered, knowing full well I could hear, "Again."

"Sorry," I forced out when he opened the door. "I'll be down soon."

"No need," he said, his slow gait agonizing to watch as he carried the tray to the table. At least it gave me plenty of time to mark my page and turn the book facedown on the nightstand. "Your uncle's conducting some business in his study with the captain, and your aunt ate early, so you may as well enjoy it here."

The scent of baked potato, steamed beans, and pork wafted through the room before he removed the lid with a trembling hand. He'd never say exactly how old he was, but rumor had it he was well over one thousand years.

Offering help would only insult him, so I sat on my hands and waited for him to finish his fussing with the cutlery and water. "Thank you."

Glenn nodded, shuffling back to the door. "Oh, and Mr. Regin was looking for you earlier."

Crud.

Moon blasted, rotten star-crusted *crud*.

It must have been while I was perusing the forbidden archives in the cellar below the library for my book on Unseelie beasts.

The door closed, and I rushed to the food as my stomach gurgled with hunger. It was late, too late to search for Regin when he'd have gone home after training. Chewing unnecessarily hard, I swallowed and pulled aside the lace curtains covering the circular window behind the table.

Down the hill, the city of Callula lined the river in the shape of a crescent moon. For years growing up, Regin would call it the canoe.

The sapphire water fell from the mountains backing the castle to wend through the villages and forests. In one of the villages just outside of the city, a small manor watched over the fields and forests across the river. I couldn't see it through the swaying trees and patchwork of huts, homes, and buildings, but I knew exactly where it was all the same.

I had to see him. Lest he thought something was wrong with me. Well, more so than usual. Excitement bubbled at the thought of sneaking out to throw stones at his bedroom window. It had been too long since I'd last done so.

Surely, just that would be enough to make him smile and forget that I'd forgotten.

And maybe, if I could find the courage, a kiss.

I'd never admit to him or anyone that I'd spent many months desperately wanting to kiss him.

The more I thought about it, the more my stomach shrank. It curdled when a pair of molten gold eyes breached my imaginings, and I set my fork down to gulp an entire glass of water.

Right. The narlows.

First, I had to check on them. *And maybe change*, I thought, wiping gravy from the breast of my gown.

I shrugged, lacking the energy to care. Regin had seen me covered in mud. He'd also seen me covered in vomit when a Jilgen—a wildflower used at celebrations—had exploded in my face, its glittering pollen and petals blocking my airways. He'd even been there when I'd woken with my first bleed while we'd been camping in the woods.

So he hadn't handled that last part very well—his face ghostly and his feet moving faster than I'd ever seen before when I'd asked for help, and he'd thought it best to fetch my aunt—but I would be hard pressed to find a male who would.

At the door, I paused and looked at the book I'd left on the dresser. Backtracking, I hid it in the loose rock of the floor under my bed. My carelessness or any curious staff would not thwart this new rescue.

The moon kissed the silverware on the table through the window as I rose and dusted my hands over my stomach, the glint snagging my attention. Indeed, the moon always knew best, so I took what remained of my dinner with me.

The hall outside my rooms was silent.

I was the only one who occupied this side of the third floor. It didn't take me long to learn to appreciate the isolation rather than lament the eternal loneliness. My aunt and uncle's chambers were on the opposite side, the main stairway of the castle between us. They slept in different rooms, but they still connected via a door Aunt Mirra liked to keep locked.

I sometimes used the staff stairwell a little ways down the hall from my rooms to avoid detection. But tonight, I'd rather take my chances with my aunt or uncle than bump into any gossiping males and females still finishing up their duties for the day.

The grand doors to the king's rooms were wide open, which meant he was indeed busy with Karn. I hacked at the thought of Regin's ever-scowling father but smiled as I sped down the azure carpet on the sandstone steps, wholly undetected.

The second floor was aflutter with remaining preparations for the next day, but everyone was too busy chattering inside the rooms, so no one paid me any mind.

On the ground floor, I ran out of luck.

I withheld a curse, nearly smacking face-first into my aunt.

"By the fucking moon, Fifi, we've spoken about this." Brushing her fingers down the frilled bodice of her cream nightgown, Mirra inspected the open liquor bottle in her hand. "You really must watch where you're going. You never know when someone might have just stolen a one-of-a-kind malt from a certain lewd lord's guest chamber."

I bit my lips, clutching the plate so tight to my stomach that it began to hurt. "Of course."

Mirra flicked a golden ringlet from her cheek, eyeing my left-over dinner. "Don't help the staff. They'll talk rotten filth about you. Here." She gestured for the plate. "It will go nicely with my night-cap. I've heard that apprentice cook Adon just hired likes to try her hand at hexes."

By nightcap, she meant the entire bottle. I couldn't say I blamed her. My mother had been her sister and only true friend. Now, she was left with a husband who was always too busy meddling in obnoxious court dramatics to care much about what his wife got up to.

"I'm getting seconds," I said for lack of a better excuse, and then I hurried down the hall to the door that would take me to the kitchens a level below.

Mirra's shrill voice trailed me even after the door had closed. "You're a lousy liar, Fifi."

She was the only soul who got away with calling me that. Mostly because I couldn't control her. No one could, and no one dared to try.

I followed the narrow hall past the kitchens into the growing dark and stood around the corner from the iron door. There, I waited and listened, unable to sense anyone on guard duty yet for the night.

Rounding the stone wall, I snatched the keys from the hook. The door unlocked with an echoing crack of metal, and I flinched, hoping no one in the kitchens had heard.

Silence.

Smiling, I rehung the keys and slipped into the stairwell before the heavy door closed. The stone passage beyond had been carved from the earth, slippery with soil as I rounded the tight curl of steps. Two sconces were lit at either exit of the dungeon, providing precious little light to guide the way as my eyes slowly acclimatized.

"She returns," the prince said by way of greeting, and for a prisoner with an uncertain future, he didn't seem the least bit morose. His eyes lifted from the fingers clasped between his knees, brightening as they beheld me. "Pity it's merely for the narlows."

"Flattery won't be of any help to you, Prince."

"Who says it's merely flattery?"

I ignored that, the silken air in his playful tone, and opened the narlow's cell. "What did they make you do? The guards."

"Clean my pail. Suppose I should consider myself lucky that was all."

"I wouldn't call that lucky." I made a face as I sat upon the cold ground, the cubs immediately stirring. "That's disgusting." The two lively creatures crawled free of the blankets and barreled toward me and the pork strips I'd ripped up. I placed them in the empty bowl that'd held the broth, their little nails scratching in a frenzy over the stone as they left my lap for the food.

"It's reasonable. I am a prisoner."

That he was, yet I looked down at the plate I'd placed on the floor beside me. After checking on the narlow still inside the blankets, I slid what remained of the food under the bottom rung of iron bars into Colvin's cell.

It was only vegetables since all the meat was given to the narlows.

But the prince blinked, his brows low, then picked up the plate. "I'd ask if it's poisoned, but I know you'd never let any near those narlow cubs."

"I'm willing to wager most poisons would barely give you an ugly cough."

Colvin paused in selecting a potato, his eyes gleaming over at me. "There's a poison for everyone, Princess."

Unsure if he'd meant that as a bad thing, I frowned, then focused on the squabbling narlows. Once they each had a piece of pork, I checked on the sleepy one again and picked it up to try offering some food.

"How did you know they could eat pork?"

"A book I remembered stumbling across years ago while playing in the forbidden cellar of the library."

There was no response for some time, but I could feel his eyes on me as I continued to nudge the tiny piece of pork at the narlow's nose.

"How exactly do you plan on keeping them hidden when, in just a season, they'll be over eight feet tall and as wide as two full-grown males?"

He was right. It would be impossible, and that I was failing to find them a more suitable home for even the time being stung like nettles. "Haven't thought that far ahead yet," I said through teeth I tried to keep from gritting. "Obviously."

A snort. "Obviously."

"But I've been reading."

"Dangerous thing, that."

My brows scrunched. "I take it your lot don't spend much time with books."

"We read," he said, licking his fingers. The sight held me captive as he murmured softly, "Some might even say I read far too much."

Unable to imagine that, to make it fit with all I'd heard of him, I found myself lost. Lost and still staring at his lips, damp with mint gravy, because I could also envision it clearly—this prince lounging on furs upon the floor before a fire with a book.

His long, slightly crooked nose flared as his gaze swung my way.

Though I should, I couldn't bring myself to look away. His sooty, butterfly-like lashes lowered, and I cursed when a narlow attempted to climb my stomach in search of more food.

"You were reading," he prompted, and I was grateful to have my attention taken away so that I didn't see the smile I could hear in his voice.

"Yes." I cleared my throat. "About where they live. I'm trying to think of a place for them to stay. At least until they've grown enough to stand a chance at survival."

"And then what?"

I clutched the narlow to my chest. "They fight, or they don't."

"Does that pain you, Fia?" The question was a velvet touch of a blade.

"Of course it does," I spat. "I might be spoiled, but I have a heart."

"Your heart has claws." But the soft insult didn't strike me as

one should, and when I dared to meet his glowing gaze, I understood it wasn't one.

His smirk faded, dark hair falling from behind his arched ear to
curtain his shadowed features. "Fia," he murmured as though tasting
my name. My heart skipped when he confirmed as much by asking,
"What's your middle name?"

"Primrose."

He moved the plate to the corner of the cell. "After your mother?"

"Yes, although I do wish it was my first name."

"What's wrong with Fia?"

I half rolled my eyes. "Besides the obvious?" I hissed when the
narlow bit me and set it back in the bedding. "Your teeth are getting
too sharp too quickly, little pig." Snatching the other narlow before
it wandered out of the cell, I put the babe into the bed with its siblings. "I don't know," I answered his question. "I just thought they'd
have picked another flower, you know, to better honor her maybe."

"You would prefer to be named after a flower?" I nodded, dusting off my skirts though it was pointless. "Fia suits you."

"Liar." I narrowed my eyes but smiled just a little.

"Not lying, fire-breather." His lopsided smile sent my stomach
swooping. "Or perhaps I should call you Violet."

I frowned. "Why?"

"Your eyes." The breath-robbing words had barely left his mouth
when his own eyes shot behind him, expression hardening as he heard
it first. A rustle growing in volume from outside.

"Fia?" Regin. "Fi, where the shit are you?"

I looked toward the unused door, then back at the prince. He
jerked his head toward it, though his jaw was clenched.

It seemed Regin hadn't gone home after all.

As quietly as I could, I closed the cell and then hurried to the
door, nearly knocking Regin over when I threw my shoulder into it
so it would open.

He stumbled back, grabbing the steps behind him before his
rear smacked them. "Fuck, Fi."

I squeezed past the door to close it. "What are you doing here?"

Regin straightened, cursing when I slipped by him and up the stairs. "What am I doing here?" he asked, incredulous, and followed. "I think the better question is, what are *you* doing down there?"

"I wasn't doing anything."

"Then why didn't you show at lunch or dinner?"

He reached my side, and we stopped above the stairs. "I've been busy, okay?"

"With what? Playing games in the dungeon?" His head shook, features twisting with annoyance. "You haven't collected another stray, have you?" When I failed to answer, he groaned. "You said it yourself, Fi. We're not kids anymore. Time to quit playing mother to all monsters."

Tears burned my throat, but I refused to let them fill my eyes.

To avoid a partial truth would mean giving myself away entirely. It was clear Regin knew nothing of the Unseelie prince sitting in a cell mere feet below the ivy-tangled steps. If his father had not told him, I had to assume it was for a good reason.

"You're right. So…" I gathered my skirts and walked into the clustered gardens. "If you'll excuse me."

His footsteps crunched behind me. "Fi, come on. You know I didn't mean to be cruel."

I waded through the wild dusting of overgrown shrubs and wisteria, the long rock-paved drive at the front of the castle in view through the curtain of a willow tree.

Then my arm was clasped. I was thrown around, my waist caught in Regin's firm grip.

"Don't you get it?" His chest heaved with a rough exhale, his eyes flitting back and forth between mine. "I'm just trying to soothe my ego." At my frown, he licked his lips and sighed. "You were supposed to meet me, and you didn't show." He swallowed. "Again."

"Oh," I breathed, now understanding why he'd lashed out at me.

But even knowing that I'd left him feeling some sort of way with my absence, it didn't remove the sting of his earlier tone and words.

"It wasn't intentional. You know I want to..." But for all the daring thoughts and imaginings I'd had, I couldn't seem to voice a thing.

"Want to what?"

My stomach squeezed. "Well, I've wondered if maybe we..."

"If we could what, Fi?" Regin urged, low and heated. "I need you to actually say what you want instead of running from me."

My chest tightened, a slimy feeling itching at my innards. "You know what? I don't want anything." I stomped away. "So just forget about it."

"I'm afraid I cannot do that."

I stepped over a small pile of branches hidden beneath the ferns and continued toward the front of the castle. "We're good friends, Regin. Let's not ruin that."

"Well, if we're such good *friends*," he said, reaching my side. "Since when do you do your crazy shit without telling me?"

"Since you don't care for the crazy shit I like to do anymore." The words hung between us, sour but true, and I knew. I just knew we were doomed before we'd even started.

This time, he didn't follow me.

Perhaps it was for the best, the ensuing onslaught of regret for my words be damned.

THREE

"**M**OTHER OF MONSTERS." THE PRINCE'S VOICE FLOATED like a sheet of silk over the skin. "Much better than spoiled Seelie princess."

Just when I'd thought I could quit overthinking the maddening exchange with Regin and that we'd walked far enough out of earshot of the dungeon, the Unseelie prince just had to go and open his mouth.

Courtesy of the two confusing males and worry over the well-being of the narlows, I'd lain awake until the stars had begun to fade.

"It's rude to eavesdrop, and I'm no mother of—" I faltered before his cell. "Is *that* what you all call me? The spoiled Seelie princess?"

"Some call you the wildling"—he lifted a broad shoulder—"but most call you Fia the feral, for not a day passes without a leaf in your hair, dirt on your cheek, or brambles stuck to your skirts."

Well, that last one wasn't exactly new or wrong. I crossed my arms and leaned against the wall outside of the narlow's cell, smirking at the prince. "Which one of the rumors about yourself is true then?"

Colvin returned my smirk. "I'll tell you if you tell me." Although we knew those rumors about me all were, I still said, "You already know which one is true."

"Mother of monsters, indeed," he purred in a way that suggested it was not something to be ashamed of. Not at all. "You'll need to tell me of these supposed rumors first."

The very thought of it made heat rush up my neck.

His eyes narrowed, and he cursed, then chuckled. "Moon melt me. How old are you?"

"The rumors don't state that?"

"Nineteen?"

"Not until the spring."

He cursed again. "Then do not worry."

"You think me too young to know of filthy things?" I said without thought or care for what might come next. "You have had a harem of lovers for many years."

But the prince just tilted his head back against the wall, arms hanging over his bent knees. Eyeing me, those golden orbs glowed, then he sighed. "I can indeed play with fire."

Knowing that was all he would admit, I nodded. "How?"

A grin revealed sharp and deadly canines. "When my body, my blood specifically, heats beyond return, it gathers like coals beneath my flesh and awaits release."

Sun squash me. The succinct yet punctured way he'd spoken those words...

I'd never thought myself much for blushing, and it angered me that he could arouse anything within me. Curiosity, a shred of kindness, and even conversation. But the blushing angered me the most, and to the point of making it worse, my skin growing impossibly hotter.

So I checked on the narlows and unfolded the handkerchief of mince stew I'd robbed from the kitchens after claiming that I did not want porridge. The cubs pawed at my fingers, too impatient to wait until I'd unraveled the soiled silk.

I laughed. "Hold on, beasts."

"They're all males."

"How do you know?"

"You get a sense for such things after enough time with them," he informed. "Bonded by land and all."

I supposed he would know.

Giving in, I let the stew fall to the ground, and the narlows ate as they wished. Then I checked on the sleepy cub, fingers carefully peeling the blankets away. He flinched, curling toward the warmth I'd stolen.

I covered him and sat against the wall, watching the other two eat and roll over one another.

"Who is he?"

The abrupt question threw me so thoroughly that I wasn't sure how to answer or if I should answer at all. Yet I did, my words curt. "My friend."

A careful curiosity darkened his next question. "Do your friends usually trail your scent in hunt of you at night?"

I gave the prince my eyes, found his already watching me, bright but with what seemed an endless yet edged patience. "Do yours?"

His lips curved.

And it grew suddenly stifling, the cool dampness of the dungeon reminiscent of a foggy summer day. I tried to look away when his eyes began to shine so bright, I thought they might explode into stars, but failed when the gold spread. It moved into the whites of his eyes, grew into a honey-colored brown, and then...

And then red.

Laughter followed the opening groan of the door up the stairs, footsteps crunching down them moments later. "...Told him he didn't know me at all if he thought I'd forget a winnings like that."

"You'll never see that coin. Gregorn's a swindler, through and through."

Colvin's brow rose, and I blinked.

His eyes... they were now normal. As normal as star-spun gold could ever be. *Perhaps I'd imagined it*, I thought as self-preservation finally kicked in, and I hurried out of the dungeon via my favored exit to the overgrown gardens.

But I hadn't.

I'd not met any other Unseelie. It was likely a common phenomenon for most of them. Especially being that so many of them relied on drinking one another's blood to fuel their magical abilities. It shouldn't come as a shock then, that the Unseelie prince might also need to feed.

I was jumping to conclusions. Conclusions that didn't even matter, I soon remembered as I traipsed back through the castle to return to my search of a new home for the narlows and overheard heated voices.

Backtracking just enough to avoid detection, I lingered on the window ledge.

A few feet away from the council chamber doors, I feigned interest in the mince dried to the beds of my nails and caught the tail end of my uncle's statement. "... wouldn't have handed himself over without protest otherwise."

"But he did so before all in attendance in a show of good faith," Karn, Regin's father, said, his voice, typically roughened with a relaxed arrogance, low and serious. "Are we to dishonor that so profusely?"

"He cannot live."

I stilled, fingers falling and my back meeting the stained blue glass of the window.

"Dangerous words, my king."

"Yet you know they are true. The last of his ilk terrorized Gwythorn for nearly a decade until it was miraculously stopped."

"That was well over half a millennia ago," Karn said. "Times have changed, and perhaps, the thirst for such bloodshed has too."

"You know our base desires never change, especially for a creature like him. And you know damned well that even if it were possible to unwind such genetically ingrained instincts, we still cannot take any risks."

"We gave Olette our word that there would be no foul play. That we would try to reach a compromise. I urge you to remember who we're dealing with here, Brolen."

I could imagine my uncle's cheeks mottling with his rising incense. "You think compromise with blood-lusting monsters is something to be accomplished?" A throaty scoff. "There's a reason we still stay well south of the border, Karn." Those last words were clipped, as if almost spat at Regin's father.

Silence.

I hoped to hear Karn's voice rise, to hear him tell my uncle that he was out of line and to indeed tread carefully. Though I knew he never would. He never did.

My teeth gnashed at the thought of Uncle Brolen sitting there, all puffed up like a crowned peacock with nowhere to parade his newfound power.

They unclenched when Karn said in an eerily calm tone, as though tempted to plead with my uncle, "Just think of the repercussions."

"That's all I've been doing, believe me," my uncle grumbled. "But even the prince himself knows what must be done."

"I don't think you're wrong, my king." My uncle's captain and longtime friend sighed loud enough for me to hear. "That's the problem."

Having heard enough, I slipped away quietly, entering the stairwell at the end of the hall.

Inside it, surrounded by shadows, I fell back against the rough stone wall. My ears rang. The flame in the sconce above my head showed a slight tremble in my hands when I lifted them to my cheeks.

They were far from warm now.

My skin was ice, my blood cooling sludge, and my heart's gallop slowing to an echoing thud.

He was to die.

The Unseelie prince in the dungeon had handed himself over, but for what reason, I didn't know. My mind swam as I pieced the timing of his arrival and the information I'd just heard together. My uncle's absence was not entirely unusual, but I hadn't so much as caught a glimpse of him since he'd returned days ago.

So Colvin had given himself to my uncle at the meeting of the courts. But why? What had happened? What was it he'd done that was so terrible they would want him killed?

It wasn't until I was lying in bed that night, the book I'd been perusing open upon my stomach, that I recalled his eyes. His demeanor. The solemn acceptance of his fate. And I acknowledged the question I'd continuously overlooked. Perhaps on purpose.

What was he?

FOUR

I WOKE WITH VISIONS OF BLOOD AND WAR STILL FADING FROM my dreams and the cover of my book digging into my rib cage.

Smacking my lips together, I tossed the book beneath my bed and rolled to the floor with a painful thud, rubbing at my eyes. Each word of my uncle's conversation with Karn pounded into my skull, relentless as I climbed to my feet and drained the water straight from the pitcher.

Prince Colvin would die.

Whether he deserved to or not. But even if he did deserve it, what would the death of the Unseelie prince mean for the rest of us?

The patchwork of blood-colored dreams was answer enough. I tried to remember them more clearly while bathing, but the suds were long gone by the time I surrendered. For there was no need.

The Unseelie were not only monstrous but also mercilessly vengeful.

We were fed cautionary tales veiled in the form of bedtime stories as we grew. Only to learn some years later exactly what they were.

Morsels of history handed down to each generation.

A shiver skittered up my spine as I dried off and dressed, my hair still wet and untouched by a brush as I made my way to the kitchens.

Adon was talking the ears off the new apprentice, who was washing dishes at the sink, but he paused when he saw me.

"Princess." He bowed, then tossed a towel over his shoulder and met me at the wooden counter in the center of the muggy room. "It's nearly time to prepare lunch." He took his time to add, to ensure the barb was clear, "Perhaps you'd like to wait for some squid stew."

"You know I do not care for seafood," I said, my nose crinkling. I continued checking the pots of leftovers intended for the staff. "I'll help myself."

Adon refused to heed my dismissal. "You don't typically care for a meaty breakfast, either."

"And you shouldn't care for my business."

"That is a little difficult when it is my job to feed you," he said, mirthful but with an undercurrent of irritation. "Dare I even ask what you might be up to now?"

Slopping some pie into a bowl I snatched from the drying rack, I merely filled it and took my leave. Adon's mutterings trailed me into the dark halls beyond. "Born rude, that one. Suppose that's what happens when there's no mother or father around to show her any better."

Most would be outraged enough to tattle on someone like Adon, but when most of this luminescent castle was filled with gnats just like him, it became but another game of ceaseless venomous gossip.

I wasn't above such things. In fact, watching people squirm and argue over stories Regin and myself had created and spread just to cause entertaining trouble while growing up had been so enjoyable that I smiled while recalling the memories.

But as Regin had grown busier with training over these past few years, I'd discovered I needed more than courtly drama to feed the things I lacked and loathed to look at.

Atop the stairwell, I paused to listen. Hearing nothing save for the muted bustle some floors above, I unlocked and opened the door to the dungeon.

"Pie?" the prince asked. He sniffed the air as I settled inside the narlow's cell. "Beef and pea."

There was no need to answer him, and I wasn't so sure I could as I peeled away the buttery pastry before letting the cubs at the meaty innards. Setting the remaining pastry in the bowl, I pushed it across the floor toward the prince's cell.

It rocked and hit the bars, crumbs exploding over the ground.

Colvin didn't reach through them. He watched me. I could feel it as I kept my own eyes plastered to the unmoving babe in the nest of blankets. "Something troubles you."

I'd thought I could ignore it. That the prince's fate would not bother me if I refused to let it, just like I had with so many other things in this eternally long life I'd been given.

It shouldn't bother me. At all.

Yet it so evidently did. A sharp discomfort, similar to that of terrible indigestion, unsettled my chest, my empty stomach. I was certain he could hear it, even if I shifted to try to hide it.

"Fia," he prompted, tone deep with knowing.

"I don't wish to talk about it."

"Is it that male?" A hair-rising wrath bit at the question. "Did he do something?"

"No," I snapped. "Nothing like that." I'd forgotten to stress about the last encounter I'd had with Regin in the aftermath of my recent discoveries. Guilt poked at me, and I inwardly vowed to find room to worry about the trivial later. I hoped I would.

The prince didn't speak for so long that I began to think he wouldn't. "Your heart races," he said, just above a whisper. "It's beating hard enough to suggest you're afraid."

"I'm not."

"Liar," he crooned. "If you do not wish to tell me what ails you, then you could at least tell me what soap you use." He drew in a long inhale, holding it as he murmured, "Lime and lily? No," he said, and I knew he was trying to distract me, to pull me free of this anxious tailspin. "It's mint and jasmine, isn't—"

"They plan to kill you," I nearly shouted, catching myself. My chest heaved, each breath burning as I dared to look at him. "I heard them talking. My uncle and his advisor."

"I see." If the prince was shocked, he didn't show it. His lips wriggled a little as he cocked his head and studied me. "I had wondered as much."

His lack of care made me glare and hiss, "Why? Why would they do that?"

"I am a monster," the prince said, though he was smiling. "Haven't you heard?"

"You're all monsters. What I want to know is what makes you any worse than the rest?"

He chuckled, and the deep sound stunned me still. "But why do you wish to know?" His eyes narrowed upon mine. "Do not tell me you've come to care about my fate."

"I care about the fate of this rotten continent and what would happen should you end up executed." I swallowed, saying softer, "Because they will do it. You know they will."

He said nothing and finally reached for the pastry.

It maddened me to the point of growling, "What the fuck is wrong with you?"

"Too much, fire-breather," he said simply and placed a piece of pastry over his tongue. He moaned and licked his fingers. "Too fucking much."

The sound and action threw me from my ire—the way his lips wrapped around his soiled digits without hesitation. My stomach bubbled, but with something far more vicious than hunger and rage.

I looked at the narlows and watched one of them attempt to climb the wall and fail while the other tugged at my skirts with his teeth. This irritating prince didn't care. He seemed resigned to it. Perhaps, he even enjoyed it. The thought of what his death would induce. The carnage our people would suffer at his hands, though he'd no longer be here to blame.

Unable to bear being in his presence, I rose and closed the cell, then I snatched the bowl perched before his. "Criminals and liars shouldn't eat."

"And how exactly have I lied?"

"By omitting the truth," I clipped on the way to the door. "So I suppose your secrets will die with you."

His low laughter stalked me long after the door had shut.

I waited until the castle slumbered before throwing off the bedding and donning my hooded robe. Sentinels roamed the grounds and stood outside of each entry and exit point.

But none ever stood guard of the unused door below the forest of a garden to the dungeon.

Outside of it, hanging upon a rusted hook behind overgrown vines, were the keys to each cell, all of them marred with disuse. I snatched them, making sure there was no jangle as I crept inside the dark rows of cells.

The prince was awake. I'd almost expected him to be asleep, given how calm he'd been earlier when I'd told him what awaited him. "Fia?"

"Up," I hissed.

"Up?" he repeated, puzzled.

"Yes, get up." He carefully straightened to sit against the wall and blinked. "Are you stupid?" Remembering he'd handed himself over, I muttered, "Never mind. You've already made that abundantly clear. Let's go."

He made an odd sound, a coughing laugh as if shocked. "Fire-breather indeed." He quieted as he paid attention to my attempts to find the right key for his cell. "What are you doing?" The question was deep and low as if he were not only shocked but far from impressed.

"Baking you a cake." I rolled my eyes. "What do you think I'm doing?" The next key fit, the mechanisms in the lock vibrating before loosening with a resounding click.

"Fia," he warned. "This is not wise."

"But staying here to await death is?" I pulled the door open slowly, relieved when it didn't creak. "I will not be blamed for any future bloodshed between our kingdoms because of you."

His eyes gleamed. "But how would anyone know?"

"I would know," I said, glaring at him when he didn't move.

He curled his lips. "A guilty conscience is indeed no fun."

"Enough. Get up." I stomped my foot. "Right this instant."

"You're truly freeing me?" he asked, still seated on the ground as if this were all in jest. "Just like that?"

"Yes, but with one condition." I squared my shoulders. "Of course."

"Of course." He grinned. "You probably should've made that clear before you unlocked the door, Princess."

I ignored that, though he was right. "You will take them with you."

A flick of his eyes to the snoring narlows. "Take them?"

"Moon murder me, you are daft indeed." I sighed. "Yes, take them. Take them back to Eldorn, where they stand a far better chance of survival."

He licked his teeth, then exhaled roughly and looked up at me.

His jaw flexed and firmed, dusted with enough hair that if given another day or two, he'd have himself a beard. A shame, a tiny voice tittered in the recesses of my mind, winding through the panic and urgency, to have the stunning severity of that jaw unavailable to the eye.

He knocked me from thoughts that made me feel like the only stupid creature here. "But your uncle is right, Fia."

"I'm not saying he's wrong. You're a monster, rotten and terrible, and you've probably committed atrocities, etcetera, etcetera. I understand." I crossed to the narlow's cell and opened the unlatched door. "Just keep it all confined to your kingdom and go."

"Etcetera, etcetera?" he repeated with a low laugh. "You are seriously something—"

"I will murder you myself if you don't hurry up," I snapped, bending down to make sure all the narlows were accounted for inside their nest. "So do you wish to live?" I asked. "Or die? You know the latter is inevitable if you remain right where you are."

He was quiet for so long that I grew worried he indeed had a death wish. Whatever he'd done, whatever he was, he clearly felt more comfortable caged and with the likelihood of dying than he did with his newfound freedom.

But then he murmured, the command gentle, "Wrap them up, ensure they can't fall free," and I heard him climb to his feet.

I did as he said, but only after quickly rubbing each little head. "Stay in here," I whispered, my eyes burning as I wound the blankets into an inescapable knot.

The prince stalked to the end of the dungeon, to the rope used for hanging criminals from the ceiling who needed extra encouragement to talk. He snatched a blade from a small selection on the wall and cut the rope down without the need to even lift his toes.

It was then I felt a belated sense of concern over my actions.

He was so incredibly tall that his head nearly met the dungeon's ceiling. Muscular, too, I acknowledged, courtesy of the large, gaping tear in the back of his tunic. He was broad-shouldered without being overly bulky like some of our soldiers, his torso tapering perfectly.

Colvin rehung the blade and collected his cloak from the floor of his cell, the fabric rippling as he shouldered it on. I stepped back into the iron bars, barely feeling their effect through my robe as he headed for the door to the gardens.

If I were him, I'd have taken the knife with me. Then again, he had certainly proven himself to be lacking in intelligence.

At the door, the prince waited. I remembered the cubs I was still holding to my chest and all but threw them at him. Again, I stepped back as he looped the rope through the knot I'd made and checked its strength before tying it around his neck.

He left enough give that the cubs rocked near his waist as he erased the space between us. I opened my mouth to bark a warning I couldn't conjure when he clasped my cheeks.

His giant hands swallowed them, and my neck cricked as I tilted it back. Our eyes met, his wild and searching. Then to my horror and complete surprise, so did our lips.

I'd never been kissed, but I'd imagined that when it happened, it would be clumsy and wet. At least at first. I'd also imagined it would have been Regin.

I'd have never imagined this.

Him.

This burning that froze every part of me, that rendered me incapable of feeling anything outside of the gentle press of his soft lips against mine. They parted, just slightly, as his mouth slid over my own, breath rushing from him and flooding my skin and lips. He was smoke and ice, an intoxicating combination that shouldn't exist.

"Fire-breather." The whisper singed, my heart unmoving in my chest. "Mother of monsters." Cupping the back of my head, he stiffened as his forehead met mine.

Our eyes opened at the same time, his wild once more and his brows low, my own stuck on the growing crimson moving over his.

Then he was gone, and my heart restarted with a rattle that shook everything into chaotic disorder inside me.

A thief after all.

Sleep captured me as soon as my head hit one of the many cushions sprawled across my bed.

It wouldn't be until some hours later, the sun blinding over the river beneath the mountains, that I felt the full weight of my actions.

The guards didn't shout or make any ruckus over the missing prisoner. I supposed they couldn't, being that few creatures had known the Unseelie prince had been here at all. But there was talk. The type of talk that I'd typically pass off as gossip.

Typically.

Heading downstairs out of curiosity and in search of food, I'd halted at overhearing, "I heard from Adon, who heard it from Gregorn, that the king seeks an escaped dragon. Can you believe it? We had a dragon right here." Shrulin feigned a shiver. "Practically lying in wait under our beds."

The two ladies huddled together as they walked toward the

doors leading to the courtyard on the western side of the castle. Their skirts, intricate layers of gauzy chiffon and stunned butterflies, dragged along the stone with grating slowness, making it nearly impossible to stalk them to catch a whiff of what they were saying.

I gave up on worrying whether they'd notice me as Froma murmured, "It has to be the Eldorn prince. I could be wrong, but being that every dragon in history was an heir of the Eldorn line, I highly doubt I am."

Oh, my bleeding stars.

A gasp from Shrulin. "No."

Froma hummed. "Dark times lay ahead." Though she sounded more intrigued than perturbed. "Last time, hundreds, some even say *thousands* of lives were lost to its frightful maw and fire-breathing rage."

I can indeed play with fire.

My head filled with a dizzying, unstoppable wave.

I turned to the nearest rose bush and vomited.

Mercifully, the ladies had moved on, their floating shawls marking their whereabouts deeper within the maze of hedges.

It was no wonder Colvin hadn't taken the blade from the dungeon. That he'd needed the rope to secure the narlows to himself. He'd need to materialize.

Or fly.

A dragon. A fucking dragon.

"Fia," Regin called, but I almost puked again, heaving as I gripped my stomach and chest. "Fia?" His hand met my back. "Shit, did you eat the apprentice's attempt at berry stew, too?"

"No," I wheezed.

"Then what's wrong?" Looking up at him beneath my damp lashes, I watched his face pale. He clasped my cheeks, and the need to expel more from my empty stomach arrived again as I recalled the prince holding me the same way just hours ago. "Fi, what is it?"

I shouldn't have said a word. I knew that.

To tell anyone what I'd done, that I knew of the prince being in our dungeon at all, was to implicate myself. Not to mention, it would make matters worse for my uncle should more people find out.

But I couldn't contain it. It was a poison I needed to evict, and so I rasped, "You cannot tell a soul."

Regin tapped his palm over his heart in promise, frowning when I still couldn't bring myself to say it. "Come on, it can't be any worse than bringing a foal into the castle with you for dinner because it had a fever."

Oh, how I wished it were as simple as a foal breaking statues and priceless heirlooms.

I shook my head, swallowing hard.

His smile waned rapidly. "It's bad then."

"Really, *really* bad."

FIVE

M Y ELBOW KNOCKED THE WALL, AND A BROOM FELL INTO the door with a clatter.

"We should—" My lips were pressed closed by Regin's, his hands tugging at my skirts. "Go," I said, breathless as I pushed gently at his chest.

"To a larger room?" Kisses peppered across my jaw, fingers smoothing up my sides. "Probably."

I laughed. "It's my birthday. We can't keep disappearing."

"Exactly, it's your ball," he said, groaning as my fingers delved into his blond hair. "You can do whatever you like."

I wished that were true. Nothing would please me more than dragging Regin upstairs to a secluded room to finish what we'd both been continuously stopping and starting since the ballroom had begun to fill a few hours ago.

He'd been gone for two weeks on a scouting mission, but for almost a month prior, he'd made it abundantly clear that not only were my secrets safe with him, no matter how much he didn't understand or agree with them, but that I was safe with him too.

In many differing ways.

I tore away when his mouth attempted to steal mine and stumbled to the door, laughing. "Enough." I moved the broom and peered out into the hall before exiting and righting my lemon and lace skirts. The bodice of my gown had been constructed from pressed bluebells and a moss so delicate and soft that it would surely begin to crumble from the soldier's rough hands if I wasn't careful.

Regin followed, adjusting himself and grumbling to my hair, "Twenty minutes, and then we're through with all this pomp."

I smirked, my hand capturing his as we raced down the stairs to the ballroom doors below. "I was thinking fifteen, but if you believe you can wait that long…"

He tugged me into his chest, nipping at my cheek.

The doors crashed open, and we separated, but our hands remained joined. It was not exactly a secret, the advancement of our friendship, for lack of a better term. But we had no better term for it. Not yet. For now, I was content with that. With the comforting squeeze of my hand that reassured me he was with me. That I had him. That this was real.

Jilgens had already exploded upon my earlier entrance, their powdery pollen staining the air with floating clouds of color. Pinks and reds, colors often chosen for celebrations, dusted the floor and many a gown and dress shirt.

I'd thankfully escaped the carnage when Regin had taken advantage of the explosion and cheering and laughter to drag me upstairs.

My uncle was seated upon the dais in the center of the table hosting the great feast. His frosted gaze met mine when we delved deeper into the dancing bodies. I forced a smile, immediately looking away when he raised his goblet to his mouth and eyed me curiously.

He still didn't know.

I'd spent weeks evading him as much as possible and waiting with bated breath to see what might happen next. If the dragon would be hunted or simply ignored until he could be ignored no longer. Whatever it was they'd decided, Regin held no knowledge, and the rumors of the dragon's existence had faded within days.

As if he were never here and did not exist at all.

I was certain it was all for show. That whatever plans my uncle and Karn had were now kept under impenetrable lock and key.

Regardless, I decided mere days after releasing the prince that, besides what was expected of me, I would finally cease what everyone deemed an endless search for trouble in all forms. I attended my lessons until they'd finished with the first notes of spring, and I made sure the only talk I gave people was that of the increased time spent with the captain of the guard's son.

Fear and regret were the key ingredients I'd needed to finally learn my lesson.

"Dance with me," Regin warned more than said, and I choked on a laugh as I was hauled to his chest. His arm banded behind my back, his hand still clutching mine as he began to sway.

"You know I loathe to dance," I whispered to his neck, feeling eyes upon us.

"Think of it as another form of foreplay."

I tilted my head back, grinning. "That is what you think of dancing?" My grin fell into a scowl as I remembered all the times I'd watched him dance with the daughters of nobles over the years.

With a slight wince, he sighed and then licked his lips, eyes leaving those around us to meet mine. "Anything with you is foreplay, Fi."

My breath caught, then fled when he spun me around and brought me back to his chest right as a scream sounded.

Wineglasses crashed to the floor.

Fiddles and flutes ceased as another scream gave way to an ear-bleeding orchestra of them.

The sky outside the glassless windows of the ballroom darkened, but not with clouds nor the gathering night.

It darkened with monsters.

One by one, they materialized into the ballroom, curling wisps of shadows and burned time clouding the air.

Regin cursed, pulling me toward the back of the room.

Guards shouted, rushing in and—

Dead.

Males with scales for beards and piercing reptilian eyes slid dark green talons across their necks, ending them quicker than a single rapid beat of a heart.

"Shit," Regin hissed, and we halted in the middle of the room.

I spun in a useless circle, my heart screaming louder than that of the fearful and the dying. Outside the windows, giant bat-like creatures screeched and flapped their wings, snatching anyone who dared to try to leap down into the gardens below.

And then I saw him.

Still seated at the table, my uncle's wide eyes fell upon me.

I couldn't decipher a thing from his gaze or if he even had the capacity to warn me of anything with a dagger pressed to his throat.

As one, we all stilled when a strange hush descended and spread across the large room. The reptilian warriors dragged my aunt and Karn to either side of the dais, talons clutching their throats in warning, as a female unveiled herself from shadow.

Her hair was bloodred, as was the hunger growing in her gaze as she lowered her nose to my uncle's shoulder, closed her eyes, and inhaled deeply.

Blood trickled down his neck to his sapphire dress robes.

The female opened her eyes and straightened. "A birthday ball? My invitation was lost to a forest floor, I'm sure."

Uncle Brolen said nothing, his gaze now fastened to his half-finished meal.

"It would seem you've been keeping quite the horrid betrayal from me, my dear Brolen." The female licked her crimson-stained lips. Her eyes, now a dark soil brown, danced over the room. "But you know what they say about that pesky thing called truth..." Lowering, she whispered to his cheek, "It will always find a way to make itself known."

My uncle's eyes closed.

The female laughed, a breathy, insidious sound that roused the bat creatures outside.

Their screeched chorus ceased when she licked her teeth and murmured, though the ballroom was so still, I was certain all heard it, "My son returned to me with lovely words of your kindness, explaining that he was sent on his way without so much as a hair missing from his lying head."

My stomach shrank and coiled.

"Oh, but it was for nothing when I was finally delivered quite the tantalizing tale." More blood ran from beneath the blade, her words hissed to my uncle's ear. "One of deceit and death."

"Olette," Brolen started. "Your son is a dragon. He cannot be permitted to—"

"Silence," the female ordered, her tone venomous. "He has not harmed a single soul from your land."

Heartbeats thundered throughout the ballroom as the unexpected guest was confirmed.

The queen of Eldorn, the kingdom of the Unseelie.

"We didn't kill him," Brolen sputtered.

The blade dug deeper. "But you intended to."

Regin's hand tightened at my waist when the queen looked up and smiled. A smile far too beautiful for a creature so grotesque.

A smile directed straight at me.

"Before a little patch of wild sunshine intervened, thus ruining all of your murderous plans."

Regin cursed, and I wasn't sure I was breathing as she beckoned to me. "Come forward, darling. I do not bite unless asked."

But I was frozen, every part of me stiff yet wilting at the same time.

It was Regin gently pushing at my lower back that finally woke me up. I could ignore Olette and face grim repercussions or take a few measly steps forward. Steps that might somehow save lives.

Without breath, without a beat of my heart, I walked into the clearing of bodies circling the mosaic of our family crest—a tree fashioned from butterflies and serpents.

I stopped some feet from the dais, a hundred fleeting thoughts suddenly crashing through my mind. I wondered if I should incline my head, curtsy, or greet the queen at all. But most of all, I wondered why her son hadn't done a better job at keeping his miraculous release a secret.

Though I already knew the answer to that last one.

It stood before me, around me, lurked outside of our windows like a storm awaiting some place to strike. Prince Colvin was a monster, and any type of deal made with a monster would result in nothing more than a game.

"There we are," the queen crooned, her head tilting as she studied me. "Fia, the feral princess." Low and rumbled laughter came from those of her lizard warriors. They quietened when she pursed her lips and then spoke. "Actions have consequences, don't they, sweet darling?"

I frowned, but self-preservation had me nodding.

Olette dragged the dagger across my uncle's throat, not hard enough to kill him but slow in warning. "I cannot hear you," she sang.

"Yes," I all but shouted, then squared my shoulders. "Of course, they do."

"Yet I hear you're not one to face many repercussions for your own."

My aunt squirmed and made to protest, but I quickly said to the queen, "I suppose you could say that."

"You suppose?" she repeated, belting out a howling laugh. It was cut short by a sudden clearing of her stone-drawn features. "There won't be any confusion here, Fia. Understood?"

I nodded, apprehension slicing through me.

"Being that you were the one to free my son from your poor excuse for a dungeon before he was executed, I will give your family one chance and one chance only to remedy this gross betrayal."

Regin cursed again, as did many others in attendance, their accusing eyes like knives penetrating my skin. I tried to tell myself I deserved it. That I could indeed only get away with my mistake for so long. That they had every right to throw their hatred at me, for a part of me hated myself too.

Yet I couldn't keep my fists from clenching, my iced blood from warming, at their judgment and audacity.

"So"—the queen released her hold on my uncle—"how do you think we should proceed? An eye for an eye. Someone must pay the unspeakable cost."

I had no unearthly idea.

Before I could admit as such, my uncle declared, "Whatever you want, she will do it."

Queen Olette narrowed an eye at our king, her upper lip lifting slightly, but he kept his enraged gaze upon me.

I couldn't blame him for his ire. I had ruined his plans, and in doing so, I'd now made him look like a fool with a niece he'd forever fail to control.

A niece who'd not only betrayed him but also our entire kingdom.

As the gravity of it sank in with sharp claws, I swallowed and lowered my gaze to the pollen-dusted tiles of the ballroom floor. "He speaks true," I said, for that was what everyone was waiting for. For me to own up to my actions and take responsibility for them.

To somehow save them.

I lifted my head. The room was deathly quiet, the pounding beat of my heart likely heard by all as I said through teeth that wouldn't unclench, hating that I had to speak at all, "I will do whatever you wish of me."

The queen's eyes glittered, her crimson lips pouting as they curled. "But of course, you will." I held her gaze, unsure if I'd meant the words, but there was no other choice. She smiled as if knowing, then looked at my uncle, the blade grazing his jaw. "A new agreement will soon be forged, *King*."

The giant bats were the first to leave, vacating the night sky outside the windows and soaring toward the moon in such crowds that it distracted most from the queen's departure.

But as shadow blended with a fast-moving air that sent the cutlery clattering, I looked over to find her still observing me, a curious glint in her dark eyes. I shivered when she grinned a moment before disappearing inside a dark, shimmering silver mist.

Within moments, the Unseelie warriors too vanished in tendrils of darkness, and healers were rushing into the room.

It was already too late for some, but others were able to be tended to. In a daze, I stayed where I was and slowly looked away from my uncle, who was pressing a handkerchief to his neck and rising from his seat.

Only to discover most of the eyes of those who remained were pinned on me.

Some were filled with glaring condemnation, and others with shining fear. Whether that fear was for themselves or for me, I wasn't sure I wanted to know.

"Fi," Regin said, closing in at my back. "What the fuck just happened?"

"Traitor," cried a male voice.

Sylvane clutched Orla's arm, both of whom I'd shared many lessons with, and sneered. "We should have known something as feral as you would one day doom us all."

My mouth fell open, and I twisted away from Regin. But everywhere I turned, more and more accusatory stares and words were tossed at me like weapons, and with such vehement hatred and fear that if they could, I knew many would already be upon me.

Before the guards could decide what to do, I backed up toward the doors, counting each step to keep the dizzying mess of my mind from weakening my knees.

"Where do you think you're going?" crowed Armen, one of my uncle's cousins.

I counted to twelve right as a feminine voice shouted, "Seize her! She is not our princess. She's a traitor to the crown."

But I ran out into the hall, pushing past bodies that failed to move in time and jumping over the injured awaiting treatment as if they were but another fallen log in the forest. Each bend and turn of the castle that had always been my home became just another tree-dense maze as my uncle's command trailed me.

"You heard them," he roared, then ordered, "Move! Seize her!"

But I made it through the staff entrance to the side gardens. Thorns and sticks snatched at my gown, and I gathered the skirts higher and pushed harder toward the woods.

The small, shallow cave was a few miles journey uphill, and my legs and lungs burned by the time I finally reached it. I'd spent too much time indoors these past months, trying to blend in hopes of keeping myself out of further trouble.

A waste.

I shouldn't have bothered. Now, I was unfit, out of options, and being hunted.

Surreal. To think that just hours ago, I was kissing Regin and lamenting my obnoxious birthday celebration. My vision blurred with tears I had no use or time for.

I concentrated on ripping the skirts of my gown at my knees with a stick I'd sharpened to better my chances at running. Although the cave sat beneath an overhang of giant rocks that overlooked the castle grounds and the land beyond, it wouldn't hide me for long.

A pointless endeavor. Yet the rip of the material gave me a brief taste of satisfaction, the cool night unable to touch me when my blood was swelling with adrenaline, with the instinct to flee.

Staring through the branches to the castle towers, the river glowing in the starlight at the bottom of the mountains, I didn't listen to it.

A mistake.

Twigs snapped. My heart stopped with my breath as I held the stick poised like a dagger and slunk back against the rock.

"It's just me," Regin whispered, and I closed my eyes, every muscle unclenching fast enough to make my head spin.

He pushed aside shrubbery and branches, ducking low and crouching to his knees before the entrance to what had been one of our favorite hiding places while we'd played in these very woods growing up. He offered a weak smile. "Hi."

I swallowed. "Where are they?"

He eyed the stick still in my fist as I slowly lowered it to my lap, then nodded to it. "Nice weapon."

"Regin," I rasped. "What am I supposed to do?"

He shook his head. "I don't know, Fi."

"They want me dead."

"The queen didn't say that," he said with a frown. "And everyone else is just scared because they know that was not what she meant. Her torment of us has evidently only just begun."

"I wasn't talking about the queen," I said, wincing at my tone. He was trying to help. He was here. He was quite possibly all I had. It hit me then, an idea that might just be crazy enough to work. "Hide me in your barn. Just until I can find a way to get to the coast without being seen."

"And then what, Fi?" he said, picking up a leaf. It changed from brown to green within his palm.

I'd always envied him for his touch with the land, so simple yet so seamless. But right now, I'd happily swallow all of my envy and attitude and judgments if it meant I'd stand a chance.

"You'll sail away to the mortal lands? No ship leaves without being searched by our forces first."

"I'll hide well enough."

"Okay." He spread his hands, the leaf falling in crumbs to the soil. "So then you arrive in Orlinthia. What are they to do with a rogue faerie princess?"

His lack of enthusiasm and his refusal to hope fueled my fear in a way that caused my temper to spike. "They trade with us." For as long as anyone could remember, the human realm had wanted our spices, our silks, our jewels, our seeds, and our lore. In return, they gave us precious metals and plastics and other various commodities.

"But they don't tolerate our presence there."

"The wild hunt visits."

"As you said, for trade and trade only. If you manage to escape the ship and hide, you will be found and either killed or..." He trailed off, not needing to say anymore.

We all knew what happened to Fae who tried their luck at living with mortals. Torture, in all its many forms, by the depraved and the murderous, or a swift death if seen by an official. There was no chance of being sent home. The same treatment was to be given to their own ilk in kind should they dare to venture here—an agreement made eons ago.

"You're not helping," I grumbled, my eyes beginning to sting.

A howl came from deep within the trees behind us, soon followed by a rush of footsteps and murmuring voices.

I looked at Regin, desperate.

His eyes were unreadable, and he didn't move at all.

Blades stacked in my stomach, scraped and stabbed at my screaming heart. My voice was brittle, my disbelief cloaking each word. "But you're not really here to help me, are you?"

His throat bobbed, and he sighed. "Believe it or not, I am. Evading capture will only hurt you, Fi."

"Asshole," I hissed and crawled from the cave. Pushing the foliage down, I saw there was no use in running.

My uncle's giant hounds lumbered downhill, tails swinging and their eyes glowing in the dark. The first wave of soldiers was not far behind them, with Regin's father leading the charge. He slowed when he saw us and nodded. "Good job, son."

The hounds pawed at the dirt, unsure what to do when I was the one who often slipped them treats and who'd spoiled many of them as pups.

I longed to use the kill whistle and have them turn on my uncle's meaty advisor, but I couldn't. I could do nothing but surrender when Karn climbed down the rocks to grab me, and Regin said, "I've got her."

I wanted to spit in his face and tell him to never touch me again. Yet I knew I was better off being escorted by him instead of another soldier who felt a raging hatred for me and my actions.

But as we trudged back to the castle, laughter and sneered words pelting me from every direction, the shock left me with each step. For what I'd done hadn't changed their minds. It had merely made it acceptable for them to openly loathe me and gladly condemn me to a potentially horrific fate.

SIX

THE CASTLE WAS QUIET, AS THOUGH EVERYONE HAD BEEN ordered to return to their rooms and homes.

There was no way they would have otherwise. This was likely the most scandalous event they'd attended since the previous city official was bludgeoned to death by his wife with a wine decanter in the courtyard beneath the ballroom balcony for fucking her handmaiden.

She'd stabbed him in the heart with a fork for good measure to ensure he hadn't healed.

I supposed I should have been relieved to be rid of the witnesses to my fall from grace. But the silence dripped too loud with every shaken step taken down into the bowels of the castle.

My heart crashed against my sternum, a caged bird in need of desperate escape all the while knowing there was none.

The door to my cell screeched to a slammed close, the lock turning.

"A true shame," muttered Gregorn, who'd been placed in charge of ensuring I was locked away, another guard I didn't know waiting at the door. The rest, including Regin, had all split toward their differing destinations once we'd reached the castle gardens. "You could've been something really beautiful if you'd spent more time attending court and less roaming about the forests."

I said nothing, just lifted my chin and waited for him to leave.

After one more lewd perusal that was finished off with a curl to his upper lip, he spat at my feet and walked away.

I watched his saliva slide down the iron bars, and when the dungeon door closed, I lowered to sit against the rough stone wall. I wasn't sure if it was intentional, caging me within the same cell as the prince I'd foolishly rescued, but I didn't care.

After whatever happened to me, I just hoped that Colvin was left to rot with incessant curses for his own betrayal.

No one. With a sharp twinge in my chest, my head upon my bent knees, and my heart slowing yet so incredibly heavy, I was forced to accept that I had no one.

No one would come for me until it was time to meet my fate.

I soon regretted hacking at my skirts.

After two days of shivering so hard my teeth clacked and my bones ached, it would seem I finally had a visitor.

But it wasn't food as I'd hoped, desperate enough to cling to the iron bars and then flinching away with a hiss. My hands were numb from the crispness of early spring, but they still burned.

I rubbed them over the bodice of my gown, moss crumbling, and blinked wearily up at my uncle.

He was alone, and after taking three more steps, as if he were merely taking a stroll over the castle grounds, he stopped. His hands were behind his back, his cool gray-blue eyes peering at me down the skinny bridge of his nose.

His white blond hair was combed back into a greasy helmet beneath the crown of sapphire thorns I wished to rip from his head when he tutted. "Fia, Fia, Fia..." He forced out a sigh, then licked his lips. "You've brought about a very unfortunate turn of events, as I'm sure you are already aware."

I didn't respond. There was nothing to say. To deny anything would be pointless.

"You not only robbed us of our chance to provide safety for our people, but you kept it to yourself for months, believing no one would ever find out. Perhaps I've let you get away with too much, and so I'm partly to blame. But I'm afraid I cannot allow you to get away with this."

I had to know, my voice roughened from days of disuse. "What will happen to me?"

He said gently, though without a hint of sadness, "You know what will happen, Fia."

He couldn't mean it.

Surely, he could just strip me of my title and send me off into the wilderness where he and everyone else believed I belonged. He'd never shown an inkling of affection or time for me, but I refused to believe he could wish for me to die. "But…" I started, words failing me as I clutched for anything to make this insanity cease. "I am the only heir."

"We both know I've likely got a few more of those lying around."

Disgusted, I glared at him, my hatred enough to finally voice what I should have minutes ago. "You always said that I needed to remember my duty to our people, to our land. Well, I did." I pointed at him. "If I didn't let him go, you would've brought war right to our doorstep by executing him."

His silence was telling, the words that eventually followed confusing. "You can spin a heroic tale such as that all you like. No one will believe you." He gave a stunted laugh as he looked around. "No one will even hear you."

"What other reason would I have?" I nearly shouted, refusing to acknowledge that yes, I'd been a fool for thinking the prince might have been somewhat decent for an Unseelie.

Brolen cocked his head. "I don't know, Fia. And I suppose we never will."

His passive expression, the shifting of his jaw as he studied me with something more akin to curiosity than sadness, made me wonder aloud, "Was it war you wanted?"

He scoffed. "Don't be preposterous."

"But you knew all too well that the queen would do more than kill you if you took the prince's life. You knew she would come for us." I smiled, enjoying his growing discomfort as I kept needling. "You wanted her to. *Why?* Are you and Karn truly that bored?"

"They're a plague on this land," he seethed, his calm veneer cracking. "The bloodletting and drinking and violent abilities. We shouldn't have to live in fear of what they can do."

"Then why provoke them?"

"To rebalance the scales by getting rid of a monster who wears them when the urge just so happens to strike. You weren't here when the last dragon existed." He stabbed a finger at his chest. "I was. I was just seven years, but I remember as if it were yesterday, the way it blocked out the sun as though it had eaten it and prowled all of Gwythorn, hunting for its next meal."

Those words sent a spear of fear into my chest. It seemed unreal—that the prince I'd met was capable of such atrocities. But I didn't truly know him, and that he'd sold me out to his mother...

A monster even without scales.

"The Eldorn line needs to end," he continued, for I supposed he considered it safe to tell me such things, being that I would soon not exist. It was the most he'd ever spoken to me in my life. "A new family must rise in their place if we are to ever rid our continent of the dragon for good."

But the prince was the only remaining Eldorn.

Colvin's mother, Olette, was indeed both queen and his mother, but it had been her late wife who'd given birth to him before she was murdered by her mate some years later. It was a topic everyone still adored talking about. When it came to love and mate-ships, both things less common with each passing decade, tales were exchanged with a fervor that betrayed the tragedies of so many.

"A new family," I murmured, nearly laughing. "That being you?"

He arched a brow. "Your mother wore the same attitude and insufferable expressions, you know. During all those intoxicating times when it would've been wise for her to remember who held the keys to her fate."

My stomach hollowed from more than just hunger. Brolen never spoke of her. Mirra seldom did either.

"It only makes the conquering all the more satisfying." His smile was smug, but it lasted a mere moment. "To answer your question, though, no," he said and turned to leave. "It matters not who replaces the Eldorn royal, just that the chance for more from that hideous bloodline is gone."

His steps clicked over the stone as I sat with all his words and tried to piece them together. Tried to make sense of what he might've done to...

Bile rocked my empty stomach, burned a path up my throat, and forced open my mouth. I hacked, twisting to hiss, "You... you raped her?"

His steps stopped. "Primrose was presented with a choice. Help provide me with an heir and her sister would need not suffer another excruciating failure to bring a babe to term. She made her decision with the agreement that Mirra would not pretend you were hers." His parting words haunted me, "Multiple times."

The door closed, and I was once again alone. Alone and forced to confront a truth that had sat right beneath my nose for my entire life.

It would be another day before I had another visitor.

This time it was Regin.

He crouched before my cage. I wasn't sure whether to be grateful or spiteful as he offered me a scone and a flask filled with water.

I chose to be neither and snatched them through the bars. Desperate for both, I choked down water while still chewing the hardened dough he'd likely pinched from the kitchens after everyone had retired.

"You're mad at me," he stated more than asked.

I just laughed, crumbs flying from my mouth as I raised the flask with a shaking hand to my lips to wash the scone down.

"I didn't have a choice, Fia, and neither did you."

Taking my time, I didn't look at him. The very idea of staring at the face I'd once adored with my lips, with my hands, with my body...

I couldn't do it. But I did ask, "Have you heard what is to become of me?"

His lack of response said that yes, he indeed had.

I scoffed and drank some more. "Just go."

"I came to warn you," Regin whispered, though there were no guards to hear. There was no chance for escape, and they all knew it. Another blade to the chest, knowing he could have visited me far sooner. "The royal guard will take you to the hanging tree before sunrise."

It was always a show—executing people via iron twined rope as the sun began to rise—the type of show no one dared to miss when it eventually came time to rid some rotten soul of this earth. Not even me.

"Lovely, thank you," I muttered and continued eating.

He sighed. "Fi, I truly am so fucking sorry. This is killing me."

"Unless you have something I'd actually like to hear, you should leave."

"If I'd have known it would come to this…" But his words faded into the useless nothings they were as he felt it before me.

The shift in the air, as if it were turning over itself.

Regin rose and stepped back. He swung his head side to side, seemingly worried someone would materialize into the dungeon. I'd have thought it nothing but an incoming storm until the walls trembled, rocks crumbled, and the dungeon grew darker.

Darker, as though the night sky was being painted black, and it was seeping beneath the cracks in the ceiling and crawling down the stairs.

Sliding beneath the same door I'd once let a prince escape through.

"What's happening?" I asked, the dough lodged between my teeth and cheek garbling my words. I swallowed to ask again, but Regin ran to the stairs that would take him up into the castle's stomach. "Regin!"

The door above the stairs closed.

The flame in the sconces rose and illuminated every bloodstain and rivulet in the stones. I scooted back to the corner of my cell as they shook and then flickered out, leaving me in complete darkness.

SEVEN

MERE MINUTES LATER, I WAS HAULED OUT OF MY CAGE and pushed up the stairs by five guards.

"Where are we going?" I asked, but no one answered.

I recognized three of them, Regin taking the lead up the stairs with his friends Kestia and Treyon. I'd never met the two behind me, who apparently found me gratingly amusing.

Their sniveling over my hacked gown and the state of my hair wouldn't usually bother me, but whatever was happening was anything but good. Perhaps they were to transport me to the hanging tree upon the lowest hill overlooking the city already.

Perhaps they were going to execute me here and be done with it. Olette was still awaiting retribution for our crimes against her son, and quite a few days had passed since her visit.

I'd spent those days getting to know my fate in the dungeon, but that didn't mean I was ready. I hadn't made peace with it. An impossible feat when all I felt was this ever-growing anger. A clawing rage that begged to be unleashed upon the stars in hopes of bringing them crashing down on this kingdom that'd been so quick to condemn and discard me.

Halfway up the stairwell, I slowed, light-headed and exhausted. I was pushed before I could tell the assholes behind me to shut up about my ungodly scent and the bird's nest that was my hair.

"Move, feral. We don't have all night." I was shoved again.

This time forcefully enough that I reached for the stone wall. My mind darkened with dizziness, and I missed, careening and turning my face to keep it from taking the brunt of the impact. My temple screamed, my skull and arm blooming with pain.

The male crouched down to wrap his fingers in my hair, then pulled. "I said, *move*—" He cursed, his hold on me wrenched away.

"Touch her again, and I'll make sure it's the last thing you do," Regin said, rough and edged from above.

I held my head, gritting my teeth as he told the soldiers to keep going. Their steps faded, and Regin clasped my cheek, lowering to the step beneath me.

Green eyes, eyes I'd found myself lost within countless times, darkened. The sight of them, of his cinched features as he surveyed my head with gentle touches of his fingers, created an instant aching sickness in my stomach.

I pulled away and continued up the stairs. "Leave it. I'm okay."

"Blood is dripping down your cheek, Fi. You've cut your head."

"What's it matter when I'm headed for execution anyway?" I said, uncaring as I added, "Thanks to you."

"They're no longer able to do that."

I stopped, swaying at the top of the stairs.

Regin grasped my elbow to keep me from falling and whispered as he encouraged me down the hall. "They're here."

I didn't need to ask who, but I did ask, "What do they want?"

"You," he said. "You said you'd do whatever they wanted." He was smiling a little, as though he were relieved when I peered at him. "Apparently, what they want isn't for you to die."

His silence afterward, the way he stared straight ahead as we passed the kitchens and met the next stairwell, grated. "Say it. Say what you know."

"They're taking you."

Dread climbed through my bones and rattled at my chest for entry. I held it at bay, turning over every reason they might want me. To use me as bait to keep my uncle in line? To torment and use as a pet? For further revenge against Brolen?

Then Regin murmured between his lips, so low, I nearly didn't catch it, "Olette's demands are not only for you to go with them but also to marry the prince."

Golden eyes crashed before me, stumbling my steps in the dim hall, their memory blurring my vision. No. Seelie and Unseelie royalty never married—never procreated. They rarely even got along. We tolerated each other for the good of our people.

"Fi." Regin pulled me from my thoughts. "Just know that he's unhinged, okay? He truly is a monster. Do not let him near you, let alone let him touch—"

"Goodbye, Regin," I said, shocking him into freezing. "Oh, and fuck you." I lifted my chin and walked on toward an uncertain future, knowing that I should count myself fortunate for having one at all.

I didn't feel fortunate.

Nor did I feel grateful as I trailed the guards awaiting us, and we continued to the throne room. If feeling were a color, then I was a dark, broiling, and bubbling red. I stopped mere feet within the room, well aware I'd never looked worse but not letting it lower my chin or shoulders.

Reptilian warriors lined the walls in leather armor and matching bulky boots, silent and imposing and so very still. Yet again, the mass of giant bats blocked out the night from the doorways to the balconies and windows. It was said that the ruler of the Unseelie held the power to force certain creatures of their land to materialize at will—to use or to merely intimidate.

Whatever the queen's reasons for bringing them along this time, I just hoped they had nothing to do with me.

"Oh, my." Olette, draped over Brolen's throne as though it were a chaise, grinned. "What have they done to you, darling?"

The male standing beside her, who'd been studying the tapestry and their embroidered poems hanging from the rafters behind the throne, turned with his hands tucked behind his back.

Burning gold flared red as the prince inspected me from head to toe.

I refused to buckle under the intensity of which he so thoroughly observed me, knowing exactly what he saw. A soiled gown with ruined flowers clinging to it, skirts that barely covered my weak knees. My hair was wilder than ever before, and I was covered in grime.

Colvin's jaw rotated, eyes unblinking as they swept back to my face. "Who is responsible for the gash on the princess's head?"

Uncle Brolen, who I hadn't seen lurking in the shadows on the other side of Olette, cleared his throat and stepped forward, disregarding the prince's question as though he hadn't asked one. "I suppose you're wondering why you're here," he said, looking at me.

I stared only at his gleaming brown boots.

He went on, his tone hardening with my refusal to acknowledge him. "It is plain to see that our people no longer want you as their princess, so"—my eyes moved to his spreading hands—"being that you seem to have a soft spot for beasts, I think this arrangement is indeed for the best."

He spoke as if it were his idea when most of us knew it was not.

I decided to play along, unable to recognize the flatness of my voice. Unable to care if it hinted at this not being new information to me. "And what arrangement is this?"

"You now belong to the Kingdom of Eldorn as the prince's betrothed."

It took great effort not to tell him his zealous delivery was in vain, for I already knew. It took even more effort not to sneer at the male who'd, up until minutes ago, had been responsible for my ever-changing fate and who'd all but admitted to forcing himself upon my mother.

But I refused to look at him.

The idea of marrying the Unseelie prince far from thrilled me, and it certainly did not fill me with any sort of confidence for my future. Though I couldn't deny that I was indeed relieved to have one, I still loathed him. After all, it was because of him that everyone had shunned me. It was because of him that I'd nearly lost my life.

So as far as I was concerned, he was almost as bad as the rest of the creatures I'd once deemed family.

I wouldn't let my fear and disgust show. I kept my features void, feeling Brolen's expectant gaze upon me as he waited for me to unfurl into a temper.

I wouldn't give him or the prince the satisfaction.

Though I did have to wonder how the prince felt about all of this and why he would agree to such a thing. There had to be more to it, so much more than my tired, malnourished mind could attempt to piece together at present.

Colvin said gently once more, "Who is responsible?"

My attention shifted to him as he studied each of the guards—studied them as if he'd not taken his eyes from them since he'd first asked about the cut on my head.

No one answered, and I certainly wasn't about to. It was all I could do to keep standing under the weight of what was happening and the exhaustion cloaking me.

Olette tutted at the continued silence.

The prince stepped down from the dais and continued to stare at the guards behind me, waiting with an unreadable expression.

Perhaps they mistook his expression for patience, as the asshole who'd pushed me stated arrogantly, "She tripped, Prince."

Colvin repeated carefully, "She tripped?"

The guard stepped forward and nodded. "She's likely feeling faint after days spent in the dungeon."

I refrained from snarling his way, my nails cutting into my palms.

Colvin looked at me, perhaps for an answer, but he didn't need it. He sighed and scratched at his cheek. "I really do wish you hadn't touched her."

"But I barely did," the guard went on. "It was just a little shove to make her move." He gestured to me, sweat dripping from his tousled milky hair. "We didn't want to keep you waiting. She's fine."

The queen released a low, breathy laugh. "Unwise."

The prince smiled, but it was almost pained. "It's the disrespect, you see, for the agreement was made before you went to retrieve my betrothed, and so now I am left with no choice."

The guard frowned.

I woke up well and truly as the prince's fingers were replaced by cascading dark talons nearly as long as his arm. Blood sprayed from the guard's throat as Colvin swiped one talon across it and then four of them over his stomach.

Wide-eyed, the dying male stared until his head tipped right back, and his innards spilled onto the throne room floor.

He toppled into a bloody heap.

The prince sheathed his talons—or rather, they disappeared with a shake of his hand to be replaced with long fingers once more. Fingers that had touched my face, I recalled with too much ease while watching him stride back toward the throne. "I think it's time we take our leave."

"Agreed," his mother said, her eyes on the mottling face of my uncle.

I withheld a smile as I finally dared to look at Brolen, as I noted the clenched hands at his sides. "You cannot just—"

Every warrior lining the walls shifted forward a step, and Brolen's face paled as he twisted toward the queen with a swift change of subject. "This wedding," he said, each word pushed through his teeth. "When will it be?"

"Why you'd care to attend when you had the princess locked in a dungeon awaiting execution is beyond me," the prince drawled, flicking blood from his tunic and cloak with a comical wince.

"I was merely trying to appease everyone. You and my own people."

"So chivalrous of you, Brolen," the queen said, watching her son with an amused expression as he continued to try to free himself of the blood. "Yet you speak as if you do not recall hearing me say that a new agreement was to be made." Looking at Brolen, she curled her upper lip, her eyes flaring. "We both know what you were playing at, and though I'm not shocked, I will admit that your audacity makes you one percent less of a repugnant bore."

"You think to insult me in my own home?" Brolen said, a touch above a growl. "And let us not forget what this arrangement truly is."

"Indeed, you should not," Olette said with unflinching coldness.

Sighing, Colvin wriggled free of his cloak and dropped it to the floor as if it repulsed him, uncaring who watched him carry on in such a peculiar way.

I tilted my head, sorry for it as it panged, but too curious. It couldn't be, surely...

Did the prince have an aversion to blood?

The queen stole my attention when she answered Brolen's question. "The engagement ball and vow ceremony will take place when we decide they will, and this time..." Olette raised a perfectly arched brow and rose from the throne like a cat after a nap, stretching her arms over her head. "It would behoove you to practice the art of patience, King."

My uncle glared but reluctantly nodded.

"Now," the queen said. "If you're quite finished with your fussing, Colvin, do escort your betrothed to her rooms to gather any belongings she might wish to take."

"There is nothing there for her," Brolen said, and my eyes snapped to him. A smirk thinned his lips, and my blood pressed into my skin with my ire. "All of her belongings were provided by yours truly, so they are not truly hers."

My aunt chortled, teetering into the throne room with a smoking stem in hand and intentionally brushing up against a warrior.

The reptilian's scaled forehead bunched as he reared back.

"Why, for the love of melting mushrooms, would you want a hairbrush or two with a grease-frenzy such as yours, Brolen?" Gesturing for me to follow, Mirra ignored the threat of retaliation in the Seelie king's gaze and said, "Come now, Fifi. Go and fetch what you need."

Grateful, even though I could think of nothing I longed to take, I did my best to walk in a straight line and fixed my attention on Mirra to keep from looking at the scaled warriors.

She waited at the bottom of the grand stairwell, a glint in her eye as Colvin followed me.

Each step was an agonizing effort I'd never experienced before, made worse by the encroaching heat of the male at my back. The energy emanating from him singed and tore at the air like that of a summer storm, his steps slow as he trailed me.

Concentrating on placing one foot before the other as we reached the second floor with his unnerving presence at my back, his question startled. "Have you eaten?"

"I'm tired, not weak."

"You are both, and it's almost painful to watch." I knew his words were not intended to insult, yet my teeth still gnashed.

They ached as I separated them to retort, "Painful is freeing a monster for I didn't know that was precisely what he was, and now I am struggling to walk down a hall I once passed in seconds after narrowly escaping death for aiding him."

"I did tell you it wasn't a good idea."

The anger that evoked threatened to split me in two and buckle my knees as we rounded the hall to the staircase leading to my rooms. Such hatred cost me precious energy I did not have, so I said nothing else as we climbed the stairs to the third floor.

I was almost too scared to open the door for fear of what I might find. Would Brolen have had my rooms packed up already? Would he have had everything destroyed?

"Allow me," Colvin said, and the door swung open without a touch from either of us.

"No need to boast," I said before I could help myself. Before I could remember just whom I was now entering a room with.

But the prince huffed, waiting for me to go on ahead.

Everything was right where I'd left it. My last embroidery failure—a patchwork of messy stars in a circular wooden disk—sat beside a pile of books. Two apple carcasses from the afternoon of my birthday, an afternoon I hadn't known would be my final one of normalcy, rotted beside them.

I didn't touch anything. I found I couldn't move at all as Colvin swept his gaze across my bedchamber.

There was an unusual beauty to him.

A fierceness subdued by the gentle pout to his mouth, the straight strands of hair falling free from their tie to mask the unforgiving edge to his cheeks and jaw, and the careful way his golden eyes observed his surroundings.

As though his talons were scraping over my soul, an intense discomfort held me immobile as he observed my unmade bed, the navy and periwinkle knitted blankets and cushions, and the destroyed curtains that hung in age-worn tatters tied to the posts.

"Did you swing from the bed like a creature does with vines between the trees?" A soft question, his voice returning to the deep, gentle quality I'd come to associate with him in the dungeon.

"When I was young," I murmured.

He smiled slightly, taking in the desk cluttered with more needlework I'd spoiled and other projects I'd never finished. Inkpots lay overturned and empty, quills dusting pads of parchment with random wonderings and findings of things I'd discovered in the woods.

But it was the dresser, still clouded with plates from my last lunch and undergarments from the morning of my birthday, that truly made my insides clench painfully.

I cleared my throat, moving slowly to the tall corner shelf where the crown of preserved wildflowers that had once belonged to my mother sat unworn. "You cannot marry me." Walking toward him was akin to nearing a forest fire, not knowing which direction it might take next. My skin no longer hummed in response to his energy—it vibrated. A tickle that wasn't entirely unpleasant but still unnerved me nonetheless.

"Apparently, I can." Colvin plucked the crown in his long fingers before I could so much as extend my arm to it. Turning, he caught me unawares, and I stumbled back when he lifted the wreath of flowers to place on my head. He tilted his own, watching. "Afraid?" he asked, brows lowering. "Why?"

"I'm not," I said too quickly, knowing that and my scent proved my words to be a lie.

Undeterred, he walked closer. My back met the wall. He stopped before me and carefully set the crown upon my head. Low and with his eyes slowly dipping from my hair, he murmured, "You were not so afraid just a few months ago." His mouth wriggled with a hint of a smile as though he were remembering. "Need I even ask what has changed?"

"I didn't know what I know now."

A nod, followed by a release of breath as he gently stroked his fingers from the top of my head to my shoulders.

To my horror, I shivered with something other than fear as they traced the long, gnarled, near-white strands down my arms to my waist.

"Hair of pure winter," he observed quietly, as if to himself. "I wanted to see you again." His eyes shifted from my waist, where his fingers fell away and back to his sides, to meet mine when I looked up. "Though I knew that was a rarity I could only ever hope for. Now I can't help but wonder if perhaps I was alone in my desire."

Maybe if things had been different, if he wasn't a monstrous beast who ravaged villages and woodland with a lust for blood, he wouldn't have been. Maybe I would've daydreamed about the touch of his lips on mine in the dungeon that final night rather than toss and turn during stolen dreams.

A trick, I thought. Deception at its finest. His ilk was well-versed in the art of coaxing their prey into believing things that would only see them bleed. Especially the blood feeders. "You were alone, and you are a liar."

He lifted a brow, tilting his head. His shoulder-length black hair was tied at his nape in a matching obsidian ribbon, but another strand fell free, soft looking and falling to frame his cheek. Rather than tell me he wasn't lying, he shocked me by asking, "Who is he to you?"

Thoroughly taken aback, I balked. "Who?"

"You know of whom I speak. The fresh-looking recruit who escorted you to the throne room and then watched you like a one-eyed hawk." His tone was mild, but there was a sharpness to the hypnotizing way his mouth moved. "The one who tracked you to the dungeon that night."

"He is none of your concern," I hissed, heated enough to dare push past him and head to the door.

His clipped words halted me. "He is if you are to be my wife."

I didn't turn back. I stood in the doorway, wishing I could tear him to shreds for all that he'd done, all the while knowing I was also to blame. "Then it is a good thing I'll likely never see him again." I seethed the last words between my teeth. "Or anyone else I might care about because of you."

"You harbor a terrible resentment toward me, fire-breather."

"I'd learn to grow comfortable with it if I were you, dragon."

His huff of breathy laughter trailed me into the hall. "What about your things? There's nothing you wish to take?"

"Brolen was right," I said, running my hand along the railing toward the curving entrance to the stairs. I looked across them to the other side, to the darkened hall that housed my aunt and uncle's private rooms. The sandstone walls, the gigantic ornamental vases perched between the arched windows, and the railing beneath my hands chipped from the dull blade Regin had carried when pretending to be a soldier growing up... "There is nothing for me here. I merely wanted to see it one last time."

But I kept my mother's crown upon my head as we descended the stairs in silence. It was all I'd ever had of her, and after what Brolen had revealed to me in the dungeon, I refused to leave it here.

When we returned, Olette smiled, beautiful and cruel as she looked from us to Brolen. "Do take care now, dear King."

I watched her materialize from the throne room, unaware of the prince's advance until his arms were around me, his scent suffocating as my surroundings began to drip away in patches of color replaced with deepening dark.

"Hold on," he said, and I wasn't sure if he'd meant to him or something else.

But the rift in the air ripped wide open, the whirling suction of it too much, and so I closed my eyes to the sound of Colvin's rough curse.

EIGHT

WATER SPLASHED, THE SCENT OF JASMINE AND buttercream clouding the cool air of the room I woke in. "Where am I?" I asked, pushing up from the bed. The last thing I remembered was leaving the throne room back home.

Home.

Sorrow washed through me like acid. Never mine again.

"You know where you are." Colvin's deep voice made me finally blink. My eyes soaked in all the black cushions beneath me upon the emerald and deep-gray bedding of the huge bed. "These will be your rooms."

My crown lay beside me. Yawning, I wondered how long I'd slept. It must not have been too long, as dawn wasn't yet glowing through the purple-stained windows on either side of the fireplace. "No cell?"

"Would you prefer one?"

I didn't answer that.

Ripping my attention from the bed that could fit six grown males, I winced as I scooted to the edge, my limbs stiff and aching.

I padded over a velvet carpet runner, likely soiling it with my feet. A door in the bedchamber's corner was open, the prince beyond. He tested the water as he perched on the edge of the emerald tiles surrounding a steaming bathing pool. "You should bathe and eat."

"I'm fine."

"You lie. I've never met anyone who passed out during materializing." A few seconds later, he added bitterly, "Scared the shit out of me."

He was right. I was lying, but I didn't bother confirming. I also didn't care that he would see me naked after he'd witnessed me covered in days' worth of filth. "Wouldn't want to lose your stolen bride in the energy rifts, would you?"

His eyes flared when I grabbed the tattered skirts of my gown and pulled it over my body.

By the time I was free, he was looking at the ground. His jaw worked as I stepped out of my undergarments with a smirk. "They should be burned."

Fire engulfed them as soon as I finished speaking, Colvin rising and dusting the ashes into nothing with a hover of his hand over what had been my clothing. "I'm beginning to think you might have preferred we left you there to face certain death."

Still staring at where my clothing had been, I remembered I was naked. "A death that would've been your fault." I stepped into the tub, needing to bite back a moan as I sank into the surprisingly deep, creamy depths. The water lapped at my shoulders, though the pool was nowhere near full.

Apparently ignoring my latest barb, the prince was busy searching the large room while I soaked.

No, I wasn't yet willing to admit he'd saved me. He and his mother might have heard of what Brolen intended for me and therefore acted sooner, but I had no doubt that whatever his plans were, they'd already been unfolding. I'd merely escaped one cell for another that was admittedly far grander than anything I could've guessed.

Towering yet fluid, I didn't deprive myself of the chance to observe this prince I'd rescued. This prince who'd doomed me.

He moved like liquid over a rock, unfalteringly graceful even as he muttered to himself about the lack of healing salts on the shelf and fumbled for a particular towel when there looked to be eight of them piled up and awaiting use.

"Why did you kill him?" The question shocked him into stillness. It shocked me too, the ease in which I'd said it when I hadn't meant to at all. When I knew better than to prod so closely to things I wished to ignore.

"He harmed you."

"But you didn't want to do it."

"What an assumption to make, fire-breather." Releasing a re-signed breath, he finally turned to face me and leaned against the tiled wall. "And an incorrect one at that."

"I saw you," I said, trying to keep my tone free of scorn and only somewhat successful. "With your cloak. You don't like blood."

Colvin laughed, brief and toe-curling in its richness. "Oh, but I do like blood." His disturbingly bright eyes remained fixed on my face even though nothing could be seen beneath the layer of milky soaps masking the water's surface. "Some might even say I love it." His tone softened to silk. "Very much."

I scowled. "Trying to scare me, dragon?"

He frowned. "Just merely stating a truth. I'll state another," he said, his long lashes shadowing his cheeks as he licked his teeth and stared at his boots momentarily. When his eyes met mine again, they shone with something I couldn't read. "I don't like it, but that doesn't change that I wanted him dead. That I needed to do it. He hurt you." An intentional pause. "Should I continue? Because I'm more than happy to."

In answer, I looked away. I wasn't sure if I was aroused or re-pulsed, but too terrified of what he might say next, I figured it was best not to decide.

A minute passed, his gaze still on me. "Rest," he finally said, sounding tired himself. "You've endured a rather harrowing ordeal. A meal will be brought to you."

I slipped beneath the water and scrubbed my hands through my hair, pushing it back from my face as I emerged.

The prince was gone.

I finger-combed the worst of the knots from the long strands with the bar of butter soap, thinking over all Colvin had said. All that had happened.

More of those stained windows lined the length of the pool, all three fogged with steam and scratched by swaying branches and vines outside. Upon the tiles against the wall was a wooden rack of bathing crystals, salts, and soaps. Between the privy and a tall ivory wash basin was a row of rusted hooks on the wall. Hand towels and two gray satin robes hung from them.

I should've been grateful I hadn't ended up in another cell, or as the prince's plaything, thrown into rooms with the rest of his harem. But I wasn't. The deliciously warm water should've uncoiled the tension in my body.

But these lavish conditions I'd been handed had me all the more wary and conflicted.

I didn't sleep.

I remained in the bathing pool until the water grew cold enough to chill and keep the drowsiness at bay. Then I wrapped one of the robes around me, the inside lined with fleece, and sat upon the bed.

The door didn't open for some hours. No steps sounded outside.

I stared at the wood. Even if it was unlocked, where would I go? Safety was but another illusion I'd believed in too recklessly all my life.

I wasn't sure what was expected of me. I was to marry the prince. But why? And then what? It would be a sham. Most marriages between royals who were not mated were all arranged and loveless. Mine would be no different.

Except it was.

No Seelie royal had ever wed an Unseelie. A tiny shred of hope told me that history would not see that changed with Colvin and me.

So I was a pawn. Though for what purpose remained to be seen.

The Unseelie queen's plans couldn't possibly only pertain to keeping my uncle on a pretty little leash. Not now that he'd shown he wished me dead for my betrayal. Perhaps she wanted to seize control of the two kingdoms. Which would require the end of my uncle slash father.

I didn't wish to call him either.

It should've sickened and shamed me that merely imagining a

world without Brolen in it filled me with nothing but bone-melting relief—the likes of which I might never taste again.

Light, scuffing steps pricked my ears. My empty stomach groaned at the sound of metal meeting stone outside of the door to my rooms.

I opened it, peering into a wide, dim hall. A door stood tall at the other end. Nothing but windows between. On the ground, a tray with a pitcher of water and what smelled like meat stew heated my bare feet.

That I wasn't typically fond of stew didn't matter. My mouth watered as I snatched the tray and kicked the door closed. I didn't bother locking it. Not when the creatures who roamed this castle were capable of more than just ruining locks.

I chose to eat on the bed even though a perfectly good, even if small, rectangular dining table sat empty with two chairs beneath.

But I didn't eat. I tipped the bowl to my lips and drank greedy mouthfuls. Forcing myself to slow down, I savored the remaining dregs of meat with the single chunk of bread I'd been given. The smoky, chewy juiciness. Then I attempted to guess the spices flavoring the sauce. A strong pepper and something musky, almost earthy.

Thinking that maybe it was best I didn't know, I finished every drop and crumb and then the water.

Afterward, I placed it all on the ground. I closed my eyes, my mind whirling with the insanity that had overtaken my life. One thing was certain, if I ever found a modicum of the peace I'd once known and had taken for granted, I'd never dare think it dull again.

Daylight had thoroughly bloomed by the time I gave in to the urge to rest.

Lying over the silken sheets and woolen blankets, I gazed at the four posts rising to hold a canopy of dark green netting. It was tied to the posts with black ribbon, giving view to the room that was supposedly mine.

Carpets, a deep moss green with charcoal whorls, covered the stone on each side of the bed that perched in the center of the room against the back wall. A chest of drawers sat on either side.

Rolling over, I studied the roses painted upon the chestnut wood, the intricate detail of each glistening petal, and the sharp tip of each thorn. The paint had faded with age in places, but it didn't detract from the overall beauty.

More stunning artwork dotted the stone walls in the form of wildflower paintings, a tapestry with a moon and sun and a familiar cursive script. The same script within the tapestries of the throne room I'd not long left behind—seemingly for good.

Beneath the sun, we have our fun, frolicking and singing until darkness comes.

Beneath the moon, we howl, and we bray, hunting and mourning the rise of each day.

Such furnishings, the detail etched into the wood surrounding the pebble work of the fireplace, spoke of unspeakable wealth. The stained Rosetta windows on either side of the fireplace offered no confirmation of what time of day it was.

There was a closed door along the wall nearest the one providing entry to the room. A dressing room, perhaps, being that a long, gilded mirror took up the entirety of the wood. My eyes roamed and absorbed the brown-and-deep-gray stone of the walls, falling upon the golden-framed paintings again, and I shifted to better see past the post of the bed to the other side.

Standing in the doorway was a male with shoulder-length, raven-colored hair.

His tall frame leaned into the engraved wood, his attention anything but comforting as he said, "You didn't sleep, did you?"

He must have materialized, for I hadn't heard a whisper of his approach. "And you didn't knock."

His only response was a slow blink and a twitch of his petal-soft mouth.

The Unseelie prince watched me with dim eyes, an emerald cravat at his neck and a fresh, long-sleeved black cotton shirt loosely tucked into matching colored pants. The lack of shine to his eyes, coupled with his slouched posture and his tone, said it was likely he hadn't rested in the hours that'd passed himself. "Can you blame me?"

He just continued to stare. "Come," he finally said, straightening. "You've been summoned."

"By whom?"

He didn't answer. He just disappeared into the shadowed hall beyond.

Knowing to remain would only anger whomever it was who'd summoned me—and willing to wager it was his ghastly mother—I hurried out of the room and trailed his irksome scent down the hall. "I am not dressed."

"You're dressed enough."

Asshole, I thought, my fingers stiff with irritation as I tightened the tie of my robe. It barely reached my ankles, but it would have to do. I wasn't sure why I cared. The Unseelie were notorious for their lack of propriety. Many a tale had been spun of their fashions and lack thereof.

Windows, arched and stained dark, provided fractals of light to guide the way. Enough to suggest it was perhaps nearing midday. The hall widened at the end, and my betrothed turned left.

I stared down the opposite, short, windowless hall and flinched when the shadows closed in to conceal a door. It happened again after we entered a spiraling collection of stone steps, maybe a floor from the bottom. When I glanced to the right, it was as if a door was fading.

"It will let you know where you are not welcome to roam," came Colvin's deep voice.

"It?" I asked, but he didn't stop. I peered back at the darkness, then followed him. "You mean to suggest that this place is alive?"

"It's seen too much to be without a soul."

He then vanished down another hall, and I picked up the pace to make sure I didn't lose him. As though eyes were watching me from places I could never so much as guess at, perhaps even the paintings of gold and bronze-eyed ancestors, I decided it would be foolish to doubt what he'd said.

Just this once.

We wound deeper into the fortress through the maze of halls, and as we did, it grew darker without the windows. Sconces, already burning, dotted the stone. Stone that seemed to lose its softer shade of brown. Almost obsidian, it glittered, and when I pressed my fingers to it, I could've sworn it shivered.

I did it again when we began to pass a series of more closed doors, murky chatter, and laughter coming from somewhere behind them. The stone warmed and seemed to lean into the press of my fingers.

"What is this place?" I whispered, not expecting a response. Whatever it was, it was becoming alarmingly evident that escape might be futile. That even if I had somewhere to run to, I shouldn't so much as try.

I received one anyway, Colvin's tone a touch snide. "A castle, of course." I scowled at his back, that hair so dark it melded with his black shirt, the only difference being the slight shine of firelight in the strands.

Annoyed that I'd even noticed as much, I tried to look past him to see where we might be headed.

After another turn, we reached a large antechamber with a mosaic crimson and purple flower for a ceiling, and Colvin slowed. Even his gait, as effortless and arrogant as if the ground carried him, irritated me.

He pushed open the imposing oak doors, and I blinked up at their unnecessary height, transfixed by the deep etchings of vines spiraling up the wood.

"Well?" a shrill voice asked, the word echoing to where I'd paused in a belated sense of feet-freezing fear. "Where is she?"

Colvin returned to view, his brows furrowed. "Do you need some assistance in entering the room, Princess?"

"Really, Col," the queen hissed. "Fia is our guest."

Col? I couldn't help but snort. Which earned me a thinning of his lupine eyes. "Precisely why I offered to help."

The word guest implied a more temporary situation than what I'd been led to believe, but it failed to provide comfort. Comfort was already a long-ago memory and as fickle as the goddess's decision-making skills.

So I moved through the doors into the vast expanse of a throne room. "Moon melt me," I murmured as my eyes flew over the room's tiled center to the deep plum and obsidian tapestry flanking the walls on either side of the throne.

Stone circled the tiles, but they gave way not two feet into the room to hug a mosaic mural of a giant dragon head. Two short horns rose from its muzzle beside gaping nostrils. Larger horns curled from its head to meet with a glowing full moon between them. A wide open mouth displayed an impressive amount of triangularly cut teeth.

Whiskers sprouted beneath the nose, long and nearly lost to the darkness of its scales. But it was the gigantic eyes, a gold so bright they burned, that made me flinch and take a step back.

"His name was Ivahn, supposedly the first monster to stalk these lands."

Swallowing, I traced the tiles to the stone dais.

A mauve gown draped aside a slender pair of feet and ankles. Each toenail had been painted a perfect shade of bloodred. Though I'd already met the creature seated upon the birch, ivy-wrapped throne twice, I'd hoped to avoid doing so again so soon.

I had a feeling a hundred meetings would not be enough to make one feel relaxed in the presence of Queen Olette of the Unseelie.

The faerie queen flung a hand over the leaf-choked arm of the chair, her long nails painted in the same shade as her toes. "Look at me."

The command ripped through me, tilting my head and shoulders back in a confusing instant.

Eyes, dark and rimmed in even darker lashes, flared. Her smile was nothing short of serpentine, bow-shaped lips painted crimson, too. "Oh, how sweet a treat you are."

Still wondering if she'd forced my compliance, I glowered. Then I remembered I wished to somehow survive this, and I quickly bent into a clumsy curtsy.

A pleased hum. "Do you find your accommodations to your liking?"

Failing to answer fast enough, the prince drawled at the window behind the throne, his back to us, "She had expected something…" His head cocked, and I wished to knock it from his shoulders as he said, "Different."

The queen tapped her cheek. "Different?"

"Well," I hemmed after a tense bundle of moments. "I just hadn't thought that I'd…"

"Find yourself in something other than a cell?" the queen supplied. "Being that was what your lot did with you and my son, of course."

Unsure if I should answer, I offered a weak smile.

Olette lowered her hand to her lap. "That can always be arranged, Fia the feral. So if I were you, I'd watch where you so carelessly step."

I blinked, frowning.

Her tone suggested she was already growing tired of this meeting when she continued. "Having said that, you may roam wherever you please, but you are no good to us dead, so do beware of the dangers awaiting something tasty like you."

I curtsied in response, though I wasn't grateful or shocked. My supposed freedom was not freedom at all, but rather just another waiting trap or death sentence.

"Speaking of," Olette said with a sigh that hinted at annoyance. "Here comes some of those dangers now."

A wretched, keening noise echoed through the halls as I straightened. I'd have thought it wind or an incoming storm until the tapestry shook on the walls.

I whirled toward the sound.

Shadows darkened the doorway opposite the one the prince and I had entered. Not shadows, I belatedly discovered, but monsters running and then rising on two legs. Mouths frothing, pointed ears twitching, teeth glinting, the two narlows slammed into the stone archway and growled.

"You know them, yes?" Olette purred as the beasts gnashed their teeth at one another and snarled. "You should, being that you were the one to save them."

A wave of icy dread thickened my blood, swaying me at the knees.

The narlows broke free of the door and advanced, and it was all I could do to raise my hands before me.

As if that would somehow stop them from reducing me to blood-ied ribbons.

NINE

THE SHAKING AND GROWLING CEASED.

Hot plumes of rancid breath blew across my raised arms. Peeking between them, I found a dark, staring eye and stumbled back.

The prince, who must have moved during the narlow's rush, caught my shoulders. "Stay still."

"And just let them eat me?" I whispered harshly, not sure why. It wasn't as if they understood me. "I don't think so." I made to escape his hold but stopped when the narlows growled, a gentle rumble if such a thing could exist, and I pressed my back into the prince's front instead.

His voice was a barely audible whisper at my ear, his hard body and heat a crackling fire throwing embers through my robe. "Trust me."

"Why would I trust a liar and a treacherous opportunist?"

His fingers curled into my shoulders. "I never lied."

"You omitted a truth that obliterated my life," I said, forgetting the queen's presence, though when I twisted in Colvin's hold to glare at him over my shoulder, I found the throne empty.

Colvin's bright eyes were trained on the narlows. And I'd have thought he had no regard for my words at all when he spoke, if it weren't for the gritted quality to his own. "They merely wish to see you."

Returning my attention to the monsters who indeed seemed to be waiting for something, I blinked at them.

The features I'd traced with my fingers just months ago were no longer cute. Their faces were mangled, tiny eyes lopsided, and their furred cheeks sunken. Snouts, once reminiscent of a pig, were now longer and upturned, their teeth permanently on display with their jaws askew.

They'd made it.

I could only hope it wasn't all in vain. That they wouldn't try to kill me, too.

"I took the liberty of naming them for you," the prince said as the hand on my left shoulder rose, a long finger pointing. An unwelcome cold filled the space he'd touched. "This is Spodge, as he's got a spongy patch of white fur under his chin, and that is Herb."

"Spodge and Herb?" I repeated, almost insulted on behalf of the grotesque giants. "But those are names you'd give to little critters."

"They were still little when I brought them home." The way he'd said the word little curled my toes. I ignored it, and the smile it tempted to birth.

Home. He'd not only followed through on that promise, but he'd named them. Raised them. Astonished, I took a hesitant step forward. "They actually survived."

"And now they won't leave," Colvin said pointedly.

The beasts grumbled, Spodge curling a large paw into his belly and scratching. "The sleepy one?" I suspected his fate before asking, but I still wanted to hear it. To know.

"Barely lasted the journey. Honestly, it's kind of miraculous these two survived. Though I think bringing them home definitely helped them to thrive. And now"—more cold swept in as Colvin circled behind the narlow brothers, pulling what looked to be a banana peel from the back of Herb's furry arm—"they can follow you around and wreck your belongings instead."

Tilting my head back, I gazed up at the narlow's faces.

Drool still hung from their mangled mouths, their eyes unmoving from me. "Do they remember me?"

"You'd be dead or in need of rescue if they didn't. They must be locked away when someone they don't know decides to pay us a visit."

"Comforting," I said, and the prince huffed at my sarcasm, stepping back when I held out my hand to Spodge. He lowered his head, sniffing me, and Herb followed when I offered my other hand. I laughed, their wet noses tickling as they inhaled hard enough to pull at my skin.

My smile fell when Herb's paw landed on my arm. It fell from the weight, and I scowled. "Ow."

He stilled. I took his paw, carefully lifting it to study the squashed toes and jagged claws, and placed it upon my overturned palm. "Gentle."

The beast stared at my hand, and Spodge edged closer, offering his and nearly smacking me in the face. I took it and did the same, then smiled and retreated a few steps, hoping they'd let me leave.

They did, but the prince laughed when they followed, and I stopped in the doorway.

The beasts collided again with a grumble, right at my back. I turned, trying to find Colvin between the minuscule gap in their large bodies. "How do I get rid of them?"

"When you find out," he said, heading to the opposite door, "let me know."

"Where are you going?" He couldn't mean to just leave me with them, surely. He didn't answer, and I'd have maybe gone after him if it weren't for the narlows blocking my path. I had no idea how to return to my rooms. "How do I get back?"

"You'll soon see," he said, and the humor in his voice made me suppress a growl of my own.

The narlows followed me down the hall as I mumbled obscenities beneath my breath, taking wrong turn after wrong turn. All the while, the beasts kept growing closer to squashing me whenever I stopped abruptly.

Trying to squeeze past them to head back to a hall I thought I'd recognized, I muttered, "This is a tad unnerving, I must say."

They just stared, likely not understanding, or uncaring even if they did.

Sighing, I walked on. They continued to lumber behind me,

bumping into walls and grumbling as they attempted to keep ahead of each other.

In need of open space, I gave up on my quest to return to my rooms at the sight of a growing wash of sunlight at the bottom of a stairwell. I'd somehow made it to the ground floor. That would be good to know if only I could've remembered how I'd gotten there.

The narlow's grumbling worsened as I reached a hall that widened into a small, bright foyer. A row of glass doors with stained green hillsides beckoned, folding open when I pulled on the wooden handle. It was indeed midday, Spodge and Herb hissing at the flare of the sun and retreating indoors.

It seemed that was one way of getting rid of them.

I smiled as I crossed the cracked terrace. No one seemed to be around. No sentinels. No courtiers. No groundskeepers.

Though the latter was to be expected, given the tyrannical growth of weeds and the state of the overgrown rose bushes. They climbed the stone and crawled along the terrace, helping themselves to the fountain at the courtyard's center. No water flowed from it, only more vines.

Turning, I spied another entrance across the stone and a rotting wooden bench seat tucked beneath a window in the corner. The walls on either side of me seemed to stretch to the sky. I couldn't look for long, my eyes adjusting to the sun's glow, but I surmised I must be standing upon a seldom used terrace close to the heart of the castle.

Though it was heavily neglected, there was an undeniable beauty to it. Pink flowers blossomed from the vines. The glisten of melting morning frost still clung to the roses, the moss along the fountain's edge and between the cracks in the stone all around me shining.

Beautiful, indeed, but otherwise evidently dull.

A feminine voice asked from behind, "Are you lost?"

Alarmed that I hadn't even heard her approach, my spine stiffened as I peered over my shoulder to find a female with cherry-red hair smirking at me from the fountain that had been empty a moment ago.

Seated on its moss-laden rim, she surveyed me as I faced her. "So you're her."

"Her?" I asked, my brow lifting with my guard. Though she seemed to lack any creature features, besides her arched ears, I still didn't trust anyone in this wretched kingdom. I quietly wondered if I'd ever trust anyone ever again.

Her apricot eyes danced. "The precious princess, of course."

"Of course," I said, giving her a smile so forced it pained my cheeks.

She snorted, the sound as delicate as her amused petite features. "Please don't expect me to curtsy. My skirts don't allow for it."

Indeed, I thought, eyeing the layers of dark blue and red lace wrapped around her shoulders and every curve. It seemed she hadn't been able to decide if she'd wanted to dress as a toffee stick or a cocoon.

"And just whom might you be?" I withheld from crossing my arms and instead kept them loose at my sides. I wouldn't be ruffled by a bored female looking for something new to entertain herself with.

"Persy," she said, her crimson painted lips peeling back to expose her teeth. "But I'm assuming you're more interested in who I might be to this family." Leaning forward, she glanced around the empty terrace and then cupped one side of her mouth, "Namely, a certain prince?"

"I hope he makes you howl at the moon," I drawled with a breathy laugh. "And I mean it."

Watching me with her lips still curved, I deduced she was trying to decipher if I spoke true. I supposed she believed me, for she rose and informed, "He does not, but his uncle Jarron?" Her next words resembled a purr. "He excels at it." Nearing me, she whispered, "Tell him that, and I'll gut you while you sleep."

Stunned, her lilac-powdered scent engulfing me as she passed, it took me a moment to keep up. "You live here?"

"Most of the time." Persy traipsed toward the glass doors I'd left open, though it wouldn't have surprised me if she'd materialized into the courtyard. "Father's one of Olette's oldest friends and her most trusted general. It has its perks."

"Like fucking a prince?"

A sharp, singing laugh as she leaned into the door with her hip. "Jarron is most certainly not a prince, though he will just love that you thought so even for a moment."

I wasn't sure if I wanted to meet this Jarron immediately or never at all. "He's your mate," I finally felt confident enough to guess.

"Yes, but it's a little… complicated." The change in her tone implied she would say no more.

So I said, "Dare I ask what brought you down here?" I made a show of looking around the leafy space. "Surely, not the scenery."

Persy pointed high behind me, and I twisted to glimpse the window three floors above. "Jarron's rooms. You did look lost, but in all honesty, we made a bet."

"A bet," I repeated, frowning.

"Seelie don't gamble?" Forcing a pout, she tutted. "You truly are terrible bores."

"We prefer to drink," I clipped. *And exchange bed partners and gossip as if they were currency*, but something told me I needn't bother telling her that.

Eyeing me, she hummed. "You don't seem like one for much drinking."

"I wasn't." A strange noise left me, a huffed grunt, and I forced my heart to steady. "Until recently."

Her brows shot up, and a shocked laugh punched the cool air. "Oh, you do detest him, don't you? I'd ask why, but I have a feeling you don't even truly understand it yourself." With a wink, this Persy turned to leave. "Good luck."

"How much?" I asked because I couldn't help myself.

Swaying back with a hand over the wooden edge of the glass door, she narrowed her strange eyes playfully. "The bet?" At my nod, she said through a laugh, "It does not involve coin, Princess."

Heat threatened to engulf my cheeks, and I looked at the ground as she laughed in earnest.

Her parting words lifted my head and hopes of finding my rooms before the encroaching exhaustion rendered me incapable of dizzying amounts of stairs. "By the way, the castle will quit playing with you when you make your intentions clear."

"And how might I do that?"

"Be intentional with where you wish to go," she said, as though I should've already known.

She was gone before I could unleash the gratitude I didn't want to give.

I found my way back to my rooms with only a few mishaps, one involving a dead end in a hallway that reeked of Colvin.

Spodge and Herb found me in the hall that mercifully led to my rooms. They thundered down it with such excitement that it took me precious few seconds while gazing at their maws to remember that they wouldn't kill me. Hopefully.

"Stop," I commanded moments before they reached me. They did, rising from all fours and blinking at me with heaving chests. "I need to sleep." Another blink, a whining growl coming from Herb. "Just..." I backed up toward the door of my rooms. "Wait, okay?" I tried to look behind them, but there was too much pudge and fur. "Or I don't know, go and find something to eat. *Something*," I stressed. "Not someone."

More blinking.

I forced a smile. "Good night." Then I opened the door just wide enough to slip inside.

I didn't bother searching for a nightgown. In the same robe, I collapsed onto the bed and listened to the narlow's shuffling and grumbling on the other side of the door until I gave in to the call of sleep.

An unearthly screeching roused me in a fright. I sat up, pushing my hair back from my face and looked at the windows on either side of the fireplace as a flock of those bat-like creatures flew past.

Their spiked wings cloaked the room in darkness for breath-rocking seconds. Then a few forgotten breaths later, the moon and stars shone once more, and right as a flying type of hound, almost skeletal in appearance, gave chase.

Not a dream. Not even a nightmare, unfortunately.

Pushing farther up from where I'd been sleeping facedown at the wrong end of the bed, I took stock of my surroundings—refamiliarized myself with the unfamiliar while my chest tightened with longing for my own rooms.

I'd known for a long time just how much I got away with and that I was beyond privileged. But I'd never felt it this keenly before, with a fragile sense of regret for not appreciating how fortunate I'd been. Now, it was far too late.

Too late to wake with the comfort of my belongings upon my nightstand, others scattered in a mess I'd known like the back of my hand around my rooms.

Now, it seemed I would wake with fear.

And the sour taste of burning resentment.

I let it fuel me as I rose and traipsed to the bathing room to relieve myself and wash up. A brush, golden and engraved with intricate leaves, caught the shine of the moon on a shelf above the sink. But I lacked the energy to care and quickly left the dark chamber.

Though I did decide, at the very least, to get dressed.

The arched door between the bathing room and the entry to the chambers indeed opened to a narrow dressing room. A small sconce shook to life at the end of the passageway, revealing rows of gowns and cloaks and tunics and sleepwear and...

Undergarments.

In frills and creams and blacks and silks, an array of them was tucked within a small chest of drawers beneath another mirror.

I didn't dare wonder who had picked them out, let alone the rest of the items. For all I knew, they could have always kept clothing designed to fit a variety of shapes and sizes on hand in their guest rooms. I chose a gown of deep blue that resembled a long-sleeved tunic, if a tunic could reach the ground, and the silk undergarments.

Remembering my bare feet on the way to the door, I returned to the dressing room and snatched a pair of black slippers from the shelf above the hanging garments. Lined with wool, they felt more like a night slipper than something one could wear wherever they so wished.

It was akin to walking upon two clouds.

I scrunched my nose, staring down at the bows upon the toes, my own wriggling inside the suede, and withheld a smile. Then I adjusted the dipping, triangular neckline of the dress, which had been embroidered in loops of purple and gold.

My breasts were large, as were my hips. The soft cotton revealed the outline of the latter and a glimpse of my cleavage. But unless I found something else to wear, there wasn't much to be done for it. So I shrugged and opened the door.

To find the narlows slumped to the ground with a soiled tray between them, dishes overturned, and eating the remnants of what I assumed had once been my dinner.

Their chewing stopped, Spodge licking his lips with his furry tongue. "Really?" Even seated on the ground, their heads were a few inches higher than mine. I didn't care. I was hungry, and they were thieves.

I lifted a finger and stabbed it at each of their snouts. "Not okay. That was *mine*." They tilted their grotesque heads, watching me, but otherwise remained still as I snatched the bowl from Spodge, who growled. I growled back, and he blinked, seemingly startled.

Herb had the decency to drop the chicken bones before I could take those too, and I decided I was no longer starving as they rolled from my palm to the bowl, covered in slimy saliva.

"By the fucking moon." I sighed and shook out my hand, taking the tray and placing everything on it, including the broken glass, before they cut themselves. "I did *not* sign up for this." For any of this, really, but they wouldn't care. I doubted they cared much about anything besides their stomachs.

They trailed me down the hall to the stairs, and I wondered if their silence, the lack of squabbling between them, meant they'd understood their scolding.

It was said that most of the Unseelie, hunters and moon worshippers by nature, slept during the daylight hours, but I had never been sure that it was true. Not until now. A somewhat comforting percussion of bustle filled Castle Eldorn. Clatter and chatter behind walls and doors and deep within stairwells.

The kitchens were not so hard to find. I followed the scent of meats and charcoal to a floor below ground level. It seemed to slope, the hall we emerged into more of a ramp as I looked to the left. To the right, the stone crawled higher to a short door, slices of light stealing in through a rectangular window in the door.

I noted it opened to a large vegetable garden as I bent and pressed my forehead to the glass.

The narlows hadn't moved from the entry to the stairwell. As I waded down the ramp, thinking they'd follow, I looked back to find them peering around the wall, watchful but unmoving. I frowned but continued with the tray around the corner to a low-hanging doorway that gave way to an enormous room with even lower ceilings.

I soon discovered why they'd chosen to stay behind as a goblin with a carrot-shaped nose and sapphire eyes the size of ants hobbled toward me. His features twisted, exposing sharp, tiny dark teeth. "What are you doing down here?"

"Returning my meal." I held out the tray. "Of which I did not get to eat."

He eyed it all, the bones and drying webs of saliva, and made a retching sound. "He was warned those beasts would be nothing but trouble." The tray was snatched from my hands forcefully, cutlery and glass clanking over the metal as he tossed it onto one of three long island counters behind him. "And I've heard you're not much better yourself, Fia the feral."

I lifted a brow, my eyes skirting over the two other goblins, a female with butter yellow braids and a male with a beard as long as him. They quickly looked away and busied themselves with mixing and washing.

"Princess," I said, and the goblin glaring at me scowled in earnest. "Princess Fia the feral." I cared not that Brolen had said no one wanted me as their princess anymore. None of them got to decide who I truly was.

"You'll find no such respect here." He waved a gnarled hand in dismissal. "Be gone, you good for nothing waste of magical blood."

My eyes widened to the size of the saucepan he dried before tucking the towel into one of the suspenders holding up his small brown pants. "But I'm hungry."

"Then teach those narlows some manners, and yourself while you're at it."

"Me?" I balked. "You're the one spouting insults, goblin." Our family had ceased hiring their ilk in our lands hundreds of years ago due to their aggressive and spiteful natures. Nevertheless, I'd always wanted to meet one, and now I wasn't so sure I was glad to scratch that achievement off my list.

"You deserve more than insults."

Leaning into the small doorway, I huffed. "And why is that?"

"You know why," he muttered, waddling to the row of four sinks along the far wall. Orbs of firelight hung from the ceiling above them, casting an orange but dim haze over his stringy brown hair as he tossed the tray into the sink, glass and all.

It grew clearer that perhaps the goblins, although evidently sour in nature, were holding a nasty little grudge against the Seelie Kingdom. "I see. But you cannot let me starve for a decision I did not make." I muttered belatedly, close to flinching as I recalled the hunger I'd felt in the dungeon, "I've done enough of that to last me a lifetime."

The butter-haired goblin glared at the male I'd been dealing with and wiped her hands on her frilled sky-blue apron. "She is to wed the prince, you blithering idiot."

"Indeed," I said, and in this case, the betrothal I hadn't quite wrapped my head around might just prove useful.

"She could wed the queen, and I would still wish she'd find herself lost in a desert wasteland of bones and dust in the worst of all heat."

Perhaps not, then.

I bit back an unexpected laugh, coughing. "Right." Then I bent more at the knees to avoid hitting my head on the low ceiling and headed for the sinks as the goblins all tripped over themselves and hissed. I smiled and fluttered my lashes. "Just washing my hands."

"Pity you cannot wash the disrespect of your forebearers from your soul."

"My soul is just fine, thank you," I said, and he gnashed his teeth when I stole an apple from a wooden crate of produce next to the sink. "Where is this prince I am to marry?"

The goblin gave a derisive snort. "Lamenting his rotten fate, I'd say."

"Orin," the female reprimanded, her brown eyes narrowed on me as she reluctantly provided me with, "The prince is probably hiding away in his chambers, as always." With one last contemptuous glance, they all disappeared through a swinging door into a room filled with ovens and stovetops and steam.

Hiding? I pondered that as I chewed on a chunk of apple. Spodge and Herb eyed the fruit, still waiting for me at the stairwell. I squeezed between them, their stomachs squishy soft against my arms, and we continued following the stairs down.

With no real direction in mind, I set free the anxiety over winding up somewhere I shouldn't and allowed myself to get lost.

Until I came upon a familiar oaky geranium scent a floor beneath the kitchens.

It seemed unlikely the prince would lurk in the damp depths. Moisture drops echoed throughout the drainpipes and dripped from sodden patches in the rock-hewn ceiling. Yet the smell of him grew more potent the deeper I traversed into the bowels of the castle.

A narrow passageway made it difficult for the narlows to follow. But follow they did, and so closely, they nearly knocked me over when I came to a stop before two mildewed doors.

Taking another bite of the apple, I nudged the door on the right with my slipper. Unlocked, it opened a fraction. "Tell them to remain outside," said the prince before I could fully open the door for him to see us.

Spodge and Herb bustled forward, nearly pushing me into the sprawling, narrow room.

"Stay here," I said and broke the apple in two, handing them half each. "Gentle."

Claws scraped against my hand, though not hard enough to slice as they took the fruit. I stepped into the room and closed the door, waiting to see if they'd listen and remain outside.

"Last time they were in here, it took me days to clean up the mess."

Taking in the room, the books towering toward the ceiling as if they were holding it up and serving as shelves for vials, jars, and countless teacups, I found myself confused and shocked still.

It was tidied chaos, the prince seated in the center of it all at a tall desk the size of a small dining table, a rusted sink in its center.

Lifting a teacup to his mouth, his eyes drifted from my toes to my hips, where they remained a moment too long before roaming to my chest. By the time he met my gaze, I'd arched a brow, about to scold him when he gave his eyes back to the parchment before him, the harsh bend of his ears a little pink. "You look lovely."

I ignored that, unable to remember the last time a brush had visited my hair and determined not to care. "Now I know why you seemed so at ease in our dungeon. You live in one." He nearly looked the part too, his hair free and finger-swept and his loose white shirt tea-stained at the breast and collar.

He scratched something onto the parchment with his quill. "Do you see any iron bars?"

I took that as an invitation to take the step down into the room. Thin but three times as long as the bedchamber I'd slept in, it stretched toward a steep flight of stairs at the back of the space. "Where do those stairs lead?"

"Outside."

"Please, spare no detail," I muttered dryly, trailing my fingers over the spines of books while eyeing the contents of the vials and jars. They contained everything from grasshoppers to butterfly wings to pollen and, to my surprise, even locks of dark hair.

Circling the room, I noted there were fairy tale and mythical stories, books on apothecaries and potions, and even some tomes on our history. Some of the spines and covers were too weathered and worn to know what they were.

But the smell of the room—the scent of books and parchment and a myriad of herbs and spices wafting from the stoppered jars—I couldn't help but gulp heaping lungfuls of it. I stopped when I noted the ingredient that made it all the more addictive.

The additive of *him*.

Shelves holding small cauldrons, bowls, more jars, daggers, tongs, and other instruments I'd not encountered before lined one length of the walls from where I stood at the stairs to the double doors I'd entered through.

The prince sat on a stool, his knee-length boots hooked into the wooden rungs and his hair slipping out from behind his ear as he wrote something else down. "Sleep well?"

"Fine," I said. "But the beasts ate my dinner."

He stopped writing. "So you found yourself an apple."

He must've seen and scented as much before I'd helped myself to his chambers. "Where's the bed?"

"I don't have one. Not here." He cleared his throat. "Why do you ask?"

"So I can ravish you on it, being that we are to marry, of course,"

I said with enough sarcasm that he shouldn't have looked at me like that.

Like I was sent merely to torment him, his jaw flexing and his eyes darkening. A hint of crimson crept in at the edges, and my heart thudded hard as I wondered how often someone like him, how often any creature like him, drank blood.

The shiver of my blood told me it was best not to ask. Not yet.

I padded back over the worn carpet, marking each faded gray whorl in the black woven wool to keep from looking at him. To keep him from seeing the curiosity in my eyes as the cool room began to heat, the energy flowing from him disturbing the flame in the ornate sconces.

"Would you like me to get you something else to eat?" The gentle question rattled me, though it shouldn't have.

"I would like to go home," I said, not intending for it to sound like a plea rather than a scathing retort.

"If I could grant you that, I would." And the solemn gravity in his voice made me want to believe him, made me look at him as I passed by his desk. I stopped, noting his eyes had returned to their golden hue. He rubbed at the growth dusting his jawline. "I did not wish for all of this to happen to you, Fia."

My eyes burned, as did my words as they rolled over my tongue. "Yet you are the reason I am stuck here. You are the reason for all of this mess."

He stared at me, unblinking, and after a few moments, it began to unnerve me. Being so close to him, just looking at him, unnerved me in a way that made it unclear if I wanted to kiss or kill him.

That he didn't refute what I'd said, didn't patch up the truth with lies, only worsened the mixture of conflicting feelings until they became a swarm of stinging nettle inside my chest. "Say something, Prince."

The quill rocked side to side between his large fingers, his attention given back to whatever work he was doing. "And what would you have me say?"

I sneered, advancing and snatching his stupid quill from his stupid hand.

I snapped it, ignoring the slight curl to his lips as I tossed the pieces to the floor. "You upended my life, stole it from me like you had the right, and then you hide down here within this, this..." I waved my hands around, blinking back tears. "This dusty cave of books, and you just leave me to roam about as if I have any idea where I am or what I'm even to do with..." I sputtered, turning side to side. "What is all of this shit even for?"

"Fire-breather," he started, his brow furrowed.

"You are the fire-breather, though, aren't you?" I raked a hand through my hair, hissing when my fingers caught in a tangle of knots, and then I stabbed one at him. "*You*. Not me. And because of that, my life is ruined. Gone as though it never even existed."

His mouth closed, and he swept his eyes to the desk, moving books and parchment around, likely in search of another quill. "Will that be all?"

Anger rose within me like a beast I could never dare hope to tame. "Will that be all?" A crazed laugh left me. "Are you fucking *kidding me?*"

His silence only made it worse as he found another quill and dipped it into an ink pot, his hand trembling slightly.

I had to leave.

I had to leave before I said something that might just make him kill instead of marry me. Perhaps, deep down, that was what I longed for. Not to die, but to make him show me exactly who he was so I could feel some solid ground beneath my extremely comfortable feet.

I stalked to the doors. "Fine, hide behind your mildewed doors and your books and your cravats and your stained shirts and your careless actions. But mark my words, dragon, I don't need to breathe fire or grow scales to make you regret deceiving me."

"Would you have still released me?" he asked as my feet met the stair to the doors, his voice right behind me. I closed my eyes and laid my hand against the wood, and he whispered, stirring my hair, "If you'd known, would you have still kissed me?"

"*You* kissed *me*," I ground between my teeth.

"Answer the question, Fia." When I failed to, his laughter rendered my heart still. Dark and gritted, the sound flowed over me like hot water on a winter's night, his hands molding to my hips. "You can't, can you?" He squeezed my waist, and I trapped a gasping breath behind my teeth. "Why?"

I shook my head, my tongue frozen solid.

The heat of his chest met my back. "Perhaps it's because you're more afraid of the answer than you are of me."

I whirled, glaring at him, but he didn't move.

His knuckles feathered down my cheek to my jaw. His fingertips and eyes followed, stopping at my fluttering pulse. "Fear," he murmured, his gaze lifting to mine with bloodred hunger. "Or excitement? The two can so often get entangled."

I smacked his hand away and tore open the door.

Spodge and Herb startled awake from where they'd been napping on the floor, snorting. I stepped over them, but not even their grunting and lumbering behind me could mask the sound of the prince's velvet dark laughter.

TEN

Colvin

GUILT WAS A SICKNESS.
I could still recall with red-hazed clarity the moment I decided to let it cease being a paralyzing plague—the moment I'd felt it transform into a broiling need to finally take what I desired. To claim that which was so fragile yet still so unshakably mine.

The sound of the doors crashing open to my study. The butter-soft pages of the worn tome beneath my fingertips. The day-old tea giving fragrance to the crisp air. All of it.

The memory hadn't left me alone for a moment as the image of Fia, bedraggled and bloodied, sat tight at the forefront of my mind.

I'd done that.

I might not have been the one to place her in that dungeon, nor had I pushed her hard enough to wound. But I had wounded her.

I'd caused it all.

Jarron delivered the message that had caused the flame to ignite, his words careful and clipped as though he'd known the fire he would start by simply speaking. "Our spies have heard word that the princess mates with a young soldier."

The book had gone up in flames, ash piling beneath my quivering fingers.

Jarron had watched it burn, watched me try to grasp control of myself, but I hadn't been able to.

The spies could have indeed heard wrong—and whoever they'd heard it from could have exaggerated the truth. Many things were always made to sound worse than what they truly were. Nevertheless, the truth was always there somewhere.

That, and I'd heard it, had witnessed it, the relationship with this soldier and Fia. A male did not track a female's scent unless he harbored a severe hunger for it—hungered for her enough to do so.

"Olette says the time is now. This procrastination must cease."

I had almost forgotten Jarron still stood there, too busy trying to keep a part of myself from perishing while the rest of me begged to be set free. To fly southeast and pluck this soldier from Callula, from existence, with my fucking teeth.

Indeed, my mother had harped since my return from Callula, warning that we could only forestall fate for so long.

So I'd nodded. Just once.

It was all the permission they had needed. Jarron had instantly taken his leave, and soon after, so did the queen and a unit of our warriors.

They'd returned an hour later, and my mother had taken one observing look at me and then smiled. "It is done. The contract is being prepared as we breathe."

Since my return, she'd been trying to devise a plan, to create an excuse for the two kingdoms of Gwythorn to come together in a way they had never united before.

Marriage.

All the while, I'd lost weeks to the sickness of guilt. I'd drowned within the plaguing peril that'd arrived with the discovery of what I'd so desperately sought and what it would cost to claim. A cost I'd not considered nearly enough during all of our searching.

In order to give myself everything I'd longed for—I would rob her of everything.

"It's the only way," Mother had said countless times while I'd remained hidden in this study more than ever before.

I'd been determined to find another way. I needed her, but I refused to force her. I couldn't endanger her.

In the end, it had all been for naught.

Fia was here, and she had every right to hate me. In fact, this might just be more bearable if that were all she felt.

But it wasn't.

Her scent suffocated, the shape of her hips memorized by my hands. They trembled, raking through my hair. The sickness had returned, but it was now at war with the primal urge to fight for her surrender.

I growled, the tower of books toppling over by the doors as I finally ceased staring at them and headed for the back stairs.

ELEVEN

Fia

I FOLLOWED THE NARLOWS TO THE FLOOR BELOW MY ROOMS.
I'd given up on asking them to wait and come with me.
Whatever it was they wanted, they weren't stopping until they found it.

I felt like a fool when they reached a set of double doors, and both turned to me, Herb expelling a grunted huff.

Of course, they needed to go outside.

As soon as I opened the doors, they nearly knocked me off my feet, barreling past and down the cluster of rounded stone steps to the grass below.

I cursed when they continued bounding toward the woods and hiked up my skirts to follow. Upon a log at the tree line, I watched them rummage and race through the foliage, still feeling the prince's parting words to me upon my skin like a burn.

One I knew would not leave with time.

The ting of metal meeting metal, followed by a rich bark of laughter that tugged at my innards, swept through the woods some minutes later.

I looked up at the castle, unable to see much of it beneath the canopy of trees above me and surrounding it. The ivy and moss carpeting the stone made it blend with these northern woods as though it was a part of the land rather than a fortress constructed many millennia ago.

My gaze swung to the left, to what appeared to be a small clearing not far from the exit I'd just taken.

A training yard, I soon discovered, as I left the narlows to play and took a few hesitant steps closer to the clang of swords wielded by grunting and cursing males.

Colvin, dressed as he had been when I'd left his cave of books not even a half hour ago, narrowly dodged a blow to his side from another male. The stranger's back was to me, but I didn't care to get a better look at him.

Not when the prince swung his sword down and up as he feigned a lunge to his right but then crouched.

Such a strike would've taken his opponent out at the knees, but the prince stopped a second away from contact, his sparring partner cursing viciously. "You always fight better when you're worked up."

At that, I frowned, but Colvin just swiped his fingers through his hair. He'd tied it back since I'd visited him, his rough fingers freeing some of the inky strands, and then he lunged at the male again.

The way he moved betrayed the senses—held me pinned behind the oak tree with my fingers clenching at the bark. He was lean, but he was all fluid muscle, the dark unable to conceal the strength and power beneath his loose tunic and tight black pants.

The two can so often get entangled.

My breathing quickened with the fluttering beat of my heart, his taunting words more than mere memory. They were a haunting burrowing beneath my skin.

I'd never felt anything like it. Never had I felt anything so acutely. This merciless combination of lust and loathing. It wasn't fear of not knowing which affliction would claim victory over me in the end but of knowing all too well.

And it made me question just who it was I truly loathed—the prince or myself.

After an eye-widening series of maneuvers, his blade glinting beneath the shine of the stars overhead, the prince lifted his tunic to his face to wipe it. In doing so, he revealed a glimpse of his defined abdominals and the small shadow of hair that trailed from his navel down to his...

The narlows growled at something in the trees behind me, or

perhaps just at each other, and I ceased breathing as Colvin stilled, then twisted slightly.

Without lifting my eyes to his, I knew that he was now aware of my presence behind the tree. I'd been caught.

But I still lifted them, coerced to by this growing entity that constantly called for my surrender.

As golden bright as if he was standing before me and not some fifty feet away on the stone terrace, his eyes snatched mine and refused to let me run.

My fingers slackened, loosening their cutting grip upon the tree. My pulse slowed to a thud in my ears as I tilted my head and watched his eyes glow a darker gold. If it weren't for the breeze that kicked at his shirt and hair, those still features would've rendered him a striking statue carved by the moon goddess.

Each breath I drew began to warm and soon burned as the dragon prince's gaze failed to relinquish its hold on mine.

"What is it?" his muddied-haired companion asked, twirling his sword and turning to glance my way.

I ducked behind the tree but peeked out from behind it again when the prince murmured with a crooked smile tossed to the woods, "Just a pretty little night bird." He then raised his sword, turning back to meet the downswing of his companion's before it could make contact with his shoulder.

Slinking back against the tree, I smiled at my toes. My heart sang through every limb as I forced myself to wander back through the woods to collect my beasts.

Curled into giant furry boulders, Spodge and Herb dozed before the fire.

Their snoring made it hard to hear much of anything, especially my own thoughts as I lay upon the bed and stared at the green canopy of netting. A blessing, I supposed. But I didn't need to hear the approaching footsteps or the knock on the door.

As soon as both happened, the narlows rose with a snorting snarl, scenting the air. A moment later, they deemed whoever it was no threat, for they soon settled, licking their misshapen maws as they placed their heads back upon the carpet.

"Enter," I said, for I didn't wish to move. I needed more sleep, more time to adjust to all that'd transpired and to unravel the twisted coil of thorns within my chest.

But it would seem that might not happen.

"Your presence is desired at dinner."

I kept my eyes fixed on the ceiling, determined to ignore the melting return of his earlier words. *Pretty little night bird.* "Didn't we already eat dinner?"

The dragon prince huffed. "You ate nothing but an apple."

True. I was still hungry. "But it was served earlier."

"There's no breakfast or lunch here, just meals and then dinner," he said. "Come, they're all waiting."

That had me rising on the bed to find Colvin leaning against the open door, his eyes on the sleeping beasts. "Who?"

"You'll see." He nodded to the narlows. "You shouldn't let them sleep in here. They'll expect it and refuse to do so in their own room."

"It's just a nap." I scooted to the side of the bed, asking, "Where is their room?"

"At the other end of the hall."

Oh.

I looked over at them, pondering how I'd get them there and if I even wanted to. They were far from cute, and knowing that they could kill me before I saw it coming was a little unsettling. But they were also company I'd found myself grateful for since leaving the outskirts of the woods more confused than I had been yesterday.

It was hard to bring myself to look at him, this prince I was sup- posed to marry, so I didn't. I stared at his leather boots, then at the tea stain on his otherwise fresh cream tunic. And as my eyes began to drift over the black cravat at his neck, I stood and walked to the bathing room.

"Time to go," the prince said, and I realized he wasn't speaking to me. The narlows whined, rousing and lifting their heads. Colvin arched a brow. "Bed. Now."

Groaning, the beasts took their time rising to their full height, Herb scratching at his chest before deciding to walk on all fours. Colvin followed them out, saying, "The dining room is on the first floor."

I peeled myself from the doorjamb to the bathing room, grateful he couldn't see my smile as I heard him lecture the narlows when they started growling at one another, and then I tried to make myself as presentable as possible.

The gown I'd donned earlier was wrinkling in places, but it would do. I didn't want to search for something new, including footwear. So I stepped into the slippers I'd kicked off at the side of the bed and finished brushing my hair.

It was still tangled in too many places, but it looked better than it had in nearly a week, so I left it in its usual haphazard mess of long and unruly curling waves and dropped the brush by the sink. The wound on my head had almost healed. I didn't prod or stare at the fading cut, a shiver threatening at the mere memory of those talons taking the guard's life.

The stairwell mercifully spiraled all the way down to the first floor.

The dining room was easy to find. Laughter and hushed murmurings floated into the hall. I followed the noise to a grand foyer. My feet slowed as the ever stretching row of arched windows gave a breathtaking view of the star-dusted forest floor outside.

To my right, the foyer shaped like a star beckoned, purple and red roses unfurling from tall plum-colored vases at each point. I entered, knowing people were waiting but hypnotized as I gazed up the grand staircase to the floor above. The stone beneath me rolled into a dark, glittering marble like the stairs. The banisters curled into the face of a dragon at each end. Atop the staircase on the wall, the late queen watched over the empty space below from a large gilded portrait.

Eyes of such familiar, eerie gold shined down at me, her hair the same shade of obsidian as her son's. Her lap was dusted with petals beneath a cluster of wildflowers. Slender fingers held them loosely, and those of her other hand smoothed over a petal.

A perfect, pink bow, her lips were upturned in one corner, giving a spark of soft mischief to the intimidating bone structure she'd also gifted her son. Queen Cherith wasn't just beautiful but also ethereal. As though some mystical presence glowed from within.

It wasn't an incorrect assumption, given her pyrotechnic abilities. She'd also spawned the first dragon Gwythorn had seen in hundreds of years.

Footfalls, clipped but unhurried, broke my trance with Colvin's voice. "Mother's quarters are up there, but I wouldn't pay her a visit unless invited."

I spun around, somewhat flustered to have been caught staring at his other mother.

He only smiled, brief but still reassuring, and looked down at the glass of wine in his hand. "If the queen is in her rooms, she's done with duties for the night, which includes talking to anyone."

"She still grieves."

He lifted his eyes, but not to me. To the portrait of his mother, a heavy exhale leaving him. "She will until she dies."

I swallowed over the thickening in my throat. It was often said that losing a mate was akin to having a part of oneself perish, dooming them to forever wander throughout their remaining days with an ache that never ceased.

"And you?" I asked, wanting to kick myself. I wasn't supposed to care, and I didn't want to care. I was just... unbearably curious.

A knowing smile glinted in the prince's eyes when he gave them to me. "The food grows cold."

"You didn't answer my question."

"I will, just not yet."

Annoyed, I trailed him out of the foyer and down the hall that ended in a large arched doorway, giving way to an even larger room.

A table, an oiled slab of thick, ginormous oak, stood dressed with dishes and beverages and crystal vases of violet roses in the center of the room. Two intricate chandeliers hung from the ceiling, their silver wrapped in threads of gold that glittered with every soft sway of the dozen candles within.

Beyond each head of the table were windows shrouded in heavy, obsidian curtains. On one side of the long room was a black marble fireplace, and on the other, a wooden bar lined with liquor.

"Don't worry, there's wine," said a familiar voice, and I looked from the glass-cased liquids to the table as Persy raised her wineglass. "Not bad either."

"There's no such thing as bad wine," said the male with hair reminiscent of burning caramel seated next to her. The strands stood in uneven, eye-catching tufts as though he'd been struck by lightning.

His voice alone told me he was the male who'd been sparring with Colvin, but that hair confirmed it.

His coal-dark eyes glimmered as he leaned back in his seat. "Perhaps there's no such thing as a feral Seelie princess, either."

I narrowed my eyes at him. "Is this audacity of yours due to losing another bet?" I smiled when his eyes widened. He glared at Persy, who coughed wine back into her glass as I rounded the table to sit before the only untouched meal on the other side. "Jarron, I assume."

"Correct," he muttered.

Before I could sit, Colvin appeared. Either I was getting too good at ignoring his presence, or he was growing more talented at surprising me. For he did so again, untucking my chair.

I looked at it, then up at him, venomous words swelling my tongue. The way he wouldn't meet my eyes made me trap them behind my teeth, and I reluctantly took a seat and let him tuck me in.

The male and female across from us stared down at their plates, their shoulders shaking with laughter they tried and failed to hide.

Seemingly at ease despite the sniveling and watchful eye of his friends, the prince sat next to me and resumed eating what was left of his meal.

A giant hunk of meat soaked in a spiced, yellowed sauce and surrounded by baked vegetables awaited me on my plate, indeed barely warm when I collected my cutlery and took a bite. Determined to keep my approval hidden as the beef all but dissolved over my tongue, I sipped from the glass of wine poured for me by the prince.

"You've left me to fend for myself since I arrived," I clipped, setting the wine down. "No need to start fussing now." Though even as I'd said it, I knew it wasn't entirely true.

Deep down, I knew he'd been helping me as much as he could while also trying to give me the space I'd needed to acclimate after so much turmoil, and in a land I'd always feared would rather eat than welcome me.

Colvin didn't respond, and a small spike of unexpected shame pricked at my chest.

Persy cleared her throat. "Have you left the castle yet?"

"Not really," I said, knowing she already expected as much, and therefore wondering what she was about to try on.

A look at the prince with a small smile on her lips, and I was growing more tense by the second. "You should show Fia the woods, Col."

Colvin smiled down at his plate. "Fia has likely spent half of her life in the woods. She knows what they look like."

"But she hasn't seen ours."

The prince set down his cutlery, and I feared he'd give me away and tell them of the spying I'd done earlier. But he merely asked dryly, "Any particular patch of trees you might be referring to?"

Persy pursed her lips, a large bite of potato held suspended before her. "Oh, I could think of one particular place."

Jarron placed his wine on the table. "I think we should get to the meaning of this lovely little dinner."

I knew it. Always with the ulterior motives. "You mean to tell me you did not wish to simply get to know me?"

His sharp gaze pierced mine, and he dabbed at his mouth with a napkin before revealing a smirk. "We know all about you, Princess."

Persy thumped his arm.

He glared at her. "What? You can goad, but I cannot?"

She rolled her eyes but then looked at me and said, "We do want to get to know you, but we also seek the book, Fia."

Confused, I slowly finished chewing, then swallowed. "And which book would that be?"

Colvin cursed into the hand he rubbed over his mouth and jaw. "Leave it."

"The Blood Bound Book," Jarron said, ignoring him, all playfulness wiped clean of his features. Which were shockingly cruel when still, his dark eyes stamped on me as he relaxed into the high-backed wooden chair and waited.

That book.

My gaze turned to the prince, who rose and walked to one of the arched windows and opened the curtain, his back to us.

Of course, he would want to ensure that particular book was out of the wrong hands. Within its pages were spells and potion ingredients—including where to find them—to aid in weakening, capturing, and even killing the most dangerous types of beasts in Gwythorn.

Including that of a dragon.

We might have been immortal, but Colvin was as close to indestructible as any creature could get. Fire couldn't harm him behind those scales when he breathed and conjured it himself. It would take an army of arrows to wound him. No one could get close enough to behead him.

But as he'd said himself some months ago in the dungeon, there was a poison for everyone.

Remembering that only made my eyes narrow further upon his back as he continued staring out at the trees.

Over many millennia, the Seelie Kingdom added their findings to the Blood Bound Book and had kept it sealed within the archives of the cellar beneath the royal library. But it was no longer there. I'd searched for the book myself. Many times. Not just because it was supposedly mine, but because I was curious.

I was also the only one with the ability to unbound the pages. The only one who could open it. It had been handed down to my mother from her own, and as she'd perished after delivering me, my mother had then left the book to me.

A fact of which these Unseelie creatures obviously knew.

Searing anger scored through me, and I too pushed away from the table and stood. "It hasn't been seen in years. I cannot help you."

Persy said carefully, "But you were the last one to see it."

Brolen had been curious about something, he'd said, but that was all. Otherwise, I might not have known of its existence at all. I'd been too young to care or remember much. All I could recall was the glimpse of my mother's looping handwriting and wishing I'd been able to read what she'd written.

Instead, I was left with the scent of damp, age-worn pages, and I'd later discovered from my aunt that the book had been hidden elsewhere.

"I was barely five years of age. I don't know what Brolen wanted with it, nor what happened afterward. Wherever he's hidden it, we'll never know. He didn't even tell my aunt. It's likely he told no one. So"—I met the prince's golden gaze when he turned, his hands folded before him, my tone as cold as I could make it—"do excuse me."

Outside in the hall, I slowed, my pounding heart quieting enough for me to hear, "She speaks the truth."

Jarron asked, "And how would you know?"

"Her reaction," Colvin said simply.

My teeth gritted. I forced myself to keep moving to the stairs that would take me back to my rooms.

Releasing my nail-breaking grip of the stone wall on the landing, I blinked back the growing damp in my eyes when I entered the hall and, one by one, flames began to dance, lighting the way to my rooms.

I swallowed the emotion clogging my throat. It sharpened my breaths, and I found myself grateful that the narlows had been taken to bed as I shut myself in my rooms.

I'd barely removed my slippers before the door opened.

"Haven't you heard of knocking, dragon?"

Colvin closed the door, ignoring my question and crossing the room to where I stood at the end of the bed. "You're mad."

I huffed, walking to the dressing room for something to wear to bed.

"More than usual."

His attempt at humor didn't work. It only made my eyes sting as I flicked all the various gowns aside in search of a nightgown. Spying a tunic, perhaps meant for riding, I snatched it from the hanger and paid no mind to the prince while I stripped.

In nothing but undergarments, I pulled the tunic on before reaching beneath it to free myself of their silken constraints.

Behind me in the doorway, he said low, "You're wearing a tunic to bed?"

"And?" I quipped. "Or do you require I dress a certain way for you, too?"

"I'm not complaining, believe me," he said, and I couldn't bring myself to turn around yet, to face him as he added gently, "I don't require anything of you, Fia."

"Except for the book." This all made more sense now. If they got the book, there was far less chance of my uncle getting what he wanted—in succeeding in ridding Gwythorn of dragons for good. "Do tell, what will become of me when you get everything you want?" For once he had that book and a permanent thumb pressed upon Callula by marrying me, he truly would be invincible.

Finished with unclipping the undergarments, I tossed them to the floor.

"Right now, all I want is to see those violet eyes."

My tunic only reached the top of my thighs, but he didn't look. True to his word, his eyes seemed to soften to a more yellowy hue when I gave him what he wanted. I crossed my arms. "What would you like next, dragon?"

"I should say nothing," he murmured. "But I'd be lying."

It was maddening—how just one look at him could spike my ire or melt my resolve. "I cannot get you that book. He'll kill me or send me right back if I return."

"Fuck the book," he said, voice rougher than moments before.

I frowned. "But you…" I lost what I was saying, what I was even thinking, as he straightened from the doorframe of the dressing room and erased the space between us with three calculated strides.

I stared at the spots of dried tea on his collar, my heart running too fast. His scent rid my brain of the ability to think, and his towering form blocked my view of anything but him.

He clasped my chin, forcing my eyes to his.

They skipped over the growth at his perfectly squared and overly obnoxious chin to glimpse the parting of his soft lips. His nostrils flared, and I surrendered, finally fusing my gaze to his. "You expected a dinner with us, with me, trusting even after all you've endured, that you'd be safe." His thumb brushed beneath my lower lip. "Instead, you were ambushed again."

He was right, so I bit back the urge to say it didn't matter.

For some reason, it did.

"I did warn them it was a bad idea, but I will admit that I am desperate enough to accept their reasoning and ignore good sense." His lashes lowered and lifted, long and calling to my fingers, which itched and curled at my sides. "Because we do need it, but that doesn't mean I didn't also want to eat with you and that I didn't want you to meet my friends." He smiled then, quick and amused. "Although it seems you and Persy had already met."

"Stop it," I rasped, but the request was feeble.

"No," he said. "I need that book, but regardless of whether I get it, I'll still need you."

His thumb traced a tear that leaked from the corner of my eye without my permission, and it grew worse, this feeling of wanting to leave my overheating skin and run. But I didn't. There was nowhere to go, so I whispered, "What could you possibly need me for, dragon?"

"Too much," he countered, and I ceased breathing. "Right now, I'll settle for your mouth on mine."

This barely contained energy inside me sprang free, pushing me to my toes and my lips to his. My hand splayed over his chest, the other rising to his head, pulling it down to feel his incredibly soft hair—to better taste him as I pried his lips apart with mine.

He was wine and heat, an explosion of sensation with just one tentative touch of our tongues.

His hand framed my face, fingers threading into my hair while the other landed upon my lower back and pushed. My body collided with his. A groan, throaty and low, tingled over my tongue as I withdrew and meshed my lips violently to his.

He met my every bruising press, our breaths loud with nowhere to tumble free. Hard and tempting me to touch, his erection dug into my stomach, his fingers a contradiction to his typically gentle demeanor, tangling deeper into my hair and digging with bruising focus into my lower back.

It gave me all the permission I needed to do the same. I gripped the thick strands of his hair and desperately clawed at his shirt, needing him closer, needing more.

A moan pushed past the punishing dance of our lips when he picked me up to pin me to the wall. Clothing fell around us, as innocuous as leaves falling from a tree.

He ground into me, and I gasped when he pulled away, his wet mouth scoring a fire-lit path down my chin to the hollow of my neck. I rocked over him, moaning again, every part of me alive like never before. Each panted breath coated in his scent, his taste, his essence, like that of new air I couldn't gulp fast enough.

"You taste like salted honey," he grunted, tongue lapping at my pulse. "A touch sour and so fucking sweet."

A shiver rippled through me. "I can feel you," I whispered, my mind vacant. He'd knocked down every shield. "With every brush of your tongue..."

"Here?" He thrust his cock into my core while his tongue swiped at my pulse again.

I shivered harder, my thighs, clutched within his bruising hold, shaking.

A dark chuckle washed over my skin. I tugged his hair, needing his mouth back on mine before I did something absurd, like erupt from nothing more than the velvet feel of his tongue at my neck. "Kiss me, Prince."

His husky words and the luminescent shine of his hungry eyes held me transfixed. "Whenever you like."

Starving as if I'd never had a full meal in my life, I clasped his cheeks, my lips and tongue at war with his. My teeth trapped his bottom lip, and I sucked it into my mouth, releasing it with a tiny daring bite.

I knew it was a mistake to toy with him in this way, but I didn't care.

I wanted, so I took.

I nibbled and lapped at his tongue. I drank him down like the rare tonic he was, the smoky essence of him making a home within my taste buds and body. He groaned, my thighs inching higher and my lower body rocking harder.

Close, I was so close, my lip stolen by his teeth, his mouth sucking and his hips thrusting with more precision. If it was this good with his pants on, without our skin even meeting, I was almost afraid to find out what might become of me if we ever truly fucked.

And then I pulled too hard, his next groan more of a snarl as my eyes flew open. His were hooded, and when his lashes lifted, a glowing red.

Our lips unstitched, covered in my blood. It began to bubble and spill over my bottom lip where his teeth had pinched it.

Shit.

He licked his lips, the action causing the red to saturate the whites of his eyes. "We should stop now." His words hung there, both a guttural statement and a warning.

For I could ask him to stay. To continue. Moon above, I couldn't remember ever feeling more desperate for anything. It was an ache felt not just within my core but everywhere, the loss of pleasure so much more acute than what I'd felt when I'd failed to find release before.

As if I were losing more than just an orgasm.

But although I was experienced, I wasn't experienced in the ways he so evidently needed. I wasn't sure I was ready for what else would happen, and he seemed to sense that.

But I couldn't help but want to be.

And that scared me enough to nod and have him carefully lower me to the ground. To watch him leave while wishing he'd stay.

TWELVE

Colvin

BRACED AGAINST THE COUNTERTOP, I TREMBLED FROM head to toe as my fingers milked the seed from the engorged head of my cock into the kitchen sink. "Fuck."

I'd never materialized to the privacy of my home so fucking fast.

But leaving her after touching her, tasting her... I groaned, cleaning myself and the mess I'd made. Then I tucked my half-erect cock away with a hiss and leaned over the sink, my breathing uneven.

The Seelie princess was rapidly overruling my every thought, my every plan, and my very existence. I'd known it would be this way. I'd been told and warned as such. For months, I'd lived with a ceaseless want I'd diligently done my best to suppress.

But it had all fallen to shit when I'd discovered she'd decided to suppress it too—with another male.

And we'd wasted no time in resurrecting this foolhardy plan.

I should still feel guilty—and I did, unbearably so, when I'd witnessed that tear sliding over the alluring crest of her cheek.

But I was now too ravenous, a hunger unlike any other writhing through my veins.

It wasn't fair to Fia. None of this had been. Which was the reason I'd stayed away when she'd freed me from her family's dungeon. It was the reason I'd told my mother we were to stop and wait as soon as I'd entered her rooms with the narlow cubs still tied and clutched to my chest.

For it was one thing to make plans, to find yourself so

desperate for something that you would do whatever it took to make it happen…

Another thing entirely to actually have that plan work and then encounter the full magnitude of what you'd accomplished.

I didn't want to hurt her. The very thought of it, of taking her away from all she'd ever known, was what had prompted me to put a pause to all this madness.

But driven by a recklessness from the itch my fire-breather had left under my skin—and a sickening jealousy that had me tempted to reduce the entire realm to ashes—I'd foolishly given Jarron and Olette permission to go ahead.

I'd doomed the one creature I wanted most.

I'd been naïve to think that finding her would alleviate my problems. To think that I wouldn't find something I wanted endlessly more than what I'd originally sought.

So I would get the book. Somehow. It had always been an option. An option we'd continuously brushed aside for to steal it was almost impossible. Not to mention what it could do was riskier than anything I'd attempted yet.

But Fia was here, and the book was in Callula, and she already loathed me. I couldn't stomach the thought of making that a permanent wound by telling her what we'd done and just why we needed it. Why we needed her. Not yet.

In her eyes, we were nothing but monsters.

She needed time, and I'd happily give her that and whatever else she needed. Moon, just the way she'd looked, pressed up against the wall, blood upon her lips and fear warring with lust in those huge violet eyes, was enough to turn all of me to stone again.

I both feared and knew it would be constant.

Never had a female undone me so thoroughly, so quickly. Just one whiff of her, and I saw the world through the eyes of a beast. A brand new monster, which she'd birthed when I'd left her dungeon, came alive. The way she walked, regal yet as if she were always on

the verge of skipping, her luscious hips swaying and her eyes forever wandering...

Guilt could no longer exist, even if it wanted to. There was no
room for it now.

This woodland creature with hair of winter and eyes of night
had snuffed it with her intoxicating presence alone.

THIRTEEN

Fia

THE NARLOWS WERE AWAKE WHEN I ROSE BEFORE THE MOON, unable to sleep no matter how many times I satisfied myself after the prince had left me wanting so much more.

I'd bathed and donned another dress, this one a violet eerily close to the shade of my eyes. The soft, ribbed satin hugged my breasts and hips without constricting. The tufted, loose puffs of organza cupping my shoulders matched that of the long skirts. They flared at my thighs in soft, nearly translucent pleats to my toes.

Not normally one to care too much for clothing, I'd forever worn what had been provided and expected of me. But I had a feeling that was changing, for I had to admit that whoever this wardrobe had belonged to had decent taste.

I added it to my list of questions to ask Colvin and laughed when Spodge offered his paw as soon as I'd entered the room.

I took it, inspecting the dank fur, his too-long claws, and turned it over to see the dark pads. "A little dry under here," I said, to which he merely tilted his head and offered it again when I dropped it.

Herb wasn't interested in bidding me hello, it seemed. His beady eyes were fixed on me in a way that suggested he'd be glaring if he could. I looked at the bowl he kicked with a growled huff. "You're hungry?"

Spodge licked his lips in response, though I hadn't been speaking to him.

Peering around their room, I smiled at the sight of the blankets I'd wrapped them in when they were babes. The tattered material lay over a large mattress in the corner, mingling with other plaid blankets and even some ripped throw cushions.

In the other corner were a basket of wood for the fire that had long gone out and a small trough of water. Balls of yarn in varying colors dotted the room, some unraveled and others squashed.

"Wait here," I told them, leaving to find Colvin to ask what the beasts ate when they woke, assuming it wasn't usually someone else's meal.

Of course, they did not wait.

They followed with a lumbered stomping that alluded to impatience. I stopped at the bottom of the stairwell, hearing voices drifting down the hall.

"... Any one of them would be willing. At least until she is."

"No." The barked response had come from Colvin.

I whispered for the narlows to stay and gestured with my hand while giving them a pointed look. Mercifully, they did as instructed, and I crept down the hall in time to hear Persy say, "You should at least consider it. He's right. It won't be long now."

"I honestly don't understand why you're doing this to yourself," Jarron said, irritation spiking his tone.

Colvin's heated words shocked me. "She resents me enough as it is. I said I'm fine, so kindly fucking drop it."

But Jarron didn't. His next words moved my feet before I could even think about what it was I would do. "If she indeed hates you, then why would she care?"

I pushed open the doors to Colvin's book cave. "Because he is my mate," I said and stepped into the room.

Persy's eyes flared, though I had a feeling she already knew. That both of them had known longer than I had been willing to understand it myself.

I moved deeper into the room, closer to the desk where Colvin sat, a quill unmoving in his hand as he stared at me with his lips parted. I cleared my throat and said to his friends, "Leave us."

Jarron smirked, eyeing me as though I were some type of puzzle he'd enjoy seeing pieced together. Persy, already halfway to the door, backtracked with a curse and a groaned, "Come on, you idiot."

Jarron followed, throwing a look over his shoulder to Colvin. One I didn't know if I wanted to decipher. Then the doors closed.

We were alone.

Colvin finally blinked, his head shaking. "I wasn't sure you were entirely aware..."

"I didn't want to be," I admitted, staring at my bare toes beneath my skirts. "I'm still not so sure that I want to be." I'd wondered since the night he'd left me standing in the dungeon after I'd set him free, the burn of his stolen kiss lingering upon my lips for days.

And when I'd seen him again, swiping blood from himself after he'd killed the soldier who'd mistreated me, it became undeniable.

Fate had spoken. This dragon prince was made to be mine, whether I liked it or not.

Colvin nodded, short and slow, and expelled a harsh breath. "How much did you hear?"

"Enough to know that you need to drink blood."

"You don't need to worry about that."

"But for how long?" I needed to know. I had to, as I teetered on the precipice of wanting to give him anything he needed while still battling all the reasons I shouldn't.

Colvin didn't answer. He rubbed the quill between his fingers, long lashes cresting his cheeks as he gazed down at its black feathers.

"What happens when you don't feed?" I asked instead, swaying a step closer. "You shift into a dragon?"

"That happens regardless, but yes," he said, rolling his lips. "Feeding can help prolong it."

"And?" I prodded.

He scratched at the thickening stubble at his jaw, the sound drawing my attention like a clap of thunder. I wanted to touch it, to scrape my nails over it while I—

"If I'm fed enough before it happens, there is less chance of me killing something."

That cooled the heat rising within me. "Less chance of you eating someone, you mean."

He winced, still refusing to give me his eyes as he shifted on the stool. "Yes."

"How many have you...?"

"Enough." The word was rough, the hunching of his broad shoulders and the warm charge in the air warning me to stop.

My mind spun back to the first night I'd met him.

Did you murder someone?

Not recently.

I could tell him it wasn't his fault. That a dragon would behave like a beast of its nature was created to. And though I didn't know if that were entirely true, I could tell this prince carried a haunting guilt large enough to eat at him for eternity—large enough to suggest it was true.

Just the thought of it sickened him, and I ignored the itch to comfort him by changing the subject. "What do Spodge and Herb do with the yarn?"

Colvin set the quill down and stretched his arms over his head, his hair a delicious mess. "Throw it around mostly." He made it worse by pulling his fingers through it, the strands falling back to brush his cheeks. "They enjoyed it more when they were babes, tearing it apart and knocking it about."

My stomach quivered as I watched his mouth finish moving.

Moon fucking melt me, I was falling ill, surely. Which was almost impossible. But I failed to find another reason for how mere—albeit intense—minutes spent with his mouth on mine could conjure such a wanton creature to unfurl inside me.

Mate.

He was my mate. He'd admitted as such. That this was indeed the curse that had befallen me.

The fate-spoken ties binding us were said to be painfully difficult to ignore, and like a fool, I'd since given into the incessant pull that awoke whenever he was near. I had only myself to blame for feasting upon him the way I so recklessly had.

There was little hope left for escape now.

Colvin sniffed, those divine lips wriggling with a smile he wisely kept contained. "I get the sense you're not here to ask me about the narlows."

"Not entirely," I admitted. "But I was curious."

His eyes dipped to my chest, then moved away as if he was silently reprimanding himself.

It bothered me—how good he tried to be. We both knew he was not. "You can look, you know."

"I don't want you to think…"

"That you want to look at me?" I asked, moving closer to his overloaded desk. "That you want me at all?"

Affronted, he reared back with a heavy scowl. Each word was clipped. "You know I more than want you, fire-breather."

Indeed, I was beginning to recognize that he did. His actions in the throne room, the aching way he'd watch or refuse to watch me as if trying to restrain himself, and the arrangement of this impending marriage. Perhaps some of his motives were not so insidious but merely a way to make sure I was near.

It should have disgusted me, the lengths he had gone to and what he'd destroyed if that were true. Instead, it filled me with something indescribable and a heady wave of confidence. I leaned my hip into the side of the desk. "Then what's the harm?"

Rather than answer, he asked, "Do you like the dress?"

"That depends," I said, and his brows rose. "Did it belong to one of your lovers?"

As though I'd slapped him, his head snapped back once more. A nearly comical expression twisted his features. "I picked it and a handful of others from a boutique in the city, and asked for the seamstress so I could have them make some more." He paused before adding quickly, "And the undergarments."

My next breath caught.

He'd picked my clothing. I didn't dare ask when, though I longed to. I nodded, knowing I should apologize for assuming but unable to. "Then yes, I like it."

He watched me observe his work while I tried to make my heart cease dancing.

I'd thought all this mess had something to do with his royal duties, though I'd never seen Brolen work a fraction as hard. Yet, upon closer inspection, I found it was a curated list of poisonous plants. "There are books on those."

"I know, but it's easier to compile everything into a list rather than search through all of the different texts again." He yawned. "Should I need to."

The sound drew my eyes. "Did you sleep?"

"Not a wink." His hand fell over mine when I pressed it onto the desk, covering it. "I'm guessing you didn't sleep much either, but Fia..."

I ignored the warning in his tone, lifting my hand free to push his list away so I could lift myself onto the desk. "You need to feed, and it seems that what we did last night only made it worse."

He placed his hands upon my thighs when I tried to inch my way to the center to sit before him, halting me. "Jarron and Persy might worry, but I know what I can and can't handle. I can wait, but I'm not so certain I can handle you this close while I do that."

I met his eyes and watched his jaw clench when I nodded. "Okay."

He groaned and caught me by the hand as I slid away, tugging me back to him. His strength shouldn't have still been a surprise, yet I was shocked when he lifted me with ease. My rear met the desk, my legs atop and draping over his thighs.

I steadied myself by palming his biceps, fingers squeezing the muscle beneath his tunic. "I thought you said—"

"Just a few minutes."

I smirked. "How often do you need to feed?"

His head tilted. "Are you trying to torment me?" When my smile spread, his jaw loosened, and his lips separated. He cleared his throat. "It depends, though on average, at least twice weekly."

I tried not to let that intimidate or, worse, excite me, unable to keep from studying his luscious mouth.

"Worried, feral?" he taunted, though his mouth thinned afterward.

"Not as much as you might think, dragon," I volleyed, then ran from more talk of it when he stiffened beneath me. "I've been meaning to ask you something."

"Ask."

"Why do you wish to marry me?"

He released a stunned huff of laughter. "Besides the obvious, you mean?" I waited, and he watched, then confessed, "We heard you were in danger. We had to act quickly." Noting my frown, he then went on. "Your uncle took it too far, Fia, with both of us."

"So," I said, attempting to better understand, "what better way to punish him than to have us both not only live but also marry?"

A lowering of his eyes, his lips rising at one side. "Something like that."

"Something?" Maybe I shouldn't have asked. Not yet. But he had an alarming way of making me more comfortable than I should ever feel around a creature such as him. "Dragon, do you and your mother want Callula?"

The prince tensed, and I withheld another smile. Perhaps I was right.

Leaning forward, I brushed my nose along his cheek. "Let me help you."

"Help me?" he exhaled the question.

"You and Olette. I want him dead."

He tensed even more. "Your uncle."

"He's not my uncle."

"Fia," Colvin said when I pressed my lips to the sharp crest of his cheek and inhaled deeply.

With a groan, he clasped my chin and forced me to meet his probing gaze, his brows furrowing. "Surely, you don't mean…"

I nodded. "He told me, assuming I wouldn't live to repeat it to another soul." I refrained from trembling when his thumb whispered beneath my lower lip. "But I suppose it doesn't much matter to anyone else."

"It matters."

"He forced her to comply." I wasn't able to voice it all.

But Colvin understood, cursing viciously. "I see. So you want him dead, and then what?"

"And then I'll be free." Yet even as I said it, I knew that wasn't true. Even if I could go home, I couldn't erase the crimes painted all over me. I couldn't forget what my people now thought of me, nor could I ever hope to change their minds.

The prince studied me so intently, as though he were watching my thoughts via my features.

I'd never cared about being seen before. I'd always preferred to slink around unnoticed until it suited me. It was an adjustment, to say the least, not only having someone see me, but acknowledging that perhaps I wanted to be seen.

Perhaps only by him.

"You're not asking me to kill him for you," the prince stated, seeming to conclude while I struggled not to squirm under his inspection.

"No, I'm merely seeking the opportunity to do it myself."

His head tilted, eyes dimming a shade. "Have you ever killed someone, fire-breather?"

I tried not to grumble. "You know I have not."

"It's a stain on your soul. Each and every time. It consumes you and threatens to spread until it grows so dark you can't see past it."

That didn't bother me. Not when I pictured Brolen's smug face. A face capable of veiling an evil so sleek and oily, it shouldn't be allowed to exist.

Somehow, I would find a way to ensure it didn't.

But it bothered the dragon prince. A fact of which he'd already made clear in Castle Callula's throne room.

"I care not what it does to my soul, for he's already darkened a great deal of it anyway." I hadn't realized how true those words were until I'd set them free, their existence an iced wind seeping beneath my clothing to torment my skin.

Colvin's fingers smoothed up my cheek, thumb tracing the bone and then dropping to the corner of my lips. A grim smile turned up his own, his focus upon my mouth. "Your heart has claws, fire-breather. But your soul?" His eyes met mine, aglow with affection I wasn't sure I wanted or deserved. "Soft as silk."

My stomach felt fuzzy, like wool left out in the rain, my chest too tight to continue looking at him. "So will you let me help? With whatever it is you're doing." It wouldn't be as simple as asking. I knew that. To gain that type of trust would be difficult, but I needed to try. I would not be blindsided by this prince or anyone else again.

A smile lingered in his voice. "Is that what you came to see me for?"

"That, and I just..." I said in a breathless rush, "Needed to."

"And here I thought you hated me."

"I do," I said, moaning when he pressed a hand to my lower back and pushed my body from the desk to collide with his. "I hate you and your strikingly handsome face."

His chuckle vibrated over my lips. "Striking?"

"And your contradictory gentleness."

"Please, don't stop," he urged, feigning pleasure.

His mouth molded to mine, my words muffled. "Your arrogantly long, silky hair."

"Silky?"

"So silky." I hummed against his lips. "This outrageous cave of books."

He said to my cheek, lips roaming to my jaw. "I thought you liked books."

"I did until you ruined them," I teased, thankful when he laughed.

The caustic yet rich bark was something I wouldn't mind hearing over and over again.

"And let's not forget the tea-stained shirts," I breathed, his tongue resting over my jumping pulse. "I really hate those."

"Fire-breather," he whispered, lifting his head and flattening my hair to my cheeks with his big hands—my heart to my sternum with his adoring eyes. "I'm beginning to think that maybe you don't hate me at all."

A brow rose. "I wouldn't be so hasty, dragon."

Another chuckle, his eyes swaying over my face, his lip stolen by his teeth. Reaching up, I set it free, and he nipped playfully at my thumb. I smiled, wide and almost laughing, and his face fell as if I'd done something wrong. "Do that again."

I frowned. "What?"

"Smile at me like that."

"I don't smile on command, Prince."

He laughed, then pulled my face to his and whispered to my lips, "But will you follow other commands I give you?"

I swallowed, my thighs clenching over his. "I guess you'll have to wait and see." His scent was intoxicating. My nose glossed over his roughened cheek while my fingers crawled up his chest in hunt of that delicious stubble, and then I froze.

He wasn't wearing a cravat. His tunic, loosely buttoned, gave a glimpse of his dark chest hair and scars. Many scars. A ring of them decorated his neck.

"Colvin," I started, gently tracing my fingers over a raised loop of skin.

"Later," he murmured, having gone still himself when he'd realized what I'd fixated on. But I couldn't leave it for later. Not when it looked like someone had wrapped a giant burning necklace around his throat, the scars raised and square and...

"Chains," I breathed, my eyes leaping to his and searching. "Who did this?"

Clasping my fingers, he brought them to his lips and kissed my knuckles, then sighed as he placed them between us. "I did."

Horrified, I could only stare.

"If you don't get those narlows out of my rooms this instant, I swear to every star you can fucking name..." The doors crashed open, Olette standing between them. "I'll make sure they're next on the menu for defecating on my plants—*oh*." Smiling, the queen swayed back through the doors, handles in hand. "Busy? I'll take care of it."

Stunned and a touch mortified, I pushed off Colvin's lap and fixed my skirts on the way to the doors. "We're not. I'll get them." Those damned beasts were going without the dinner I should've already hunted down for them.

"No, stay," the queen called, the doors slamming with an oddly sweet, "I insist."

Colvin's lips were pressed so tightly together, I wasn't sure if it was to keep from laughing or if he was also embarrassed, his cheeks an adorable shade darker. "I don't think she knows the word subtle exists."

"What do you mean?"

He shook his head. "Never mind." Then he stood, adjusting himself without a morsel of shame as he prowled toward me. "Where were we?"

I folded my arms and leaned back against the doors. "You were telling me why there are scars in the shape of a thick chain around your neck."

He stopped a few feet from me. "I wasn't, but perhaps another time."

"Colvin," I hissed.

"Any chance we can just resume?"

"You said you weren't sure you could handle it." I lifted a brow, then opened the doors and skipped out while saying, "And the narlows are hungry, which is also why I came down here."

"Didn't think so," he muttered as the doors slammed again.

FOURTEEN

Colvin

IA'S WORDS LINGERED WITHIN MY MIND LONG AFTER SHE'D left my study.

I didn't doubt she'd spoken true when she'd stated her desire to have Brolen wiped from existence, but it was the way in which she'd admitted as much that haunted me. Fia had been wounded in more ways than one, but she loathed to show it.

Perhaps she didn't realize that she wore her hurt as armor. Armor I fully intended to peel away until the only weight she could feel was me.

When I'd confessed to Olette that the Seelie King had indeed planned to do away with me, I'd thought I'd have myself a battle on my hands in making her acquiesce to what I needed.

Time.

I'd expected rage, a pacing, snarling queen who would have already begun strategizing and sending the call out for our warriors to report to duty. We'd known Brolen would be a nuisance, that he would do as arrogant kings did, but we hadn't known just how deep his hatred for our family ran.

I hadn't expected my mother to smile and simply murmur, "Oh, how beautiful indeed," before reluctantly giving in to my request to wait.

But I'd been a dazed fool to think that any amount of time would make this easier.

The fear that accompanied the incoming change was different from what I'd typically experienced before I turned into something

I couldn't control. It was no longer the people in the surrounding towns and villages that I worried about.

"We need to think this through some more. Devise a better plan," I said upon entering Mother's private balcony, where I knew I'd find her watering her beloved plants at this time of the evening. "It's too much too soon."

I was so wound up, overflowing with nothing but longing and hunger and exhaustion. It pinched at my skin, my joints, every part of my fucking mind. I could tell this change would be worse than any I'd had in a long while.

Olette inspected the leaf of the giant flesh-eating plant blocking out the moon. "What has you so bothered, darling?" The plant snapped its thorny teeth, narrowly avoiding her finger. She gave it a gentle smack and hissed, the plant recoiling and closing its pinkened maw.

When at rest or lying in wait, it appeared to be nothing more than a giant green almond, its enclosed leaves the size of a grown male's head. I had the scars on my own finger to prove it was not.

Annoyed I had to even say it, I did so clipped and low, "I shouldn't have to spell it out."

Unbothered, though she'd reprimanded me for far less growing up, Mother shrugged. "But it must happen the only way it can. You cannot lose sight of that after all we've already accomplished." Moving on to her crowded cluster of poison-barbed flowers, reminiscent of giant daisies, she said exactly what I predicted she would, "As I've already told you, you must continue to believe."

I was glad her back was to me so she couldn't see the roll of my eyes. My teeth gritted, my jaw aching. Talons threatened to erupt from the fingers curling into my palms. There had to be another way.

A safer way.

At the very least, I would prolong it. Fia could remain within the wards.

I unclenched my teeth and rotated my jaw, but I knew the ache wouldn't leave. Like the others overtaking my limbs, it would grow worse until it happened and I returned. "Not this time. This time will be all the more dangerous, Mother."

"So is continuing with your asinine backup plans, Col." Finally turning, the queen set her watering can down and tightened her robe, inspecting me. "Have you fed?"

I didn't answer. There was no need.

"Then you've only yourself to blame." Eyes alight with fury, Olette whispered harshly, "Don't be a fool. Go now." She flicked her hand. "Find Gesna. She lives with her family this side of the river, just a few miles from the cottage."

Gesna had been a member of my harem, which now did not exist. "I'm not visiting any villages right now." Not when it was so close, too close, my chest burning. Not ever. "I'll be fine. But please, keep Fia in the castle this time."

"Colvin," Olette called, but I had to leave, and she knew that.

Though her intentions were not cruel, she knew encouraging me to feed from anyone when I was now mated was pointless.

I needed Fia, and in ways she was only just beginning to wake up to, but not yet.

Not like this. When I was too close to tipping into new skin, and she was still trying to make sense of all that had and would come to pass.

Unlike my betrothed, I'd had a few months to imagine it—to plan for her. Though I'd never planned to marry, I couldn't deny I was glad that I now would.

But never would I sire an heir for fear of delivering them the same punishment my late mother's bloodline had bestowed on me. Even if this Seelie princess of mine could somehow find it within herself to stomach my presence, to enjoy me as I did her, any future she might find herself able to envision would not arrive.

No matter how much I wished to give her everything.

FIFTEEN

Fia

THE NARLOWS HAD ALREADY BEEN RETURNED TO THEIR room by the time I'd left Colvin, annoyed, flustered, and riddled with questions I hadn't asked.

Fresh bones hung askew from their teeth and sat on the floor between them. It took one look from their deformed, bear-like faces for me to give in. "Fine. Come on, then." Those beady eyes aglow, they bounded across the stone floor, claws scratching, drool swaying, only to collide with each other in the doorway and end up in a brawl.

"Enough," I said, but of course, they didn't listen. That or they hadn't been able to hear me over the snarling and snorting. I clapped my hands twice, repeating myself in a growl of my own, "I said enough."

They broke apart, Herb shoving Spodge before making sure he was first behind me down the hall to my rooms.

Now, Herb dozed before the fire that had already been started before I'd returned. Spodge played with a spoon I'd given him from my meal tray, licking and pressing it to his nose with a huff, then tossing it to the stone to hear it clang and repeating the actions.

Hours crawled by as I watched them while not really watching them at all, perched upon my side on the bed. I could barely stand to look at the walk-in robe, let alone find something more appropriate to wear for lounging around.

His scent still stained the room as though he'd just left—as though he'd made sure I carried it with me after leaving him. He would, too, I surmised, my nose crinkling at his stubborn yet endearing audacity.

Soul connection or not, I didn't want to care. From what I'd secretly read during the months after freeing him from the dungeon—for I hadn't dared ask anyone, not even Aunt Mirra—we didn't have to care.

We could reject a connection and hope the fates, the sun and moon goddesses, would eventually deliver us a new one. Though such connections were growing rarer the more fickle we grew as a species.

Perhaps I could've rejected it. Maybe that was also partly why something inside me still resented the dragon prince. For if he'd never sold me out to his mother, then we both could have gone on with our lives to potentially find someone else to fixate on.

But it was painfully apparent now I was here and unable to escape him, that any attempt to make myself believe that I didn't want him, that I could do without him as my mate, was futile.

Especially after the way I'd reacted to seeing those scars, to his need for a book only I could open, and to his mere presence. I understood why he needed the book, but I failed to make sense of the urgency when no one could access its contents without me.

There was nothing left to do but ask him, and the other questions vying for first place at the forefront of my mind. But the most pressing need, the most frustrating for it shouldn't have been one, was my desire to get closer.

To get as close as possible.

I couldn't. He'd made it clear that he needed a blood source. That he was struggling to wait, but wait he would. I wondered long after the midnight meal had been delivered to the door of my rooms, just how long the prince had been waiting.

I wasn't sure it was wise to find out. For although I hadn't been here and I wasn't yet entirely willing to demand he drink from me, to think that he'd so much as placed his mouth on the skin of another sliced at my innards.

The intimacy of drinking another's blood, of having him take anything he needed from someone else…

I saw enough red that it wouldn't have surprised me if my eyes had turned crimson with the lust for blood. A different, far more violent type of bloodletting.

Fia the feral indeed.

I shared the meal with the narlows, allowing them half a piece of bread I'd dunked into the soup each, then I took them to bed.

I had a prince to hunt down.

I knocked once, then slowly opened one of the doors when I heard nothing, a smile already tickling my lips as I tried to guess at his expression upon seeing my return.

He wasn't in there.

A cup of tea was overturned, its contents still warm when I lifted it from the parchment Colvin had evidently left in a hurry. I threw my eyes around the narrow room, noting nothing else out of place. If anything could even be out of order in such disarray.

But the door atop the stairs at the back of the room was wide open, leaves dancing onto the small landing and floating down the stairs.

"Colvin?" I called, walking up them and peering outside.

No answer. Nothing but the call of night birds and haunting howls in the woods beyond. His scent lingered on the breeze, so I followed it, grasping at my skirts when they got caught on twigs as I turned and looked up at the castle.

It was barely visible through the vines carpeting the stone. Its spires and towers were mostly hidden by the giant treetops surrounding it.

The door opened to nothing but forest as far as the eye could see.

I trailed his scent down a worn, leaf sprinkled path through the trees. Not half a mile from the castle, I discovered where it led.

A cottage.

Tiny, as though the nonexistent groundskeeper had once lived there, the home was reminiscent of a mushroom. Its mossy stone exterior was covered in crawling ivy that draped across the circular windows with peeling white wooden trim. The roof was a dome of darker stone, heavily concealed by the greenery falling from it in thick curtains.

I breached the trees, twigs and wildflowers dusting the grass and steppingstones leading to the door. A faded white, it was nearly as tall as the roof. I slowed when I saw it had been left ajar, then stopped entirely as a bell sounded from the castle.

The ringing grew in volume as more and more bells in the distance chimed in response. My ears threatened to bleed. I placed my hands over them and spun back to the trees, unsure what was happening.

Colvin had left in a hurry via the study door leading northeast into the woods.

Toward the cliffs.

Go back, something inside me screamed alongside my racing heart. But his scent traveled toward the cottage, so he couldn't have...

A swift wind blew my hair across my face and carried the call of his scent to the side of the cottage.

There, behind it upon the ground before an overgrown vegetable garden, was the prince.

He was on his knees and shirtless. The clearing granted the moon permission to highlight the clenching muscles in his arms and back. I watched them bulge and shine, moving closer. He was agleam with sweat.

It glistened from his skin as though he'd just left the creek I could hear gurgling beyond the ignored gardens.

A twig snapped beneath my foot.

Colvin's head turned. There was no white visible in his eyes. They'd been engulfed by a gold so bright it was like staring straight at the sun and nearly as painful. He then lowered his head with a groaned, "Fuck."

I stopped, though I wanted to run to him and ask what I could do to help, to ease his evident suffering. To stop the convulsing that tore back his head and spread his arms and dug his fingers into the soil.

"Fia," he gritted, the command that followed an animalistic growl, "*Run*."

And then it happened.

His head tilted farther, nose aligned with the moon and his entire body shaking. Shaking as if he were a leaf being rattled by a storm—or possessed by an evil spirit.

He was.

And I tripped backward as it took hold.

As it swallowed him in a cloud of smog so dense, all I could see was growing darkness beyond. All I could hear was the howl of the wind stirring into a frenzy, swirling around the cottage clearing in a whirlwind, followed by a monstrous groan.

Then crunching, like twigs underfoot. His bones. Stretching, reshaping, changing entirely...

The groan became a low, unearthly rumble. A growl of soil-disturbing thunder rolling along the ground.

My heart kicked back into the correct rhythm and succumbed to the fear, and I finally ran.

Too late, something within me warned as I skidded through the trees beneath a growling, growing darkness. It advanced too quickly, soon swallowing every inch of light from the moon and stars and making it nearly impossible to see.

I veered too far from the path in my panic and tripped over two crossed logs. But the castle was just up ahead, the door to Colvin's chamber hopefully still open. I climbed to my feet and pushed forward, telling myself not to look back. I could make it, could run straight through that door before—

A roar cleaved the night, and it melted like butter as the sound rained from the sky above.

From right above me.

I slammed into an invisible barrier, hard enough to make my ears scream again. My head spun as I bounced back to the ground and blinked up at the impossibly dark sky.

At the underbelly of a dragon.

I rolled to my hands and knees, a scream trapped in my throat as I scrambled to crawl around the base of the nearest tree. Panic bleated through my blood, coiling my limbs so tight that I wasn't sure I could move or what the point was when the monster was right there, watching.

Rocks rolled and leaves jumped off the ground. Trees curled and snapped as the dragon lowered onto all fours and prowled to the edge of the clearing housing the cottage.

Pushing to my feet, I ran to the next tree, and then the next. A furious roar covered the scream I let loose as I moved faster. Faster than I ever thought myself capable. But it was in vain.

A giant, clawed foot landed right next to the tree I attempted to hide behind. A thick hind leg flexed as the beast lowered and turned his head.

And stared straight at me.

Familiar gold eyes stared back at me, but on the face of a scaled and snarling beast. The dragon opened his mouth, another growl displaying rows upon rows of razor-sharp teeth. I was fairly certain I knew what he wanted. He was warning me—telling me just who was in charge here—but I had to try.

I ran again, hurtling from tree to tree.

The dragon stomped forward, reaching me in just two giant steps.

I froze and whimpered, knowing I was playing a losing game, but there had to be a way. There had to be a place to hide until he found something else to hunt or changed back.

The tree's exposed roots next to me appeared larger, so I launched for them, ducking into the deepest crevice and wincing as my head hit the tree root behind me with impact.

Dark wings stretched through the clearing, each sharp apex rising into curved spikes, and I prayed the beast would fly away.

He didn't.

He tucked those wings into his sides and lumbered toward me—a hunter who knew his prey had been sufficiently cornered.

I could run again, perhaps even climb the tree, or I could stay put and shield as much of myself within the tree roots as possible. My panic ebbed into something else entirely as I realized I was doomed no matter what I did.

The dragon could not only fly but also breathe fire.

And I had his full, undivided attention.

Webbed feet hooked into the soil, carving trench-like grooves with each seemingly patient step. My eyes swam up his legs and the mass of scale-covered muscle to his huge, swaying head. It was so dark, so unforgivingly dark, as his towering form slowed to a stop right before the tree, his scales an impenetrable black that made it hard to study his features. To gauge what might happen next.

Then he lowered to the ground with a growled, steaming puff from his nostrils.

Soil and leaves dusted the air. The dragon leaned forward with a tilt of his head, and I knew exactly what would happen next.

"Colvin," I shouted, throwing an arm over my face and pushing myself deeper between the roots. "Stop," I begged, though it was pointless. It would seem the fates had indeed decided that I'd wrongly escaped death after all.

The idea of making history for being eaten by a dragon, and by my mate no less, was so much less appealing than being strung up by iron at the hanging tree.

The beast grumbled, each breath it took similar to an incoming thunderstorm. Breath so hot, the soil beneath my hands and legs melted into mud. Sweat slid down my forehead, collected over my chest and stomach. But his snout didn't touch me. His teeth didn't pluck me from the ground.

So I peeled an eye open, my lungs expelling gulped, heaving, painful pants.

To find the beast that had stolen my mate's body simply watching me.

"Oh, fuck," I whimpered, ransacking my empty brain for what to do.

Move. I should most definitely move, or at least quit staring at him. Perhaps play dead. I had a feeling that last one wasn't something I would get away with, nor did I wish to try if it meant he might throw me around like a toy doll.

The creature huffed, the plumes leaving his cave-sized nostrils burning briefly and drenching my arms in more sweat. He shifted closer, however that was possible, his snout looming over me and tilting down, almost in line with my head.

A mass of black scales, each as large as a shield, and whiskers were all I could see. But when I dared to break eye contact and look down, I noticed the scales at his chest faded into gray and then silver. They cascaded toward the belly of the beast and hugged his sides.

The monster grumbled again, louder this time, and my head snapped up. His golden eyes were still upon me and narrowed slightly.

His mouth remained closed, mercifully, the skin around his nostrils like that of leather. It grew thicker closer to his eyes, his cheeks— if you could call them that—and rolled into scales that fanned over the back of his horned head.

The moon could be seen again between the two giant milk-white arches behind his small pointed ears.

I was thankful for that much at least. To see it one last time.

"If you're going to do it, you'd better make it quick. Bite my head off and swallow it whole because I'm not a juicy treat," I warned, leaning forward to stab my finger at the beast's snout, "I'll be the most bitter thing you ever fucking tasted."

The dragon blinked, but otherwise, it remained wholly still.

I was an idiot.

An idiot crazed with fear. For I knew talking to a monster such as he was futile and just plain stupid. But the apprehension spearing through my every vital organ would kill me before he could. So I scowled up at him, shouting, "Well? What are you waiting for?"

Instant regret stopped my heart when the dragon finally moved, and I screamed, slinking back and wondering where in the fuck I'd lost my brain.

The ground shook. The tree above me swayed as the beast rose to his full stomach-turning height and seemed to peer through and above the treetops. Then he gave me one last glowing look before turning and lowering to the ground again.

This time, facing away from me.

His tail flicked. The spikes along his spine fell into a mace of sharper ones at the tail's tip that would club me into next week if I dared move.

So I didn't. The creature was waiting for something. Maybe a better, less foolish meal. I curled into the soil, sweat drying to my skin as I shivered and watched the mountain of scales watch the forest.

SIXTEEN

Fia

STARTLED AWAKE TO THE LOUD SCREECH OF A BIRD AND SAT UP instantly.

My head swam. My bleary eyes blinked half a dozen times, absorbing my surroundings as I remembered exactly where I was and what had happened. It had been too much, the ache in my muscles and neck from sleeping beneath a tree wrapped in nothing but fear, to be anything but real.

I rubbed my eyes, the cool tip of my nose. The sun was rising, bringing warmth and chasing away the dark from the forest floor. In its absence, there was no more dragon.

There was a naked male asleep on the grass, surrounded but untouched by fallen leaves and debris, where a beast had once been.

"Colvin," I croaked, crawling free of the roots and across the grass to him.

I pressed my hand to his shoulder, knowing my cool touch would likely startle him but not caring if it meant he'd wake up.

He wouldn't. "Colvin," I said, louder and close to his ear, shoving his arm.

Nothing.

This wasn't what was supposed to happen. I knew little of shape-shifting, but I knew enough to know he was supposed to be awake and moving. He was supposed to be just fine...

Warmth left his nose when I placed my fingers beneath it, and after trying to rouse him once more, I knew it was time for help.

I climbed to my feet and ran.

Remembering the barrier I'd hit just hours ago while running from Colvin's dragon form, I slowed when I saw the castle and placed my hands before me. Within seconds, they met a vibrating warmth that would warn off most creatures looking to roam too close. It shimmered.

And then it fell to reveal a queen.

Olette stood there, a fur-lined cloak draped over her shoulders. Her cheeks were stained pink from the cold, as though she'd been waiting behind the wards for quite some time. "You're okay." She dragged her eyes from the trees and set them upon me. "It's done?"

"He's…" I struggled to find the words I needed to use. "Help. He needs help."

Olette's hand clenched at her chest, at the bronze clasp of her cloak. "Jarron," she called, her eyes not straying from me. The question was low and clipped. "What happened?"

"I thought he was asleep, but…" I looked back to the forest. "He won't wake up," I said, my voice strangled with ice that had nothing to do with the crisp morning and everything to do with a newfound taste of fear.

Gripping her lace nightgown beneath her cloak, she said while looking at the trees, "Go inside," then called for Jarron again.

The male came running from a side courtyard I'd yet to visit. Skidding through a leaning arch of roses, Persy nearly collided into his back when he neared us and slowed suddenly. "Where is he?"

Their wide eyes assessed me. My torn dress and my wild state.

"Just over here," I said, and led the way.

Jarron and Persy hurried ahead when they spotted Colvin through the trees, and all I could do was watch as they hefted him back through the foliage toward the clearing.

To the cottage.

Olette walked inside ahead of them, and slowly, I followed, numb to my core though certain the early spring weather wasn't entirely to blame.

"You should go," Olette said when I entered. "Return to your rooms."

"This is normal," Persy reassured me when I didn't move from the doorway.

Jarron snorted, grunting out as he shifted the prince over the large bed at the back of the cottage, "He'd already be awake if he'd just fucking listened to me."

"Don't," Persy hissed from the kitchen nook, where she finished filling a pot to place on the stovetop. "What's happened has happened. He's okay. That's what matters."

"He's out cold and barely breathing," I retorted heatedly. "That is not fucking okay."

At that, Olette quit fussing with the patchwork sheepskin blanket. Her chin lifted as she surveyed me. "When I said you should go, it wasn't merely a suggestion."

Perhaps I'd run out of room to care, having narrowly escaped death twice. I didn't know.

But my own chin lifted as I said without an ounce of regard for what the consequences might be, "I do think that after surviving half the night stuck behind a mass of muscle and scales that I have earned the right to more than just making sure he wakes."

I waited, breath bated, and wondered if the shrieking beat of my heart could be heard.

But the queen's mouth fell open. "You were right there?"

Incredulous, I almost shouted, "Where did you think I was?"

"Hiding in a burrow or cave because of course, there was nothing else for you to do," Olette said, placing a hand to her forehead. "He'd scent you and hunt or wait you out."

None and all of that had happened. He'd guarded me like a watch hound. The irony wasn't lost on me.

The queen snorted, then shook her head, seeming as if she might collapse into a fit of laughter or tears at any second.

Sensing this too, Persy intervened, setting a cloth by the stove before collecting Olette's arm in hers. "He'll be fine now, so let's get you home."

Olette nodded, curses muttered beneath her breath as she left, while I wondered how many saw what I guessed was such a rare sight. A vicious, bloodthirsty queen reduced to shaking tatters.

It was obvious those rumors lived on for a reason, for I didn't doubt she was all those things and more.

But perhaps only when she needed to be.

Jarron, finished with throwing logs on the fire, was standing by a chest of drawers opposite the end of the bed, his arms crossed over his chest. He eyed me with a heavy amount of skepticism. "So you survived."

"Disappointed?" I extinguished the burner and dunked the cloth into the water, feeling his gaze like hot coals at my back. I wrung the cloth and rounded the cluttered dining table to the bed. "I'm just as surprised as you are."

He remained where he was while I gently pressed the warm cloth to Colvin's forehead and cheeks. The prince's lips parted when I reached his shoulder. "Do you wish to stay until he wakes because you don't trust me?"

"I don't know you, and you refused to feed him when he was in need, so yes," he said, taking a seat in the armchair below the window and crossing his legs, "I think I will be staying."

I didn't argue. I didn't care to. I returned to the kitchen to soak the cloth and wrung it out once more. "We don't drink blood."

"But you're willing to spill it," he countered.

I couldn't fault him for saying that, but his attitude was beginning to rankle.

Sighing, I climbed onto the bed this time and scooted close to lay the cloth upon Colvin's head again. "Perhaps you should spend more time wondering why you're so concerned about a mating connection that isn't your own."

"He's not just my nephew. He's my friend. Has been since he could talk."

"How sweet," I muttered. "And how long have you known Persy?"

Clipped words turned scathing. "That's none of your business."

"And my relationship with this dragon prince I've found myself tied to is none of yours, so you can either make me a pot of tea or find someplace else to be."

Jarron cursed with a short laugh. "You're serious."

"Deadly."

He stared at me for endless minutes, but I hadn't the energy to bother saying anything more to him. When I next left the bed, my skirts brushing the rim of a large bathing tub beside it, Jarron decided to finally take his leave.

He paused in the doorway, perhaps tempted to say something else, but left instead. I couldn't say I was sad about it. Not now that I had the prince and this cottage to myself.

If I hadn't known it was his by scent alone, then the bookshelves lining the walls between the bed, the rusted tub, the plush-looking armchair, and the dining table would surely give it away. All of them towered toward the ceiling in a matching twisting oak.

More books and parchment covered the table and even the countertops. The latter was overflowing with various teas and tea-cups, some cups clean, others used, and many chipped.

Rounding the circular dining table in the kitchen nook, which took up the front half of the cottage, along with the fireplace, I smiled down at the prince's messy, curling scrawl. Hurriedly drawn pictures of certain plants and creatures danced across the piles of parchment. More lists with chunky paragraphs below hastily drawn graphs were covered in drops of tea and splashes of food.

One particular piece of parchment was titled *new potions*, but before I could read it, Colvin groaned.

Wetting the cloth once more, I returned to him with a glass of water in case he woke, and waited while warming his skin.

He likely no longer needed it—likely hadn't needed too much attention at all with the type of blood coursing through his veins—but maybe I needed it. The excuse to touch him while still marveling at all that'd happened. At him.

This prince I'd found in my family's dungeon was certainly

something. Nothing I would have ever expected to happen to me. Not even in my most dizzying daydreams. And it would seem that in my anguish, I'd easily forgotten that I'd happened to him, too.

That the fates had decided we were fit to be knitted at the soul.

I wondered how he felt about that, although he'd made it clear he was far from disappointed. I still wasn't sure what I felt about it. What I did feel was foreign—earth turning and impossible to fight in a way that frightened me the more I gave in to it.

Watching him, the severity of his hewn features at ease, it was hard to believe he was the creature who lurked beneath his skin. Though, even when he was awake, I was beginning to see that the two couldn't be more different.

Yet it was him, the dragon who'd watched me so carefully, who'd growled when I'd dared to look away from him. It had been so very much him. A monster, most certainly, but he hadn't hurt me. Not at all. Perhaps I'd merely been lucky. Perhaps, even with the instinct to hunt and feed himself, he'd recognized me.

So he hadn't eaten a thing.

Colvin's eyelids fluttered, and I reared back as he reached up to grab the cloth. He squinted one eye open to the wet material, then opened both wide to look at me. A whisper accompanied a quirk of his lips. "Mother of monsters."

Unbidden and intrusively unwelcome, tears filled my eyes. I closed them, willed them away, and when I reopened them, I could only stare.

He stared right back, unblinking and his features soft with sleep. His voice was rough, a little hoarse. "I can't decide if I should kiss some sense into you or growl at you."

I grinned. "You could always do both."

His eyes thinned. "I could've killed you, Fia."

"You didn't."

"No." His brow furrowed as if he were remembering. He smiled then, but while still frowning, a burst of laughter freed with his astonished words, "I knew you."

"How?" I asked, eager to know. "Sight alone was enough?"

"The bond, or maybe your blood," he said, seemingly perplexed. The cloth was thrown to the floor. "Perhaps both."

Of all the wildest things to happen...

It made sense, yet I was still astonished myself.

Leaning over the pillows beside him, I studied his broad, hair-dusted chest. "The scars." I reached up to trace them. He shivered, an arm breaking free of the blanket to hold my hip. "You chained yourself with iron."

He didn't answer, but he didn't need to.

"Don't do that again."

His lips curved. "Worried about a dragon like me, fire-breather?"

I scowled.

His smile widened, displaying his perfect teeth and those sharp, pointed canines. It fell after a moment, gold eyes dimming to a dull orange as he stared at my mouth. "Desperation makes one try some dangerous things, but I haven't been able to restrain myself with chains for some years." He swallowed, his voice thick with exhaustion. "I grew too..."

"Gigantic," I supplied. "Powerful." In awe at the mere memory, I stared at him in wonder once more. "I cannot believe..." I laughed, breathy with disbelief, and trailed my finger over his jaw to his cheekbone. "You're truly magnificent."

He narrowed his eyes, perhaps thinking I was toying with him. "I'm a monster, Fia."

"My monster, apparently." Pushing him to his back, I rolled over top of him, my hair falling to curtain our faces. Then I pressed my mouth to his, hard and still and just feeling the supple warmth of his lips before whispering, "And you're weak. You need me."

His brows flattened. "Fire-breather."

"Please."

"I don't think you quite know what you're asking for."

"But I am asking for it all the same."

He shifted my hair behind my shoulder to better gaze up at me, searching my eyes. I shivered at the merest touch of his fingertips upon my skin. "You'll want release."

"Then you'd better make sure I find it," I warned, and his eyes flared a warning red in response, but I snuffed any further protest with my lips against his.

He groaned, rolling us and pinning my hands above my head with his. "Fia," he whispered to my cheek, grazing his nose against my skin. "This isn't something I want you to feel as if you need to do."

"But I do feel like I need to," I whispered in return, skimming my hands over his smooth torso to his defined hips. "I'm beginning to feel like I might need it even more than you." It would hurt, I knew that, but I wanted it anyway. The drugging sensations that were rumored to make some careless creatures lose their minds to addiction.

Colvin trembled. No—he shook.

Then he slammed his mouth over mine with a violence I hadn't expected. His teeth pried my lips apart and rubbed along the underside of my upper lip, then they pierced.

The groan that left him was pure animal, all trace of my refined, gentle prince gone.

He licked and shivered again beneath my hands, which were now clenching, my nails scoring into his waist. Copper soaked my tongue and flooded my mouth, but his tongue roamed with velvet strokes between my lips to lick every morsel of blood.

Breathless, I could only gape up at him through heavy eyelids when his head rose. His hair hung in dark ribbons around his cheeks. His eyes were entirely red save for the dark pupil. His mouth glistened with my blood. The sight of it running down to his chin awoke something I'd never met inside me.

I clasped his face and pulled his chin to my lips to lick it from his bristle-coated skin.

"Fia," he rasped, trembling harder as he pushed himself up on his forearms and opened my legs with his knees.

I finished licking him clean and then bit his lower lip—hard but not enough to draw blood. I knew enough of mating connections to know that once there was an exchange of blood, it was accepted. No matter how small.

It then became an agreement stronger than any marriage.

My skirts were shoved up to my waist. Something sharp brushed against my inner thigh.

A talon, I realized, my mouth leaving Colvin's and my breath coming fast. "I'd have liked to see you in these, but…" that talon running over me, so light, so careful as he stared down at me, accompanied by his husky words, tightened the coiling heat at my center. "Perhaps another time."

"Just…" I said, my voice throaty, clogged with want. "Touch me."

He grinned, teeth coated in blood. The sight should've repulsed me, but instead, it made me squirm beneath him and grasp the back of his head to pull his mouth to mine. After one taste, he tore away, his hair kissing my cheeks and his nose brushing mine. "And just where would you like to be touched?"

"You know where," I said, impatient.

"Fire-breather," he whispered with a rub of his lips over mine. "Would you like me to touch your cunt?"

That horridly crass word—in his voice—I moaned out a pleaded, "Yes."

Talon sheathed, his fingertips skimmed my mound, teasing. "Then you'd better open your legs nice and wide for me."

I'd never thought I'd like being told what to do. With Regin, I'd taken the lead any chance I could, but with him, with this prince, it wasn't just different. The command whispered through me and grew thorns that tickled my flesh into swelling with desire.

"Good," he murmured, then kissed me softly, sweetly, taking his time to build me up so thoroughly that when his finger spread me, slid through me with ease, I failed to keep from whimpering.

He breathed in the choked sound, a satisfied glint to his ever-reddening eyes. "So slick. Maybe you do need this after all." My every breath grew tighter as he watched me, as he explored me so delicately, as if he were savoring the first encounter. He confirmed as much when he reached my entrance, the tip of his finger toying but not entering. "I've been imagining this."

"You have?" I asked, and I'd have been annoyed by the eager surprise in my garbled words if I weren't so invested in all he was doing.

Colvin hummed, licking my jawline. "Every fucking day since I left you in that dungeon. Every fucking hour I've failed to sleep since you arrived because you're here." He dipped deeper, but only to his nail, and I couldn't remember if I was breathing. "Every fucking time I scent you, taste you in the air I breathe greedily like a wanton beast whenever you're near."

My thighs shook when his finger carried what he'd coaxed from my body to my clit and circled around it.

At my ear, he murmured, "But Fia?"

"Yes?" The word was exhaled in a trembling rush.

"Nothing I imagined comes close." His nose trailed over my cheek. "Kiss me."

A chord of lightning struck through me, and I did, my fingers curling into his hair at the back of his head. His mouth devoured mine with bruising efficiency. A dizzying contrast to the way his finger continued to swirl through the mess he'd so expertly created between my thighs.

He broke away to slide his lips over my chin, whispering, "Now show me that pretty neck."

I tipped my head back into the pillows. He inhaled deeply with a soft groan while his mouth trailed from my chin to my neck. A rough exhale seared my skin. His tongue dipped into the hollow at my throat, lapped, and then shifted to my pulse. Beneath it, he sucked at my skin in warning, but I didn't need it.

"Do it," I pleaded, desperate—desperate to give myself to him in that way, desperate to have his finger finally enter my body, desperate for more.

Both happened at the same time.

A fractured cry scraped my throat raw, his canines and finger plunging deep.

Pain mixed with pleasure, and the room blackened, but only for a moment. His tongue soon soothed the sting, and I began to dissolve into nothing but feeling with the first suctioning pull of his lips.

He rumbled approvingly, his finger curling inside me and rubbing, his thrusting cock pinning my thigh to the bed.

An avalanche of sensation coursed through me the more he drank. My mind drained of all thought. My mouth dried. My stomach quivered violently with my legs. My fingers fell slack and then clutched him to me when it felt as if he might move away.

His chuckle was dark and followed by a groan. The sounds, and that of him swallowing, of the slow torture between my thighs...

Colvin's mouth slipped from my neck, his eyes heavy-lidded as he watched me fall. "Fuck," he breathed, rocking faster against me now. "You're shaking so fucking hard, Fia."

My eyes closed, and I succumbed to such an overwhelming orgasm, it almost hurt. A silent scream was swallowed by Colvin's mouth as I pressed his face closer to steal his bloodied lips. He pulled free with a growl. "I have to see you."

A panted, "Shit," flew free as his finger was clenched by my body.

"I can't wait to feel this with my cock," he rumbled.

There was no way. Not yet. Not when I was so sensitive that just the slightest movement of his thick finger caused me to flinch. My eyes opened as I swallowed, my throat dry.

But then he returned to my neck, and I shifted over his finger to make him move again. "More," I croaked as he coaxed me farther away from reality with gentle laps of his tongue. "I want you inside me."

He ignored me, content to keep sucking at my neck—content to torment me as my body rewarmed with too much ease and swiftness. My very blood tingled, licked at my skin and bones in ripples that shot right to my core with every drugging pull from the prince's lips.

Then his finger curled again, stroking the sensitive, swollen depths of me. The sucking ceased, his mouth gliding down my neck to my chest. His head rose, and he gazed at my breasts, which were concealed, but my nipples pushed at their confines.

He stared as though at war with himself, his finger retreating and then entering slowly, his thumb pressing into my swollen nerves.

"Colvin."

"You're too fucking much. Look at you," he rasped. "What I've done to you…" He blinked and flared his nostrils, eyes fixed upon my neck. "Feral, indeed."

I rocked my hips and gritted, "Just fuck me, please."

"Please?" he said, eyes meeting mine and a brow raised. I'd have praised his restraint if I hadn't seen how his jaw worked, crimson still lingering within his lust-stained gaze. "You can't have my cock, but you will come on my hand again."

"Why?" I gasped as the aforementioned cock dampened my thigh with sharper thrusts, his need for me leaking from him.

His mouth fell over mine, his hair over my cheeks. "Because I'm about to explode, Fia."

Then he did. He kissed me, our lips failing but desperate as he tensed, his teeth clenched. And the sight—his widening nostrils, the caustic, rumbled sound climbing from deep in his throat—sent me spiraling all over again, and this time, it did hurt.

He was right. This was too much.

But I knew, even as my head pounded in time with the throb ricocheting from between my legs, that I would do terrible, atrocious things to ensure I experienced it over and over again.

My nails clawed at his back, and a pained moan slipped free.

Both seemed to make him roar louder as his head fell to my shoulder, mouth seeking my ravaged neck. "Fia." Colvin hissed as though it were so much that it pained him, too. Warmth tickled and dressed my thigh. He groaned, jerking as it continued. "Fuck…"

Breathing hard and fast, I opened my eyes and splayed my hand over his clammy back, stroking. "Agreed."

He chuckled, lacking breath and sound. "Not bitter," he said, heaving, and his eyes once again white and gold. "In fact, I think you might just be the best thing I ever fucking tasted."

My heart bounced. "You understood me."

"Every word anyone says. My instincts just don't care, especially if I haven't fed. If it moves, I chase. If there's meat, I'll want to eat it. But you..." He gently removed his finger from my body with a groan, and said hoarsely, "My instincts knew exactly who you were." His bloodstained lips met mine when I smiled.

They stayed until I grew limp beneath him and yawned, and he then cleaned my thigh before forcing me to sleep.

SEVENTEEN

Fia

COLVIN CURSED WHEN A KNOCK SNATCHED US BOTH FROM sleep.

His arm, which had been wrapped tight around my waist, slid away. Cold drenched the top of my head when he carefully removed it from beneath his chin to leave me.

"Col," Jarron called. "Better be decent. I'm coming in."

The prince pulled the blanket higher over my body to my neck, and I withheld a smirk. "Do that and it'll be the last thing you fucking do."

Jarron's laughter floated through the wood. "Touchy this morning. Did the feral princess not stay to satiate your beastly appetite?"

Snarling low, Colvin tripped into a pair of black pants and plucked the tunic hanging over the dining chair, storming to the door. Too fast for me to steal a good look at anything other than a teasing glimpse of his firm ass. The door slammed before I could give Jarron a little wave and a piece of my mind.

Colvin surprised me by taking care of that. "You'd be wise to stop calling her that."

"Everyone calls her that," Jarron retorted.

"Who?" Colvin asked as though he'd take names.

Jarron's laughter sounded nervous. "Relax, shit. I just came to check on you, you unfed, cranky fuck." A pause. "But it would seem she did stay after all." Another pause. "And she's still here."

Colvin didn't answer, but I could picture one of his rare, rather delicious glowers.

I held the pillow beneath my head and closed my eyes, far too comfortable to even think of leaving, and I had no reason to.

Until Jarron said, "Olette's been looking for her. Something about a dress fitting in the tea parlor on the third floor."

Now I do, I thought with a sigh.

I knew my gown would be ruined, but I'd forgotten about the bite at my neck until I sat up and looked down to find a few drops of blood staining the material. A small mirror hung from the wall by the bathing tub, and I pulled my thick tangles aside to glimpse the mark.

There was no blood, of course. Colvin had made sure to lick every last drop from my skin. But even after some hours had passed, my quick healing hadn't erased all evidence. A bruise remained, faded and with two dark pinpricks inside it.

I should have cringed, and perhaps I would have days ago.

But that was before. Before I'd been cast aside and condemned and given away like property that lacked value. That was before an oddly endearing male had shown me that he thought otherwise— that he was my mate, and he was seemingly more than okay with it.

Now, I couldn't help but smile. It spread when a small shiver raised the hairs on my body at the memory of the mark's maker.

The door opened as I finished readjusting the soiled and ripped dress as best I could, my torn undergarments now ill-fitting beneath. "Did you hear?"

"That your friend is an asshole?" I slid my hair back over my shoulders. "I was already well aware."

Colvin nodded, watching me while gripping the back of the dining chair. His tunic was rumpled, and I could smell some type of tomato-laced sauce on it as I stepped closer. Though tousled and a little tangled, his hair swept around his face and shoulders as if it too enjoyed touching him.

I didn't envy him, but I wanted to touch him, so I crossed to where he stood. His jaw unclenched, eyes lifting from my neck, and I wondered if he wanted to see it—the mark he'd left—as I tugged at the front of his tunic.

He lowered his head for me with a smile in his eyes. "Beautiful mess."

A brow rose, my nose nudging his. "And here I'd thought you were against name-calling."

"I'm allowed."

"Are you now?" I whispered.

His mouth curved over mine, his eyelids lowered. "I'm the only one." Just four barely audible words, yet their roughened sweetness threatened to melt me into a heated puddle.

I evaded the caress of his lips, skimming my own over his cheek. "Then I guess I'm allowed, too." I muffled his huffed laugh with my mouth and pressed closer with his groan.

He broke away, murmuring, "Mother is expecting you, so unless you wish for her to scent what happened here..." He stepped back, chewing his lip as though it pained him to do so.

"Don't worry," I said, smiling as I forced myself to the door. "I'll wash every last trace of you from me."

He smirked, collecting some teacups from the dining table. "Some things never wash off, fire-breather."

"We'll see about that, dragon."

His rumbling laughter gave me a boost of much-needed energy as I bounded out of the cottage and over the patches of stone through the clearing toward the castle.

Olette was indeed waiting.

My hair dripped to the carpet when I curtsied upon entering the tea parlor. It was an oval-shaped space with curved wooden shelves where the cornered edges of the room should have been. Instead, there were rows upon rows of books and dried floral arrangements.

Many books seemed to be missing, and I knew instantly it was because of a certain golden-eyed prince.

Olette noticed what gained my attention, setting her tea cup down. "He's relentless," she said. "And you're extremely late, but given your ordeal in the early hours of this morning, I won't hold it against you." She gave a thin, crimson smile. "Much."

"What does he want with them all?" I asked.

Olette pursed her lips, leaning back into the ornate two-seater chair with roses etched into the dark green velvet. "Who really knows." She waved the hand of the arm bent over the wooden crest of the chair, her smile curving higher into her cheek. "It's always something new with him."

I frowned, not entirely sure I believed her but certain I should've perhaps looked closer at Colvin's studies.

It was then the cherry-red gown caught my eye behind her. "Is that...?" I crossed the room, the organza pleats of the bronze dress I'd hastily plucked from my dressing chamber held tight within my hands.

"For your engagement ball, yes. Which will be held tomorrow night."

Tomorrow night.

The shocking words attempted and failed to stop me from admiring the voluminous gown. A gown fit for a queen and made just for me.

I was not normally one to care much for fashion, but the masterpiece hanging from a wooden rack by the wall left me without words. The overflow of skirts was a seductive concoction of overlapping silk and lace layers. The bodice was a corset of patterned lace spun into the form of vines and roses over silk to match. Black ribbon ties hung loosely at the back, with no straps or sleeves seen nor necessary.

"It's..." I blinked and tore my eyes from it when a male with silver hair and matching eyes entered with another gown, this one covered, in hand.

"Oh," he said, bowing deeply. "Our bride has arrived."

"Fia, this is Golan, my talented dressmaker."

Golan turned a humorous shade of bright red, and I realized then that his ears were atop his head, similar to a cat. He was short for a faerie, his nose upturned. "What have I told you about making me blush, Majesty?"

"Show me," Olette simply said, and the creature plucked the covering free of the garment.

My jaw fell all the way open.

Olette clapped. "Place it next to the other."

I turned, unable to remove my eyes from the sorcery this creature had created. Golan carefully stretched up on his toes to hang the black gown next to the other, their skirts, never more different yet somehow expectantly similar, brushing.

The wedding gown was entirely black but with a glittering hue throughout the giant extravaganza of skirts reminiscent of staring at the night sky. "Pixie dust," he exclaimed. "Costs a fortune, but it's most certainly worth it."

No pixie in Callula would ever sell their dust, but I had to remember just how far from home I'd traveled. The gown was a dark reminder. The bodice was also a corset in a plain yet perfect dark plum. At the back were more black ribbon ties, but that wasn't all.

A giant bow sat where the corset met the steep rise of the skirts, falling with them to the floor in gold. A gold similar to a certain prince's eyes. A gold that acted as a striking train, Golan plucking the silk ribbon from the floor and carefully hanging it on a rung behind the dress.

"Mother of moons," I breathed, reaching out to touch, then thinking better of it and retracting my hand.

Golan sighed as if relieved, a swollen hand pressed to his vest-covered chest. "That's the type of reaction I live for."

Olette laughed low. "You've indeed done splendidly, as always."

Golan bowed in gratitude. "Do let me know what adjustments might need to be made as soon as you're able."

Olette nodded, an acknowledgment and dismissal, the dressmaker heading to the doors.

Once they'd been shut, she rose and walked over, inspecting both gowns with tilts of her head. Her crimson hair fell over her shoulders like butter, as though every move she made, perhaps simply breathing, caused it to shine.

"You seem to like them," she murmured, pulling at the skirts of the wedding gown to inspect them carefully. The pixie dust glimmered and distracted, and I was tempted to tell her not to touch such finery.

"Like is far too meager a word, and I'm not one to care much for such things as fancy gowns."

"I've noticed," she said, tone dry, and her eyes flicked to my feet, which I'd thought were covered by my skirts. "Nor footwear, it seems."

"I was in a hurry," I defended.

"Of course," she said, a touch too knowing for my liking. "You are always in a hurry, aren't you, darling?"

I didn't answer, for she was mostly right, and she knew it.

"You're immortal, yet you seem to live as though the sky might squash you at any moment."

"Stranger things have happened," I stupidly argued.

That evoked a genuine, shocking burst of laughter. I tried to keep my eyes from widening at the musical sound. Dropping the skirts, Olette tapped her chin, her eyes shining as she surveyed me. "Like surviving several hours with a giant dragon?"

"Amongst other things." I nodded, my clammy hands squeezing my skirts. "Yes."

Mirth still dancing in her eyes, the queen pressed her lips together, then sighed. "Let's try these on, shall we? I want you to tell me all about it."

Her curious tone unnerved me, but I wasn't about to protest.

The gown was far from easy to get on. Fearful of ruining it, I was grateful when Olette assisted, her question little more than a whisper as she tied the ribbons at my back. "You didn't hear the bell?"

I winced, the corset binding to me. "I did. I just hadn't known what it was for until it was too late."

She hummed. "And just what were you doing out there?"

"I was looking for Colvin after noticing he'd left his study in a

KINGDOM OF VILLAINS | 157

hurry. I found the cottage. I found him outside of it as he was about to shift." I withheld a shiver at the memory of the smog-like smoke, the crunching and otherworldly sounds. "I didn't... I couldn't seem to move. I watched him change."

"Hideous, isn't it?" she said. "Not his dragon form, but how it takes hold." I pulled my hair aside, nodding. "When he was small, when he wasn't yet grown enough to kill me, I'd make sure I was there." Her tone had softened, a sadness to it.

I tried to imagine it. Something like that happening seemed horrible enough, but to a youngling? "He must have been so terrified."

"He was, but he's never complained," she said. "Not about that."

"But it upsets him," I said, knowing it was true. "What he does when he's not in control. When he's a dragon."

"It slowly kills him," she said, then nothing more for long moments. "I hated leaving him, even after he'd broken nearly every bone in my body, but I had to. I would've endured it, but of course, he vehemently refused. He grew stronger, more monstrous, and then there was nothing any of us could do."

"You had to leave him."

Her fingers paused, then pulled. A sharp breath rocked through me as my lungs squeezed. "So you eventually ran," she prompted.

"Though it was pointless, yes. I hid in a trench between the roots of a tree, but he could've burned me to ashes and pried me out with ease."

"And what did he do?"

"He watched me, growled and grumbled a lot, and then..." I smiled, thinking of it and wishing I hadn't been so understandably scared—wishing I'd have appreciated all that he was a little bit more. "He watched the forest."

"He guarded you," she confirmed, and turned me to face the mirror that stood on a stand beside the hutch housing an array of teapots.

"Yes," I said softly. In disbelief, over what had happened and at what greeted me in the mirror, whatever else I was about to say vanished.

My violet eyes were wide, as large as always, but aglow with an unfamiliar shine. My cheeks still sat too high but were no longer too pale. Color stained them, riding along my cheekbones like a permanent, subtle blush. My unruly, damp waves fell over my shoulder to my waist, kissing the rise of the skirts at my hip. A mess, just as Colvin had adoringly stated, but I didn't mind. The near-white was a shocking contrast to the cherry red of the gown, but in a way I couldn't help but marvel at.

Quiet but seeming as if she were also absorbing my appearance and all I'd said, a smile bloomed in Olette's reflection behind me. A smile I was growing too familiar with. One that once appeared condescending and a touch cold. But now, I could see she was merely pleased, though perhaps still slightly amused.

I decided against telling her the rest. I was certain she'd put those pieces together just fine. The mark on my neck did not go unnoticed, with my hair scooped to one side to better fasten me into the gown.

Done, Olette stood back, circling and inspecting from every angle.

My hands swept over the waterfall of cherry red, unsure where they wanted to journey first. "This is unlike anything I've ever seen before." I trailed my fingers over the intricate design of black vines in the corset, the lacework even more impressive up close. "Beyond beautiful."

"You sound surprised," she remarked with a hint of snide. "Did you think we'd dress you in cobwebs and bones?" A stunted burst of laughter followed when I failed to answer. "Really, darling. I know it's been mere days, but after everything you've witnessed so very closely, I thought you'd have realized which kingdom contains the true villains."

She wasn't exactly wrong, but the urge to refute her claim still soured over my tongue. I kept my mouth closed and turned to the side to view the corset. It held my hips and breasts so tightly, the latter threatened to spill from their confines.

And I adored every breathtaking inch of it.

Olette bent at the knees, lifting the hem to inspect the needle-work beneath. "The slippers will need to be without much height to keep them from showing."

A knock interrupted us, followed by Persy's voice on the other side of the doors. "Olette? Do you have Fia?"

How she got away with calling her that, I didn't know. But I assumed it was due to her father's position and that she spent so much time in the castle.

"You know I do." Olette scowled at the doors, rising from the ground with liquid grace. "Why?"

"Just, uh... would like her help with something."

The queen rolled her eyes, unfastening the ties of the gown. "Where?"

After a long pause, she answered, "In the city."

Olette looked at me in the mirror with a perfect auburn brow arched. "I suppose the wedding gown can wait, for there are stranger things for you to experience yet." Tossing her hair to her back, she sashayed to the doors. "But I highly recommend some footwear." She then left the room with a strict, "Do not damage that gown while taking it off."

The doors closed, but I still heard her say to Persy, "At least try not to get her injured or killed."

Interest officially piqued, I carefully but quickly shimmied out of the gown. I left it swaying as I pulled my dress back on while rushing from the parlor.

EIGHTEEN

Fia

Kicks and Velvet were a mated pair of Pegasus, and unlike the few I'd glimpsed in rare sightings back home. Those had been magical, their feathered wings and manes a match for the moon, but they'd never allowed me close enough to see much else. To marvel at their deep gray, almost blue, coat and their staggering height, which was twice that of a horse.

Eyes of liquid ink watched me as I slowly inched closer. "I've not seen one since I was a youngling."

The Pegasus were native to Eldorn, and Callula royals had stopped encouraging their breeding in our territory upon discovering that the beasts would forever fly toward the calling of their souls—home.

Persy cursed. "Careful, they don't take too well to—"

But Velvet nudged my extended hand, an indication that I was welcome to touch her.

I needed no more encouragement and gently pet her soft nose before moving to her neck. Her mane, silver beneath the moonlight, was next. "Moon-washed silk," I whispered, then moved to the wings tucked into the creature's side. Reverently, my finger stroked down the spine of a single, long and thin moonlit feather.

Velvet shivered, and I breathed, "Magnificent."

Boots crunching over the damp soil, Persy snorted as she walked to Kicks. "You'll give her a big head."

I smiled at Velvet, running my fingers over her moss-soft cheek. "How far is the city?"

"About an hour by air. I can't materialize," she said. "Never had the patience to learn how, so"—she pulled herself into the saddle—"I call these guys when I want to get somewhere quickly."

"What has you so impatient?"

"You'll see. Hurry up and climb on." I hardly knew this female, yet the shine to her apricot eyes told me I wouldn't be disappointed with whatever she had planned. It told me to trust her.

What shocked me more than how this evening was unveiling was that I wanted to. I wanted to try. "Wait," I said, moving to Velvet's side and eyeing the huge saddle. "I've never ridden a Pegasus."

"But you've ridden a horse."

"Well, yes."

"It's much the same," she said with a shrug. "Just far more traumatic if you fall off." I glared, and she laughed. "Hurry up."

The height of the beast was daunting, but I tucked my dress into my undergarments and gave it my best shot, hauling myself up into the saddle.

"Sleek," Persy observed. "Like that of a forest cat."

Realizing it was not a jesting insult—at least, I didn't think it was—I refrained from handing her another glare. My toes curled over the gleaming stirrups, and I settled into the saddle. Velvet's hooves carved at the wet soil, eager to move.

Persy said, "Just tell her to…"

"Rah," I hollered, already gripping the reins. Velvet took off, running toward the end of the clearing.

And then the cliffs came into view.

Kicks galloped past, Persy squealing with delight as they raced off the cliff's edge, her hair sailing behind her with the deadly drop.

We followed, and I screamed. My stomach fell so swiftly, I half-expected it to fall through my toes to the dark sea crashing against the patches of jagged rocks below.

Then Velvet's wings spread wide, and we soared toward the frothy cliff line. As we traced it, my heart began to beat again, a fast patter as I smiled. The wind hurtled through my hair and slapped icy fingers across my face.

Persy raised her arms up ahead, her laughter like that of the morning birdsong I missed from back home.

Endless sky and sea stretched far into the distance, but below and to the left, the Kingdom of Eldorn was a patchwork giant of darkened treetops. Dense with greenery as far as I could see, I was surprised when the first village came into view below the canopy of trees.

Castle Eldorn loomed behind us, deep within the northern woods of the kingdom and closer to the Crystal Sea than any map had suggested, its dark spires barely visible through all the foliage.

The wind became less blistering the farther south we traveled. More villages populated the land and even small towns, the closer we flew toward the giant mass of lights in the distance. Trees grew sparse, some watchful sentinels surrounding the snaking river and city in the shape of a gigantic glowing clover.

The fiery lights soon grew within that clover. Kicks and Velvet speared toward it as if they'd visited the city that awaited a few miles inland a hundred times before.

I was almost sad to arrive, all the while burning with nervous excitement to lay eyes on it. Time had never fallen away with such ease, for it was not normal to enjoy the passing of time within such clear sight of the stars.

Velvet slowed, wings spreading wide against the wind as the ground rose up to greet us. I braced, prepared for impact, but her hooves hit the earth with a graceful gentleness I should've expected from her elegant ilk.

We'd landed in a cornfield, and I gingerly dismounted with a slight wince.

Kicks hit the field with a little more zest than Velvet, wet soil spraying and a growled huff leaving his nostrils in a plume of steam.

Persy immediately jumped free of the saddle and patted the beast's side. "Thank you."

Apparently, that was their cue to leave. Kicks and Velvet began to trot into the trees beyond the field.

"Where are they going?"

Persy, wearing a frilled cream blouse and flowing emerald pants that could've passed for a skirt, gestured to my dress, which was still tucked within my lace garments. I pulled the skirts free as she walked toward the cluster of lights through the tree-lined road. "Back to the stable hands to have their gear stripped, then home."

"Where's that?" I asked, watching them fly side by side toward the moon.

"Caves within the cliffs beyond the castle."

"But how will we get back?"

Another shrug, her tone a tad too nonchalant. "We'll catch a ride with someone later."

I didn't ask how, though I wanted to, for she seemed impatient to get wherever it was we were headed.

The gowns I'd been given might have indeed been more comfortable than what I'd worn in Callula, but I couldn't help but envy how relaxed Persy looked—the ease in which she moved. "How did you get those pants?"

"Bought them, of course. I'll show you where next time. Tonight, we've got other things to do."

I struggled to keep up, jumping over a stretch of rocks at the edge of the field. "Such as?"

"Stop asking," she said and waited behind the shrubbery for a wagon filled with cackling females to pass. "You'll ruin the surprise."

The growing volume of noise had me tearing my eyes from the barn house a little ways behind us through the trees and looking straight ahead. Across the dirt road was the river I'd seen from the sky.

A river that encircled the giant, luminous city of Eldorn.

An arching bridge built for foot traffic gave us passage over the algae-blanketed water. Farther up, I noted a larger bridge. Reptilian warriors stood at either end, ensuring each wagon and carriage waited their turn to cross.

Up the slow sloping hill, the city seemed to blaze brighter and appeared larger, so I assumed this was just one of many entry points due to its size. This area still shined, but with that duller orange I'd glimpsed from high above. To the left, the river rolled on, hugging this bottom portion of the city, and spread toward the tree-dotted valleys in the darkness.

"So he didn't kill you," Persy said.

I frowned at the stone arch we neared, a warrior watching us walk toward the entrance. "You didn't need to drag me across the kingdom to ask me about that."

"I know. I'm just extremely curious."

"Well, I'm still breathing." Her pinched lips made me admit with a crinkle of my nose. "Likely because I'm his mate."

Persy snorted, and I felt her eyes on me when I looked forward. I refused to acknowledge them. The warrior was now well within earshot, and she thankfully kept her mouth shut.

Squat stone buildings appeared to have been placed atop one another, staggering crookedly toward the sky. They lined the riverfront in a zigzagging fashion, leaning against each other. Many windows were dark and patched over with wood or only barely illuminated.

We stopped at the arch, the black metal gates beneath it open and creatures darting through the cobblestone street beyond.

"Persy," the male said, the scale-like skin at his jawline and forehead creasing. A long, scaled tail flicked behind him. "I'm not covering for you again."

"Nothing to cover if you didn't see me, Dolcom. Just passing through."

"Uh-huh," Dolcom grumbled, his fluorescent yellow eyes pinned on me. "Just passing through with the queen's captive."

"She's not a captive."

The male lifted a brow, further scrunching the roughened skin at his hairline and upper cheeks. "Can she confirm that for herself?"

But I was still staring at his forehead, imagining what it might feel like. "Sorry?"

Dolcom tilted his head. "Never seen a real warrior, Princess? I would've thought enough of us had paid that pristine palace of yours a visit that you'd be able to quit gawking by now."

"Not gawking," I clipped with a scowl. "Merely curious, actually."

He chuckled, and it was similar to that of a wheezing set of smoke-affected lungs. "Dare I ask what you're curious about?"

My eyes widened, and Persy laughed, using my mortification to drag me past the smirking warrior and through the entrance.

He called out behind us, "I'm here until dawn if you find you're still feeling curious, Princess."

I spun back to glare at him, but a tall carriage similar to a small hut ambled by. Four giant workhorses tugged it uphill toward the brighter side of the city.

"Crude as fuck, he is," Persy said through a laugh, then stopped upon the break in the hill that split two ways beneath us. Larger buildings that also looked like they'd been dropped from the sky atop each other sat between the two streets, rolling unevenly downhill. She chose the street on the left. "This way. More obvious but quicker."

Having no idea what she was talking about, I tried again to keep up.

"By the way, your feigned lack of enthusiasm regarding our prince doesn't fool me. You reek of his feeding mark, and the lust still shines in your eyes."

Her goading was beginning to rankle. "Just admit that Jarron told you."

She veered around a puddle of something unsavory smelling, her voice noticeably lower as we ventured deeper downhill into the dark. "Of course, he did."

Passersby became fewer, and I could no longer hear any horses or the crunch of wheels. There was only the faint percussion of walled revelry and the sizzling of meats at a vendor cart perched in an alleyway. The cook eyed us with one eye, a patch on the other, as he spoke quietly with a female wearing a trench coat.

The female turned. Sleek raven hair fell away from a harshly angled face with the breeze to reveal a glowing set of orange eyes.

"That's Madam Pond," Persy said beneath her breath. "Look

away. She'd like nothing more than to recruit something as innocent and well-known as you."

Madam... "Are you referring to a brothel?" Pleasure houses had been outlawed from Callula long before I was born.

Persy gave me a pointed look, but she nodded when she saw I was merely surprised.

"And what gave you the impression I'm innocent?"

"Oh." Persy laughed, then caught herself when a group of goblins exited what looked to be a tavern to our right. Her voice dropped to a whisper as beady eyes fell upon us. "So she admits to giving in to her mate in more ways than just *sustenance*."

"We haven't done that."

Her brows shot up. "No fucking?"

I shook my head and looked forward, the hill growing steeper as it rolled toward the lake that waited through the tall pine trees at the street's end.

"Who is he then?" she asked carefully.

Just thinking of Regin both pained and angered me. Two feelings I'd managed to ignore for days, and I wasn't too keen to have emerge right now. "He was my friend, then more, and now I don't wish to even talk about him."

"Noted," Persy said with a slight whistle. "But does Colvin know about him? It seems it was perhaps something serious."

"There's no longer anything to know," I said firmly. But then I reassured her with a reluctant, "He does." To keep from falling prey to the memory of Colvin's questions and displeasure regarding my life-long friend, I demanded, "Now tell me why Jarron has such a chip on his shoulder."

"He's protective of Colvin," she surprised me by supplying with ease. "Not just as his uncle, but almost in a big brotherly sort of way. He watched him grow up. He's been there for it all."

That made sense, and though I still didn't care for his attitude, it was good to have a little more understanding of it. "I came in a bit later," she continued. "When I grew old enough to realize I preferred being with my somewhat absent father more than my flippant and overly obnoxious mother."

"How old are you?"

"One and twenty," she said with a faint smile in her voice. "Not too much younger than Col. But I was nearly twelve years when I moved to the castle. Far too young to find a mate, but I'd just started my bleeding..."

She needn't have bothered explaining more.

Although it was rare, anyone could find a counterpart in another soul once they'd begun to mature—no matter the age of when that happened. She needn't have explained the rest either, but she'd poked at me, so I had no issue returning the favor. "Jarron wasn't happy about it."

"No," she said, and I knew her quiet tone had more to do with how she felt than our surroundings. "He still struggles with it. He's thirty years older, and although age isn't usually something to feel shame over, he knew me when I was still maturing, still so young, so..."

So shamed he would most certainly feel, even if the mystical laws of nature couldn't be helped.

"He treats you well?" I wasn't sure why I felt compelled to ask, but something about this female who'd saved me from Olette's interrogation to play in the city had me feeling unexpectedly protective. That, or maybe it was that her mate seemed to be the truest form of an asshole.

Of which she confirmed by saying, "He's better now."

My steps slowed. "What do you mean now?"

"He used to take lovers." The words were said quickly, quietly, as if she wanted to avoid hearing them herself. "He stopped a few years ago."

"A few years ago?" I said far too loudly, but mother of monstrous moons, he was an asshole indeed.

Persy shushed me and halted by a cluster of broken steps.

The street sconce above her didn't need to glow for me to see her cheeks pinken. Leaning against the railing, she waited as a group of males tumbled from a three-story dwelling across the street.

The sign one of them reached up to smack swayed in their laughing absence. The Red Garden. "Can people go there to feed?"

"Why, is Callula's exiled princess a blood feeder now?"

I rolled my eyes, and she grinned, watching the males sing their way up the street. "Madam Pond aims to satisfy whatever need you might have, but I wouldn't step a foot closer. Colvin will scent it and burn it to the ground."

I snorted. "All right."

Her brows furrowed. "You don't believe me? He might appear anything but when not wearing scales, but he is certainly still a beast."

I swallowed as I looked at her and recalled all he'd said and done, especially in his bed and in the throne room back home with that guard. "No, maybe I do believe you." I veered back to the subject we'd strayed from. "Did he do that to push you away?" I asked. "Jarron."

Persy looked down at a weed crawling up and around the whorls in the railing, a tiny white flower resting over the metal. "Yes, and it worked. After the first few rejections, I let it be."

"But he didn't."

She shook her head. "It's impossible to repair, I know. We've vowed time and again to just stop so it might fade, but that's hard to do when in such close proximity and all." Forcing a smile I saw right through, she added, "Like I said, complicated, and though it made me proud of him, I couldn't help but feel excruciatingly jealous at how quickly the prince got rid of his harem when he returned from Callula."

The swift change in conversation threw me, but the topic rocked me. "What?"

Persy peered down the street, eyes narrowing on a building at its end. "Just packed them all up with a bunch of coin and sent them on their way." She looked back at me, frowning. "He didn't tell you."

"I knew he had one." And I couldn't deny wondering where they were since my arrival at Castle Eldorn, but I never would've guessed he'd act with such speed.

A sickening shame slithered into my chest. For I hadn't.

In my defense, I hadn't known for certain, and really, I hadn't wanted to. I'd thought I'd never see him again. I'd hoped I wouldn't after finding out what he was and what I'd done.

But none of that made the heavy weight settling into my chest lessen at all.

"Oh, shit," Persy hissed and snatched my wrist.

Before I could see what had startled her, I was tugged to the other side of the stairs and forced to duck down behind them. "What?" I whispered. "What's wrong?"

She pressed her finger to her lips, her eyes squeezed closed as if that might help her hide better. Unsure whether to laugh or follow her lead and remain quiet and still, I popped my head up to peer between the stone landing and the metal railing.

A reptilian warrior with long brown hair walked downhill, dressed in the same uniform of leather and ginormous bulky boots as I'd seen on the rest, but with a plum patch at his chest.

Persy opened her eyes and pulled at my arm, then pushed at my head. "Stay down."

"Who is it?"

"My father."

But it was too late. Maybe he'd seen me. He could most certainly scent us with Persy being his daughter. "Persy." A sharp, rough command.

Persy winced, then rose, inspecting her nails. "Oh, hello."

The male's piercing eyes narrowed. "What have I told you about sticking your nose in these parts?"

"Uh, well…" Persy looked at me, and I made a face because what was I supposed to say? Looking back at her father, she finished with a smile, "Not to? But the princess got lost, so I was just searching for her."

I scowled but then smiled when she elbowed me in the ribs, shrugging with an unconvincing, "Whoops."

The male huffed, smooth lips twitching. "The princess would not be here if you didn't bring her, though, now would she?" he assumed correctly. "Get back uptown now, or I'll take you home myself."

I followed Persy when she rounded the steps and asked her father, "But what are you doing here?"

"Hunting something for Olette."

"Another murderous plant?" He didn't answer, just turned to cross the street. "Or are you seeing Mother?" Persy's accusatory tone swayed my attention to her, and she folded her arms defensively.

"Pers, mind your business and get moving before I make you."

Persy hollered to his back, her voice bouncing off the stone buildings into an echo. "She's only going to chew you up and spit you right back out again." She then dragged me up the street and darted into an alleyway, where she muttered, "Hugest idiot to ever exist."

"Why?" I whispered and peeked around the edge of the building in time to see the door to The Red Garden close. "Did he just...?"

"Mother works there. She's made it her mission in life to break his heart, I swear." Sighing, she gestured for me to follow her back onto the street. "Come on. He'll be gone for the remainder of the night."

We continued downhill, and I looked back at the wooden overhang and sign to the pleasure house. Every window was aglow, some duller if the curtains had been closed, in the building that towered higher than those on either side.

"He does this every other full moon, but she'll never commit to him." I couldn't help but wonder if her parents were the sole source of her evident frustration or if her own situation was also to blame.

"Because he's reptilian?"

"That's what she says. Though it's not because of what he is, but more so of what it requires of him."

"A lifetime of service to the kingdom," I said, unable to hide my feelings about that with my harsh tone.

Persy paused outside of the last building at the end of the street. It was shorter than most we'd passed, only one story, and it appeared unoccupied.

"They're born into service, yes," she confirmed. "But they need it, crave it—the loyalty and the brotherhood. None are known to leave unless it's via death, and even then, they have their own ideals on what happens after." With a roll of her eyes, she said, "Eternal honor and glory and all that dull shit. My father is Olette's most trusted and favored general, and my mother is an all-or-nothing type." Taking a breath, she eyed me up and down. "Ready?"

Failing to keep up, I didn't get the chance to ask what I needed to be ready for. Persy stomped on a metal drain covering beneath her boot three times.

My brows scrunched in confusion. "What are you—?"

But the covering rose when she stepped off it, revealing a dimly lit staircase beneath.

Her gleeful smile was contagious as she finally hinted at her plans. "I heard you like beasts, so let's see if we can win you one."

As soon as we descended deep enough, the metal covering closed above my head. The stairs stopped midway down a hall. A goblin with a smoking stem in hand pushed the wooden casing closed over a lever and greeted us with a sharp grin I wished to never glimpse on such a creature again. "Evening, ladies."

"I thought goblins served the crown."

"Who do you think owns this place?" Persy said.

"Olette?" I asked, trailing her down the narrow hall. Cobwebs hung from the damp ceiling, mildew speckling the rock and packed soil.

She slowed upon entering a room that seemed to stretch halfway up the street we'd trekked down.

A long wooden bar lined the far wall, dartboards and glasses hanging beyond it. Before us stood tables, all of them varying in size and most of them occupied with card players and drinkers and creatures of all ilk.

A gambling den.

"Colvin."

My eyes widened upon two females groping a faerie with the face of a boar and the body of a typical faerie male. "That's impossible."

But I was beginning to see that there truly was no such thing as typical in Eldorn.

"He inherited it from his mother, so I guess you can say it belongs to him and Olette." Seeming to know exactly where she was going, and as though she regularly frequented this den that sat beneath the darkened part of the city, Persy hurried toward a table near the bar's end.

Another reptilian warrior sat there. This one with cropped brown hair and arms the size of small tree trunks. "You're too late. Game's over."

"Define late," Persy stated, gesturing to a seat beside the one she pulled out. "And I know when you lie. You get a little twitch in your…" She reached out to poke his cheek, and the male grunted, swatting her fingers away as she laughed.

He sighed and shuffled the deck of cards. "What I meant is no one wants to play with you."

"Why?" she said, collecting a spiced peanut from the bowl in the center of the table. "Because I always win?"

"Because your father has been visiting your mother again, not ten floors above."

Persy waved him off. "He won't know, Fen. Besides," she said, looking up, "we can always count on one creature to seek any chance to annoy me."

A finely dressed reptilian female and Fae male made their way to the table, hand in hand.

Fen cursed. "You two better fucking behave."

Persy delivered Fen a glower. "It's him you need to worry about." Beneath her breath, she muttered, "The filthy cheat."

I didn't get the chance to ask who the male was, but it was

evident that both he and Persy visited this den often and therefore knew one another.

The male arrived, the female dropping his hand and taking a seat with him across from us. Delighted surprise lifted his copper brows, the hair combed back over his head a shade darker. Dignified yet far too arrogant, he lowered to the chair with a miserable excuse for a greeting. "Oh, my." His charcoal eyes swayed between us. "Have I already won?"

The female laughed and plucked a stem from the jar on the table, leaning over to light it on the candle. "You're a dreadful flirt, my love."

Persy feigned disinterest, but I didn't miss how she'd tensed. "What could you possibly want with an infant woon, Lorr?"

A woon?

I'd never encountered the miniature and rather vicious bear, being that it was a smaller monster of Eldorn and therefore not so easy to come across in both kingdoms.

This Lorr ignored her question and looked at me, a gleam in his eyes. He was handsome, but the air he carried with him made you take notice. This male was far from good, and he didn't seem to mind who knew it. "A Seelie princess brightens our den."

I just stared, not agreeing with the greasy energy permeating from the stranger who couldn't decide what female at the table to blatantly ogle.

"She's all ours now." A server placed a large glass of purple wine before each of us, and Persy tipped hers to her lips. "Drink up, princess. We've got ourselves a furry babe to win."

It probably wasn't the right time to let her know I'd never gambled, so I didn't. I picked up the glass and sipped.

Fen tossed the cards across the table.

Lorr eyed Persy with unabashed hunger, his purr more of a threat than a request, "Roll the dice, Persy."

NINETEEN

Colvin

THE QUILL SCRATCHED AGAINST THE PARCHMENT HARD enough to tear it.

I cursed, tossing it to the desk and staring at the sentence I'd butchered and violently crossed out. I could still scent her, still feel her beneath the pads of my useless fingers. She was a haunting so vivid, the restraint it took to keep from stalking through the castle halls in search of her made more than my hands shake.

My very bones quivered. Hunger and exhilaration coursed through me like a river over a cliff, too much to tame. This entity surpassed the need to feed, to unleash pent-up desire upon another's flesh. It was unconquerable and impossible to ignore.

From the moment I first laid eyes on her, I knew that should I ever have such a wish granted, then I would never again taste anything quite like her.

And I'd been right.

Exquisite, a rare wine gifted from the goddesses themselves, Fia Callula was the poison I'd spent most of my existence searching for.

She was both life and death, for after one drop of her blood had touched my lips, it was instantly apparent that I'd never get what I so desperately needed anywhere else.

It had to be her, and I was still thanking the fates I'd once cursed for allowing it to be so. Her taste was imprinted upon my tongue. A song that called deadened parts of me back to life inside my veins. But touching her...

I groaned, reaching for my teacup with trembling fingers.

The tea was a poor replacement for what I'd spent hours devouring, so I set it down with a clatter in the saucer.

She still loathed me. There was a good chance a part of her always would. I'd stolen her from her life, and I'd brought her here to make my own easier. For I had to, and I had to have her.

She had every right to blame and despise me, but I'd never know she did either when I'd scented her desire. When I'd felt it drench my fingers. When I'd felt her already swollen, incredibly soft flesh flood with desperation for more.

For more from me—for more of me.

Jarron's steps clipping down the hall outside ignited a spark of annoyance before he'd even opened his mouth. "You're still bothering with that even though everything is going to plan?"

"It's going to plan because she's my mate," I said before I could help myself.

She was my fate-given counterpart, and I'd spent hours staring at the same stupid piece of parchment, coming to terms with the fact that she'd given in to me because of that.

It was hard for her to deny herself or me, and therefore barbaric and cruel of me to succumb when I knew. I knew she hadn't forgiven me and that there was so much, perhaps even too much, to forgive.

"And?" he said, his features creased with confusion as he took the step down into my study. "That's been the whole damned point."

"And I'm still a dragon." I didn't bother giving voice to more of my turmoil, but I had something else I needed to say. "Care to tell me why the fuck she was out there?" I'd avoided leaving this very room since I'd arrived not long after Fia had left the cottage. I couldn't until the anger had subsided enough that I wouldn't snarl and snap at everyone. "You were put in charge of watching her when it began to take hold."

Jarron's brows lowered. "I know, but she went looking for you."

I'd already assumed as much, and my teeth clacked together. I said through them, "And none of you thought to go looking for her when you realized?"

He stiffened at the barely leashed fury in my words. "Col, Olette said it needed—"

"Olette wouldn't have risked Fia's life," I immediately barked. "Especially when I'd told her not to." She shouldn't have been in the forest. I didn't doubt she had found me of her own accord, but we should've done better. Somehow, someway, we were supposed to make this safer. "She didn't even know about the bell."

It was then I knew I was most angry with myself. I should have been the one to ensure Fia was thoroughly aware of the danger—to ensure her safety. But that was easier said than done when I was the one she needed protection from.

And it would've only been a matter of time before we could no longer avoid it.

Even so, the shame and fear multiplied when my mind drifted to what could have happened if the beast within me hadn't recognized her as ours. We had. I had. But the relief and amazement were short-fucking-lived upon remembering what typically happened in the past.

The murder and the mayhem.

"She knows now." Jarron leaned against the desk. "So where is she? Scrubbing you from her neck until it bleeds anew?"

I slurped my cold tea, the fire illuminating my eyes warning enough.

He raised his hands and grinned. "Just playing with you."

"I'd really fucking rather you didn't, but to answer your question…" I set the teacup down with an intentional clatter. "She was stolen for the gown fittings, remember?"

Jarron's smile fell. "But I just saw Olette chasing the narlows out into the courtyard. No sign of Fia."

In her rooms then, I surmised, yet I stood and stalked past him to the doors. I had no doubt this princess of mine could fend for herself should she roam too far from the castle, but her aptitude for finding trouble had me wanting to at least lay eyes on her.

I materialized to the hall outside her rooms to find the door ajar and her scent hours old.

I still entered to be sure, and as I left the bathing room, I nearly slammed into Jarron. "Pers isn't here, either." His jaw ticked, barely unclenched enough for him to mutter, "And it's beast night at the den."

We both cursed and materialized to the city.

We needn't have bothered trailing their scents down the street to the gambling den, but it was a comfort and a thrill to the monster that lurked within to know I was so close to hunting her down.

Both scents smothered the stairs beneath the drain cover, the goblin at the bottom startled into a deep bow at the sight of me. "Sire, I wasn't aware that you'd be—"

"It's fine, Richan," I said, hardly recognizing my voice when I heard her laughter.

The smoky, low chiming timbre staked talons into my chest and propelled me forward with longer, more impatient strides.

Patrons, both at the bar and tables, scrambled. Some bent at the knees, some merely stared. I didn't frequent the city. Unless I was not a Fae prince but a dragon, I'd seldom left the castle grounds for the past three months.

The females were seated at a table in one of the darkened corners of the den.

Persy was first to notice our arrival, growling a myriad of curses when she sensed us and stilled. She then removed her hand from the dress shirt of a male across the table from her, the ire draining from her features as she looked over her shoulder.

Fia, who'd been watching the two argue, turned her smile my way when she caught on a moment later.

Her grin was a glimpse at rare magic that quickly faded when it dawned upon her that I'd come to collect.

The wineglass in her hand slipped, the little that remained splashing across her gown and over the table. She looked down at it, then righted the cracked glass and whispered to Persy, perhaps too riddled with wine to remember that I could hear, "We've been discovered."

Jarron didn't ask questions, nor did he pause to assess the situation. I supposed he'd seen enough. He untucked Persy's chair and hauled her up and over his shoulder. "Wait," she came close to screaming. "That asshole has our woon."

I looked at Fia, but she was scowling at the copper-haired male. "He does. He's a rotten cheat."

The cheat in question was eyeing Persy as if he'd take her from Jarron at any second, his fingers curling into fists upon the table. "If you want it, Persy, then you know where to find me."

Jarron had already started materializing from the room, but I didn't miss the threat of death that entered his eyes as he drilled them into the audacious male.

I held a hand out to Fia, waiting for her to quit glaring at the male who'd lost interest in much of anything now that Persy was gone. He rose from the table and forgot the reptilian female, who scrambled to keep up as he left, a crated creature in hand.

Fia watched them go with a huff, then finally looked up at me. "Dragon."

I smirked.

Fia glared, even as her lips wriggled.

I helped her up from the chair, enjoying the easy way she fell into my arms. Then I took us home before she could deliver any threats of her own, of which I might then need to rescue her from or backup.

"That slimy fucking slug," she immediately said, her arms unwinding from me far too soon for my liking. "He cheated. I swear. Shouldn't he be handed to the warriors for punishment or something?"

I loosened the cravat at my neck as I watched her whirl and frown at the walls and my belongings. "We all know what's likely to happen when you visit a gambling den, especially in that part of the city. It's just how it is."

"It's stupid," Fia hissed, her tone brightening a moment later. "But I do like this cottage."

"Stop spinning," I gently warned. "You'll be sick."

"Don't tell me what to do, beast."

I chomped down on my lips to keep from smiling.

As if regretting her harsh words, she stopped moving and blinked up at me with glazed eyes.

Moon above, she was beautiful. All that creamy hair. It was everywhere, always, dancing around her shoulders and lower back in tangled curls. Yet it didn't detract from her allure or make her any less of the princess she indeed was.

It only heightened my extreme desire to explore more of her with my eyes.

Her tiny, freckle-speckled nose crinkled. "What is it?"

"Nothing," I said, stepping closer to brush my knuckles down her cheek. "I just really enjoy observing you."

Fia flushed, her cheek warming beneath my touch. Long lashes fluttered as her eyes closed. "Mates."

"Before knowing that, I still did."

"You knew when you kissed me in the dungeon, didn't you?" she asked, so softly it was mostly breath.

I couldn't help but assume she hadn't meant to voice that thought aloud. "Yes," I admitted, husked as my mind skipped back to that first taste, the overwhelming heat it had created within my blood. "I kissed you to be certain of something I already suspected." I breathed her in now as I had then, as though her scent alone was all I needed to exist. "That you were mine."

Fia swallowed, the sound thick. She reached up to place her small hand over my cheek, her eyes opening and now glazed with something else. "I think I need to lie down."

I grinned. "I think that would be wise."

I helped her climb into bed and seated myself on the side to pluck her slippers off. Then I placed her feet over my thighs to rub them.

She moaned, but I was merely the beast she'd said I was, one with an insatiable appetite for this princess. I wanted to see every part of her, no matter how much it painfully hardened me. So it was for selfish reasons that I admired the arch of her feet, her soft toes, and slender ankles with my fingers.

"How did you find us?" Fia asked.

"Persy likes to try to capture rare things she'll never bother to keep."

She giggled when I pressed firmly into the arch of her foot. "I want that woon."

"I think you'll find they're more trouble than they're worth."

"Like me?"

I pinched her toe, and she squirmed with a heart-stalling smile. "You're the only kind of trouble I find myself desperate for."

"Desperate?" she questioned, and it was low, as were her lashes as she eyed all of me with blatant slowness.

Growing harder than stone, I stood from the bed and tucked her feet beneath the blankets. I then pulled them over her and whispered to her forehead, "Fucking famished."

But she wouldn't let me leave with a brush of my lips across her skin. A fist clenched my shirt, pulling with more strength than I knew she possessed. I teetered, placing my hands on either side of her head just in time to avoid falling over her.

"Then why don't you feast?" she whispered, lifting her head while pulling at my tunic in an attempt to make our lips connect.

I wanted nothing more than to let them, but I knew one taste would be all it would take. One touch and I'd find it nearly impossible to stop. "You've had too much wine."

"Says who?"

My mouth itched to curve at her fierce scowl. "Says the cauldron-sized glass I caught you drinking from and the fumes threatening to intoxicate me from your lips alone."

"Fair." The princess meshed our noses together. "But I still think you should kiss me."

"I think you should sleep, and we'll save the kissing for tomorrow." I inhaled her, growing more intoxicated by the second, and eyed those rose petal lips. "Should you still want to."

"I want to now." That was the only warning she gave. Swift and soft as satin, her mouth fused to mine and pressed.

For lung-tightening seconds, she just felt my lips against hers, and I did the same. Then with a breath that caught, she pried them apart to touch my tongue with hers. Softly, lazily, she teased and provoked me mercilessly.

I had to stop. I knew that. But one kiss from her made me wonder what the fuck I'd been doing my entire life if I'd never been kissed in such a way before. Kissed as if I were the air she needed to breathe, and if I didn't cooperate, I'd be the one to perish.

A slight whimper sent a barrage of blood straight to my already engorged cock. Despite all my plans, when it came to this female, I had no idea what I was doing—just that I'd do whatever was necessary to keep her. I was fucking addicted, and it made every muscle ache to pull away and stand from the bed.

Fia did something I'd never expect from her, and whined. "Why?"

"You need water," I rasped, my voice breaking like I was maturing all over again. "And I need to keep the beast inside me from mauling you."

"But I do enjoy being mauled."

I stopped by the dining table, liquid wrath flooding every vein.

My eyes shot to hers, and hers widened at what she saw in them. "It kind of excites me," she whispered, grinning into the blanket. "To see you get so mad."

"I'm glad the idea of me hating the thought of you with someone else enthralls you so," I muttered dryly and felt my cock mercifully deflate by the time I'd reached the kitchen nook.

"But I was referring to you, you beast. I want to be mauled by you." I was hard again, my teeth meeting from the searing, instant ache. But with an exaggerated exhale, my mate promptly ran from the subject. "And I really do want that woon."

I smiled down at the glass I filled with water.

"If I were queen, I'd have five of them."

"Just five?" I asked, setting the pitcher down and peering through the lace drapes to see the first touch of the sun within the starlit sky.

"Okay, maybe ten," she said, followed by a loud yawn.

I let the drapes fall closed. "Is that what you had planned? To collect as many creatures as possible when you one day became queen?"

Her answer came a delayed moment later. I turned back to deliver the water as she mumbled with her eyes closed, "I just want them all to live and roam wherever they wish."

I set the glass down on the nightstand, then took a seat in the armchair across the room. We'd slept in the same bed before, but it wasn't only out of respect that I chose not to join her this time. It was also that I couldn't pass up the opportunity to watch her surrender to sleep.

Her lashes shadowed her freckle-dusted cheeks, and her hands slipped from their tight hold on the blankets. One fell over her stomach. The other across the bed. Her fingers unfurled as if seeking something.

I didn't delude myself into thinking that something was me.

All that hair was scrunched behind her head in a near-white nest. Some strands tangled around her arm and draped over her chest. Her breathing soon evened, her journey into her dreams complete. Awake or asleep, this Seelie princess was quite possibly the most beautiful creature I'd ever laid eyes on, and not due to the usual qualities, though no one could deny she held that type of beauty in volumes.

But due to her soul.

The sun had brightened the world outside of this new one I'd fallen into by the time I decided to let my eyes close. Though even as they did, I still couldn't keep from marveling over the nettle entwined jewel in my bed—couldn't shake the overwhelming feeling that I'd found a treasure more rare than anything I could've expected.

TWENTY

Fia

A WHISPER CARESSED MY CHEEK. "FIRE-BREATHER."
I curled closer to the sound, into the brush of affection at my hairline, reaching for it with a sleep-heavy hand.

A low, velveteen chuckle. "I'm afraid you must wake up. We've an engagement ball to prepare for." My eyes flew open, the dragon prince looming over me with soft golden eyes. "You forgot."

"Well," I hemmed, pushing up when he leaned back to offer me a glass of water.

I drank it greedily as he said, "You were informed it was this evening, yes?"

"Someone might have mentioned it," I muttered and handed back the glass. He was so close I could bend my head to inhale the headier fragrance of him at his neck and allow the dark stubble at his jaw to kiss my skin...

I forced myself to move the opposite way, scooting to the edge of the bed and groaning when I swung my legs to the side. A dull ache lingered in my skull and limbs. "How long did I sleep?"

"The sun was rising when you passed out," Colvin supplied. "And it's now set."

"Shit." That would explain the grogginess. Well, that and the wine I'd consumed while watching the entertaining sparring match between Persy and Lorr at the gambling den. I stood, searching for my slippers and giving in when a glance around the cottage failed to reveal them. "I need to go."

Colvin said nothing as I raced for the door, but as I opened it, he called with irksome humor, "Your shoes, fire-breather."

I ignored him and jumped over each moss-touched stone into the forest, racing down the path made by many a journey from the castle to the cottage.

The door to Colvin's rooms, or study, whatever it really was, was mercifully unlocked, and the halls outside my rooms were empty. Though the preparations downstairs for the evening's event carried a thickening tension upon the air.

I soaked and washed the previous night from my skin and hair in the tub, knowing I was running out of time but too comfortable in the hot water—too thankful for its waking yet relaxing embrace. When I heard a light tapping outside on the door to my chambers, I called to whoever it was to enter.

They did, and I knew without moving an inch that the dress had been delivered by some of the staff. Its skirts whispered over the floor, the scent of excitement from those who'd delivered it lingering in their wake long after they'd made their exit.

It was just an engagement ball, I reminded myself.

It was merely another excuse for everyone to gather and indulge themselves stupid. I hadn't been informed of when the wedding would occur, but it wouldn't be long after tonight's celebration. It could be days or weeks, though usually no longer than a month.

I could easily have asked someone. Colvin, Olette, Persy. Anyone. I just didn't want to.

It would happen whether I was ready for it or not, so there was no point in giving myself a looming end. There also wasn't any point in feeling forlorn or anxious over it. It was a price I had to pay, and with a male I was rapidly discovering I did not totally despise.

But it would mean it was done. That soon, there could be no going back.

I knew such a thing was already impossible, but I'd done too thorough a job at ignoring its permanency as much as I could over the past few days.

The increase in volume from downstairs and outside drew my eyes open. Baying hounds called to one another through the night.

Outside the window alongside the tub, a flock of those bat creatures flew in the distance, heading toward the castle. The commotion and heightened emotions would capture their interest and lure them like moths to a flame. That, and their queen had likely summoned them for another layer of defense.

I wasn't sure what the Unseelie thought of their prince wedding a Seelie princess, but if the disgust of my own ilk was any indication, then I was sure many would not attend.

I would soon discover just how wrong such judgments were.

A pixie half my height with glowing orange eyes entered after a sharp tap on the door while I struggled into the overabundant gown.

Her voice was reminiscent of the chimes strung outside some of the shops in the city of Callula, which many believed would ward off evil spirits and tidings. "Allow me to assist you, Lady."

Stuck halfway in the corset with some of the skirts tangled within my slip, I didn't protest. Her long, claw-like fingers were nimble, the dark nails painted with some type of glitter. "Is that pixie dust on your nails?"

Shrewd fiery eyes lifted to me, the paper-thin skin of her nose crinkling like silk over the bone. "It is." Her thin lips lowered over sharp teeth as she finished fixing my skirts and moved behind me to begin the tedious work of trapping me within the corset. "We do not have the time to strike a deal, though."

"It is your own, then?" I guessed, lifting my arms to give her more room.

"Yes."

"I do not want any, don't worry."

A tense silence ensued until the ties were tightly affixed to my back, and my lungs shrieked. I turned to find the pixie gazing at the gown with wonder. "You are to have some regardless. Her Majesty has asked that I dust your eyelids."

"It's not necessary if—"

A bony hand rose. "It has already been paid handsomely for."

I couldn't refute then, although I'd never worn much in the way of rouges and paints upon my face. All that changed as the pixie instructed me to sit on the edge of the bed so that she could get to work.

"What is your name?" I asked, my eyelids struggling to stay closed as the creature scraped dust from the tiny, brown-and-blue mothlike wings at her back. I wanted to see, but as her clawed finger came for my eyes again, I wisely shut them.

"Ilena," she said. "Her Majesty's beauty technician."

"I've never heard of such a thing," I murmured, tempted to blink as the thickening layer of pixie dust dried to my skin. "We have handmaidens at home."

"That is not your home anymore," she said curtly and without any remorse to follow as she pressed the sharp pad of her finger to the corner of my eyes.

When I opened them, I found I had glittery wings of my own staring back at me through the mirror across from the bed, but upon my eyes. Kohl was plucked from a holster at her thin waist and applied to my lashes.

Too shocked by what I saw, the glitter giving a sparkling, snowy backdrop to the long dark lashes I fluttered, my irritation at the pixie's reminder of my fate faded rapidly. "Wow," I breathed.

"Not done yet," Ilena clipped, her wings beating as she rose from the ground with a rouge-tipped brush. The crimson paint was sticky but dried quickly over my lips. "No talking for a minute." The pixie used that minute to make herself scarce. "Do enjoy your evening, Lady."

I stared at the closed door, then slowly rose from the bed. I hadn't found any suitable footwear, and I didn't care to remember to when Persy opened the door with a half-laughed, "Well, well."

"I know," I said, suddenly self-conscious that I had to now leave the privacy of these rooms to venture downstairs where everyone would see me. "It's far too much. I feel ridic—"

"Quiet," Persy scolded and moved behind me to drag her fingers through my hair. It was still slightly damp from the bath. "Ilena didn't brush your hair."

"She doesn't seem too fond of me."

Persy snorted, heading to the bathing room in search of a brush. "Most pixies don't like anyone outside of their own families. Even Olette is barely tolerated."

That was true, though I'd never dared to speak with one before. They kept to themselves, so I'd never had the opportunity. Returning, Persy gently pulled the brush through the worst of my tangles, but then paused. "I think it should stay out."

"I agree," I said with relief I couldn't hide.

Persy tossed the brush behind her to the bed, then shifted thick strands over the bodice of the gown and my arms. "It wouldn't be you without a little wild on display."

I laughed, but it died quickly as my nerves constricted my breathing more than that of the corset. I attempted to distract myself by asking, "What happened with you and that male?"

"Which male?"

She could try to play coy, but her stilling fingers gave away what I already suspected. "Lorr."

"Oh." Sighing, she studied her own gown. The sleek and alluring slip of black silk draped over one shoulder and leg to reveal a silver slipper with a short heel, the straps crawling around her ankle. "Well, nothing."

At my raised brow, she leaned against the bed post and pinched her lips, which had been painted a dark, nearly brown, red. "Okay, a handful of somethings, but it was a few years ago. I've not gone there, or anywhere else, since Jarron promised he wouldn't do anything like that either. Not while we're…"

"What is it he's doing?" I asked without a trace of shame, for after all that male had done to her, I had to wonder what beneath the darkest moon he truly intended.

"He's trying to…" Seeming without words to explain it, Persy crinkled her nose and lifted a shoulder. "He's just trying, and before you get all judgmental, so am I."

"I am being judgmental," I admitted and waded to the door

beneath the mountainous volume of skirts. "But I'll try not to be, I suppose."

"You suppose?" Persy said with a laugh and opened the door as I struggled to reach for the handle.

"Get me that woon, and then we'll talk of certainties."

"Lorr won't budge, not without good incentive." There was no need to imagine what that incentive would entail. "So"—she slid her arm through mine—"I suppose I just accept you the way you are, feral."

I shoved her gently, and she laughed again.

Our smiles soon fell as we took the stairs down to the main floor to find a small reception awaiting us.

Jarron stole Persy, an unreadable look cast my way as I descended the last two steps into the star-shaped foyer and lost my breath anew.

In a black so dark it shined, Colvin waited for me in the center of the mosaic floor.

A pair of fitted pants hugged his muscular thighs, and pointed leather boots reached his knees. His crimson cravat matched the shade of my gown. It also hid the skin the loose-fitting button-down dress shirt should've revealed at his throat. The frilled edging of its bell sleeves peeked out beneath the gray fur-lined cloak draped across his broad shoulders.

Whatever the Unseelie prince wore, even his tea-stained tunics, he wore it well. Too well. So although I was impressed, I was far from surprised.

It was his face that stunned.

His stubble had been trimmed close to his skin to display the unforgiving angles of his square jaw. His eyes held a sheen, a luster similar to what I'd seen after he'd spilled himself upon my thigh. Each strand of hair had been carefully combed back into a small bun at his nape, leaving the sharp blades of his cheeks available to ogle.

He was handsome, to be sure, but he was also quite possibly the most interesting creature I'd ever laid eyes on.

I wasn't sure what came over me. I wasn't sure I wanted to know.

The admission left me without my permission. "You're fascinatingly breathtaking, dragon."

He finally blinked, his eyes thinning. "Me?"

"Coy doesn't suit you," I said and left the bottom of the stairs to close the distance.

He met me halfway, shaking his head with a slight laugh. "You constantly threaten to knock me from my feet, fire-breather." He offered his hand, and I placed mine within it, grinning when he finally allowed his eyes to travel down the expanse of my body. A whisper, his lashes beating hard when his gaze lifted to my chest, he said, "But this is just…"

"A lot," I offered and arched a brow when his eyes rose.

He smirked at being caught, cheeks shifting and coloring, and then pulled me close, as close as the gown would allow. "A vision of divinity," he murmured, pressing his hand to the small of my back while the other stayed folded around mine.

"Don't get too carried away." I turned us toward the doorway as footsteps sounded in the hall. "I might have conveniently forgotten my shoes."

His rich laughter stole into every part of me, twined around my chest cavity, and squeezed.

The ballroom awaited us at the opposite end of the hall to the dining room. A large and grand space that had been decorated sparsely with violet roses and vines. They looped from each column in the circular room and the railings of the banisters on the floor above.

A whole head taller than me, the prince whispered to my hairline once we'd breached the first layer of guests encircling the room, "Ready?"

"You know I'm not."

His lips brushed my skin, his hand squeezing mine as everyone bowed and curtsied and watched our journey to the waiting thrones beyond the dance floor.

Olette was already there, wearing a burgundy gown that resembled a silk bedsheet, and in conversation with Jarron. The queen glanced at us briefly, but that one quick look and quirking of her ruby lips was enough to convey her surprise.

Gazing up at Colvin, who I found already looking at me, I murmured, "Are you?" His brows rose. "Ready, I mean."

His answer was a blinding, brilliant smile. My lungs tightened painfully at the sight and at his tone's heated timbre. "I'm ready for whatever comes, as long as it involves you."

With that, he left me stunned as Persy joined me. We watched Colvin lean down to kiss his mother's cheek, Jarron looking our way as Persy grumbled, "I'm fucking starving. Come on." She then dragged me to the edge of the ballroom.

Refreshments awaited in crystal jugs and bowls with ladles— wine and water and what smelled like whiskey and gin. An array of tufted pastries, gleaming fruits, and cheeses were placed within clover patches upon trays.

Eyes, from the railings above and behind, were warm and heavy upon us. My limbs uncoiled somewhat as Persy grabbed us a plateful of appetizers and escorted me away.

Colvin, who'd since finished talking with his mother, turned to find us heading upstairs, where Persy spent the better part of the first half hour pointing out each noble and creature worth discussing. But although the crowd grew thicker, there was no Seelie to be seen.

Reptilians lined the walls, silent and stoic, but some also wove amongst the throng, laughing and talking with all manner of Fae.

Pixies intermingled with faeries. Some even appeared to be more than friendly with one another. Centaurs remained on the lower level, and I couldn't blame them given their hooves and height. My eyes caught on a female with a serpentine body, and I nearly mistook her for a mermaid until Persy noticed who had garnered my attention. "That's Wolinda, lady of the serpentrolls."

Indeed her upper body was bulky, her gray-tinted skin more muscle than curves. A jeweled and tasseled cloth hung from her neck to cover her chest. Below her navel, a darker gray tail of scales held her upright, growing slimmer as it curled around her into a lethal point.

"I have no words," I said, low and in awe. "I've only ever heard of such creatures. I never thought…"

"That they actually exist?" Persy supplied. "They certainly do, and though most are friendly enough, do watch that sharp tongue of yours. They're easily offended."

"Noted," I said, thankful for the warning as the lady of the serpentrolls turned and lifted her crystal-blue eyes to where we stood above her. I tried to smile, but I must have failed to do so correctly, for the female's features creased as she smirked with dark lips and looked back at the queen.

Persy laughed, snatching us each a glass of wine from a goblin passing at our backs.

The bearded creature pulled his plaid vest tighter at the sight of me, and I recognized him as one of the three I'd met in the kitchens. I nodded in greeting, but he just blinked and shuffled away in his pointed ankle boots.

"I don't think I'll be winning any of the goblins over."

"No one can," Persy said, sipping her wine greedily. Swiping her fingers beneath her lower lip, she watched Jarron, who walked away from Colvin downstairs toward a shadowed exit beyond the thrones. "You can't add every monster to your arsenal."

"But it is fun to try," I drawled, smiling as I remembered the outrage on the goblins' faces when I'd entered their kitchens.

Persy snorted, then cursed and looked behind me.

I didn't turn, but I made a face, curious to know what had caused her to tense up. She just shook her head and curved her lips into a beautiful smile. "Rain."

The newcomer stopped beside us, and I twisted to see the strawberry-scented faerie.

Hair as red as fire cascaded from two pearl clustered clips at either side of her head to fall upon slender shoulders and breasts. Far taller than us, she inspected me over the tight bridge of her porcelain nose. Glittering coal eyes gave me a perusal slow enough to suggest she was indeed assessing me.

"The Seelie princess." Long, jewel-bedecked lashes fluttered, her eyes meeting mine. "I must confess, I could hardly believe what our prince had gotten himself into, but I'm beginning to understand why." Extending her hand, she said, "Rain, friend of the prince."

The word friend didn't quite sit right, but I wasn't about to deny her when it seemed she was willing to be friendly. I placed my hand in hers, and she gently shook it with a smile as I said, "Fia."

Persy, clutching the stem of her wineglass tightly, swung her gaze between us. "How have you been?" she asked Rain.

"Good," Rain said, releasing my hand and eyes. "I was sad to leave, of course, and I miss you all and the others, but it was for the best. I cannot live my life for the prince's pleasure forever."

The wine soured over my tongue, and I nearly choked.

Rain cast an apologetic look my way, but I swallowed and cleared my throat. "I'm already aware."

Rain nodded, smiling slightly as though relieved, then asked, "What do you think so far?" And my eyes bulged before she laughed and made herself clear. "I mean of Eldorn."

"Of course," I said, on the verge of blushing. "Uh, it's..." *been both nothing and everything that I expected.* "It's been surprising," I finally settled on.

"Fia had her first city trip just last night." Persy thankfully intervened, then whispered behind her hand, "She drinks like a fish and watches cheats like a hawk."

I scowled, but it fell as Rain and Persy laughed.

I listened idly as the two females who'd evidently been friends chatted while looking at the ground floor again, unable to stop my eyes from searching. Unable to keep from thinking of the unexpectedly sweet prince entangled with the lithe, incredibly beautiful Rain.

I drank more wine as I remembered she hadn't been the only member of his harem and that I shouldn't be annoyed. Rain was nice enough, and Colvin hadn't known me.

And I'd been with my traitor of a best friend more times than I could count before the prince had returned to flip my entire world into something I could no longer recognize once more.

Rain soon said her goodbyes, and I smiled in farewell, finding that it felt genuine as guilt for my insidious, unjustified jealousy subsided. Even so, I had to ask Persy, "How many were there?"

"A lot," she said, joining me at the railing as I caught a flash of blue and black in the shadows beneath the opposite balcony. "Four in the last one."

"The last one?"

She took her time to say, "It was always ever-changing. More would come, and others would leave."

I wasn't sure whether to be impressed or sickened. My gaze was stuck to where I'd last glimpsed Colvin. An instinct, unfelt before but strong, emerged, and I murmured, "I'll find you later," before walking to the steps to follow the biting feeling down to those shadows.

I left my glass with a passing goblin on the stairs and helped myself to a new one, doing my best to ignore the many eyes upon me as I descended them far slower than I would have liked, courtesy of the enormous gown.

Weaving between groups of guests as best I could, I slowed when I neared the less populated space beyond the stairs and heard Colvin's voice.

"Gesna."

"I'm sorry, it's just..." a female whispered, and I barely heard her next words over the chatter and laughter and glass clinking in the grand room. "I thought something might've happened, but nothing like this."

My hackles rose, the wineglass warming in my hand as my blood began to heat.

"But it has happened, and I'm happier for it. I cannot apologize for that."

"Are you cared for, though?" There was a pause. A reptilian warrior with braids passed me at the side of the stairs, staring with unveiled curiosity. I ignored her, trying to hear the female talking to

Colvin as she spoke again. "She is Seelie, so she cannot know what you need, and rumor states she does not even like you."

Colvin cleared his throat, and I could picture him adjusting the cravat at his neck. "Please believe me when I say that I am fine, Gesna. But I do thank you for your concern."

Swarmed with a poison I knew wouldn't shake easily, no matter how much I told myself I needn't feel anything about their conversation, I walked to the open doors they stood by.

A raven-haired female with bright opal eyes stood back from Colvin and inclined her head, but she needn't have bothered if it was for me. I didn't look at either of them as I passed through the large arched doors and into a small courtyard with several bench seats perched along the stone walls.

Some seats were occupied, while other attendees stood amongst the hedges of roses at the courtyard's edge. I didn't want to sit or linger. I wanted to walk until this feeling abated, and my mind grew clear again. The wine wouldn't help matters, yet I still drank more as I made my way to a path that veered around the circular tower.

A wall greeted me.

I fell into the thorny vines encircling the tower, the wine spilling and the glass cracking in my hand.

"Fuck. I'm sorry, Fi. Here," Regin said, lowering to the ground where I'd caught myself on the pebbled path.

I blinked at him in disbelief while he pried the broken glass from my hand and tossed it to the grass. He was here. "You're here," I murmured out loud.

Dancing teal eyes lifted from my hand. Familiar roughened fingers inspected my skin. "You're surprised?" He grinned, but it wavered. "I wouldn't dream of missing such an event."

I smiled, tears filling my eyes. Relief, unexpected and bittersweet, held me immobile and torn. I hadn't forgotten. I could never forget what he'd done. But I could never forget what he'd been to me for most of my life, either—the only real friend I'd ever had.

His smile fell, his own eyes glossy. "I've missed you, Fi," he rasped. "So fucking much."

"I'll bet you've been too busy with both of your swords to find such time for little old me, soldier."

He didn't laugh as I'd expected, though. His thick brows lowered, and he squeezed my fingers with his. "No, Fi. Nothing is the same with you gone. Nothing."

I didn't doubt things hadn't changed, and it hadn't even been a week since I'd left, though it felt far longer. So long that the life I'd once had now felt like a dream. But it was somewhat comforting to think my absence wasn't celebrated by at least one person.

I squeezed his fingers in return and felt wetness trickle between my own. "Shit. I can't ruin this gown."

He rose with me. "Since when do you care for gowns?"

"Since this one contains more than a few hours of needlework." I shook the droplets of blood from my hand, but Regin caught it and brought it to his lips. A cold and prickling sensation twisted into my body, rendering it uncomfortably tight. "What are you really doing here, Regin?"

"We were invited, of course, but being a hostile territory, your uncle thought it best to only send me with his regards." He lowered my hand. "Given how close we are."

I didn't take the bait, busy mulling over the first words he'd uttered. The word hostile seemed ill-fitting after the short time I'd spent here. "We both know Brolen wishes me nothing good."

"Regardless, I couldn't pass up the opportunity to see you and make sure you're okay. The wedding will be held at Halfway Hall." Neutral ground would make the Seelie feel safer in the midst of blood feeders and a dragon. "So just hold on, okay? I'll be seeing you again soon." He clasped my cheek, his lips parting as he swayed closer and lowered his eyes to mine.

I knew what was coming, and I turned my head.

His mouth skimmed my cheek.

"I deserved that," he said roughly. "But I promise, Fi. I will find a way to fix this and make you forgive me."

"You can't fix anything, Regin." I stared at my hand in his, smiled at the familiarity of it, of his touch, and gave him as much honesty as I could when I met his gaze. "And I don't want you to try. It's a waste of your time and far too dangerous."

He just looked down at our hands and studied mine with gentle fingers. "I think you'll live."

"No thanks to you," I muttered, but the words were more jest than scorn.

"I was a fucking idiot," he said, smiling. It waned as he bowed deeply and, once again, left me all alone. "I'll take a proper kiss next time, Fi."

I watched him go, itching with indecision as he followed the pebbled path into the patchwork of overgrown rose gardens and wisteria dotting the grounds rolling toward the stables skirting the woods.

The darkness swallowed him, and I'd never felt more homesick since arriving in this kingdom. I'd been given a taste of what I once had, what I so desperately missed, the place I'd once called home, and all I could do was watch it leave me to the wolves all over again.

The creature at my back remained silent.

The prince's energy was a presence alone, so I'd known he'd been lingering within the shadows for some time. But I hadn't cared to be cautious, nor worry over what he'd thought of my visitor.

I looked down at the cut already healing on my finger, then brushed off my skirts as I turned to face the male who'd stolen my future.

His eyes were similar to what I'd seen in the throne room back home in those minutes before he'd ripped open the throat and stomach of the guard who'd mistreated me. Red-rimmed gold, his gaze was hooked upon the dark that'd taken Regin.

My heart thundered, though I wasn't sure why I was nervous. I wasn't sure why a stabbing prod encountered each beat. I hadn't done anything wrong, and perhaps Colvin hadn't either. Yet the feeling still sharpened each breath, as well as my tone. "Did you invite every lover you've ever had to this celebration of ours, dragon?"

He blinked, his brows lowering when his attention finally fell upon me.

For long moments, he simply stared. I stared back, my chest rising and falling too fast. Too fast for me to hope to control. Those eyes slowly returned to their usual luminous gold, and his jaw remained fixed. Low, he then ordered, "Walk with me."

"If I refuse?"

He stilled, a maddening curve to his mouth to match the knowing gleam in his gaze, and then he held out his hand.

Anger and that curdling, insidious feeling that'd overtaken me when I'd witnessed him talk so softly to his once beloved Gesna curled my fingers into my palms.

Heavy drums began to pound, a lone fiddle sparking and dancing above the haunting beat. It was time for the betrothed couple to take to the dance floor.

But Colvin slid his fingers around mine when I didn't move. We walked the opposite way, deeper into the lantern-speckled gardens and the awaiting dark night.

"We should head back," I said belatedly, knowing he had no intention of rejoining the festivities.

The prince was too quiet, each long stride too determined, as we encountered the woods surrounding Castle Eldorn and the privacy of the shadows within. So rather than demand he tell me what we were doing, I remained silent and lifted my skirts as best I could with one hand.

We soon reached a small clearing containing the debris and corpse of a giant, fallen tree, and only then did he slow. Upon a patch of branch-and-rock-free grass, he stopped and lifted my hand.

The same hand Regin had held. "What happened?"

It had healed, but he must have scented the dried blood and glimpsed it beneath the sodden light of the moon and stars. "I ran into him," I said carefully. "Quite literally, and I cut myself on my wineglass. It's fine."

Colvin, seemingly trapped amongst his thoughts, didn't respond. But he lifted my finger to his mouth.

And sucked.

A cord of tickling tension scorched directly from his warm mouth to my stomach, making it jump sharply. The gathering heat spread lower, and I shifted, scowling when the prince's golden eyes shined with satisfaction at what he'd done. Slowly, languidly, he dragged his tongue over my forefinger, watching every reaction I couldn't hide, scenting it.

I pulled free, but he captured my waist before I could retreat. "I cannot help but wonder if he is capable of arousing you so promptly, so"—pulling me to his body, he traced his thumb down my cheek, his eyes aglow on my flushed skin—"fucking thoroughly."

"Stop it," I said—almost begged.

His brows rose, jaw rigid as he inhaled with a slight flutter of his eyelashes. "You weaken me terribly, fire-breather."

I sensed he meant more than just arousal, but fear clutched at my vocal cords.

"Did you allow him to touch you because you saw me talking with Gesna?"

Just hearing her name elicited shameful feelings, but I didn't allow them to become the weapons they nearly did. "No," I said, the word thick. "He just wanted to see me, to talk."

"Given how few attended from Callula, it seems he must have been desperate to... talk."

"He wanted to know if I was okay." Which wasn't exactly a lie, though the prince waited for me to say more. "He feared for my safety and still does."

"I heard," he confirmed what I'd already suspected, and my blood cooled. "Everything. He misses you. You can never be his, yet he hungers for you regardless."

I chose not to give that a response.

The prince surprised me by taking my hands and placing them over his chest, his own at my waist. He then began to rock side to side to the distant beat of the drums.

Frowning, I looked at my hands upon his shirt. He'd abandoned his cloak, and the material was thin enough that I couldn't resist curling my fingers over his hard pectorals. "Will we get into trouble for running away?"

"We haven't run away, and we've shown our faces long enough." He lowered his head to the side of mine, his lips stirring tendrils at my temple as they grazed, and he breathed me in. "I'm sorry they were in attendance."

I focused on the clumsy movement of our feet in an effort to ignore the clenching in my chest.

"Most nobility and friends throughout Eldorn were invited, but I should've realized that would mean old friends, too."

"Friends," I said, the word acidic and dry. "Surely, you held stronger feelings for some of them."

"Would it make you feel better if I lied and said I did?" he taunted.

Blistering relief loosened my bones. I supposed it was time to admit what I knew. "You got rid of them before you stole me."

He huffed as if the way I'd worded the confession humored him. "I told them it was time they moved on, and I made sure they had the means to do so if they didn't already, yes."

"When you returned from Callula." He didn't answer, and I pushed, "Colvin."

"As soon as I returned," he said, a tad reluctantly as if knowing what I would reveal once he did.

I didn't have to. He seemed to know.

Yet to stay silent made what I'd done feel like a betrayal.

My eyes closed. "Regin…" Though I'd half-hoped to maim this prince, to exact some type of revenge for all he'd done and all he stoked to life within me, the admission was too gentle, too laced in fear, to be anything but an attempt at clearing some of the weight in my chest. "We were together even when I suspected that you were…"

Colvin tensed beneath my hands, his hold at my hip and back tightening.

An owl hooted overhead, the drums pounded into a new rhythm, and the beasts within the woods sang from a safe distance.

Finally, the dragon they could likely sense and chose to keep away from murmured with noticeable grit, "You might've suspected, but you didn't want it. I fucking hate it, but I also understand. You didn't think you would see me again, nor did you even want to."

"But I did want to," I whispered, the confession a promise breaking over my lips. "I hated you, but I still thought of you. I couldn't stop, no matter what I did."

Colvin was quiet again for some time. Then he asked, "And do you still think of him?"

"Regin?"

He hummed, and new guilt struck as realization dawned. I hadn't really thought of Regin at all. "No," I said, the word barely a sound.

"Judging by his attempt to kiss you, I'd wager he still thinks of you." Gritted, he added, "And often."

But I couldn't stomach it, thoughts of Regin and the conflicting emotions they provoked. Not now. I was here, and he was there, and despite his faulty promises, that was how it would remain.

A quiet part of me recognized that this was how it was supposed to be, so I turned to the prince's jaw and murmured against it, "You're a terrible dancer."

He lowered his head, pulling me closer. "I'm terribly distracted." His nose kissed mine, and my eyes closed, his words drugging breath. "For I find myself needing to erase his scent from your skin, Fia. To make sure I'm the only creature you ever touch."

Those words cascaded into my bleating heart to pour into all of me, and I failed to suppress a shuddering exhale.

Nothing escaped him, for he murmured, "Run away with me, fire-breather."

My lips slammed against his in answer, and my arms coiled tight around his neck as the earth gave way, and we fell through it.

TWENTY-ONE

Fia

I DIDN'T NEED TO OPEN MY EYES TO KNOW WE WERE NO LONGER in the forest.

Well, not that particular part of it anyway.

Colvin dragged his tongue over my lower lip, which had been stolen by his teeth, then groaned when I broke away. "The gown," I said, close to panting already. "Get rid of it."

Eyes of golden fire gazed back at me in the dark of his cottage, his chest rising fast. "You're certain?"

"You know what I want."

"I'm not sure you understand. If I am to have you…" He curled his lips as he rounded me, stalking slow to my back and shifting my hair over one shoulder. Reverent fingers trailed the strands down my arm as rough words were murmured to my bare shoulder with shivering heat. "I will make you irrefutably mine."

"I know," I said, breathless at just the thought, the fear of what he intended fading fast beneath the undertow of anticipation.

Deft yet slow, allowing me time to reconsider, the dragon prince pulled at the ribbon ties of my corset. "Tell me, fire-breather."

Each breath that should've come easier with every tie unfastened only grew more labored. His fingers climbed to the top of the corset and slowly slipped inside as I lifted my arms. "That I want you to make me yours?" I turned as the material slid over my chest, and I pushed it to my waist, pushed it all to the floor in a mountain of fabric with the skirts.

I'd never seen his eyes so bright, so feverish as he watched me pull at the waist of my strapless slip and lift it. "Prince." I let the silk fall from my finger as my toes met his boots. I seized his shirt, buttons popping as I tore it open, and rose onto my toes to say to his chin, "You speak as though unaware that I wish to make every inch of you all fucking mine."

I was in his arms a failed breath later, and he turned to lower us to the edge of the bed.

His hungry mouth devoured—my lips, my jaw, my neck, his hands just as starving as they roamed my sides. He trembled over me when I pushed him with my feet at his ass, forcing his clothed length to my naked center. "Fuck, you feel incredible."

"And you're still clothed," I said, grasping the back of his head when he reached my breasts. Moaning, I let him introduce his lips and tongue to each nipple, his teeth gently scraping and his every breath rumbling.

Then I pushed him, relying on his distraction to succeed, or perhaps he'd merely allowed it.

He rolled to his back, fire in his eyes as I removed his cravat. I fumbled at his pants to free his cock while he struggled out of his shirt. He groaned, pushing up and forcing me back over his thighs when I gripped it and marveled at its weight in my hand.

I didn't wait. Desperation pooled at my core with just the thought of placing the engorged, thick member inside me.

"Fia," Colvin rasped.

But I ignored him, rising to my knees and watching him as he watched me place him at my entrance. I rubbed him over me, spread myself over him, and he cursed. His lashes shadowed his cheeks, strands of escaped hair curling toward his parted lips, and his eyes unblinking.

His crown breached me, and I moaned, his fevered eyes jumping to mine then back down. Every muscle in his arms convulsed—as though it were costing him to restrain himself as I slowly swallowed inches of him within my body. "Fuck," he groaned, nearly whined, when I stopped with little more than half of him inside me.

The fabric of his pants at my rear, my fingers clutching at his

shoulders, and the sheer size of him beneath me, sinking into me...
I tried to find the courage to fully seat him—needing more but needing a moment first.

"Fire-breather." He kissed my shoulder, the sweet action contradicted by his next words. "This lover of yours, was he the only one?"

"Yes."

"Did he ever make you scream?" When I didn't respond, struggling to say anything as my heart stopped, he growled, "Answer me."

"No," I croaked, the burn of his words combined with that of his cock scalding and delicious.

"Good." At my mouth, he warned with gentle wrath, "Allow me to be the first." Then he gripped me behind the shoulders and pulled me down over him.

Until I was thoroughly filled with the thick, throbbing impossibility of him.

My head fell back, a silent scream choking me.

He released a groaned laugh, the wickedly hoarse sound heating my neck as he dragged his teeth down my chin and throat. "Feel me." His lips pressed to the underside of my chin, large hands sliding to my ass and bruising the flesh within their grip. "Feel every fucking inch of me."

There was indeed so much of him to feel, the burn slowly subsiding but still distracting as he gently wound my hair in his fist to tilt my head back. "Your beautiful cunt is pulsing, Princess." The brush of his lips over my breasts was all the warning I had.

Another scream left me, this one riddled with sound—with both pleasure and pain—when his fangs sank into the sensitive flesh.

The prince groaned and growled. The hand still at my rear squeezed, moving me gently over him, while the other held my hair at my upper back to keep me from falling.

But I'd already fallen, deep down into a darkness so dizzying, the flames that had ignited in the candles of the cottage hurt to see when my eyes opened and the prince ceased sucking blood from my chest.

I shook in his arms, rocking over him and beyond ready.

His lips slid up my jawline, my blood accompanying and smearing. "Would you like to kiss me, Fia?"

In answer, I immediately placed my lips over his, my own essence sliding down my throat when our tongues touched. Taking his face in my hands, I held him to me as my teeth tore at his lips.

But before I could taste it, he pulled away and stood.

Then he turned with a groan as he slowly pried me from his body to lay me over the bed. "What are you doing?" I nearly whined, curling up to sit.

"Tasting all of you." He climbed onto the bed and leaned back on his knees, his cock glistening in the moonlight as it swayed. "Open those pretty thighs."

Lying back down, I did, and he swiped at his mouth, blood coating his stubble and cheek.

His eyes darkened to a dusty gold. "You're going to end me, fire-breather." He said nothing else, just lifted my thighs over his shoulders until my ass rose high from the bed and buried his nose in me. The tickling heat alone robbed a weeping sound from me. "Fuck, I've spent too many hours dreaming of this." His eyes opened, a fire within as he flattened his tongue and slowly dragged it over me.

I mewled, thighs shaking beneath the punishment of his fingers.

He did so again and again, watching me grow more desperate until finally, he parted me with his tongue and did the same to my swollen opening and clit.

Three swipes and I was there—trembling and squirming and moaning.

"Did he do this to you?" he taunted, pausing as I began to fall from the precipice. "Did he adore you this tenderly?"

I shook my head, my ears ringing and my hips rocking, needing his mouth back on me.

"I don't know if I believe you," he said, his voice all wrong, strangled and edged with both need and animosity. "You can't seem to speak."

I was shaking all over now, a hollowing yawning open inside me.

One touch was all I needed, and I'd give him anything he wanted for it, but I didn't need to lie. "Nothing like this."

"Good." He licked me but stopped below where I needed him. I was about to beg or touch myself when he blew a heated exhale upon my clit.

And I fell apart.

A low, pleased chuckle rode along my skin, causing more goose-flesh to rise while I moaned and twisted. My thighs closed as soon as he released them, clenching tight to ride out the torture he'd inflicted upon me.

He opened them before I could finish finding relief. His towering form hovered above me, and he wrapped my legs around his waist. Nostrils flaring wide, he entered me in one slow thrust, his lips parting with a hypnotizing groan and widening of his eyes.

I spasmed around him, smiling as he felt it while sinking as deep as he could delve. "Fuck, Fia." Studying me with hooded eyes, he stopped with a heaved exhale, and then he smiled too.

The sight caught my slow to return breath, my finger rising to his mouth. He kissed it, then scooped his arms beneath me to lift me with him. He settled on his haunches, perspiration dusting his shoulders. "You can take me again now."

I curled my arms around his neck, squashing my breasts to his chest. "You're done with being jealous?"

"Far from it." He kissed me hard in warning. "So don't lose patience with me."

"On the contrary," I whispered, smiling when he scowled. I tightened my legs around him. "I like your bruising fingers."

"I can tell."

"And I really like how you feel inside me."

He groaned, licking at the blood he'd left on my jaw. "I can feel that."

"But I won't fuck you into forgetting another creature, dragon. I will simply do without these things I like by removing all of them from your body should you place them anywhere near another's."

The prince raised his head, eyes absorbing mine, his hunger a wilder energy stifling the room as he twitched inside me. "Noted, Fia the feral." He lifted me by the hips, grinning when I slowly ate all of him again. "Let's see just how feral you truly are."

I stole his mouth and rose over him, wanting so much more. So I took it. I pulled his lip into my mouth. Our eyes met, his daring, as I sank my teeth into his flesh. He didn't seem to breathe. He waited, likely doubting I would do it.

"You might think I don't have the stomach for it, that I don't truly want it, blood feeder…" I sucked and pulled, blood filling his mouth and flooding into mine. "But you're wrong."

He growled and took me to the bed, his teeth piercing my lip. "Last chance," he warned, and we both stilled as our blood combined—seconds away from sealing our fates forever.

There was no way out. Despite what Regin had said, there was nothing and no one to hold on for. No way home. So I'd surrender the shreds of hope I'd unknowingly clung to like a shield. I'd quit fighting against a connection that would keep winning.

I wanted this prince. I more than wanted him.

I was in desperate and dire need of him, so I closed my eyes and swallowed.

A white noise infiltrated my ears, emptied my mind, and brought every sensation within my body to the surface beneath my skin.

Colvin cursed, his chest meeting mine and his arm sliding beneath my shoulder.

Then he moved.

With an efficiency that rendered me mindless, he withdrew his cock and plunged deep, over and over. As my cries grew louder, muffled against his mouth and tongue, his hair tangled within my fingers, he drove into me harder.

The bed shook, and the dark brightened.

Without mercy, he ground into me. He fucked me like the beast he was while I scraped my nails down his smooth back and allowed the poison I'd swallowed to awaken every hidden thread of my soul.

It tethered to his when my eyes opened and fell into his own, a painless yet excruciating connection that brought us both to climax instantly.

Every flame in the cottage extinguished. The dark seemed to shine with a gathering of stars.

They exploded when Colvin roared.

His body stilled, deep inside mine and grinding. Bared teeth gritted, he trembled violently. I swam beneath the surface of my humming skin and clung to him. My nails had dug grooves deep enough to wound, the pads of my fingers slippery with his blood.

The room spun, and my chest heaved.

As did his, and his hair curtained his cheeks when he rose onto his forearms. The ribbon that'd contained it all was long gone, courtesy of my fingers. Dragging them over his back, I brought them to my mouth and licked them clean.

His eyes lifted from my breasts to my lips. His own were blood-stained, and they parted in response to what he saw. A harsh breath was expelled with his warning. "It's going to be a long night."

"Indeed." I grinned and painted his lower lip with my finger, never wanting him to leave. "You're still hard."

He nipped my finger, then kissed it before leaving my body and the bed.

My scowl fell at the sight of his perfect backside, and I watched him walk to the kitchen for the pitcher of water. I hadn't needed it until he turned back, and my mouth dried. His cock stood rock solid, bouncing as his lean legs carried his impressive physique back to me.

Flame danced from two candles on either side of the bed with an absent flick of his fingers, the fire restarting in the hearth.

I marveled at the ease of it—at the power he possessed. The power he hid behind a veneer of books and unexpected gentleness and the guilt he harbored for things he could not control.

I sat up when he reached the side of the bed, gulping greedily from the pitcher while he waited. He took one sip himself before setting it down upon the nightstand, then roamed the length of the bed.

A predatory gleam lit his eyes, which hadn't unfastened from me in the slightest. He stopped at the end of the bed, and I rose to my elbows to better see what he was up to.

"Open your legs." As he stood there with his hand wrapped around his cock, his dark hair falling around his shoulders and his gold eyes red-rimmed, I forgot to breathe.

He was every fear I'd ever had and every wish I'd never known I'd longed for. A soul as dark as night and a heart of cloudless mornings, this contradiction of a male had me tethered tightly to him long before he'd made it irreversible.

And the smug thickness to his voice said he knew it. "Wider. I need to see everything."

I did as I was told, wanting to please him, for doing so pleased and excited me.

"Touch yourself, fire-breather. Touch yourself and—" He cursed when I did and then lifted my fingers to my mouth to suck them clean.

Then he pulled my ass to the edge of the bed and gripped my spread legs, watching me watch him. "The sheer fucking sight of you, Fia," he whispered as though memorizing me. "Those eager eyes. All that snowy hair kissing those beautiful tits. Your perfect cunt leaking with me and still so incredibly swollen..." He shivered, rasping, "You undo me like nothing else in existence."

I failed to speak, to find room for thought, as my fingers slipped from my mouth.

He grinned knowingly, aligning at my center. "You need me."

I nodded, moaning when the head of him entered my body.

He stopped, and I writhed, attempting to wriggle closer to sheath myself on him. But his hold on my legs didn't allow for it. "First, my greedy creature, there is something I need to know, and don't you dare lie..."

I frowned, impatient and desperate, but the possessive glow to his eyes warned me that he was indeed far from able to forget the male who'd traveled a great distance to visit me at our engagement ball. "I see no point in lying, but there is nothing more to tell."

"Nothing?" A brow rose. "So he didn't kiss you first?"

My entire face flamed instantly, giving me away. "You already know the answer to that."

The prince's eyes flashed with lethal satisfaction. "And he didn't tend to you in this way?" He withdrew and then pushed forward, slowly ruining me as he eased all the way in while watching my eyes flutter. "He didn't make your legs shake as hard as your heart when he stuck his undeserving cock inside you?"

"You know the answer to that, too," I rasped, whining when he pulled out to the tip. I gnashed my teeth, but he only grinned. Stunned by his otherworldly beauty and debilitating magnitude, I stilled completely.

His features softened then, and he slid inside me a fraction more with a roll of his neck and a rumbling groan. "You really need to be more careful, fire-breather."

"Oh?" I breathed. "Why?"

With utter seriousness, his fingers spreading over my hips and stomach and pushing higher to squeeze my breasts, he admitted gruffly, "Because when you look at me like that, I don't just forget what I'm doing, I forget all that I fucking am."

I clasped his chin and kissed him, using the distraction to wiggle over his cock. I gasped when he rubbed against a pleasure spot. "Then I shall remind you."

"Will you?" he whispered with humor, mouth brushing mine.

I lifted my feet to his ass and pushed. He cursed, losing his hold and spearing inside me as he fell over top of me. With my hands framing his face and my legs climbing his back, I vowed to his lips, "I'll remind you that you're all mine."

TWENTY-TWO

Colvin

WATER SPLASHED.

Peeling an eye open, I struggled to keep from leaping out of bed and onto the female climbing into the bathing tub.

My mate.

It sang through me like an endless drumbeat. It changed the taste of the air I inhaled as I watched Fia pluck a sponge from the basket on the shelf closest to the tub and dunk it into the water before dragging it over her chest.

Without moving, without a glimpse at anything else, I knew that everything was now flavored and fragranced with her. It already had been. But now, it wasn't just a fading taste. It was a stain. Now, I wasn't just addicted—I was wholly at her mercy and never more thankful for it.

She could wash the blood we'd greedily spilled from her skin, but she would forever never be clean of me.

Content to let her believe I was still asleep so I could watch, I lay still and observed, although my blood thickened with the need to join her in that tub. Lifting her long, curling locks to her back, Fia scrubbed every inch of herself without looking my way.

It didn't occur to me to think that was a problem until it was far too late.

"Get a good eyeful, prince," she said, her tone cool. "For it could be your last."

Such words were pointless after binding souls in the way we had last night and in the early hours of the morning. Yet a spark of panic still flared, causing me to ask with feigned amusement, "Did I sleep too long, fire-breather?"

Violence flooded the violet eyes she shot my way, threatening to make me both smile and wince. "You were the one still needing attention until a mere few hours ago, dragon."

She was right. I'd had her more times than I'd ever dared to hope for, but it wasn't enough. I feared an eternity wouldn't be nearly enough.

Fia dropped the sponge into the water and rose from the tub. That full, round ass caused my already hard cock to ache against the bedding. "I suppose I can understand your desire to fuck like a savage beast."

Bruises bloomed on the creamy skin, blue and dotted from my fingers. I groaned, turning my face into the pillow to rid the red haze that drowned my vision, each muscle seizing to act. To take a closer look at those bruises, to trace them with my tongue—

"But the desire to bind yourself to a mate? Not so much." My stomach dropped, and she paused before continuing. "I didn't know Foxglove…" The gentle scraping of parchment sounded. "And a third of an indigo mushroom could induce a weeklong fever, hallucinations, and horrific vomiting, but why should I?"

Fuck.

Fia went on, her sour tone softening with something else. Something that sounded a little like hurt. "Being that when combined, both are enough to kill you within hours."

"Fia," I started, throwing the bedding aside and myself to my feet. "It's really not as bad as it seems."

"Not bad?" Next to the dining table, she stood in nothing but my green towel, her cheeks flushed with ire. Reports taken from the mountain of research I'd recently attempted but hadn't had the chance to finish tidying were clutched tight in her hand. "You're right. It sounds like a screaming good time."

I lifted my hands, knowing I was stark naked but not giving a fuck. "Fire-breather, just listen—"

"No." As I advanced, she backed up toward the door, and my work fell to the floor. "You're poisoning yourself. All the books and all this parchment…" Her eyes, coated in a damp sheen, flitted behind me to the table. Swallowing thickly, she looked back at me as she rasped, "You've been poisoning yourself for years." Her eyes searched mine, and the growing wet within them stirred my beast, riddled me with rage and disgust for having put it there as she whispered, "Why?"

There was nothing left to do but speak the truth. I should have told her sooner, but I had hoped to find a way to make it seem anything other than what it was—insanity. "You know why, Fia."

Her golden brows lowered, anger strengthening her voice. "You let me bond to you all the while you plan and plot ways to murder yourself?" She then turned to the door and opened it.

I closed it, and she spun to glower at me as I pushed her against the wood. "I have no intentions of leaving you, believe me, but you must understand that I can't do this forever."

"Do what?" she asked as if she couldn't comprehend the problem.

As though she couldn't see that I was the fucking problem. A plague upon my own people and our lands and my family.

"The guilt, the unpredictable nature of the slumbering asshole within me, the death tally that will only climb, and the fear." The reactions of those who'd realized or heard never strayed far from my mind. "Everyone's fucking fear. We need to ring a damned bell to let everyone know to take cover and hide from me, for star's sake."

Even worse were the bloodstained memories of those who'd been in the wrong place at the worst possible time, and now they were no longer.

"I've killed people, Fia. Undeserving people. My own people." She blinked, a bead of water leaving her long lashes. I caught it with my thumb, rubbed it into her cheek, and kissed the damp skin. "I can't live like this, and neither can they. If nothing changes, someone will undoubtedly take on the same mentality as Brolen, as others have with every dragon before me."

My chest clenched when her lips trembled.

But I still said it. "They *will* kill me, Fia, and I can't even hate them for it, for they absolutely should. So if I do so myself while trying to find a slice of freedom by stopping the change, then so be it."

"And how long will this freedom last if you find some type of antidote that works and you somehow survive its wrath? Days?" she asked, strangled. "Months? A decade or two?"

No one knew. I was willing to try regardless.

"Exactly." Fia's nose scrunched adorably as she hissed, "I forbid you to try again."

I almost laughed, but the vehemence in her eyes warned against it. "Fire-breather, I can't—"

"Fine," she said, turning and attempting to open the door once more.

I splayed my hand over it, and I did laugh when she growled and turned back. "Let me go."

"Why? You're upset, and I'd like to make sure you're not before you walk away from me."

"Just looking at you is upsetting me." Her tits rose, loosening the towel's hold, her heaving breaths threatening to expose them. Tempted to help them free, I thought better of it as she said, "I've saddled myself to a dragon with a true death wish."

"Fia." I released the door and took her hip and face, gently tugging her close until she gave me those huge eyes. "Beautiful, fire breathing, Fia."

"Flattery won't work, Prince. You're ignorant and insane."

Fuck, she was breathtaking. All the more detrimental when she was angry—when she was worked up over me.

"This is why you want the Blood Bound Book, isn't it? Not to make sure others can't kill you, but to try to kill the beast within you. To poison yourself some more."

My lack of response said enough, and she laughed without a shred of humor. "By the fucking moon, Colvin, have you ever stopped for one rotting minute to think that maybe there is nothing wrong with you? With the dragon who didn't harm me in these very woods?"

Remembering how afraid I'd been when she'd found me and it'd taken over helped me stand my ground even more. "It's not that simple."

"But it is. He is you, and you're him, and you have me."

My eyes widened. "I don't think you quite understand what you're saying."

"No." She stood toe-to-toe with me and stabbed a finger at my bare chest. "You're just refusing to believe it when you know it's true. When you change again, I'll be there. You'll be too preoccupied with me to eat anything."

A different poison pooled within my stomach. I could barely comprehend that this was unfolding in this way. "I don't want to endanger you on the off chance that might be true."

"But it is true." Her eyes narrowed. "You know it as well as I do."

My jaw tensed, making each word rougher than I'd intended. "Regardless, I still need to find a way to stop myself. I won't take advantage and continuously put you at risk."

"You're not taking advantage. I just said you have me."

I wanted to believe that, but even after the promise we'd made in blood that outweighed any form of commitment, I still saw it and felt it in the energy clouding us both. Anger still lived inside her. A resentment she hadn't yet released. "I have you, and I don't. You haven't forgiven me for robbing you of your life."

Fia's features slackened, her lashes bobbing as she blinked heavily. "That doesn't mean I can't," she then fired back, and the force within her words stilled me. Her tone softened. "But that can't happen if you keep letting your conscience get in the way. You didn't before, so quit pissing me off by letting it now."

She'd barely finished talking before I pounced, and she was in my arms.

Her own looped around my neck, her nails scoring into it, her other hand twisting in my hair as our mouths collided. I reached between us, felt her wet and waiting, and was welcomed with silken ease inside her magical body.

Fucking Fia was like being shown what true pleasure was—a paradise too exquisite for words and as necessary as breathing. She was sunlight and snowfall, the most bittersweet poison, and I lost more of myself with every taste she willingly gave me.

"You infuriate me," Fia breathed out, nipping at my upper lip.

I chuckled, my mouth dipping lower and my hips rocking when I reached her neck. Her head tilted, and her pulse raced in invitation. "I'm under your skin, and I suspect I've lived there far longer than you'd care to admit."

A whispering moan. "Just fuck me."

My fingers sank deeper into her thighs, and I did.

I pounded her into the door like the monster I was, but I couldn't stop. Not when she began to unravel in my arms. Her breathy cries increased as I feasted on her neck, drinking her down with relish while I made slow but slamming work of destroying her with my cock.

I wouldn't let her leave, but when I finally did, it was the following evening to accompany her on a visit to the woods with the narlows.

"Do you truly hate being a dragon?"

It took me a minute to answer. Not because I didn't want to, but because the horrors I'd committed had never allowed me to properly consider it. "I don't hate it," I admitted for what might have been the first time in my life. "Just certain parts."

Understanding what parts, Fia nodded. "What does it feel like?"

"Well," I started, unsure but willing to try. "I'm no longer me, yet I've never felt more like myself. A red sun stains everything, yet I've never seen and sensed things so clearly." I stopped, intending to say no more, but the burning curiosity widening those big violet eyes had me conceding, "The bloodlust is overpowering, especially when I haven't fed for a while, and it lingers when I return to this form, but it's more…" I rubbed at the bristle over my jaw. "Then it's more of a need to fuck and feed than kill."

Fia blinked rapidly, her scent changing with her harsh exhale. "That explains a lot."

The warming sweetness that arose from her skin and the growing heat in her core hardened me in an instant. "You make me feel that way all the time. Just the thought of you conjures a similar hunger." That type of want was the slowest fall into true madness, the hoping and itching and silently pleading for just a touch of relief.

"A beast indeed," Fia whispered, a smile thrown toward the leaves she kicked.

I brushed my fingers over hers and reluctantly let her be.

The late afternoon downpour we'd woken to had left its glowing mark upon every twig, wildflower, leaf, and tree. We slowed as Spodge stopped to scrape his claws across the mossy patches of a fallen tree. Tiny insects fell to his belly when he lifted them to his mouth.

"You explained Spodge's name, but dare I ask how you settled on Herb?"

"A week after we arrived home, I made the mistake of thinking they were still too small to climb. I was wrong." We walked on as Spodge grew bored with the critters and went in search of his brother. I laughed a little as I remembered the tiny creature sitting in a plume of mess in my study, sneezing and snorting. "He climbed onto the shelves to get to a particularly potent jar of herbs."

Fia's mouth spread into a breath-knocking smile. "Gnome flecks?"

I nodded. I kept some to aid in pain relief should I need it after a bad experiment, which she seemed to guess, for her smile slipped, and she looked back at the lumbering beasts ahead. "I was so mad and honestly a little concerned, but now, I can't help but laugh. He was stumbling and sleepy for days."

Fia's laughter eased the weight that had arrived with the removal of her eyes, a dusty song I'd never tire of hearing.

"What did Olette think when you arrived home with the cubs?"

"That I was insane," I said, recalling her annoyance. But it hadn't lasted as long as I'd expected. "I'm actually surprised she's never kicked them out to live in the woods."

"They would stand less chance of survival after being hand-reared."

"That wouldn't typically stop her. I think she's secretly fond of them." Fia was quiet for some moments, and I saw her tense as the cliffs came into view. "They'll be fine," I promised, and she released a weighted breath when the narlows finally sensed the steep drop down into the crashing sea ahead.

"She's not as cruel as everyone believes, is she?" Fia murmured, as if fearful of the queen herself hearing, though the castle was a few miles behind us. I gestured to a large boulder, and she watched me take a seat with a raised brow. "Not much room there."

"Should it matter when I've touched every inch of your skin numerous times?"

The princess's cheeks colored, but only a little. Relenting with a sigh, she took a seat. Her plum skirts draped over my leg as she surprised me by twisting to lay both of her legs on my thighs and her head against my shoulder.

"And just in case I haven't made it clear." I tightened my arm around her to pull her even closer. "You're the best thing I've ever touched."

Fia pinched my stomach, and I chuckled, snatching her fingers and bringing them to my lips. She traced them while I watched Spodge smack Herb with a branch.

Herb growled but continued to try to turn over a log to get to what lay beneath it in the damp soil.

I answered her earlier question. "Olette is as cruel as she needs to be, and she's never cared what skin she must wear in order for people to understand that." I linked my fingers through Fia's, but she unwound them to gently study my hand. I let her be, content to have her touch me however she wanted. For that she even wanted to made my chest swell. "My mother, Cherith, did not have the heart for such things."

"A fitting pair, then," Fia said.

I smiled, the few memories I had of them before Cherith was taken roaming forward. "They were mates, though it wasn't until Cherith rejected her first mate that she could truly bind herself to Olette in that way. But he wouldn't let her move on."

It shamed me that such a male was my father. I'd long wished he'd never taken his life after taking my mother's so that I could ensure he died slowly myself. "So Cherith did the only thing she could."

"She married Olette."

I nodded. "There was always a hostile edge to Egorn. He didn't carry the dragon gene. That came from Cherith's grandfather. But Mother says his primitive nature, the aggression he could never quite control, was why Cherith never made permanent ties to him."

"That would've been extremely hard." I squeezed her, knowing she'd fought doing so herself, and she asked, "When did Cherith meet Olette?"

"They were close friends for most of their lives, but Olette's father leads the wild hunt, so she was often never in one place too long. Not until Cherith fell pregnant with me, and I guess something clicked."

"She grew worried?"

"Protective, being that Egorn became more hostile and unpredictable after impregnating her. He demanded he be placed on the throne. To have what he deemed his rightful position beside her. For years, Cherith was condemned by many of our people for not giving her mate the respect he thought he was due. Not accepting him and their bond was one thing, but to refuse to wed him when she carried his babe..."

Fia traced my knuckles. "It would seem knowing how to mind one's own business is a trait that neither court possesses."

"Indeed." I smirked. "Most couldn't and didn't understand. But word continued to spread, and Olette soon returned. It'd been some years since she'd last visited Cherith, but it was instant." I smiled then, watching Spodge join Herb in plucking worms from beneath the overturned log. "It was perhaps why Olette never settled down in one place and never stayed too long when she visited the castle. She knew long before my mother had the space and state of mind to realize it entirely herself."

"They say Egorn killed her. I'm assuming that's true?"

"It is," I said. "He was gone for most of my early youth. I have one particular memory of him snarling down at me with cold near-black eyes while muttering hateful words."

"What did he say?" There was no hesitancy. She wanted to know, so she asked.

And her boldness, that she seemed eager to know as much as possible, made it painless to repeat. "He said I would grow without a spine, nor a shred of real power, for it would be robbed of me in being raised by two females."

Fia snorted. "Moon above, what a toad."

"I was too young, too shocked, to say anything in return. The next time I saw him, it was with his axe in his chest inside the caves he'd taken my mother to."

"He stole Cherith?"

I nodded. "From the city after she'd left a meeting with some nobles regarding their pointless quarrels over land in the far west. She was last seen being led by him into the woods. She hadn't been able to materialize. She was found wearing iron bindings at the wrists and ankles, her heart pierced and her body next to his."

Fia absorbed what I'd said with her fingers still twisting through mine. I swam to and from the memory of Olette's screams, the howling cries that haunted the castle halls for months on end. Yet even in her grief, she'd made sure I wasn't entirely alone in mine.

Jarron, her younger brother, had been called to the castle to watch over me, and he'd remained ever since.

"How old were you?" Fia asked.

"I'd not long reached six years. I missed her terribly, and I still do," I confessed. "But now it's with the confusing sense of missing someone I never had enough time to truly know, all the while feeling their absence within the marrow of my bones."

She brought my fingers to her lips, kissing the tips of each one. Every soft caress was a tugging squeeze at both my heart and cock, and I exhaled a tight breath. Herb and Spodge hadn't moved, now digging at the wet soil for something we couldn't see.

"Olette never got her vengeance," Fia said. "So she never misses an opportunity now."

I frowned at that, not so sure I understood. "She has her reasons for all she does, and they're fairly obvious to most." I let those words linger there, awaiting them to land where they would.

"But having us marry won't aid any plans she has for Callula unless Brolen is removed from existence."

"Why do you think we want Callula?"

"Because…" She exhaled heavily and released my hand. "What else could you want? Things are never this simple."

"And by things, do you mean this?" I tucked some of that wild hair behind her small arched ear and stole her hand back, encouraging her inquisitive eyes to mine. "That no one could want you merely because they want you? For they cannot be without you?"

"Everyone wants something more. Not one thing is ever enough."

She looked back to the narlows, but I continued to stare at her profile—at her long golden lashes and the faded freckles dusting her cheekbones. I could tell her until I was breathless, but she wouldn't hear me.

A creature like Fia had to learn the truth of most things by discovering them herself.

TWENTY-THREE

Fia

COLVIN WAS EXACTLY WHERE I'D LEFT HIM WHEN WE RETURNED from taking the narlows on one of our evening walks.

"So I've been wondering."

He smirked at the parchment. "Dangerous."

Ignoring that, I jumped up onto his desk. "You can change whenever you want to?"

"Why do you ask?" His looping handwriting left a lot to be desired. I smiled down at the parchment, grateful it wasn't one of his poison reports but a letter he was marking and seemingly proofreading. Whoever had written it, their handwriting was small, and I struggled to read it upside down. If I had to guess, I'd say it was Olette's.

"You know why I'm asking." I snatched his quill and stuck it between my teeth, then placed the letter behind me.

Colvin sat back and stretched his arms over his head, gifting me with a tantalizing glimpse of his defined hips and stomach when his cream tunic rose. It was unsullied, and I wasn't sure why that bothered me, but it did. I tossed the quill, then loosened the black cravat at his neck.

He didn't stop me. He placed his hands upon my thighs and watched me with a curl to his lips.

"I can," he said, and I dragged my eyes off those scars at his neck to meet his gaze. It was amused but also aglow with that familiar hunger. My stomach jumped as he pushed my skirts over my thighs and pulled me off the desk to his lap. At my cheek, he murmured with tickling lips, "Miss me?"

"You're evading the subject."

"It can wait," he said, low and with his hand climbing my back to my hair, the other sliding up my skirts to meet the bare skin beneath. "It will have to now that I've discovered you've also taken a liking to wearing no undergarments."

Every word singed like a touch of burning velvet over my skin, the fingers trailing idly over my inner thigh a cool compress tempting my heated flesh. "Does it end?" I wondered aloud to his whiskered jaw, unbuttoning his tunic and flattening my hand over his pounding heart. "The wanting even when you're taking?"

"I've heard it doesn't, but I welcome it," he said to my shoulder, the hand at my back tugging the dress that scooped around my shoulders down to expose my breasts. He groaned at the sight of them, his cock twitching beneath me. "I'll gladly never tire of you."

I concurred, though I didn't say so. He already knew by the way I nudged his chin back with my nose and sank my fingers into his hair to inhale his scent at his neck. One by one, I kissed each scar he'd given to himself, a melting occurring in my chest when he paused in digging between us and grew so very still.

His breathing turned ragged, a rasping groan vibrating against my cheek as I kissed a large raised square of ruined skin at his throat. The idea of him in chains, of poisoning himself... I still couldn't wrap my head around it all. It hurt to even try.

And it confused and angered me to hurt at all when all I wanted was to get lost in him.

He might have been my mate, but I refused to fall prey to the looming mountainous risks that came with complete surrender. I just wanted him in every maddening way, and perhaps I was delusional, but I was determined to have him without losing myself entirely to the suffocating feelings he ignited.

But there were no filthy words, not even so much as a taunting smirk when he lowered his head.

As golden as a brand new day, he watched me beneath sooty lashes while I struggled to keep still and watch him in return.

As I was about to say moon only knew what, he kissed me. He

kissed me and stood to lift and lay me on the desk. Parchment protested. Teacups and inkpots clanked and clattered. My skirts were bunched over my stomach. My thighs opened without being told.

And the prince unbuttoned his pants, his cock joining with my entrance and his hands pulling me up to sit…

Right as he slid inside my body.

"Colvin," I moaned, shocked but nowhere near unhappy.

"Look at how greedily you take me." He gathered me with an arm at my back, my legs tight around his waist. "Now, look at me."

But I couldn't remove my eyes from the sight of him slowly filling me.

"Fia," he warned and clasped my chin. He lifted it when I lifted my eyes. His gaze darted down between us, pausing on my breasts, then collided with mine. "Your lips quiver," he whispered, "every time I fill you."

They parted in response, indeed still trembling.

He brushed his thumb over my lower lip. "I have to see it." A harsh breath fled me as he pushed deeper, slowly invading me completely. His head lowered for his mouth to skim mine. "You fray me at every seam, and it's the sweetest fucking torment I've ever experienced."

"I don't wish to torment you," I breathed, unable to keep from tasting him, from clutching his biceps as he seated himself and ground into me.

"Liar," he whispered with an amused spark in his eyes. I squealed against his mouth when he picked me up and took a seat on the stool he'd not long vacated. His fingers caressed the exposed skin of my back, dragging through my hair. "Torment me, fire-breather. Ride my cock until you can't fucking breathe."

The command washed through me, euphoric heat cascading throughout every limb. I clung to his shoulders, moaned into the heady skin of his neck while his hair tickled my nose and cheek, and I rocked and lifted my body over his.

He nuzzled the crook of my neck, fingers kissing my back as

they roamed down to my rear. He tugged my skirts higher to hold my ass, assisting my efforts with a grip that made my thighs shake.

He didn't feed this time. I supposed there was no need, given how many times he had over the past few days. But I found myself wishing he would, craving that closeness, the magic that would slither into my veins to propel me toward a violent release.

In slow, room-tilting maneuvers of his hands at my hip and rear, I began to drown within the undertow of him.

His harsher breaths sank inside my ears, forcing me to press harder into him. His mouth grazed my shoulder, tender enough to hurt. His cock rubbed every swollen and sensitive part of me, coaxing louder exhales from my lips to heat his neck.

But his silence tormented, another form of torture he inflicted with a low groaning satisfaction.

My head lifted as it came—the onslaught that would soon ripple through me. His own rose from my neck. Our eyes met, his hand sliding up my back to hold me over him as I shook apart, as I rocked into fragmented pieces of who I once was atop him.

He watched it all with parted lips and a rigid jaw, his nostrils flaring and his clouded eyes never leaving mine. He followed with a low curse, my forehead meeting his as we trembled and twitched.

An unexpected though not unwelcome silence rose in volume over our calming breaths.

He opened his mouth. To say what, I would never know for certain.

I kissed him with my hands cupping his face, with my heart in my throat, and until whatever he'd thought to place upon me like a curse disappeared.

"What is it with you not telling me where we're going when you kidnap me?"

Persy had insisted, rather loudly through the door of Colvin's cottage, that I was to accompany her on another journey.

Knowing she wouldn't relent until she'd gotten what she wanted,

Colvin had unwound his arm from my waist. But he'd made her promise no more gambling dens, to which she'd said there were worse things to show me.

He'd grumbled, but a little sore and dazed from days spent with only him and brief visits with the narlows, I'd climbed out of his bed and into the gown he'd peeled from my body at sunrise. We could do with the break.

Well, I could. The fact that I'd recoiled so quickly at the idea of leaving him and his small home unsettled me.

It was time for some fresh air that wasn't tainted with the scent of a princely dragon.

"Kidnapping would suggest you aren't interested in what I have to show you." Persy held a branch back for me. I caught it, releasing it when she'd stepped farther down the narrow trail through the trees. "Yet here we are."

"Where is here?" I asked for the fourth time. My steps slowed as the soil-packed path wound deeper and grew firmer toward the cliff's edge. "Are we going to visit the Pegasuses?" For they apparently rested in giant caves overlooking the sea, and wherever we were going had a lot of water.

It crashed with a boom down below the weed-dusted cliffs, but undeterred and seemingly familiar with the steep terrain, Persy scaled the stone steps we soon encountered with envious confidence.

"Not tonight."

"Then whatever it is, it better be good," I grumbled. "This doesn't seem wise."

"People come down here from the nearby village all the time. It's a popular spot for fishing."

"Are we fishing?"

She turned and laughed at the face I must have made, the wind whipping red strands free of the bun atop her head. "Not so fond of fishing, Fia darling?"

"It's just…" I gripped a groove in the rock to my left, swallowing as I glanced through the shrubbery to my right to the frothy spray from the waves far below. "Boring."

"Anything that doesn't involve your mate is unlikely to rouse much excitement right now."

"Not true," I said, and far too quickly.

Persy laughed. "Well, if anything will, it might just be this."

I tried to keep up as she disappeared into a narrow cave. The cloying darkness lasted only a minute before the moon reappeared, the breeze ruffling Persy's skirt-resembling pants. I stepped out of the gloom to her side and felt my jaw unhinge.

Above us, a waterfall pressed between groupings of monstrous, glittering obsidian rocks. It cascaded with gentle fury into the enormous pool of water beneath. The pool bubbled and gurgled toward the rocks we stood on, wending between them into another waterfall that met with the sea behind us.

But it wasn't just the beauty of the water, the stalactites hanging from the rocky overhang surrounding the circumference of the cliffside pool, nor the luminous ferns and moss that spun my heart into a riot.

"Fishing?" I said, arching a brow at Persy.

Laughing, she said, "Just wanted to see if I'd get the reaction I suspected I would." She shrugged. "I did. Come on."

Crustaceans, some with shells that glimmered like jewels, roamed alongside the rocky banks. Bending to take a closer look, I leaned on what I thought was a large rock, only to flinch when it moved.

The stone-backed creature could've been mistaken for a giant tortoise until it hissed and revealed a serpentine face and dagger-sharp teeth. I inched back, and Persy laughed again as it crawled away from us with torturous slowness. "What is something like that doing in here?"

"He was probably washed down and managed to get out. Now he's stuck unless he wishes to head out to sea." Persy reached into the water and ran her finger over a bright pink mound of fluff. "Happens a lot."

"We should help him get back up."

"With teeth and an attitude like that?" Persy huffed. "No, thank you. Besides"—gently plucking the fluff from the mossy rock in the water, she brought it to the surface—"he's likely enjoying having all this food to himself."

I reached down to stroke the slimy creature in her hand, smiling when it wiggled beneath my touch. "Is it a furlish?"

Persy nodded, then placed it in my hand when I lowered to the damp stone at the pool's edge. Droplets sprayed my arm and dampened my hair against my skin, but I didn't mind.

Above us, the rocky walls of this hidden gem danced with the shine of the stars and moon who watched on between them. I would've gladly sat there for hours to greet each creature, providing they weren't inclined to maim us. But we left as midnight neared, knowing both Colvin and Jarron would be on edge until we returned after dragging us home from our journey to the city.

Persy sensed it first. Atop the trail leading from the cliffs, the woods stood still, too still.

Waiting.

"I haven't heard a sound," I whispered when she slowed at the first thick line of birch trees.

The look she passed me over her shoulder stiffened my spine with fear. Every sense rose to high alert, and as she unsheathed a blade I hadn't seen tucked in one of her billowing sleeves, there was a slight crushing of leaves.

Footsteps over leaves.

Red eyes pierced through the shadows between the trees before us, Persy whispering, "I don't suppose you have any handy abilities none of us are aware of?"

I swallowed, my answer rasped. "No."

"Didn't think so," she said, her breathy laughter born from fear rather than humor. "It's okay. I've bested one before."

"One?" I was too afraid to blink as several pairs of glowing eyes swayed closer to the tree line, growled breaths now within earshot.

"Get a stick or rock," she said. "Aim for the eye or break their skulls and ribs."

Air rushed from my lungs as I knelt with trembling knees on the ground and patted blindly for any of the items she'd mentioned. I refused to take my eyes off the trees. "What are they?"

"Bloodhounds. They're usually too busy hunting more fitting prey, but they must have caught our scent right as we returned." She took a quick step forward to grab a small stone, then braced her feet apart. "Rotten luck."

"I'll definitely say," I muttered, brushing at the leaves and hardened soil and finding nothing. But over by a small fern near the cliff's edge stood a sharp-looking rock, decent enough in size to do considerable damage.

Yet the idea of using it sickened me, and I hesitated.

Persy shouted my name as the beasts grew tired of their slow advance.

They crashed through the trees with preternatural speed, and I scrambled for the rock at the sight of their towering skeletal frames.

Small ears flicked back over their long, bony heads. Teeth, as dark as their brown, striped fur, gnashed. Spittle sprayed as they met the ground before us and licked their maws. Unlike other hounds back home, theirs didn't cover their teeth. They were left on display to remind everyone of what they were.

Hunting canine corpses.

My fingers wrapped around the rock, and I threw it at the beast launching through the air toward Persy's face.

The hound yelped and hit the dirt as another sprang toward her blade. The other two rushed at me, and without a weapon, I fell to my ass and lifted my feet, ready to kick them in the head, when a roar sliced through the night.

Not merely a roar but an unleashing of anger ferocious enough to shake the treetops and the sandy dirt beneath my hands.

The bloodhounds halted, the larger one's face mere inches from my foot. Its breath plumed over me, as sour as old milk, but its beady red eyes grew enlarged. Web-like wings of bones spread from each creature, confirming them to be the same beasts I'd seen flying past the windows of my rooms, and they all ran for the cliffs.

But they were too late.

A dragon rose from the distant treetops.

Wings of darkness unfurled between a curved framework of bones and spread wide, flapping. Branches groaned and broke and scattered beneath the force, trees and plants swaying. Bells began to ring, from the castle to the nearby villages and what sounded like every populated area of the north.

But the dragon cared nothing for the rest of us.

He launched toward the sky with a growled screech and flew over the cliffside, his vast wingspan taking him out to sea in chase of the bloodhounds.

There wasn't time to watch the giant mass of scales and wings stir the waves. Persy yanked at my arm. "Quick."

"We won't make it," I warned, unwilling to lose sight of Colvin. "You go. I'll wait for him to return."

"Just because he didn't kill you the first time doesn't mean he won't now." Persy tugged harder, urging me into a reluctant run. "He's known us for years, and it doesn't matter. All he knows now are his instincts." She tripped over a small ditch, cursing. "And every single one makes him nothing but a stranger—a hunter."

I didn't doubt she spoke true, but I couldn't forget how he'd watched me, as if he'd been assessing me and then seemingly protecting me. Colvin had said himself that he knew me, remembered me. And after everything, I would've believed it even if he hadn't confirmed it.

"We need to stop running," I said, knowing it would only provoke him.

Persy just ran faster, and we jumped over a narrow creek. "I wish to live, thank you."

As if knowing we'd moved, another roar came rolling in a rumble toward the forest. Persy stopped, eyes slowly rising to the canopy of trees above us. "Fuck. We need to hide."

But Colvin crashed through the trees, smaller ones crushed beneath his clawed feet. A prehistoric growl echoed through the woods, creatures skittering and screaming. Persy cursed again, her hand shaking around mine.

The beast dropped those enormous, bone-woven wings to his sides. Smoking, growled huffs left his nose with each ground-pounding thud of his feet as he lowered to all fours.

I pulled at Persy's hand. "Get behind me."

"Are you insane?" she hissed, and the dragon snarled in response. She whispered, "He'll just fire-fry us both."

My eyes traveled over his gray chest, my head tilting back to meet his golden gaze. He scented the air, a long tongue sliding out to taste it while he slowed to a stop before us. "He won't."

"You might survive, but he'll see me as a threat, or worse," she swallowed, gripping my hand so tight that the bones in my fingers protested, "a treat. I don't want to be a treat, Fia. I haven't finished the book I've been reading, and the last time I saw my mother, I called her a fucking idiot."

I snorted, and the sound stilled the beast. Those giant eyes fell upon me, and we both waited without breathing, without moving, to see what he would do next. But he just watched, heated breaths leaving his snout.

Slowly, I murmured, "When I tell you to, walk away. *Walk*," I emphasized. "Don't run."

Persy didn't listen. Her scream drowned beneath Colvin's screeched roar when she made to dart out from behind me, only to encounter a wall of fury-fueled fire blocking her path.

I hauled her back, and breathing hard, she wheezed, "I'm staying with you."

Eyes wide, I looked at the dragon, who merely licked his maw, the fire he'd breathed mere feet from us crackling with unearthly heat.

He lifted his front paw as if he'd come closer to be rid of the female at my back. "No." I stepped forward, taking Persy with me. "Stop."

The dragon lowered his head and released a rumbling breath, his huge nostrils twitching as he scented me. I remained still as he did and met his eyes. My own face reflected back at me in the dark mass surrounded by luminous gold, my hair curling in the breeze and Persy barely visible behind me.

He exhaled a breath that coaxed sweat to immediately coat the skin, and then he shifted back. But only a few inches.

He was waiting. Either for Persy to leave or for me to move so he could attack.

"Walk backward with me," I instructed quietly, not moving my eyes from Colvin as we retreated a few steps. He remained where he was. "We leave now," I said. "Slowly."

"Fia, we can't—"

"Then we stand here like this until he changes back, and we hope he doesn't tire of the game we're playing and eat you or roam elsewhere to hunt."

Persy cursed as we continued to retreat toward the stretch of cliffs at our backs, away from the gradually dying fire. Then we ducked into the trees.

The beast snarled, rushing forward and only stopping when we did.

"Mother of many fucks, Fia," Persy whined. "Let's just wait and hope he finds something else to play with."

But as I looked up over the heaving chest and the silver scales swallowing the night sky's shine to glow a deathly black to his eyes, he knocked his head side to side slightly. "Colvin hasn't shown any need to change," I told Persy. "He did so because he knew we were in trouble."

"He knew that *you* were, you mean." She huffed, her hand clammy in mine. "This beast doesn't give a shit about me."

"You're right," I said and gently encouraged her to part from me, releasing her hand. "Go. He wants me to stay."

Persy side-stepped toward a giant elm. "I swear, if you're wrong…"

But I wasn't.

The dragon trained his attention on her, his tail flicking into the shrubbery behind him with impatience, spraying dirt and leaves and rocks. When Persy had enough distance between us, her pace picked up, and the dragon tensed, growling low in warning.

"Colvin," I called, walking forward.

He was so tall, so large, that I barely reached his chest. Nearing him seemed to work, though. He shifted his attention to me and lowered closer to the ground until one of his eyes was almost level with mine.

I smiled even as my heart trembled in my chest. "Hello, dragon."

He blinked slowly, whiskers twitching with his dark nostrils when I showed him my hand. It wasn't much larger than one of his eyes, but he saw it and watched it as I gave him warning of my intention before placing it upon his scaled cheek.

It ceased shaking when it encountered a smoothness unlike any other, a deadly sharpness at every edge of the perfectly overlapping shapes. Impenetrable, I knew, and at just a glance, but touching those scales made it clear why everyone thought him to be nearly indestructible.

Not even the night sky could touch what lay beneath.

He grumbled, but it was a soft sound. An endearing sound. I wondered if perhaps this bond had robbed parts of my brain, the instinct to flee and live another day, for there was no longer any fear.

Just a healthy dose of intimidation and near-excruciating awe.

I lowered my hand to my side, the pads of my fingers rubbing together. They were smooth, different somehow, for having touched him.

Colvin exhaled a rumbling breath, his giant head tilting to better stare me down with both eyes. "More?" I asked, offering my hand to the air before him.

Another blink was the only response, but combined with the heart-seizing purr vibrating throughout his body as I ran my hand down his neck, it was enough. I reached the top of his front leg, tracing the boulder-like muscle beneath the scales.

He turned his head, watching as I continued down his body.

Reaching his back leg, I stopped when his tail flicked to the earth beside me. I marveled at the row of sharp spikes that curled toward each other like a rib cage and carefully placed my finger on one. The dragon's eyes were on me as I murmured, "Beautiful."

Something nudged my rear, and I braced a hand on his tail, perilously close to the spike I'd just touched. Turning, I found his chin nearly upon the ground. Unsure of what he wanted, a startled yelp left me when his tail pushed me into the side of his body.

"You want me to climb on?" I asked, tapping his side.

He pushed harder, so hard I was nearly squashed between the mass of muscle at his side and that of his tail. "I don't think—*whoa.*" Teeth pulled at my gown until I was hanging upside down and almost sliding free of the material. The rows of spikes upon his back glinted in the moonlight as I was lifted over them.

Just when I thought he'd drop me and I'd impale myself on them, he carefully lowered me until my hands reached out and I could maneuver myself between them.

Then he was moving.

I screamed, sliding over and down his back.

My hand caught on a spike, slicing open, but I managed to grip it. It would seem he didn't approve of this part of the forest. His wings spread, moving fast. My stomach fell into ash, the cliff looming and...

Then open air. A freefall toward the sea raging against the rocks below.

Birdsong and a gentle prodding at the stinging skin of the palm of my hand roused me.

My eyes fluttered open to find there was no longer a beast curled around me and only a cool breeze. Dawn was bathing the sky. Gloriously naked, Colvin crouched before me, my hand in his.

A quaking smile curled one side of his mouth. "The mother of monsters awakens."

Searing breath parted my lips as I gazed at the wonder before me. My prince. My mate.

My very own dragon.

The gentle wind knocked strands of his obsidian hair from his cruel cheeks to sit behind his broad shoulders, revealing the relief and worry lowering his thick brows. It darkened his bright eyes and firmed his already harsh jawline.

I leapt and took him to the ground beside the gurgling creek behind the cottage, where he'd brought us just hours ago. "You flew me home."

"Fia, you're injured."

"I'm fine."

His frown eased. "Home," he said, tracing the bone of my cheek to my jaw, his lips twitching with a smile he held at bay but couldn't keep from his eyes. His finger reached my mouth, and he lifted his head to whisper to it, "You just called it home, fire-breather."

It scorched a path over my tongue, the desire to refute him. To take back what I'd said and correct myself. But I didn't.

He clasped the back of my head, pulling my nose to his. I kissed him before he could torture me more—before the tightening inside my chest could become so painful, it would cause tears to spring to my eyes.

Colvin pulled me over him, his hand clutching my face and his mouth urgently claiming mine. Moaning, we twisted and tugged at my dress. We slipped and rolled down the bank, both of us laughing as we broke apart in the shallow, rocky depths of the creek.

It faded as I climbed over him, my dress sodden and heavy like my heart when he curled some of my hair behind my ear and captured my chin. Our mouths collided again, the sun crawling through the trees as I gave another inch to this thief who continuously defied every stubborn beat of my heart.

The world birthed a brand new day, but I didn't want it.

I longed for the night—for the stars and the moon and the beastly prince who'd gifted me both.

TWENTY-FOUR

Fia

COLVIN FOUND ME AS DAWN BEGAN TO GREET THE NIGHT sky once again.

His shirt and hair deliciously tousled, he leaned against the doorway while Persy finished braiding my hair. She'd insisted when I'd left my bathing room to find her on the end of my bed. Then she'd insisted on hearing all about what had happened when she'd escaped Colvin in the woods the evening prior.

I'd told her some of it, but we'd been interrupted by a tired-looking prince.

I knew that was my fault. We'd only slept for a handful of hours at a time each day since the engagement ball. But he was just as to blame and just as insatiable, if not more, than me.

Persy clucked her tongue. "Come back later, Prince. We're not done."

He raised a brow at the ribbon she tied to the ends of my hair. "My eyes see differently."

"I meant we're not done talking about you, you murderous beast, and you know it."

With a feigned sigh, the prince drawled, "Then by all means, allow me to leave so you can continue."

"That would be the gentlemanly thing to do."

He cocked his head, eyes meeting mine. "I'm not quite sure I qualify as such."

My skin warmed, and I chewed the inside of my lip while recalling the morning hours spent with him on the bank of the creek, then on the kitchen counter in the cottage. I forced my eyes from his and to his britches.

That wasn't much better. Muscle bulged in his thighs as he hooked one boot behind the other while leaning into the doorjamb.

It failed to conceal his erection.

Persy laughed, then patted my shoulder. "Fine." Marching past Colvin, she tugged a strand of his hair and whispered, "You owe me."

Smirking, he said to the floor, "You know I didn't mean to almost kill you."

"Not for that," she called, and I stood when her steps faded within the stairwell down the hall.

I pulled the ties of my satin robe tighter over my stomach and the long braid over my shoulder as I crossed the cool stone to where Colvin waited at the door.

His eyes brushed over all of me, then both of his hands rose for his fingers to do the same with my cheeks. Reverently, he traced them along my jawline to my ears. "You need to stop this."

Leaning into him, I whispered, "Stop what?"

"Ruining me from noticing anything in this world that isn't you."

My heart stalled. I laughed, and then I jumped.

He caught me, holding me beneath my rear as he walked us down the hall. To my exposed neck, he whispered, "I'm going to enjoy making you look wild again."

His threat heated my skin more than the gentle press of his mouth. "We need to sleep," I chastised, though I clenched at just the thought.

He kissed my skin again, leaving his mouth there. "Soon."

"Soon?" I said, smiling against his shoulder.

"I missed eating with you," he said, heading into the stairwell. Indeed, he'd been tied up with finishing neglected tasks during the evening's final meal, and I'd eaten with Spodge and Herb. "So we'll have us some dessert."

Realizing where we were headed, I gasped. "The goblins."

He chuckled. "If there's anything they hate more than us, it's the sun. They've long retired."

The kitchens were mercifully empty as promised and completely void of light.

Colvin seemed to know his way around just fine, though, and set me upon the first island counter. Hunched down to avoid knocking his head on the low ceiling, he inspected the leftover dishes in the cold chest beneath the sink.

I jumped down to join him when I scented the fragrant creams and fruit, nudging him out of the way when I found what I wanted.

"Lemon tart," he commented, closing the lid.

I placed myself and the nearly untouched pie upon the stone floor. "Who would waste such a thing?"

Colvin rummaged through a drawer in the counter beside us, then lowered to the ground with a fork. "You should thank them, being that you're quite excited."

"You're right." I snatched it, grinning as I stabbed the tart. "It's my favorite."

"Figures." He snatched it back, and I scowled. "A little sour and oh so fucking sweet." His grin was more mouth-watering than the dessert he offered to my quickly parting lips. I closed my eyes, savoring the buttery crust, the perfect consistency of the sugar-loaded tart eroding over my tongue.

His question was throaty. "Good?"

I nodded, slowly opening my eyes to find him right there, whispering to my mouth, "Show me."

I opened for him to taste the remnants on my lips and tongue, but I pushed him back when he groaned and made to move closer. "Don't squash it."

He laughed low, digging at the tart and offering me more. His eyes darkened, lids weighted as he watched me eat mouthful after mouthful. After several, I took the fork from him and licked my lips. "Your turn."

The energy emanating from him to heat the dark kitchens grew harder to ignore, but I wasn't done watching his lips wrap around the metal prongs. The glimpse of his tongue as I withdrew quivered my stomach.

"Are you nervous?"

I knew what he referred to. The wedding was three evenings away. Persy had told me that people had already journeyed from all over Gwythorn to attend. A historical event, the merging of two kingdoms, wasn't one to be missed.

Even if rumor spread that the groom was a dragon.

But surprisingly, as I absorbed his question, I found I wasn't nervous. Not for the reasons he thought. "I don't want to see them."

He knew who I meant, nodding once and swallowing when I gave him another bite. I watched his throat bob, wanting to stuff my nose close to it, to lick it. Before I could, he asked, "Regin?"

I licked tart from my teeth and lifted my shoulders. "I don't want to see any of them."

"Then, after it is done, you won't have to ever again," he vowed, and the vehemence to it forced my eyes from his mouth to his.

"Would you stop me?" I asked cautiously. "If I saw Brolen and there was a chance?"

His brows scrunched. "Fia—"

"Would you?"

He sighed. "If that is what you need to do, then I would only ever support you, but I'd thought that maybe after these past few weeks, you'd have changed your mind."

I hadn't. It might have tempered, but the hatred was still there. Like an extra shadow at my back, I wasn't sure it would ever leave. Not after what he'd divulged to me about my mother when he'd thought I would die. "He doesn't deserve to live." I stabbed the tart and fed some to myself.

Colvin took my hand when I lowered the fork to the dish, watching me closely. "Come here."

I crawled into his lap, not wanting the comfort but relishing what he gave all the same. My legs looped around him, the robe falling open as I tucked my nose into his neck and held him tight. "Are you nervous?"

"No," he said, sure and strong. "In fact, I wish it were here already."

I laughed and pulled back to lay my forehead on his. "Why?"

He frowned as if that should have been obvious. "You'll be mine in every possible way, and I'll be yours."

My eyes stung and narrowed. "You're far too sweet for a male who shifts into a dragon and fucks like a beast."

"Not sweet," he said, reaching beside him for the tart. "Just…" He lifted his fingers, the dessert coating them, to my mouth. "Content."

I sucked the tart from his fingers, his eyes upon my mouth and his harsh exhale warming more than the skin of my face. Loosening my hold on his shoulders, I reached between us to free him from his pants. "Fia," he warned, but my name was more of a whispered plea.

I kissed his lips and jaw, murmuring as my fingers encountered his silken thickness, "Yes, my Prince?"

A groaned, "Fuck," as I squeezed him and dragged my hand up and down his long length. Then it was my turn to curse as he took me to my back, the tart squashed beneath my arm while his mouth ravaged mine, and his cock rubbed through and against my waiting flesh.

"You murdered it," I complained when his mouth left mine to trail a path of fire down my chest. I grasped his head, fingers tangling in his hair, when he inhaled and kissed my center.

He hummed. "Shame." Something cool met my mound before his heated mouth licked it clean. "As it's now my favorite, too." I melted, quivering as he painted me in the tart again before cleaning it with slow vigor from my core.

I was close, my back arching as he swirled his tongue around me, then flattened it over the knot of need he'd created and rocked it back and forth. A dark laugh accompanied my moans as I ruptured. As I clenched his head within my thighs, trapping him while I tried and failed to quiet myself as the low ceiling loomed closer.

Needing him, I pulled at his tunic until he finally relented and gave me his mouth. I licked every cream and lemon crumb from it, his hips lowering to mine and thrusting. Not entering but teasing me until I was ready and moaning for all of him.

But I was always ready and wanting more. I feared it might never cease, this hunger that had blossomed to life inside me. With just one look, one touch, I came alive with a ferocity I knew extended far beyond lusty greed.

This prince of mine had gifted me with more than I'd ever thought I'd wanted.

He unearthed hidden desires I'd have never dared acknowledge myself, let alone admit aloud. He fed every starving facet of me, places I'd never known needed such devotion. With careful coaxing, they'd been handed a freedom to exist and to also grow.

So much so, courage bloomed—outweighed and erased the fear-laced reservations I'd been wearing as a shield for far too long.

Taking my prince's face, I let my lips linger at his mouth and ran my fingers over the corners of his glowing eyes. "Maybe you didn't rob me of my life." Colvin's entire body tensed, braced for bruising words. I smiled and felt him relax over me as he waited for my eyes to fall into his. "Maybe you gave me the one I needed, the one I was destined for, instead."

Time swam and crashed, but it couldn't touch us. Nothing could touch me when he looked at me like that, as if he'd been hunting for treasure his whole life, only to have it land before him in a beautiful earth-shaking mess.

I didn't delude myself into believing I was anything special. I'd always known I wasn't, and though it had often bothered me, it hadn't ever truly mattered. But this prince seemed to think I was. Somehow, that was better than any magic I'd lamented not having, any crumb of attention I'd lain awake at night hoping for.

It was enough to believe I'd never needed any of those things. That I'd only ever needed myself.

And perhaps a lot of him.

"Fire-breather," he whispered thickly, his body heavy over mine as he finally blinked, his smile falling as he breathed me in. Kisses were pressed to the corners of my mouth, to the tip of my nose, and spread across my cheeks.

I laughed, clutching his back and smoothing my fingers down it.

As if remembering he was squashing me, he pushed up onto the forearm beside my head, his hair falling over his cheeks. I lost the ability to breathe as he loomed above me, as he pressed into me, his gaze unwilling to release mine.

Then he stilled, dropping to squash me again when shuffling steps sounded.

A moment later, a gnarled voice snarled, "What beneath the rotting moon do you think you're doing?"

Colvin quickly pulled my robe closed and helped me to my feet, tucking himself away while I struggled to keep from laughing.

In a striped nightgown, Orin gaped at us, a lamp swaying in the goblin's hand as we raced for the door.

Colvin knocked his head on the low-hanging frame, and my laughter rang through the hall as I dragged him down it to the stairs.

My dragon was leaning against the headboard when I woke with the afternoon sun, a knee raised and a book pressed to his hair-dusted thigh.

My voice was still hoarse with sleep, even though I'd been awake and watching him for some minutes. "That better not be more research on how to successfully poison yourself."

Colvin smirked, then turned the page. "It's a recount of one of the largest mortal wars."

I frowned at the weathered novel. "How did you get your hands on such a thing?"

"My grandfather, Gayle, who leads the hunt," he informed. "I've accompanied him a few times to Orlinthia."

The continent nearest our own. A mortal realm.

Rising to my elbow, I pushed my hair from my face to better

inspect the gray, worn, and thinly bound manuscript, unable to keep from inspecting the prince holding it. Stunningly naked, the book blocking my view of his manhood, he looked as though he might have been posing for a lewd portrait.

One I'd pay a lot of coin to possess.

"What makes you want to study their wars?"

"Curiosity." Looking down at me, his lips curving wryly, he murmured with his eyes fixed upon my mouth, "I like to read, and I like to spar, so you may cease your worrying, fire-breather. It's purely for enjoyment."

I relented with a huff, my eyes closing when his knuckles grazed my cheek. "What's it like?" I asked, taking his hand when he made to give it back to his book. "The mortal realm."

He pondered that for a minute while I stroked his fingers with my own, the fire dying with low crackles in the hearth. "Intriguing but also quite dull."

I snatched his book and placed it beside us as I climbed over him to straddle his lap, forcing his knee to the bed. His hands immediately found the wide flare of my hips—as though they'd been crafted just for his touch. "Tell me more of these mortals."

His eyes danced and lowered to feast upon his marks at my chest, his teeth scraping his lower lip. He released a heavy breath, hard as steel beneath me. "They have no magic, but they have far more buildings and cities. Places called churches, and unbearably crowded markets that reek of refuse and desperation."

Colvin laughed silently at the twisting of my features and poked my nose. "But these mortals carry a rare hope—a type of frenzied liveliness—as if they know their lives are too short, but they'll still do whatever they must to live them."

Entranced by his voice, the whispering of his fingers as they traced my ribs and the soft curves of my stomach, I relaxed against his knees when he lifted them for me to do so. "What are these churches like?"

"They're often the nicest structures in most cities and towns," he said, eyes upon his traveling fingers. "It's where they convene to pray and marry and seek solace from their gods."

I hummed and shivered from his touch. "And what of the mortals, are they nice?"

"To us?" He huffed a breath when I nodded. "Scared, overly well-mannered, and distrustful."

He twitched beneath me when I ran my fingers over the light smattering of dark hair at his chest. "They permit the hunt to visit, but nothing and no one else unless they are human. Once a year," he said. "And only for trade. Most of what I've seen of their land is from the skies as we arrive and leave."

Via Pegasuses and flying carriages that blended within clouds and darkness.

As he trailed his fingers down the strands of hair falling over my breasts, his voice grew rougher. "It's a giant continent. We set up camp in different places each time, along varying coastlines and within thick forests. But I don't doubt that to many of them, we're still but a myth only the desperate and curious choose to barter with."

"You are truly terrifying," I teased.

He grinned. "Am I, fire-breather?"

Breath sat tight in my chest as I nodded and leaned forward to trace his soft lips. "With all those scales and your fire." Excitement hit me like a stone bouncing into my stomach, and I exhaled in a rush as I sat back. "Show me."

His brows dropped. "Show you what?"

"Your fire."

"You've seen it."

Indeed, in fleeting doses and in the woods when he was a dragon. But he knew that was not what I meant. I plucked his hand from my stomach and turned it over between us. "Please."

He chuckled, the gravelly sound deliriously delicious. "Since you asked so nicely..." Fire erupted and danced upon his palm. In a small, swaying arc, the flame warmed my skin through his as I refused to release him.

Slowly, I dragged my fingers over the back of his hand, daring to inch them closer. They halted at his thumb when Colvin tensed. But I wanted to know. "Will it burn me?"

"All fire burns, no matter who wields it."

I arched a brow. "Does that mean I shouldn't try?"

He laughed. "Yes, Fia. It most certainly means you shouldn't—"

I touched the flame, and he cursed, extinguishing it with a fold of his fingers.

He then snatched my forefinger, inspecting it thoroughly— adorably. But I had felt nothing but warm air. He scowled at it, then up at me in disbelief. "You excel at finding ways to make my heart stop beating."

I smiled. "Has that happened before?"

"No," he said, and seemingly reluctant to admit it.

"What does it mean that I can touch it without being burned?"

Glaring slightly beneath his long lashes, my prince remained silent, petulant, and I laughed, low and breathy. His features eased, then tightened when I rose to settle onto his cock, which was still erect and throbbing when I speared myself with it.

His knees lowered to the bed as I sank down, his gasped curse an edged blade skimming my skin as he watched me take him.

Once he was seated, I leaned forward to whisper to his lips, "I think you cannot burn me because you are mine, dragon. Every part of you—all mine."

"You think so?" he taunted.

"I know so." I brushed my lips over his, gently rocking my hips.

He cupped my face, eyes meeting mine and his thumb caressing the curve of my mouth. "I want you here always."

"On your cock?" I smirked, then moaned when his other hand squeezed my ass.

"In my home," he whispered to my mouth and pressed his own to it softly. "In my bed." His lips moved to my chin. "In every fucking corner of my life. Every night. Every day. Always."

My heart melted and seized, strangling my words into a barely existent rasp. "Then it's a good thing you are to marry me."

"Marriage doesn't automatically grant me what I want," he said roughly. "What I need."

"Then by all means…" breath fled me when he rocked up into me, his tongue crawling over my jawline. "Let's see if you can convince me to surrender to such a horrible fate, dragon."

His eyes and nostrils flared with the challenge, and I laughed when he flipped me to my back. Our bodies stayed joined, my legs winding around him. He kissed a path from my lips to my throat, and my head tilted back into the pillows. "I'll spend the rest of my nights convincing you if I must."

I moaned through a shuddering exhale, clasping his head to my neck. "I think you must."

"Then I will," he vowed with an unexpected gravity, and pressed his lips beneath my chin. "Until every star burns out."

TWENTY-FIVE

Fia

O N THE EVENING BEFORE THE WEDDING, THE PRINCE WAS called away not long after we woke for preparations regarding security.

It was almost impossible to believe that come morning, as dawn kissed the land, we would be wed. But after the impossibility of everything that had already come to pass, perhaps it shouldn't have been.

I was ready.

As ready as I could be to officially make this kingdom my new home and promise myself to the prince who'd given it to me in this final way.

The castle was aflutter as staff prepared the final packages, which would need to be materialized to the border—to Halfway Hall, where the ceremony and celebration would take place.

The frantic energy had Spodge and Herb on edge, who'd been waiting in their room with the door open, seemingly content to remain inside rather than brave the busy halls.

Though I'd asked, there was nothing for me to do, so I'd gladly taken the brother beasts outside to play in the clearing of the cottage. All three of us had been grateful for the reprieve, but it couldn't last.

Midnight came and went, and Colvin still hadn't returned to the cottage.

After taking the narlows back to their room, I decided it was time to find him to discover what I needed to do before we left. He'd told me we would be materializing to the forests surrounding the hall, but I knew little else.

Colvin's study was empty, void of even a used teacup, and I whirled when I felt the presence at my back.

Jarron stood in the doorway, wearing a frown I was beginning to think might be perpetual as he observed me while eating a peach. "You seem happier."

I didn't deign to give that a response.

"But I do find myself wondering why," he said, then chewed a fleshy chunk torn from the fruit.

He was right. I was happier, but that didn't mean I would ever be in the mood for skulking males with bad attitudes. "Kindly make your point or cease trying to piss me off."

His frown worsened as though that hadn't been his intent.

I almost believed him. Almost.

"It's the evening of one of the biggest events in Gwythorn history, given the two courts have never unified in marriage before now." Another bite was taken, my shoulders stiffening as he spoke while chewing. "Therefore, we expected that not all would be pleased by this, so we await the inevitable."

"I'm already tired of listening to you." I made to leave through the door behind me to the woods. I'd wait for Colvin at the cottage.

His next words stopped me. "We wait for someone to spoil it." I spun back when his implication settled deep, ready to set him straight, but he continued. "We know that won't be Eldorn. Not after what happened the last time our people chose to ignore one of our queen's wishes." He smirked, stepping down into the study. "Ah, he has told you of Cherith."

"He has," I said. "But I don't understand what any of this has to do with me."

"Nothing, of course." He stopped, shrugging. "And everything. You see, our people might be eternally loyal to Olette after what happened to Cherith, but that doesn't mean they wish to live beneath the threat of a ruthless dragon."

Gesturing to me with his half-eaten fruit, he said, "Word has spread since you arrived. So they welcome you with open arms, no matter your blood, for the safety they hope your bond to the prince will bring them." He paused intentionally. "Which leaves only one court not to be trusted…"

"You think I don't mean to marry him." Not a question, for he'd heavily implied as much.

"Can you blame me?" He leaned against Colvin's desk and eyed the piles of books and parchment. "You're far too content with the lot you've been forced to accept."

I pushed through my teeth, my heart slowing, "You know we are mated, and I've grown to care for him." I would give this asshole no more than that.

Jarron smirked at the shelving as though he knew of my reluctance, then looked at me. "But the creature we took in a mere few weeks ago would rather tear the world apart with her teeth than be used as nothing more than a shield and a cure for the remainder of her days, so tell me what you intend," he said, his low tone hardening. "Better to do it now than when chained in another dungeon." He shook his head. "Ours is not so pretty."

A ringing echoed in my ears, struck through me to stake a hollowing pit inside my stomach.

At my silence, he huffed out a rough breath. "You cannot tell me you haven't figured it out." A ruddy brow rose, and he laughed in quiet shock. "My, he really must be taking good care of you." With one last perusal, one of confusion and pity more than anything else, he rubbed his hand over his mouth.

Then he made his way to the door with an earnest, "Do forgive my assumptions."

"Wait." With my heart sinking for reasons I couldn't yet grasp, I followed him. "Stop with the riddles and just tell me what you mean." He turned back when I shocked us both by saying softly, "Please."

He took so long to answer that I feared he wouldn't. "I never intended to confuse you, nor is it my place to inform you of anything," he said, and I found myself believing him. "I merely thought you were…"

"Up to something," I said when it seemed he wouldn't.

He scrubbed a hand over his hair-dusted cheek, cursing. "I've spoken out of turn. Please just forget it, okay? And forgive me." As though not wanting to chance I'd follow him again, he materialized, leaving a smoky, acidic energy in his wake.

In a daze, I lowered to the step and watched fireflies dance inside the jars upon the shelves. The door at the back of the room remained closed, shadows swaying in the sheet of thin glass at its top from the trees outside.

The woods and cottage beyond beckoned.

But I didn't move.

By the time I was found for my final dress fitting by a surly goblin who seemed irritated to have been given such a lowly task, the nausea of confusion had clouded too thoroughly.

So I angered the creature further by declining and heading to my rooms.

The Unseelie queen tapped twice upon the door before letting herself in.

I remained on the bed with my back to the post, my knees to my chest, and my mind in tatters, trying to discern the truth from Jarron's careless words while battling with the desire to ignore them. I wanted so desperately to ignore them.

But there was no escaping them.

In lace robes that whispered over the stone floor, Olette gave me a cursory glance before standing by the window nearest the door. "My dear brother has informed me that he said something he possibly shouldn't have."

To ignore her when she'd made the effort to seek me out after I'd snubbed her with the gown fitting would not be wise, even if I wished to tell her to go away.

"He said I am a shield and a cure." I chose my question carefully, selecting it from the splinters of my thoughts like a twig from a rain-damp web. "For Colvin, I know, but what I'm failing to comprehend is why? How could you have known it would be me?"

For they couldn't have, surely.

"Finding you has been a quest, indeed, Fia. One that has spanned more than a decade." Her fingers folded behind her back. "Fable says that the only way to tame a dragon is to find his mate. Have you ever heard of such a thing?"

I hadn't, and my silence said as much.

A smile sang in her voice as she said, "I didn't think so. Very few knew, being that we are lucky to see a dragon once a millennium. Many of them are slain while they're younglings, before they can even hope to find such a fortune."

A fist clenched around my heart at the thought, and squeezed.

"When Colvin first changed at the tender age of four years, Cherith and I feared he'd share the same fate as those before him. She was taken from me, my queen, and I'd sooner see this entire continent swallowed by fire than await the same fate for our son."

My heart ceased racing. It slowed as if it needed to hear every word said.

"So the search began when he was just ten years of age. He was exposed to females of all statures. We traveled. We invited them into our home as weeklong guests." Nostalgia stained her voice. "I'd watch them play and sit awkwardly side by side at meals, and I'd wish it could've been that way for different reasons."

"Years went by, and nothing sparked. Colvin soon grew too dangerous, and word slowly spread, no matter how much I warned people not to speak of it. Nobles and even village folk in need of the coin wouldn't hear of having their beloved offspring come anywhere near this castle. So for a few dark years, my son hid away in that cottage with his books and parchment, and he rarely left. It wasn't until he began to recognize the signs, to hunger with a feeder's bloodlust and drink, that he decided to trust himself. Just enough to try again."

My eyes lifted from my hands in my lap to the queen, who still had her back to me, seemingly lost to memory as she gazed out of the stained glass to the night beyond.

"He joined my father and the wild hunt, paid visits to nearly every town and village, including that of your precious Callula." Her shoulders rose and fell with a tight breath as if recalling the disappointment. "Nothing. It was my idea to give him the harem under the guise of making him seem the typical rake of a prince. By then, he and his lovers were of an age to do as they wished, no matter what fears their guardians or others whispered about, and oh how they came…"

My nose crinkled, as did my stomach, as I remembered seeing some of Colvin's past lovers at our engagement ball.

"By the dozen, we'd turn them away, but only after taking their details with a promise they likely assumed was feigned to contact them if he was ever in need." A humorless laugh. "And needed they were. As each year passed, we'd bring in fresh meat and pay those who'd been here too long handsomely before sending them on their way."

Olette sighed. "I'd been so certain, with the ever-changing harem, all the balls and events and his continued quests throughout the land, that we would succeed. I'd even implored him to look at males, all the while knowing his preference because there had to be someone for him somewhere."

Her head lowered, ruby red hair slithering over her robed shoulder as she lifted a hand to touch the stained glass of the window. "Alas, I soon had to face what I couldn't bear. Like so many other souls, there was a severe likelihood that Colvin would never find his mate."

But he did. He had.

He'd found me.

As if hearing my thoughts, she went on. "He found you himself, really, and long before entering that dungeon. Within one of his many beloved tomes lies a rough recount, so fragile in its age and rarity, of the last dragon to have found a mate." She paused. "More specifically, just who she was. A village female."

Olette finally turned away from the window, her dark eyes

agleam upon me. "A Seelie female. She died, of course. Both her and her dragon were slain in the final war without many knowing of her existence. All anyone has ever known is that a dragon ravaged our lands for decades too long. So an army rose to take him down, unaware that he'd recently found his counterpart—a way to keep from endangering others."

I didn't doubt what she'd said. I'd forged such a bond with Colvin and had experienced it for myself, but I was growing too incensed to care. All this time, he'd said nothing. All this time, I'd let him take everything, believing it wasn't premeditated but fated. I'd lost myself so thoroughly that I couldn't see what everyone else appeared to have already known. "You should've just let me be."

"Why?" she asked as if I were the mad one. "So you could continue to rot away beneath your uncle's," she paused, her smile one of knowing, "unjust tyranny veiled as heroic boredom?"

The queen tutted. "You were made for more than such simple evils, Fia, and you know it. You might loathe that you were not told all of this sooner, but you cannot deny that if you had been, then perhaps this might not have unfolded how it has…" Her smile widened and appeared shockingly genuine. "Into something real. More real than any plan or magic could've brought to fulfillment."

Venom crawled and curled into my chest. "Plan?" I scoffed, close to snarling. "You sent your son to me knowing they would wish to kill him. That is not a plan. It's…"

"It was a calculated risk," she cut in. "One we both agreed upon for Callula Castle contained a Seelie princess who harbored an affection for things she was eternally talked of and put down for enjoying." A smile lingered with her next admission, "How do you think those narlow cubs ended up along that woodland trail you walked so often?"

It was rare for creatures such as them to roam so far from home, let alone make it to the mountainous terrain beyond Callula Castle. My burning eyes flared wide. "You put them there."

Insanity, I thought. All of it. The babes and the blood in the snow.

The calm prince in his cell and how reluctant he'd been to leave when I'd thought I was rescuing him.

The queen brought me back from dizzying memories made in a dark dungeon. "Those who knew of Colvin's true nature were well aware of their fate if they chose to speak of it to the wrong people." Meaning any Seelie, or even Unseelie, who wished to use the information for their own gain.

"As the whispers began to spread farther, I made sure to spread some myself. Colvin became Eldorn's secret, and they have protected him while knowing of the immense threat he poses. Still, a secret can only remain one for so long. At the meeting of the courts, we took the risk. We exposed him to every power-holding creature in attendance, knowing they would wish to take control by taking him."

Despite everything, the thought of it sickened me with fear. "He just handed himself over to Brolen?"

Olette smiled. "A good game is never won by playing out in the open, Fia. We had one of the lords enter the hall in a fluster, swearing to all that he'd seen it for himself—that the Eldorn prince was a dragon. The look in Brolen's eyes..." A weighted, wicked laugh. "He'd already known, of course, or at least suspected, but he'd never been able to do anything about it because he could never prove it."

"But this time, Colvin did not laugh the accusation off, nor did he dispute it. He agreed to be escorted to Callula with Brolen, knowing he could leave whenever he wished." My stomach turned. Her tone softened. "It is easy, I know, to forget all he is and all he is capable of. But he doesn't have the luxury of forgetting, not even for a second. If he didn't want to be there, he wouldn't have been, and no iron nor stone would have kept him."

When you look at me like that, I don't just forget what I'm doing, I forget all that I fucking am.

But all along, he'd known exactly what he was doing.

"I don't care how you dress it." Tears pressed like thorns, but I held them at bay. "You still destroyed my life to save your son's."

My mate had destroyed my life to save his own.

Olette's chin rose, dark eyes burning down the bridge of her slender nose. "I would destroy far more than that, my darling." Allowing that statement and warning to hang there, she smirked and made her way to the door. "You might be furious, and that is fine, but let us not pretend that you suffer for all this, Fia."

The door closed with a quiet creak.

Rage filled my chest and my eyes. It shook my fingers into fists, my nails scoring into my palms. I hadn't doomed myself by saving a prince.

I'd fallen into the trap of a desperate monster.

TWENTY-SIX

Colvin

"THERE'S BEEN A SITUATION."

Jarron's words were the last thing I wanted to hear. We were just hours away from preparing to leave for Halfway Hall, and I hadn't seen Fia since I'd left her in bed this afternoon. "Walk and talk," I said, moving past him to the stairs, annoyed his need to see me meant I couldn't just materialize to the fourth floor.

Fia hadn't been in the cottage when I'd returned, and unless she'd taken it upon herself to explore the woods again, she'd be here in the castle. Even after her encounter with the hounds, I didn't doubt she harbored no fear about venturing into the dark once more. Though right now, she was likely anxious and enclosed in her rooms.

"I might've accidentally spilled some milk..."

I paused on the landing, as did he. "Spit it out."

He raised his hands. "Olette's not long left her rooms. She explained everything, so don't worry."

"Don't worry?" I breathed more than said and felt my heart sink. "Tell me you didn't..." Not now. Not until I was ready. Not until Fia was ready. She'd only just surrendered to it all, for fuck's sake. Uncle or not, friend or not, I'd tear his tongue from his throat without a sliver of remorse if he'd done this intentionally.

Jarron rubbed at the back of his neck.

I gripped his shirt. It ripped as I pushed him into the stone wall and snarled, "What the fuck have you done?"

"I didn't fucking mean to, okay?" he said between his teeth. "I swear. I just..." He shook his head, and I pushed harder upon his chest. "I thought she knew."

"Did I tell you she was aware?"

"No, but come on, it's obvious, isn't it?" His eyes searched mine. "She'd have to be under some type of heavy spell not to see it by now. That"—he swallowed and dared to make this worse—"or perhaps she didn't want to see what sat right before her very nose."

"She thought we wanted Callula," I seethed. "You fucking prick. Only recently has she started to wonder if that wasn't the case. I've been hinting." I released him and dragged a hand through my hair. "But I couldn't do it. I wanted her to trust us before we demolished all chance of that ever happening."

"And how would that make it any better, my prince?" he gritted.

"Who are you to judge when it does not even concern you?"

We both stiffened then, the stairwell flooded with fading rage as Jarron whispered, "You dare say that after all these years of watching you nearly destroy yourself?" His dark eyes shined with disbelief. "After I've been here to help you recover from every asinine quest to intentionally harm yourself?"

I stepped back, at a loss for words, because he was right. He was right, but he was still wrong for what he'd done. "You should've just left her the fuck alone."

"I've been doing that, but when I saw her..." He groaned. "She just seemed so content, so suddenly at peace with this new life she'd once loathed you for, and I've been worried about this wedding. I didn't think. I just reacted."

"Because moon forbid anyone should be happy while you continue to choke on the weight of all your mistakes."

His features creased, teeth bared, but I was done wasting time with him.

His voice stalked me. "All your careful plans and apologies won't mean shit when she chooses not to trust us, Colvin."

He spoke true, but it didn't help.

It only served to rile me further as I continued up the stairs to Fia's rooms. My blood pulsed in my ears and thickened within my veins, but there was no way I would give in to the beast clawing for freedom when it was the very reason for all of this.

I couldn't even say I was sorry. I knew that was what she was likely expecting to hear, but no matter what excuses I formed in my mind, remorse wouldn't fit. Such a thing was impossible when I could never regret one moment we'd spent together, nor how it had all come to be—not even when she'd despised me.

I wanted to keep everything that came with her.

A book was thrown at my head as soon as I opened the door. "Get out."

I caught it before my nose and blinked to where Fia sat on her knees in a robe upon the bed, her eyes red and her cheeks stained with ire.

A quick glance at the thick volume in my hand revealed it was one of mine from my study. "Do you hate me so much that you've taken to researching poisonous plants?" My attempt at humor fell flat.

Fia gripped the post of the bed as though it kept her from leaping at me to claw my eyes out.

I set the book on the chest of drawers by the window. "Firebreather, allow me a few minutes to explain before resorting to violence."

"There's no need. Your mother told me all of it. The harem, the balls, the traveling..." She swallowed. "The endless search for someone to cure you. For *me*."

Unwise, yet I couldn't resist reminding her, "We both know nothing will cure me, and the one thing that might is not within our reach."

Her fiery expression banked, delicate features falling lax. I took the opportunity to move two slow steps closer to the bed. "You still seek the book? To poison and potentially kill yourself even after all you've subjected me to?"

Her tone, the way she'd implied that all we'd discovered together, found in each other, was nothing more than a bad dream, strangled my lungs like a threat. "I didn't want this."

"Bullshit, Colvin," she growled. "You've spent most of your life looking for *just* this."

I couldn't dispute that.

Many years had been committed to finding the one who might tame the bloodlust of my inner beast via mating connection, someone I might listen or respond to when I was no longer in control of myself. The poisons had been a last resort, a desperate excursion into madness to try to keep me from transforming into the scaled monster in the first place.

"I mean," I started, then stopped, casting my eyes to the ground as I tried to find the right words to explain. "I didn't want *this*—for you to feel as if you are nothing but a leash for a beast no one else can tame. I did want that, and desperately. I won't and cannot deny it, but then I met you…" I lifted my gaze, meaning every word. "I truly did want the book, Fia. I still do."

Her brows lowered, her chest heaving slower now. I wondered if perhaps she was too confused, still too unsure of all she'd discovered and how she felt to be having this conversation. But the idea of giving her space, of not seeing her at all when she was evidently hurting, and before we were married…

Unfathomable.

"I wanted to find you. Of course, I did. I wanted to make this stop in the only nearly certain way we knew how, but wanting to find you and actually accomplishing it…" I walked another step closer. "The repercussions of what we'd done became painfully clear when we received word of what Brolen intended for you. I then hated myself for different reasons, but not enough to stop. Not enough to keep from falling—"

"Stop," she rasped, her hand slowly unwrapping from the bed post.

"Fia." I erased the remaining distance between us and clasped her damp cheeks. "You're my mate, Fia, but you're also my heart. You're in my blood as much as I am yours. You don't just belong with me. You belong here with me. With all of us."

KINGDOM OF VILLAINS | 259

Soft hands fell over mine at her cheeks, as though she'd remove them but couldn't find the strength. A throaty whisper scratched at my heart. "Belonging is irrelevant when you plotted and stole what wasn't yours to take."

"But is it?" I questioned carefully, my voice deepening. "I'd do it again. I'd deceive you and steal you and enjoy every fucking moment over and over again if it meant making you mine."

Long, wet lashes spread wide. "You…" Violet eyes swam all over my face. "You barbaric asshole." But the insult was too gentle to sting as her venom had done in the past.

"I'll be whatever I must, fire-breather. Always."

"You have some fucking nerve," she seethed between gnashed teeth, attempting to pluck my fingers from her face. "Leave. Right now."

I let go but stopped her from leaving the room by snatching her around the waist and trapping her against the wall by the door. "Do not run from me."

"Why?" Fia glared. "You won't kill me, and you won't kill anyone else so long as I'm around." Her laughter broke. "You can live with a clearer conscience now that you've completely destroyed my life to make it so." Disgust sharpened her tone and weaponized the hatred in her eyes. "You lied to me, had me shunned and almost killed by my own people, and here you stand, acting as if all of that is okay because you finally found the mate you've spent so long hunting."

Each word was a blade to the chest, but she wasn't wrong for saying them, for wanting to hurt me as I'd done her. All she'd said was true, but it didn't deter nor guilt me. I tightened my hold on her waist, and whispered to her temple, "Does knowing what I sought make finding it any less real?" I pressed my lips to her cheek, urging her to melt. "Does knowing all of this really change anything, fire-breather?" Her silence was slaughter. "Answer me."

"I don't want to."

"Because you don't want to see it. You don't trust it because you don't trust anyone, and rightfully so, but you do trust me." I traced the flare of her hips and smiled when she shivered. "Deep down, you know within your beautiful fucking bones that you can always trust me." I trailed my lips to the corner of her mouth when she didn't respond, the stalling of her fast beating heart response enough. "I've wanted you from the moment I first laid eyes on you in that dungeon, holding those cubs as if you'd lay down your life to protect them."

"Colvin," she warned, my name all breath.

"I've wanted you since the start, I need you in ways I never expected to, and I've fallen too deep to regret a damned thing." My lips pressed, then brushed her skin with every word. "Hate me as much as you need, but you'll have to do so with me. Everything, all of you, forever with me."

"Right now," she whispered, swallowing. "I need you to leave."

It killed me, but she'd meant it, and I could sense she wasn't far from fraying. I wanted to stay, to hold her while she felt all she needed to, but I'd certainly done enough.

"Fine, but don't you dare forget…" I inhaled her deeply, stirring the hair over her ear, and murmured with vehemence, "I fucking love you, Fia. I'll love you regardless of what you choose to do with me." I stole her hand and placed my lips upon her palm. "Until every star burns out."

She just stared, her lips parted and a lone tear sliding down her cheek. I smiled, then I left before she could see it fall with me to my knees.

TWENTY-SEVEN

Fia

DISAPPROVAL GLOWED FROM ILENA'S ORANGE EYES, WHICH I continuously tried to evade, and in her rough touch as she fastened me into my wedding gown.

The pixie jumped down from the chair she'd been standing on to inspect every inch of the gown, rounding me slowly. "Beautiful, yet you act as if you're on the way to a pyre for the dead."

My eyes lifted from my wrung hands to the reflection awaiting me.

Just as stunning, if not more so now that I was wearing it in earnest and it was complete, the black and purple gown shimmered with night. The gold bow falling into a lace train could be seen from the front, its ribbon like that of wings on my lower back.

I both hated and loved it.

I fucking love you.

Such simple yet unnervingly powerful words were not enough to fix anything—yet I hadn't been able to keep them from infiltrating my every thought. The way he'd said them, so low and weighted, shortened my every breath, rendering my lungs too shallow and my eyes too swollen for what awaited me.

Everyone who was anyone in all of Gwythorn would be in attendance. In mere minutes, all would bear witness to the sealing of my fate.

To the accomplishment of a monstrous court.

But my deceptive prince was right. My fate had been sealed long ago, and I could once again try to fight it, to deny it, but I knew

262 | ELLA FIELDS

I would surely fail. There was no chance for victory when I didn't truly want it.

When all I wanted was everything I'd already surrendered to.

Ilena tutted as I wiped a tear from my cheek. "Bend down, Lady." Quickly, she inspected the silver dust she'd said had been traded with a friend, dabbing at the corner of my eye to ensure her work remained unspoiled. "No crying."

I scowled. It wasn't as if I wanted to.

A bony finger swayed between my eyes. "No frowning, either."

Indeed, she'd carefully laid a faint dust across my brows, the effect, with my kohl-lined eyes and lashes, reminiscent of a winged mask.

"Come on, then. Best be leaving before you ruin yourself anymore," she ordered, snapping her fingers toward the door.

I lifted the heavy weight of my gown, but I didn't move. The pixie watched me with an impatient flutter of her wings while my heart and mind battled for dominance.

I'll love you regardless of what you choose to do with me.

Colvin had spoken as if there ever had been a choice—as if there was once a time in my life when I'd had the power to decide what I wanted for myself. But I'd known what he'd truly meant. We would marry, but it was what I would do with him after that he feared.

And I didn't know.

I wasn't certain of anything anymore, but although I struggled to come to terms with all he'd hidden from me, I was also undeniably glad. Out of all the creatures in this land, his soul had chosen mine.

He'd stolen everything I'd known to give me everything I never knew I needed.

I dragged my heavy gown and heart to the door.

Outside, I was surprised to find Persy waiting in a slinking gown of what appeared to be dried roses and rubies. "Wow," she breathed, her eyes lined with dark shimmering dust.

Jarron stepped forward from behind her with a slight clearing of his throat. He bent at the waist, adjusting the sleeves of his dress jacket as he rose. "I am to escort you straight to Halfway Hall."

Persy, still smiling at me, elbowed him.

He shot a glower her way, but his expression softened marginally as he looked back at me. "And I must also offer my sincerest apologies. It was not my place to speak of things better discussed with you and the prince."

Persy coughed.

Jarron straightened with a smirk. "Nor should I have been a rude, arrogant toad during our other encounters."

I withheld a smile and refrained from biting my lips, which had been painted a gentle nude pink. "Do not apologize for your honesty." I gave a sidelong look at Persy. "I prefer it."

She winced, whispering, "I'm sorry, Fia. It just all worked out so well, and I couldn't betray him or—"

"But you would betray me." It was unfair of me to say as much, I knew. Colvin had been her friend first, not to mention her prince. I closed my eyes momentarily, then opened them and took Jarron's arm when he offered it. "Don't do it again."

Persy nodded, giving me a grateful, tremulous smile, and slid her arm through Jarron's.

"Are we ready?" he asked.

"No," I said.

At the same time, Persy gave an enthusiastic, "Yes."

Jarron's low chuckle accompanied us into the twisting wreath of darkness that tore us from the hall outside my rooms to transport us halfway across the continent.

Halfway Hall was aglow through the thin line of trees we materialized before.

Fire danced toward the brightening sky from tall maypoles in the shape of circles and stars. The outline of the long, wooden hall was made clear by the twinkling orbs of fireflies hanging from the roof upon looping string and vines.

Many a gilded and plain carriage, horses, and even some wagons, were parked within the woods encircling the clearing. Even a cluster of Pegasuses stood tied to elms, two reptilians with smoking stems standing guard over them.

Jarron loosened his tight hold for me to pull free. Persy remained at his side as he said to me, "Your uncle awaits you outside the entrance to the hall."

The pieces of bread I'd forced myself to eat before Ilena's arrival turned to little stones in my stomach. "He will escort me to Colvin," I said rather than asked. That I hadn't thought of that before now was a testament to how thoroughly enmeshed in Colvin and this new world I had become.

Jarron's eyes narrowed while Persy slowly nodded. Attempting to defuse my discomfort, she said, "I wouldn't be surprised if he doesn't even recognize you." Jarron's attention went to the trees as a dark carriage arrived on the other side of the clearing. "You look like an Unseelie queen."

I scoffed, but my feigned smile flattened when I quit trying to catch a glimpse of the giant carriage and looked at Persy. Her eyes dipped over me, filled with what seemed alarmingly a lot like tears. "Beautiful."

"Don't cry," I warned, and I knew she understood why when I looked away and straightened my shoulders. It was hard enough to believe this day was here, let alone manage the onslaught of anxiety I hadn't but perhaps should have expected.

I nearly jumped when a soft hand wrapped around mine and squeezed, and I glowered when Persy laid her head upon my shoulder and grinned. "You're magnificent. So just let everyone see, and then we can go home."

Home.

The anger I'd sat with for hours until it had become a small ember in my chest threatened to spark anew. I swallowed it down by reminding myself that I wouldn't change anything even if I could.

I would still choose him.

Maybe that was love. Maybe I was still too afraid to know. But

I did know with courage-spurning certainty that if I was capable of such a feeling, it was because of him. That this soul-seizing entity gripping each tender beat of my heart was because of him.

So when Jarron began to lead the way through the trees, Persy lifting my skirts from behind to keep from gathering forest debris, I followed instantly.

A path of glowing emerald grass, leaf-lined as though intentional, soon met us at the edge of the woods. None of us spoke as we trailed it toward the tall open doors of the hall.

It was teeming with energy, and though it might have been large, it evidently wasn't large enough as we soon passed finely dressed guests who waited and watched from outside. Those of Seelie blood stood on one side of the path and the Unseelie on the other. Surprisingly, neither gave any indication of harsh judgment. Though the Seelie attendees, some of whom I recognized from Brolen's many balls, did ogle with overt curiosity.

The skies behind us began to swarm with those giant bats. In slow loops and with keening cries, they darkened the dawn but didn't dare breach the clearing to find their queen. Being neutral ground, the hall itself would be empty of guards unless they were guests bearing witness to the nuptials.

Across the clearing, the silver armor of the Seelie soldiers gleamed in the growing absence of night. Reptilian warriors came forward to stand watch in leather and scales along the tree line we'd left at our backs.

The hall might have been a place for both courts to convene in peace, but given the events that had brought us to this day, it was clear neither was taking any chances.

Brolen awaited us some feet from the doors, Jarron stiffening and turning back to look at me.

I nodded, and he and Persy walked ahead while I tried to keep my hatred from permeating into something so obvious that conflict might arise.

As if sensing it anyway, Brolen's mouth curved. "You survived."

I walked on, even though the flute I'd been forewarned about by Ilena hadn't yet sounded.

Brolen took my arm, still smirking as I stopped and curled my upper lip. "We can do this without you touching me."

"But that would be in poor taste," he muttered between his lips, smiling at one of the nobles who eyed us carefully from the side of the cleared path. "You do not wish to make a scene now, do you?" Then he huffed, murmuring, "But of course, how foolish of me to forget how much you adore trouble."

Before I could respond, the haunting call of the flute sounded.

Within moments, the drums followed, pounding in rhythm with my descending heartbeat when Brolen leaned close to whisper in my ear as we entered the tree-shaped doors. "Uncanny, isn't it, feral Fia? How the goddesses always find a way to deliver us that which we covet." With a hard pat on my hand he'd draped over his arm, he guided me forward.

My attempt to unravel his words failed as he led me down a long runner of gleaming moss. It lined the center of the cavernous hall, row after row of vine-wreathed tree stumps spread either side in a circular formation, and delivered us to the makeshift dais.

It too was covered in moss but with white flowers surrounding the edging. Beyond it, two large hexagonal windows, one blue with a butter yellow sun and the other violet with a silver moon, watched over all.

In a petal-trimmed gown of dove gray silk, Olette sat cross-legged in the front row with Jarron and Persy, Persy's father beside her. On the other side of the walkway, my aunt waved with wriggling fingers. Grim-faced and stiff-shouldered, Regin was staring not at me but at the dais. His father sat beside him in a similar fashion, an empty stump beside them awaiting Brolen.

Light danced from more fireflies in vials and jars, the vines and twine holding them hung from the patchwork of rafters in the ceiling. Beneath a skylight of a moon meeting a sun, we slowed in the growing puddle of dawn.

And I finally allowed myself to look at the male who'd been watching me since I'd entered the hall, his attention akin to the sun's kiss upon my skin.

Perhaps that was why I'd never miss it—living within daylight hours.

My prince stood with his proud chin high and his hands behind his back in a long brocade jacket of deep obsidian and plum, a matching black cravat in rippling silk at his throat. His burnished eyes fastened tighter to me upon gaining my attention. Though he kept his expression carefully blank, he shifted slightly in his smooth leather boots.

A sidelong glance at my uncle fractured his calm veneer, and rather than wait, Colvin stepped down from the dais to take me from him.

Brolen made a sound of distaste, but it was barely heard beneath the slowing beat of the drums.

The Unseelie prince swept into a deep bow, a strand of hair falling free from the ribbon at his nape when his head rose with his offered hand. I hadn't been wholly informed of the Unseelie wedding traditions, but I did know that this particular wedding of ours would be a blend of both kingdoms customs.

Regardless, Colvin's actions didn't just shock me. A few murmurs erupted from those in the audience behind at the show of submission.

I placed my hand in his and pulled my arm from Brolen, who stood still as stone as if trying to withhold a scathing remark. The prince's eyes refused to release mine as he brought my hand to his mouth for his lips to graze my knuckles.

Brolen made another noise, but he was ignored.

The entire hall fell away as Colvin turned my hand over to press his mouth to the inside of my wrist. He inhaled deeply, his lashes lowering to a close. Then he finally straightened.

But he did not relinquish his hold, whispering to my hair once Brolen had marched to his seat beside Mirra, "I wasn't certain you would show."

I said as quietly as I could, a twitch to my lips, "Was there another option I was not made aware of?"

Colvin's head reared back enough for his eyes to search my face, his brows low. I looked at his parted lips, releasing a shaken breath, and squeezed his hand. It was all I could manage, unwilling to be overheard and unsure what to say.

He escorted me up the steps of the dais and to the awaiting priestess.

The white-haired female laid dark cobalt eyes upon our hands and cleared her throat. "Very well." A band of thorns had been inked into her forehead and I noticed her teeth were all sharpened to perilous points when she parted her stained ruby lips to smile and murmur, "Let us begin, then."

Colvin took my other hand, his fingers sliding over mine and clasping them, and though I tried, I couldn't not look at him as the priestess paid homage to the goddesses of night and day. Everyone rose, repeating after the priestess, then seated themselves. My gaze lifted from the silk covering Colvin's neck to his jaw.

He'd shaved, but only enough to present respectability, that thick strand of hair falling over the harsh rise of his cheek to brush against the dusting of facial hair below. His porcelain skin remained still, free of markings gifted from the sun, but his lips spread as if the touch of my eyes upon them prompted them to.

Our hands rose and fingers linked when instructed, and I could no longer avoid the fierce pull that lured my eyes to his. They met, and the sun seemed to awaken further. It fell through the windows and skylight in a milky, bone-stirring flood.

Even the priestess wavered in her hymns, but only momentarily.

I swallowed when she finished and said, "Repeat after me."

Colvin was first, his smooth and unfaltering voice drawing all breath from my lungs. "By the dark of the sky and the light of the stars, I vow to protect and cherish thee, Fia Callula, until death do we part."

I was to repeat the same verse. An Unseelie scripture, for that was whom I was to become. A princess of the dark court.

I lifted my chin and tightened my hold on Colvin while the priestess finished entwining our folded hands in a spider silk so soft it was nearly translucent. My voice was far gentler but no less resolute as I exhaled a leaden breath and said, "By the dark of the sky and the light of the stars, I vow to protect and cherish thee, Colvin Eldorn, until death do we part."

Colvin's mouth curved, a flash of his teeth appearing.

The sight kept me from noticing the priestess, whose blade broke the spider silk and sliced between our enclosed hands. It nicked our flesh and pierced it. But we didn't let go as a goblet collected our combined blood. "Seal your pledge, and so it shall be," the priestess murmured, but her voice carried into the deathly silence of the hall.

She turned to the podium behind her and twisted back with two large goblets. With an incline of her head, the priestess retreated while Colvin turned us to our audience. Following his lead, I raised my goblet when he did, and we both drank.

There wasn't much, and I drained the contents. Our goblets were collected when we turned back to one another.

Colvin captured my hand, drew my palm to his mouth, and kissed the cut. His eyes aglow on mine, he gathered me at the waist with his other hand until our chests met. "A bride is not expected to kiss her groom during our ceremonies," he whispered to my hair, his head lowering for his nose to skim my cheek. "But I know they are in yours, so I find myself desperate to make sure we pay respect to both customs."

"Desperate?" I teased, barely a sound.

He hummed, releasing my hand to tilt my chin high. My eyes swam into liquid gold and then fluttered closed when his mouth brushed across mine.

Before I could kiss him back, he seized, and his touch fell away. His heat fled so rapidly that I shivered when I opened my eyes in time to see Colvin's flare wide and turn red.

A flood of accusation narrowed them as he placed a hand over his chest and coughed, then wheezed, "Fia…" He stumbled backward.

I called his name and made to follow as he fell and hit the ground to the sound of gasps and murmurs, but I was grabbed from behind. My arms swung to smack whoever it was until they too were caught, and I was pulled backward from the dais.

The hall exploded into uproar—seats overturned, feet scurrying, and then the room began to grow dark.

Not with the encroaching creatures and armed forces from outside, but my vision.

"Regin?" I mumbled, recognizing the face that swam into half-focus as I was dragged toward the rear exit behind the dais. "Regin, what—"

"Hold on, Fi." Then I was in his arms. His scent was wrong but comforting until I remembered and pushed, trying to get free. "Wait, Fia. Almost there. It'll be over soon."

It was akin to being trapped within a nightmare I couldn't escape, my efforts in vain and only causing Regin's hold on me to tighten.

"Colvin," I yelled or thought I did, but it was a garbled rasp.

A roar ruptured the sickening sludge entering my limbs and mind—and the ceiling of the hall.

Wood splintered, and it groaned like a dying beast as it flew in burning shards into the clearing. Some guests screamed and ran, but not from the raining debris.

From the dragon who rose from the hall.

His wings blocked out the sun as they spread, and he released his rage. A screeched, thunderous roar shattered my next breath, forcing my eyes to open when I hadn't given them permission to close.

"Hurry," Regin barked, running now, running and cursing as he tripped on my dress.

Brolen's mocking warning from earlier returned, but too late. This wasn't merely trouble. It was bad. Really bad. A thousand times worse than bad. I groaned, my tongue too thick in my mouth. "Regin, take me back."

He either ignored or didn't understand me, for he didn't falter, and he didn't respond. My heavy eyes begged to close. I surrendered, and they didn't reopen until I was placed upon the ground while Regin mounted his horse. "Pass her up," he said to someone I couldn't see.

Strong arms hefted me over the saddle, but I flopped, the world twirling with both shadow and sunlight. Regin cursed again, turning and tugging me until I was half draped over him, my head at his shoulder.

Hooves pounding against the soil roused me what could have been seconds, minutes, or hours later. My eyes opened one last time—in time to see the dragon prince flying north, two screaming bodies within his grasp.

My roiling stomach heaved, and I forced back the urge to vomit upon the grass I woke on.

A tent enclosed me. A bedroll, still tied and untouched, and a lamp sat to my right, but I'd been left on the ground in my gown like a sack of overflowing grain. A sticky residue coated my mouth and glued my lips together.

I pried them apart to call for Colvin when murky patches of memory stitched together enough for me to form a pale understanding of where I was.

I wasn't with Colvin.

My eyes closed over the threat of tears when I recalled how I'd last seen him—flying through the brightening sky with his next meals.

I was certain Colvin hadn't needed to change. He wouldn't have ignored the signs and put so many people in peril if he'd had any doubts. Remembering the way he'd clutched at his chest while staring right at me...

He had to have been poisoned.

I reached for the canteen by the tent flap, scenting it before deciding it wasn't worth it. Whatever it was Brolen had given us still crawled through my veins like a sickness. Why he'd done such a thing, I didn't know. Perhaps to separate us.

Perhaps to kill a dragon.

But he hadn't. That alone was enough to help me focus on taking calm, even breaths. Voices drifted around the crackling of a campfire outside, and I stilled to listen.

"...should leave now, just to be safe."

"He survived," Regin said. "We all saw it. Nowhere is safe."

There was silence, and then a feminine voice I hadn't expected murmured, "It needs time. He changed because he entered survival mode." Sylvane paused, then said firmly, "It will work. We created more than what was necessary, so it has to."

My heart splintered.

So both of our goblets had been laced, but evidently not with the same thing. For they hadn't just poisoned us to tear us apart—to attack or take the dragon prince while he was in Fae form and weakened.

They'd poisoned Colvin with the intent to kill.

Regin said gently, "But then what, Syl? The repercussions of this..." his words faded into a rough curse.

"Brolen said whatever comes our way cannot be any worse than a dragon's wrath."

"We've done our kin a favor," a voice I didn't recognize said. "Even if war comes for us, they will call us heroes."

No one spoke for a time after that, as if none of them quite believed what the male had said.

It took every remaining morsel of strength I had to keep from charging out of the tent to smash the lamp beside me into each of their heads. Not only would I fail, being that soldiers were snoring in tents within feet of me, but I would likely end up bound or, worse, drugged again.

And if what they'd said was true...

Fear tied a noose around my heart. I needed to find Colvin as fast as possible.

When it seemed only Sylvane and Regin remained by the fire, their soft murmurs making my skin itch and my blood boil, I knew

I might not be presented with a better opportunity. I crawled out of the tent and feigned a yawning groan as though I'd just woken up.

And then I froze.

Regin did, too, pulling his mouth from Sylvane's. Upon his lap, her hands clasped to his shoulders, the noble's daughter scowled my way. "Why wasn't she tied up?"

Regin set her down on the grass, then rose. "Fia's not a prisoner, Syl."

Sylvane eyed me with overt hostility. "She wed a dragon." Disgust twisted her porcelain features. "*Kissed it.* She's not to be trusted."

"She did so because she had to," Regin said, exasperated enough to suggest he'd had to remind her of this a few dozen times. "Hi, Fi," he said, crouching before me with a sheepish smile.

"Sorry to interrupt," I said in a way that implied I wasn't sorry at all. "But where beneath the moon have you taken me? And what gave you the impression that you could do so in the first place?"

With a glance over his shoulder at Sylvane, Regin sighed and then offered me his hand. "Come on. I'll explain."

I refused his hand but followed.

I watched Sylvane foolishly disappear into a tent—leaving the encampment under little to no guard as Regin escorted me deeper into the trees toward the river. I knelt upon the vegetated bank to splash some water over my face and rinse my mouth.

I choked and spat it out when Regin had the gall to say, "I'm still waiting on a thank-you."

"A thank you?" I growled, rising on shaking legs.

Regin rubbed at the back of his head. "Look, I can explain about Sylvane—"

"You think I give a shit about you and Sylvane?" I marched closer, seething as he frowned. "You poisoned my husband and me, and then took me against my will."

"Fi." Regin's laughter was more of a nervous release of breath. "We *saved* you."

"Did I look like I needed saving?" I stopped before I could get close enough to punch him. "By the moon, what is wrong with you? I didn't want any of this, Regin."

"I know." Regin licked his lips, still misunderstanding. "Brolen said he'll pardon you once the dragon is dead. So now, we take our time in journeying home and hope that happens along the way."

I nearly screamed with both frustration and fear. "Regin, please, I need you to actually listen to me." I waited until I had his full attention, his arms crossing over his chest and a small twitch to his mouth. "Brolen is not my uncle. He's my father. He forced my mother to fuck him when Mirra couldn't provide him with an heir."

"What?" Regin laughed out, then blinked when I just glared. "Fia, no."

I reared back, his refusal to believe me like that of a blow to the chest.

He stepped forward, hands raised. "Why would he order your execution if you were his daughter, Fia?"

"Because I'm nothing more than what was expected of him, a tool, Regin," I said. "And the moment I became more of a burden than I already was, he took the opportunity to..." I stilled as it dawned.

He knew, I didn't say.

"To be done with me," I finished, the words but a whisper as my eyes fell upon the sodden leaves catching at the tattered hem of my wedding gown.

Brolen had known, or he'd at least suspected, that I was the prince's mate. Which meant he too was aware of the only record of another dragon in our history to have found a mate.

"Fia?" Regin questioned. "Are you okay?" I shook my head, stepping away when he made to touch my arm. "I'm sorry, okay? I've only ever wanted what was best for you. You have to believe that."

I did believe it. That in his own arrogantly warped way, he did want just that.

But I was too afraid, too enraged, to keep from asking, "Then has it ever occurred to you that I might not be miserable, Regin?" His features scrunched. "Has it once crossed your mind that I might not want to be rescued? That what's best for me is to simply leave the prince and me alone?"

"Fi," he protested, disbelief widening his eyes.

My words thickened with anguish. "Has it occurred to you that I might want to lead the army Olette sends to Callula myself if what you've all plotted comes to fruition and my mate dies?"

Regin balked. "Mate?"

My chest heaved, tears scalding my cheeks. I nodded.

He swallowed, his eyes closing. "Fuck, Fia. No."

"It's true, and because of it, he's not a monster. Not when he has me." My lungs tightened painfully at the thought of him suffering, of not reaching him in time to find a way to reverse what they'd done to him. For there had to be a way. I refused to believe there wasn't.

I had to go.

Regin glowered, seemingly still in shock. "You can't stop him from changing into a bloodthirsty monster. He's a dragon, Fia, not a critter or a mule."

"But I can stop him from hunting what he shouldn't when he does change."

His features fell lax. "The mating connection?"

I nodded, taking his hand and squeezing. "If you truly want to save me, then give me a horse." I squeezed harder. My voice croaked as I tried to keep the rising terror from clawing free. "Let me go. I have to go."

Regin swiped at the wet on my cheek. "Fia."

"Please." My eyes closed, but more tears still escaped.

Regin watched me for chest-cinching moments when they opened, then exhaled heavily. "I don't think you can fix this, Fi," he said, sounding as though he was beginning to feel remorse for his part in it. "I'm sorry."

I released him and ran toward the horses tethered to the trees upstream, unwilling to waste another moment or fall victim to the creeping darkness that told me my efforts would be in vain.

TWENTY-EIGHT

Fia

HALFWAY HALL WAS IN SMOKING RUINS BY THE TIME I reached it some agonizing hours later. Tendrils curled toward the starlit sky, reaching for the clouds rolling across the scythe moon.

Keeping to the deeper foliage of the woods in an effort not to be captured again, I tried and failed to see much.

But I heard them. Reptilian warriors patrolling the border of Eldorn in the trees up ahead.

Rather than avoid them, I dug my heels into the mare I'd stolen, and we took off in a gallop straight for them. It would take days to reach Castle Eldorn, and that was time we didn't have.

Perhaps being captured wouldn't be so bad, so long as it took me where I needed to be.

We slowed, and I lifted my hands as soon as they heard my approach, calling, "It's me—Fia."

A warrior turned, a second running with stunning speed from his post near the clearing of the hall to join him. The first warrior had a torn tunic and a scar cutting through his scaled cheek. He sneered. "Decided to turn yourself in, traitor? Wise. The queen might let you live a few minutes longer."

The other warrior drew his dagger from a leather sheath at his waist, releasing a sound like that of a growled and gargled exhale.

My mount tried to retreat, but I held her firm and said, "I come with no ill intent or guilt. I simply wish to be taken to the prince."

"So you can finish him off?" the scarred male asked, huffing.

"Un-fucking-likely, *Princess*." He spat at the ground, his vibrant eyes thinning.

Fed up, I slid from the horse, and the warriors growled in warning.

My aching thighs cramped and shook, and I gripped the saddle to help steady myself. "I need to materialize back to the castle, but I don't have the ability. If you won't help me, then take me to someone who will."

The creature with the dagger flicked out a slightly forked tongue as if scenting where I'd been. He confirmed as such when his thin brows lowered. "Smell that? She's been with her own ilk."

"Smells like a Seelie whore." His comrade scrunched his features and came forward. Menace gleamed within his bright eyes. "And they're always more fucking trouble than they're worth."

I swallowed but remained where I was, frowning when the advancing warrior froze and turned his head over his shoulder.

Shadows coalesced and separated behind the males, a familiar warrior with long, braided hair appearing. "If the princess doesn't want your rotten tongue, Kilros, I'll surely take it." Persy's father snarled at the shocked males, and they begrudgingly retreated a healthy distance from me.

Kilros directed his enraged glower from the queen's favored general to me. "She's no princess of ours. She conspired with her family to take down our prince."

The other male nodded, but he sheathed his weapon. "You saw it yourself, Morthan. You know they're saying this will kill him."

My throat closed, the little resolve I'd held on to fraying fast.

Morthan ordered, "Enough." Then he eyed me. "Regardless of what she may or may not have done, she is still the prince's wife, and you will treat her with the respect she is owed unless ordered otherwise."

"Can you please take me back?" I asked as soon as he was done speaking.

Morthan cocked his head, sharp nails scraping over the scales lining his neck and jaw as he pondered me. "And what is it you hope to accomplish, asides from more upset? For everyone is in a right state as it is."

I didn't doubt they were, and clearly, he was too worried and wary to help me. Though I couldn't blame him, I didn't have the luxury of waiting while he tried to gently deny me. I turned to mount the mare. "Forget it. I'll take myself."

But Morthan said, "Send the horse back."

The two males behind him cursed, but the withering look he gave them made even me pause as I climbed off, my limbs no better than quaking liquid once my slippered feet hit the ground.

Morthan appeared at my side and gripped my arm to steady me. "What happened to you?"

"My goblet was laced too."

The queen's general immediately smacked the horse's rear, and she charged back through the woods to Callula.

He gave his glaring warriors orders to return to their posts, then clutched me to his side. "Best hold on tight, then."

I hadn't known what to expect, but to arrive outside of the moss-and-ivy-covered wall encircling the front half of the castle was not what I'd had in mind at all.

"Stay here," Morthan ordered, ensuring I was stable on my feet before marching toward the gates.

I was tempted to argue, but I understood that his brethren must have been right when he materialized again. I was now considered a traitor, even though I'd done nothing wrong. Otherwise, he'd have materialized straight to wherever the prince was being cared for with me.

A few torturous minutes later, the imposing gates creaked open, stirring night birds from their nests in the trees surrounding the expansive grounds.

I half-wondered if more warriors would appear. There was only silence as the wisteria-heavy gates ceased their screeching, the over-grown rock-paved drive with its empty fountain exposed within.

The giant oak doors didn't open. I was certain they rarely did.

The queen materialized into the courtyard, still in her gown, but her intricate updo was now disheveled. Her crimson lips were raw with worry. "Morthan tells me your goblet was laced," she said by way of greeting.

Extending my wrist, I offered it to her.

She stared at it, a ragged laugh bursting free. "You think I need to drink from you to believe it?" Disapproval thinned her mouth, and she wrapped her arms around her waist. "I don't doubt it's true, but I still wonder why you bothered to come back when you now have no reason to."

My knees buckled.

Olette's eyes lowered to them as I forced myself to move a step forward in fear of falling. "He can't be…" I would've felt it, surely. I couldn't be too late. I could still do something. I refused to believe there was nothing to be done.

And it infuriated me that everyone seemed to think that was the case.

"Not yet," she said with a shaken sigh. "But there's nothing we can do but wait."

"Let me see him," I urged, closing some of the distance between us. "I need to see him." But Olette wouldn't move, wouldn't relinquish the cool press of her eyes upon my every feature. I stumbled back a step. "You think I meant for this to happen?" I asked, so bewildered that an incredulous laugh escaped. "I knew *nothing* of this."

"We know you didn't have a hand in the ceremony sabotage, but to create bone milk, someone had to have had access to the Blood Bound Book." Her eyes darkened. "And only one creature can open that book, Fia."

"It is the poison he sought, then. Bone milk," I said, so soft, as though the name itself might extinguish the hope I was clutching to keep from drowning.

Olette nodded. "No other concoction would make him this ill."

"But I can get the book. There has to be something in there that we can—"

"We stand no chance of getting that book without enormous force. Even if we did, some poisons are designed to stay with their hosts, even long after they…" She stopped and released a breath. "It's clear he was given quadruple the amount he would've tested upon himself, and even that tiny amount would've likely been enough to…" She needn't have said it, and I understood why she couldn't— was grateful for it.

The thought alone, of existing when he did not, not only stopped the beat of my heart—it shadowed everything he'd colored. I couldn't do it. I couldn't imagine this life without him. All that had come before seemed a dull dream I'd finally been shaken awake from.

I wouldn't survive in such a state again.

I'd thought after everything, I could survive anything. That I'd never be so weak again. Yet what I'd endured and found had made me both untouchable and never more vulnerable.

To lose it, to lose him…

Unconquerable.

The queen watched me. Then she swallowed and turned to the doors, defeat thickening her voice. "Beneath the castle, there are two tunnels. One leads into the woods, and the other to a cave housing healing springs—you'll find him in the springs."

She vanished not a second later, and I swiped furiously at my eyes before racing toward the opening doors. They slammed behind me, sconces flaring to life upon the walls as I raced through the portrait-lined foyer and skidded into the adjoining hall to the stairwell.

I followed it down as deep as it would go, knowing I'd need to search the lowest level for another set of stairs to reach the cave.

I didn't need to.

I halted where I should've had to leave—where the stairs should've ended. But the wall was a hidden door made of stone.

And it had been left ajar.

I pulled it open. The steps upon the other side were rockier and damp, winding down beneath the foundation of the giant fortress above. The tunnel was riddled with rusted pipes and so dark that I could barely see what lay below my feet, let alone what awaited up ahead.

My slippers were soon submerged in water, the hem and ruined train of my gown sodden.

But I moved faster when I heard it—bubbling water and groaning. Leading away from the castle, the tunnel opened into a giant cave, the night sky peeking in through small gaps in the rock formation to light the space just enough to see.

Giant boulders encircled the crystalline springs that nearly filled the entirety of the cave.

Rocks, sharp and ancient and watching, pressed in from all sides of the space, overlooked it with moss markings and age-worn grooves. They curved and smoothed toward the cave's ceiling to welcome the elements and the moon via a hole wide enough for a large male to fit through.

Directly beneath it, not in the water but shivering upon a flat rock in the shadows on the other side of the largest pool, was Colvin.

The only way to him appeared to be through the water. I didn't stop to think of how I might accomplish that while wearing a gown that weighed almost as much as me.

I hiked up my skirts and stepped into the warm, shimmering depths, readying to tear the clothing from my body when he spoke. "Leave."

"It's me," I said, water sloshing as I slipped and stumbled to a stop.

Sweat gleamed upon his back, muscle bulging when he spasmed violently. His warning was growled. "I said leave."

I shook my head, though he couldn't see. "I'm not going anywhere until—"

"I think you've done enough, Fia." His voice was guttural, not only with anger but also with pain as he pushed the words free. "I was just too fucking intoxicated, too jealous…" He groaned, and my every limb tensed, wanting to move, needing to get closer to him. "I couldn't see what you'd done, and right beneath my nose."

My rasping question echoed. "What do you mean?"

He laughed, then coughed out, "The fucking book."

"I haven't touched the book, Colvin."

"Turns out, you never needed to," he said. "You just needed an opportunity to give your blood to someone within reach of it."

About to refute that too, words dried over my tongue when I stopped.

As surely, that was the only way it could have been opened. I skimmed through my mind, desperate to recall when I'd injured myself, and my stomach soured. "The engagement ball," I whispered. "Regin." The remorse I'd glimpsed from him at his encampment now made more agonizing sense.

He hadn't attended the ball to check on me, to reassure me that someone wanted and missed me.

He'd been on a mission to steal my blood to murder my mate.

Colvin said nothing, just curled deeper into the overhang of a jutting rock in the wall—farther out of view.

"Regin, he…" I tried to remember, but there was nothing. I hadn't seen him take it, but he must have. There was no other way. "I cut my hand on my wineglass when he ran into me, but I didn't see him do it."

"How uncanny," Colvin drawled thickly. "That a creature with such instincts, a soldier no less, can simply walk into you hard enough to accidentally injure you."

"Colvin, I promise I didn't—"

"It's a little too late for promises, fire-breather. A part of you has loathed me from the moment I returned to take you and will eternally think me nothing more than a monster moon-sworn to ruin your life." I tried to speak, but he continued, scathingly gentle, "And I was a blind fool to even try to make you believe otherwise."

"I don't hate you," I stated, my chest unbearably tight. "I hated what you made me feel and that you took me away from all I knew, but you never really took anything—you gave me everything." Tears burned down my cheeks, flowing harder when he refused to respond. "I didn't mean for any of this—"

"Do you know what hurts more than dying, Fia?" he asked, but he didn't wait for an answer. "The sound of your voice."

My eyes closed. My fingers squeezing my skirts too hard.

I had to go. I should've already left, yet the idea of doing so drew more blood than his cruel words.

"Fine," I eventually said, my tears splashing into the water before I swiped them free of my cheeks and retreated. "Refuse to believe me, but don't you dare leave me." I waited, knowing I was wasting time but unable to make myself move—to remove my eyes from his heaving form. "You promised, dragon." Hoarse, I whispered and watched him grow still, "Until every star burns out."

His silence echoed louder than the water I waded through to head back into the tunnel.

Persy was leaning against the wall inside the stairwell, and I flinched, awaiting her own accusations and anger. But she whispered, "I believe you. I'm sure he does too, Fia. He just..." her head shook, eyes reddened from crying. "He can't right now."

I blinked, then I surprised us both by leaping at her to wrap my arms around her neck. "Help me."

She squeezed me. "Whatever you need."

"I need that book." I stood back and brushed my hand beneath my nose. "And I need your father to take me to it."

"I'll do it," a voice said from above, and we both looked up at Jarron, who stood atop the stairs. "I've been inside that castle more than Morthan anyway, which will help with hopefully going unseen."

I didn't wait, nor did I question whether he believed me or not. He wanted to help, and that was all I needed as I raced up the stairs, and we materialized to Callula.

TWENTY-NINE

Fia

MY SENSES CRUMBLED AT THE RETURN OF WHAT I'D ALWAYS known.

But there was no time to appreciate the home I'd thought I might never see again. No time to marvel at the library's enormous, floor-to-ceiling shelves that stretched far beyond the second floor we'd materialized beneath.

Nor could I give room to nostalgia for the paintings I'd once poked fun at with Regin, and the aroma of worn pages, freshly cut wildflowers, and clean linen upon the air creeping in from beneath the library's imposing entrance.

There was little point.

It was not my home anymore.

"Wait here," I whispered, indicating the dark alcove behind a statue of an ancient Seelie scholar. "If someone comes, then leave and return later."

Jarron gestured ahead. "I'm not going anywhere. Just keep moving."

I wasn't sure if he was following for my safety or because he still didn't trust me. So long as he didn't get us caught, it didn't matter.

But as I'd begun to suspect, the library was curiously empty.

I still wove through the aisles of books I'd once danced between with quiet caution, my wet skirts dragging over the flagstone with a scraping hiss. Jarron followed, a silent comfort at my back as we slowly wended our way closer to the goblin-sized door hidden beneath the absent clerk's desk.

"No one's here," I said, stopping a row away from the desk and turning to Jarron. "That's not normal, especially given what happened. Unless," I felt my heart droop, though I had known it was a likelihood, "the book isn't here."

I had hoped with far too much certainty that in my absence, and after what he'd done, Brolen would have surrendered the Blood Bound Book to its rightful home in the library. We'd need to search his study, then, and perhaps his rooms, which did not bode well—

"No one is here because I sent them away," said a familiar voice.

Jarron gripped my arm, ready to leave.

But I looked at him, gesturing to wait, as I lowered my head to peek over the row of books we stood behind.

There, on the floor behind the desk, was a pair of legs. A crystal decanter sat beside them. "Mirra?"

"Cease dawdling, darling. Everyone knows I'm not to be trusted with a priceless heirloom for too long." A shrill laugh was cut short by a gasp when Jarron and I revealed ourselves at the end of the aisle. "Oh, Fifi." I took a hesitant step closer to where my aunt sat on the floor, her frilled skirts placed just so and her hand pressed to her bosom. "I know you're not typically one to appreciate the art of beautiful clothing, but what you've done to that gown is a traumatizing tragedy indeed."

I needn't have glanced at my wedding gown to know what she'd meant. I was well aware. My eyes stayed glued to the book in her lap.

The open book.

"Is that...?"

"The Blood Bound Book?" Aunt Mirra smiled. "But of course it is. They refuse to close it just yet." She feigned doing so herself, her slender fingers tilting the worn edges of the hardback tome, pages falling, then she laughed. "Oh, stop it. Here," she laid the book back down and offered the decanter, "have a drink. You look as though you need it and far more than usual." Her ice-blue gaze swayed from me to Jarron. "Just who might you be?"

Jarron stiffened beside me, and I withheld a snort at his comical, dumbfounded expression.

Mirra just wiggled her fingers.

"This is Jarron, and he's mated, Mirra."

She pouted. "How dreadful for you, dear." Then her eyes fell upon me, some of her mirth fading. "They scour half the land for you, you know."

I didn't need to, but I still asked, "Why?"

"He wants you dead, Fifi." She shook her head as if I should've known. "So here, come take your book and leave before someone discovers you. You're not safe here."

"Has anyone been guarding the book?"

"No one but Frensloth," she said, referring to the library's clerk. "I sent him on a fool's mission to the city in search of a historical artifact so rare, it does not exist, but it won't be much longer before he realizes."

"Why wouldn't the book be better protected?" Jarron asked.

Mirra fluttered her lashes up at him, a finger dragging over a faded page of writing in her lap. "Why should it be? It remains open just in case the dosage is wrong and the dragon does not die. Brolen knows there is nothing you or anyone else can do with it now." Mirra's dancing eyes drifted to me. "I might have forgotten to remind him that he has a bad habit of underestimating you."

Tempted to smile, I couldn't. I needed to know. "What do you mean there is nothing else we can do with it?"

In answer, she held out the book, and I lowered to the ground beside her.

It was lighter than I'd expected for its size, which was possibly three times that of a regular hardbound book. The edges were worn, soft although stained with the blood of its many owners, and I needn't have bothered trying to find the pages I needed.

They already awaited me.

Jarron read over my shoulder, faster than me, and cursed. "Turn it over."

I turned the page, but there were old depictions of rare flowers—a different poison for a different beast. A cross-species of large, blood-lusting felines that had been wiped clean of Eldorn over half a century ago.

"But there has to be something." I refused to believe that was it. That all of these potions and poisons and pages were for nothing more than inflicting harm—that there were no instructions on how to heal.

I flipped through as many pages as I could, not realizing I was crying until a hand fell over mine and stopped me near the back of the book.

Mirra said with surprising gentleness, "When you were a babe, you didn't cry. It was the most peculiar thing. The nursemaid thought you sickly, but I knew better." Turning my chin, Mirra brushed at my wet cheeks. "You were too curious, too amazed at even the tiniest things. A fly buzzing too close to your nose. A patch of sunlight dancing upon the ceiling. A storm grumbling in the distance..."

I tried to make the tears stop, but there was no stopping what caused them. A chasm in my chest had yawned open. It widened and hollowed with every useless breath taken and page turned, and I couldn't make it close.

Its very existence warned that it would never close.

"Don't let that curiosity fail you now, Fifi. Turn those pages the other way."

I blinked, gazing back at her with blurred eyes.

She nodded to the book. I looked down at the tearstained pages in my lap and lifted them, letting them fall through my fingers like time.

Until I encountered the inscription in the front.

"Every time a new inscription is made, the previous one is erased by their blood," Mirra said, her long fingers reverently seeking what I hadn't seen before.

My mother's handwriting.

In her blood, she'd written as neatly as one would have if using a trained hand and ink...

For my dearest daughter, Fia,

May you always live in favor of your heart and never lose sight of its chosen path.

There was nothing more. Though I ached for it, that was it.

But it was enough.

I traced each thick letter while Mirra murmured, "Primrose was not much older than you when she left me. She never had the chance to wonder, to dream, to explore all this land has to offer, but as I've watched you grow, it's impossible not to believe that she passed on those lost desires to you."

Mirra touched her sister's handwriting, too, stroked it with trembling fingers. Then she sighed, reached for the wine, and took a hearty swig. "Want some now?"

I shook my head, smiling. I closed the book and clasped Mirra's hand, squeezing it. "Thank you."

"Go save your dragon husband, Fifi, and by the moon," her face creased as she drank some more and observed my crumpled, damp state, "treat him better than you do your poor gowns."

Jarron, who'd been as still as one of the library statues beside the desk as he watched us, leaped into action to help me rise from the floor. With one last grateful look at Mirra, I hugged the book tight to my chest, and then Jarron took us home.

"But what will you do?" he asked as soon as our feet met the stone floor atop the stairwell on the lowest level of Castle Eldorn. His eyes dipped to the book I held. "There is no remedy in there."

I smiled at the book. "But there is. Here." I gave the troublesome tome to him. "Let Olette decide what to do with it."

Jarron frowned but gingerly took the book they'd all sought for so long, his eyes still upon me and riddled with questions. "I don't understand, Fia."

"You will soon, but there's something else I need to ask of you."

"Fix him, and I'll personally see to it that you get whatever you want."

"You're certain?" I questioned with a raised brow. "Whatever I want?"

Jarron tilted his head. "What are you implying?" He studied me for a few moments when I remained silent. Then finally, understanding darkened his eyes. "Just fix him, Princess." He vanished with the book.

And I hurried back to my prince.

Colvin was right where I left him.

He didn't so much as stir at my arrival. Nor when I tore free of the gown to enter the water in nothing but my tight shift. I crossed to where he lay and hauled myself onto a lower rock beside the one he'd curled upon.

I tried not to let panic take hold and, instead, forced myself still to try to listen.

He was breathing—short, rasped heaves of which the trickling water nearly veiled. Scalding relief warmed me, and I crawled up onto the giant rock to lay next to him. "Colvin."

There was no response, but he had to know I was here.

I pushed his sweat-slicked hair back from his cheek. Still, he remained silent, but my heart jumped when he opened his eyes.

They were a dark crimson, bloodshot with pain and flooded with hunger.

Veins pulsed at his temple, and as I dragged my fingers down his shoulder, I noted the same in his twitching bare arms. "I think I know how to help you," I whispered, unsure why, but it was likely his head ached. That everything ached wretchedly. I was also scared—worried he might send me away.

But I wasn't going anywhere.

I shifted closer as if he'd know what I intended when I tossed the wet ends of my hair over my shoulder. But he didn't move. He continued to watch me as he trembled, so I gently clasped his clammy bicep and pushed him to his back.

He finally spoke when I climbed atop him, careful to keep my knees astride his waist. "Fia, stop—"

I silenced him with my mouth on his, quick, hard, and breathing him in as I lifted my head for my eyes to meet his. "You need to drink as much of me as you can stomach." His eyes narrowed, lips parting to protest, but I said before he could, "Trust me."

Daring words considering all that had happened—all he'd thought I'd had a hand in doing.

He stared for so long, so still beneath me, that I feared he truly would push me away. As though he wanted to but couldn't, he snapped with a caustic snarl. He turned us until he was looming over me, my wrists gripped within his large hand above my head.

There was no warning, no gentle coaxing of my skin in preparation.

I didn't care. I wanted him to take what he needed.

But I still cried out when his teeth pierced the flesh at my neck. My back arched as he sucked, my blood rising to meet his greedy tongue. With sounds akin to an animal, a grunted series of groaning, moaning swallows, he drank me down with desperate relish.

And I held on to him for dear life as pain sliced me into tense, heaving ribbons.

My eyes closed. My hands trembled as I gripped the back of his head, fingers tangled in his hair.

Time passed in thresholds of pain and numbness, for the more he drank, the less it hurt. My shift was ripped down the center of my body by a talon and pried wide open. My mind began to swim with shadows, and I opened my eyes to stare up at the rock-hewn walls. The jagged ripples and sharp edges were brushed by the moon and stars, who watched through the small ceiling opening above the water.

What might've been minutes or hours later, a hand crawled down my side to my thigh, lifting it higher to slip between our bodies. Colvin licked at my neck. His trembling had ceased, but it was clear he wasn't done. That this was going to be far from an easy fix.

Fingers brushed over my core, both featherlight and bruising—my flesh too sensitive, painfully primed from his feeding.

His voice was edged, guttural, and I flinched at the sudden sound after so long without it. "You taste different."

"My goblet, it was—"

"And you reek of him." His mouth pressed to my skin, then his tongue, dragging and drugging. "Yet you crave me."

Another glide between my thighs, this time with his knuckles, and I opened for him like a flower meeting spring. "Yes."

"You will always crave me," he groaned into my neck. "But you've never wanted this."

I clutched his hair, fingertips firm at his scalp. "You're wrong. I've never wanted anything quite like I want this, which terrifies me. You terrified me." I swallowed, my throat unbearably dry. "You still do. Not your scales and fangs and talons, but your unrelenting heart."

His head lifted. Dark hair fell over his feverish gaze as it burned into mine.

I trailed my finger over his cheek. "I've never allowed myself to wholeheartedly want anything, Colvin, for I've never truly had something of my own." My smile shook, as did my voice. "Not until now."

His lips parted, brows hovering low.

"I do want this," I whispered, staring into his eyes. "Why won't you believe me?"

"You left me," he rumbled, lips moving down my chin in search of a new place to puncture. "You left in his arms while I tore someone's limbs from their body."

My lungs emptied, my heart ceasing to beat.

"You left with him, and I was left wondering if that was the last I'd see of you before I died." About to speak, I was hushed. Then lethally soft, he said, "Do you know what that does to someone like me? I fucking swear it's kept me alive." When I failed to find a quick response, he continued, voice rougher, "Do you know what made me return for you? What made me cease my futile hesitation and finally take you?"

His fingers grazed my clit, and I spasmed. "Colvin..."

"I'd heard." His finger slid lower, his whisper menacing beneath my ear. "I found out you'd been with him." His words raised every hair on my body and froze my seeking hips, his fingers leaving to skim my side and breast. "While you were riding his cock to forget me, I was here, struggling with guilt for what I'd need to do with this mate I'd searched so tirelessly for." A wicked laugh. "Filling your rooms with soaps and books and gowns..."

My eyes welled while I struggled to settle on how to feel about that. Anger and shame swept through me like a double-sided blade. "You took me for being with another male?"

"I did, and I'd do it again," he said, teeth nipping at my earlobe before his lips dropped to my racing pulse. "For it was only a matter of time." He licked it. "But now, my obsession, this horrific love I've fallen into that was supposed to save me..." He groaned. "It's destroying me."

"Colvin, I didn't leave you by choice," I said in a rush, tempted to scream. "My goblet was laced with some type of sleeping draught. I was taken."

"Oh?" he questioned, and though his search of my skin stalled, his tone was mocking. He didn't believe me. "And where were you taken?"

"To an encampment in Callula. But I told Regin everything, and he let me go."

"He just let you go?" he asked, disbelief hardening his words. "You mean to say after going to such lengths to steal my mate, he didn't so much as try to keep you for himself?" A dry, baffled laugh. "Fascinating."

My teeth gritted. "It was nothing like that."

"Nothing like this?" A hard thrust of his finger inside me.

I moaned. "Nothing at all. I would never." I grabbed his face and forced his eyes to mine. "I'm telling you the truth, and while I don't like that you took me because of Regin, I cannot deny that I'm glad you did."

His brows rose. Reddened, heavy-lidded eyes blinked slowly. "Then you must not have truly loved this Regin."

"No." I pulled his nose to mine, my confession searing. "But I do love you."

Colvin tensed and reared back.

"You made me fall in love with you, dragon, so please"—I sniffed, smiling up at him—"spend more time making sure you live and less being an archaic, possessive beast."

His throat bobbed, his eyes narrowed and cruel as if he still wouldn't quite let himself believe me. He stared, nostrils flaring and his jaw tight, for aching moments. Then his mouth slammed over mine. His cock impaled me, hard and punishing.

There was no other response to my words, nothing but a throaty hum, as though the beast within him warred with his typical rationality.

He chose the curve of my shoulder, groaning as he sank his teeth into my skin and his cock harder into my body. This time, it didn't hurt. He ground his hips against me while I moaned and fell limp, stolen by sensation.

Nothing was said for a long time.

I fell apart continuously, my back numb and scraped from the rock, but he didn't stop. He feasted as he needed—as I'd hoped and needed. He continued to fuck me even though he'd spilled himself inside me countless times. He drank from my neck and even my chest until I was fighting to remain conscious.

I must have failed, for I woke in the warm springs with a gasping start, Colvin holding me tight to his chest. "You shouldn't have done this, Fia."

That was the last thing I heard. My eyes closed again, and he cursed and carried me from the water.

I woke in my rooms, sore and nauseated.

My heart calmed when I saw Colvin asleep next to me, naked and mercifully breathing evenly. I pressed my hand to his shoulder, finding his skin cool and the tremors gone.

Then I rose from the bed and grabbed a riding smock and the first pair of britches I touched in the dressing room. I pulled them on as I quietly left my chambers. My thighs screamed, and I needed to place a hand on the wall in the hall to finish pulling the tight pants on.

I donned the navy smock and left it untucked, drawing in a few steadying breaths as I headed down the hall to the stairs. Spying a pitcher of water in a sitting room I passed on the level below, I back-tracked and drained half of it before continuing my search.

Jarron was in the grand foyer, appearing to have just left Olette's rooms. He slowed upon seeing me. "You look like shit."

I didn't care. "Are you ready?"

He stopped, boots squeaking on the mosaic floor, and arched a brow. "Are you?"

I smiled in answer, reaching back to braid my knotted hair.

He sighed but offered his arm. He'd changed into a dark tunic that matched his pants. Noticing the question I was too afraid to ask, he said, "It's been two days, Fia. I'd ask if he's okay, but it would seem it's you we should now be concerned about."

Two days.

My head spun a little faster, and I must have teetered, for Jarron steadied me. "You've lost a lot of blood. This can wait."

"It can't," I said, and just the thought of putting it off filled me with enough anxious anger to give me a renewed burst of energy. "We go now." It was late afternoon. There was no better time to catch Brolen alone.

"You're not even wearing shoes."

I waved him off. "That's not exactly unusual."

THIRTY

Fia

MOMENTS LATER, WE MATERIALIZED INTO THE HALL leading to Brolen's study.

It was locked, of course, but Jarron fixed that. Heat rippled from his hand as he turned the door handle, but he didn't allow it to melt completely. He stopped when we heard it, the fracture of the mechanisms in the lock, and we slipped silently inside.

"You're sure about this?" Jarron asked, closing the ruined door as best he could behind me.

Sickness climbed my throat. Just the scent of this room, pungent with rose oil and leather, curled my hands into fists. "Positive. He'll arrive any minute, and he won't be expected to leave for at least an hour while he pretends to be perusing and signing documents."

There were none on his long desk. The brown leather armchair behind it was made more for rest than work.

"I mean what you're about to do," Jarron said.

"Yes." I peered around the book-lined shelves at the giant maps on the wall opposite the desk. There were three—one of Gwythorn and the other two of Callula and Eldorn. "Give me five minutes with him before you return."

Jarron exhaled a curse, then inclined his head and left. The sun erased the shadows of his exit as steps sounded out in the hall.

They paused, and though my heart began a wild beating inside my chest, I roamed to the doors of the small balcony and peeled back the velvet drapes.

Ever the arrogant king who believed himself untouchable—even after all the turmoil he'd caused—Brolen chose to enter despite knowing his study had been tampered with. "I thought I scented a traitor."

I didn't turn. I continued to stare beyond the gardens to the woods, my hands clasped behind my back.

He forced the door closed, humming when it wouldn't latch. "Where's your accomplice then?"

"Do you see anyone else in the room?"

Brolen huffed. "I scent a male, and we both know you've not one crumb of magical talent, let alone the skill to melt a lock." His voice grew closer. "Was he also the one who stole you from those who tried to save you?"

Of course, he'd twist it to sound that way. I didn't take the bait. "There's no saving me," I simply said.

"It would seem we are in agreement for once."

I smiled and turned to face him, taking satisfaction from his confused frown as he watched me dare to move two steps closer to him. "You're not really afraid of the dragon, are you? In fact," I said, circling where he stood on the patch of woven carpet before his desk, "you do not even fear for your people's safety."

Brolen stiffened, even as he laughed. "Don't be absurd. What are you—"

I tutted. "No, you care for something far greater." I released a breathy laugh, then sighed. "Oh, the power those Unseelie can wield. And now, with a dragon no longer lost to bloodlust, but to his mate's every desire…"

"I always knew I gave you far too much lenience." A hand grabbed me by the throat, one of the framed maps falling with a crash to the floor as I was pushed up against the wall. "That one day I might live to regret it."

I smiled when he scowled, his face a mottled red. Then I grinned when Jarron appeared at his back.

With an already snarling Herb and Spodge.

The narlows instantly assessed the situation and decided they did not approve, their outrage growing in growled volume.

Brolen froze. His fingers slowly unclenched. Enough to help me breathe, but not enough to free me.

It didn't matter. I watched his face pale farther when I rasped, "Fear not, my dear king. I have no need of my dragon to be rid of you." My eyes moved over his shoulder to the drooling, unhappy beasts.

Meeting their beady gazes, I commanded, "Dinner time."

Brolen released me as he whirled. I snatched the crown from his head before I slipped away from the wall the narlows pinned him to with a cracking thud.

His screams were immediate and ear-shredding, but I listened to each one with a slowing heart. Jarron watched me, his hands behind his back, and I gave him a nod while I rubbed my neck. The crown was lighter than I'd expected. The sapphire thorns woven around the circlet of branch-coated silver were warm with ancient knowing.

"Enough," I said, and the narlows paused in their feasting, but they didn't stop. I winced as I glimpsed what remained of the Seelie King who'd sired me—bones and tattered meat. "No more," I growled.

The beasts growled in return but backed away when I advanced. The faceless mess slid down the wall, Spodge snarling when Herb made to swipe for more shredded flesh.

Jarron watched on impassively as if the grotesque slaughter didn't bother him.

My stomach turned. I swallowed over the acid climbing my throat, and said, "Take them home."

He dragged his eyes from the remains of Brolen. "I'll take you first."

But someone would have surely heard, and soon, the soldiers would come. I couldn't leave when I wasn't done. "I'll find my way back."

"You're still weak."

True, but the relief already invading my chest made that easy to ignore. I smiled down at the crown in my hands. "Believe me, I've rarely felt better." The times I had were courtesy of my prince, but I kept that to myself and hurried to the door.

Jarron cursed. "Just don't get yourself killed before we find a way to get you out." Then he materialized back to Eldorn at the first sound of the incoming soldiers.

Pounding boots on the stairs echoed like distant thunder, and I walked right to them, holding the crown before me like a shield. It would do nothing to save me, but I didn't need saving. I needed to place it upon the rightful head of the true ruler from the Callula line.

I met the four guards atop the stairs, three of whom I recognized.

Treyon, a friend of Regin's, shouldered past his comrades. "Fia?" He stopped upon spying the crown in my hand. "What are you doing with that?"

"Take me to my aunt."

"Hold on," Kestia said, her bright blue eyes surveying me with distrust as she climbed the stairs and headed down the hall. I waited for it, but to her credit, she merely cursed viciously before marching straight back. "He's dead," she rushed out. "The king is dead."

Treyon paled, looking at me with both horror and doubt. "You killed him?"

"Think me incapable because I don't wear a fancy weapon?"

"That was not the work of a blade," Kestia said roughly, as though trying not to retch. "Not a weapon at all."

Still watching me, Treyon said to Kestia, "Guard the princess." Then he gestured for the other two soldiers to follow him up the stairs.

I was grateful Spodge and Herb were gone, for they entered the study with their swords drawn. But they exited not a moment later with them sheathed and their stomachs threatening to empty, cursing and coughing.

Treyon was especially pale as he hurried to me and seethed, "By the fucking moon, Fia. What did you do?"

I exhaled and blinked slowly. "Just take me to Mirra."

He scoffed, incredulous, and gripped me by the arm. "She couldn't save you from execution or the Unseelie, so you know damned well she won't be able to save you from this."

I hadn't known she'd tried, though perhaps I should have. I couldn't let it distract or deter me. Unwilling to tell Treyon that I didn't wish for rescue, I kept my lips sealed tight.

I was led downstairs and straight through the grand foyer to the front courtyard, where more soldiers arrived after the belated call out. Eyes fell upon me and the crown with suspicion and confusion, my feet tripping down the steps to the drive.

Regin's father jumped from his steed, his green eyes flicking from my face to the crown in my hands. "What is the meaning of this?"

"The king," Treyon said, still gripping my arm. "I don't know how, but she killed him."

"He was no king," I said calmly. "He was a murdering opportunist who forced himself on others and planned to have his own daughter killed to garner a power balance that will never exist between the kingdoms."

Murmurs arose from the thickening crowd, but Karn merely glowered at me, evidently unmoved. I huffed, squinting up at him as the late afternoon sun caught its final fire. "But you already knew all of that, didn't you?"

His jaw flexed. "Move her to the grass."

Kestia argued, "Why? She must stand trial before the queen."

"The queen doesn't yet wear the ruling crown," barked the captain with a sneer at me. "Which was likely stolen from the king's head. So take this traitor away from the doors. We will not have her blood taint the entrance to our royal home."

Treyon hesitated, and my stomach sank with my heart when he did as commanded.

Jarron would return at any moment. He likely already had, only to discover that I'd been taken. But though I knew he would be doing all he could, I still surveyed the endless sprawl of green grass that rolled away from Callula Castle toward the river below.

My knees met the edge of the pebbled drive, and Treyon attempted to take the crown from my hands.

He glared when I wouldn't let go, tugging. "Fia, hand it over."

Thorns ripped at my fingers. He was strong, and he would get it, but I wasn't yet ready to quit.

Only when I knew he would stumble back once I released my hold on it would I let go, so I could then run and roll downhill toward the city. They would catch me—of course they would—but I had to try.

I had to buy myself time until Aunt Mirra arrived.

"For the love of the sun," Karn groaned. "Are you a male or a mouse? Someone get the fucking crown from this miscreant, miserable excuse for a princess."

Talk and shifting sounded, and above it all, a familiar voice. "Fia?"

Regin.

I turned, forcing Treyon back with my elbow, and refused to allow all Regin had done to stop me from pleading, "Find Mirra, Regin. Quickly." She wouldn't let me die, and she needed the crown before someone who couldn't be trusted decided it shouldn't be worn by her.

Regin scowled when his father placed a hand on his chest, halting him from reaching me. "She killed the king and has now seized the crown for herself," Karn told him. "We've no choice but to take her head, son."

Regin hadn't removed his eyes from me, and they widened as he forced his father's arm away with a shove. He stepped closer and crouched low beside me. "You killed him, Fi?"

I hadn't, not exactly, but I also had. So I confessed, "I might have told my narlows to eat him." I lifted a shoulder. "They did."

"Might have?" Confusion wrinkled his lowered brow. "Narlows?" His head shook. "Fia, what were you thinking..."

The sky darkened.

The sagging remnants of the sun were erased completely as a screeching roar sent many of the soldiers scrambling. Some screamed, racing for the castle. A few remained, drawing their weapons as the beast landed upon the hill beside the drive with a thunderous boom.

Grass and soil sprayed. Fire erupted from the dragon's mouth, blocking the soldiers' path to me as he released another roar and prowled uphill.

"Run," I yelled, using this unexpected visit to my advantage, and those who hadn't already did as I said. "Get out of here." Then I smiled and stood, telling a paling Regin as he slowly backed up toward the castle's doors, "I was thinking it was time for a much-needed change."

Colvin snarled at Regin, lunging forward a step and expelling a bellow of flame.

"And you should definitely go."

Regin leaped and rolled to the side, narrowly avoiding the inferno, then raced into the castle.

The flames ate at the statue of the sun goddess in the center of the drive, melting the stone and the pebbles beneath.

"Oh, my stars, Fifi," Mirra shrieked from the front steps. "You must tell it to leave."

Colvin growled at my back, the ground shaking as he stomped in warning. I looked at him and raised my hand, hoping he would wait before burning or hunting any of the archers preparing to shoot at him from the windows and parapets.

"I will," I said, hurrying to Mirra. "But first…" I rose to my toes and lifted the crown.

Her eyes widened. "Oh no, you really don't want to do—" It fell onto her head, the silver writhing and the thorns embedding. She winced and whined, blood trickling into the nest of ringlets pinned atop her head, "That."

I hugged her briefly, whispering, "Just think of all the fun you'll have."

Mirra scowled when I pulled away, reaching up gingerly as the thorns released their bonding hold on her head. I laughed, and her annoyance eased with a wriggle of her painted lips. "Troublesome princess indeed."

Then I walked across the now empty drive to my prince while Mirra told her soldiers to stand down.

Colvin watched me, his tail ruining the grass with each impatient flick. He watched me, yet he seemed all too aware of everything else, every threat. "Dragon," I said, smiling wide.

He lowered to the grass, an arrow bouncing off the scales at his back. I placed my hand upon his heated snout, then my head, and sighed. "Take me home."

I slept throughout the night and much of the next day, waking only to eat alone before falling asleep again.

The sound of running water roused me for the final time, and I rose and stretched, then reached for the fresh glass of water on the nightstand. My limbs were stiff. The warm bath awaiting me would help with that, so I stripped out of the smock on the way to the bathing room, the britches long gone.

"I feel like we've been here before." I slid into the creamy water. "But this time, I'd like you to join me."

My request was ignored.

Colvin placed the salts back on the shelf, then fetched a fresh towel and set it within reach on the corner of the tub. He licked his teeth behind closed lips, his gaze fixed upon the window, and cleared his throat. "I suppose you can now return."

Some moments washed by as I frowned up at him, and he continued to keep his eyes from me. I understood what he'd meant. Now that Brolen was gone, I could go back.

But there was no going back. Callula was no longer where I belonged, and I could now see that it never had been.

Perhaps I had misread him, and he was still upset with me. Just asking felt wrong, but I had to know. "Do you want that?"

"No," he immediately rasped, hands curling at his sides. "Never."

A relieved burst of breath left me. "Then look at me."

He did, and my heart swelled. Color had returned to his features, to his beautiful eyes, but a hesitancy lingered in the firmness of his jaw.

I wanted to erase it, to ease whatever still ailed his mind, though I knew he wouldn't come any closer until he was certain of what I wanted—of what I would do. "I don't want to be anywhere else." His throat dipped when I added tremulously, "I don't belong there, Colvin. I belong here." I reached for him. "I belong with you."

He searched my eyes, and I watched some of his turmoil slide away with his heavy exhale.

Then he stripped, and I smiled but busied myself with cleaning my body to keep from growing too excited. I should've known it wouldn't work.

He stepped into the tub, and my eyes swam over his lean legs and his muscular thighs to his hard cock and abdominals. I swallowed, and he lowered into the water with a smirk on his face, his feet sliding under my legs. "Come to me."

He reached beneath the water to grasp my waist, and I slid forward, my legs climbing over his to curl at his back. "Would you let me go?" I felt the need to ask, though I knew the answer.

"Yes," he said, surprising me, but he continued, "Then I would follow to convince you to trust what you mercifully already know and feel."

My eyes welled. Of course, he would.

For magical moments, he just watched me—the way each breath lifted my chest faster and how the touch of his eyes upon my lips made them part.

"Magnificent," he whispered, trailing a sudsy finger down my cheek. It danced over my breast, his palm flattening over my pounding heart. "This heart." His awe was soon replaced with a hardening of his every feature, his voice deepening. "But it's my heart, Fia."

I placed my hand over his. "It is."

"And you were too reckless with it." His brows lowered. "Do you have any idea how terrified I was to wake and find you weren't in bed next to me but in Callula on a mission to murder?"

Regardless of how I'd unintentionally hurt him, I'd known that he would have been worried. But I didn't want to risk having him stop me. "You needed to rest, and I had to. He wouldn't have stopped, and he should've been for his numerous crimes and wasteful existence long ago."

"You needed to rest, too. I'd all but drained you." He glowered. "You should have waited."

I smiled up at him. "Would you have helped me?"

He framed my face, brought it close to his, and murmured vehemently, "I would've made sure you never had to leave these rooms to get what you wanted."

I nodded, knowing that was true. "But then that would make you the monster they believe you to be."

"So be it," he seethed quietly.

I pressed my mouth to the corner of his. "But you're not a monster, Colvin." I took one of his hands from my cheek, curled my fingers through his, and slid even closer. So close, I could feel him hard against my stomach. "The monster has always been me."

"Fia," he breathed, visibly tensing, his hand squeezing mine.

I shook my head. "But if it means there is one less corrupt creature in this world with the audacity to try harming you, then a monster I am happy to be."

Colvin swallowed thickly, his eyes coated in a wet sheen. "I care not what you are." His hands slipped down my arms to my hips, lifting me until I aligned myself over his cock. "Just that you're here, and you're mine."

"All yours," I whispered to his mouth, and I slowly sank down to swallow him inside me with a gasped, "Husband."

Air sliced between his teeth. He groaned. "Say that again."

A breathy laugh was choked by a moan when I pressed down on him, my arms wrapping tight around his neck. "Husband." I peppered kisses over his cheek to his ear and whispered, "Forgive me for not being there."

Colvin tensed. "Fia." I kissed the corner of his eye. "Fia, look at me."

I did, and I smirked when his eyes closed briefly as my hips rocked over him. They opened with darkening fire. "I shouldn't have thought that you would've opened the book, not even for one second. That you would've helped him in any way."

"But you did, and I understand." I pressed my forehead to his, wanting to move—needing to. "It's okay."

"It's not, and I'm the one who requires forgiveness. I hurt more than your heart." He kissed my cheek, lips lingering. "Down in the springs, and I'm sorry."

"You didn't," I lied.

"Fia," he said, barely a whisper, then deeper and guttural, "I was not myself. We both know that, but that's no excuse. I fed from you when you weren't properly prepared—"

"You had to, and you just said yourself that you were in no state to cater to me." Tears gathered. I willed them to retreat and grumbled, "I don't want an apology."

A dark brow rose. "Oh?"

"But I do want a thank-you."

He laughed, the sound deep and soaked thick with heart, and I could only stare, enraptured and falling impossibly harder than I already had. There was no way out, and I didn't want one, so I let go.

I traced beneath his eyes when his cheeks and lips lowered and whispered, "You have captured my heart too thoroughly, dragon."

"Then all is now fair." He took my fingers and brushed his lips over my knuckles. "Your heart is safe with me, fire-breather."

I knew it was, so I squashed his lips playfully with mine, my breasts to his chest, and he groaned, fingers crawling up my ribs to join his other hand at my back.

Then I kissed him with a newfound urgency that rushed through me with tickling wings and demanded freedom. Fear was no longer. Not because he'd made such a promise—but because I'd witnessed as much from him.

All I was and desired would always be safe with him.

His mouth moved to my chin, tipping it back while he pulled my body down upon his with a hand at my waist. His tongue flattened against my throat, but he wasn't in search of my blood. He kissed my neck, the curve of my shoulder, my chest—every place he'd ever marred with his teeth. "Tell me you love me."

Breathless, the words shook from me as my body grew taut. "I love you, Colvin."

He groaned and held me tighter, closer. "Show me." A low order I gladly obeyed.

His tongue dragged up my throat to my chin, urging my head to tilt down as I began to unravel. His nostrils flared, his arm spasming as he further tightened his hold on me and felt me seize his cock while a silent cry crept through my parting lips. "Fuck," he exhaled gruffly and unleashed inside me as soon as his mouth captured mine.

We remained that way long after our breathing had settled, content to listen to the slowing tempo of one another's hearts. "Can we just stay like this?"

His huff heated my shoulder, a finger running up the length of my spine. "Careful." He kissed my damp skin. "Or you'll never know a moment's peace."

I smiled, tucking my nose under his chin. "But you already give me that." He stilled, the beat of his heart thudding loud in my ear. "Peace. You were looking for it, but I was the one who found it."

His head turned for his mouth to skim my forehead. "I discovered far more than that."

Some minutes later, we cleaned off and left the water, and I was laid gently upon the bed.

Colvin brought a towel with him, but it was forgotten when he decided to lick every water droplet from my body instead. He started at my ankles, and while his tongue and lips worshipped my skin, his fingers roamed over my other leg. Those fingers warmed, and I gasped when I realized he'd called forth his fire to sit beneath the pads.

By the time he reached my stomach, chuckling when I laughed from the dipping of his tongue in my navel, I was starving again. Pushing my fingers into his hair, I ensured he stayed right where he was, his knees upon the ground and his torso between my legs.

He needed no more encouraging and lapped languidly at my core. Gentle fingers pried me open for his greedy gaze and feasting tongue. My thighs shook as release loomed, but he ignored the tug of my hands in his hair.

"Need you," I protested feebly, but it was too late.

A lone, thick finger entered me to toy with what remained of his own release. He curled it as his tongue flattened ever so softly over the swollen knot of tortured nerves. From my toes to my scalp, I came apart in a slow, near-painful wave.

Colvin kept my thighs spread as he cursed and watched me writhe and moan.

My eyes opened when he nudged his cock at my quivering entrance. He rubbed it over me, and then he pushed himself inside. "One more," he said. "Then you eat and sleep."

Dazed, my tongue too thick behind my teeth, I could only manage a tremulous smile.

His head lowered, inky hair dusting my cheeks. Laying his forehead upon mine, he asked with amused, hungry eyes, "Can't speak?"

I swallowed and reached for him when he rose and pushed my thighs toward the bed, his gaze upon where we'd joined. "You're still convulsing, you breathtaking creature."

"Come back," I said.

He groaned, a shiver shuddering through him and against my skin as he watched himself leave my body and then enter it again. This time, he sank as deep as he could go, and I gasped as he ground into me. "You take me so well, wife." A shaken exhale left him. "So fucking well."

"Colvin," I attempted to growl, but it sounded more like a fractured moan.

Another chuckle, this one huskier, as he finally conceded and gave his torso and mouth back to mine. I clasped his head tight, scraped my nails up his side, smiling against his lips when he cursed and began to fuck me in earnest.

We soon rolled, his hands at my hip and face, my name a

whispered murmur tingling over my tongue when it dipped into his mouth. "Fia."

I slid my lips over his, then pushed against his chest to sit up. Breath burst from my lungs as I adjusted.

He rose, too, pulling my legs behind his back and watching.

My eyes widened, and I almost cried out at the sharper, deeper angle. His large hand roamed up my back to gently grip and push at my shoulder, forcing me to take him as deep as he could get. He groaned and kissed my jaw, soaking my skin with taunting words. "You're panting, fire-breather, and swelling more around my cock by the second." He licked at my upper lip. "Feeling okay?"

The beautiful burn subsided, and I trailed my fingers over his broad shoulders, swallowing hard. "Never felt better."

He studied me beneath heavy eyelids. His lips quirked. "Never felt anything better?"

I smiled but admitted as I bumped my nose into his and captured his lips, "Never."

"And you never will," he vowed, his mouth rubbing in a whispering caress over mine. "My mother of monsters." Though we weren't really moving, I shook—so full I began to ache in a blooming, desperate rhythm. "My fire-breathing Fia." I rolled my hips to its call, but my prince stilled them and tilted my head back with a hand gathering my hair around his fist. He pressed his mouth under my chin. "You saved me after all."

"No," I rasped, his tongue licking over my chin to my mouth. I caught it as his hold on my hair loosened and sank my teeth into it, moaning when his blood bubbled and encountered my taste buds. "You saved me."

EPILOGUE

Colvin
Twelve years later…

F ATE WAS FICKLE, TO BE SURE.

But it was creatures like myself who sought it with desperate hearts who were to blame. We wanted, and so we yearned and hunted for all we desired.

And in the end, we were cursed or rewarded in ways that no amount of desire could've prepared us for.

I'd spent a large portion of my life searching for a mate, and with such desperation, I'd never stopped to think about what finding one would truly mean. I'd known about the fate-gifted connection—had witnessed the fragile yet near-unbreakable bond between others— but I'd not thought of what it would do to me outside of what I'd needed from such a bond.

I'd cared only to find the soul who could help me protect others from myself.

And I found so much more than that.

My mother's laughter rang like a chiming bell through the windows of the tea parlor. Mirra's soon joined, shrill enough to make me wince and chuckle.

Halfway Hall had been restored and rebuilt. During the reopening ceremony before the annual meeting of the courts, the two queens of Gwythorn had formed an unlikely truce and friendship.

One that involved a lot of wine and cackling laughter.

Olette would claim annoyance at the first sign of a visit from Mirra—who took it upon herself to do so frequently under the guise of duty and checking in on her niece—but I couldn't remember the last time I'd ever seen my mother smile nor laugh so much.

So we didn't comment. We let her pretend it was whatever she needed it to be. We were just glad that she'd managed to make room for a little more happiness.

Especially being that the rest of us had found plenty of our own.

Fia feigned a scowl as Cherith painted another flower upon her cheek but grinned when our daughter leaned in to place a kiss upon her nose. "Now I can call you daisy."

My heart both shrank and swelled at the memory Cherith's words brought forth from all those years ago in that dungeon. One of a young princess who'd once told me that she would have preferred to be named after a flower.

As though Cherith had triggered the same response in her, Fia looked my way. Her fingers curled into the grass on either side of her legs as she said with damp eyes, "Did you hear that, husband? I'm officially a daisy."

"I heard," I said and cleared the thickness from my voice before leaving my book upon the stump and walking over to join them. Though I liked to believe I could, I never read much when either shards of my soul were near anyway, too often happily distracted by them.

And though I still read, it was no longer in search of a remedy, but merely for enjoyment. The only remedy I'd ever need had never once left my side when I shifted, so the dragon I became never left hers. "Do you not approve of your mother's name, Cherry?" I teased.

Her violet eyes darted up to me, a glower within. "I didn't say that."

I smiled, curling her near-black locks behind her ear. "I suppose you didn't." Her expression softened at my touch, her skin silken beneath my fingers—all of her a blessing I'd never once dared to hope for. "Tell me, why a daisy?"

We weren't yet entirely certain that Cherith didn't possess the dragon gene. Although she was already six years of age and hadn't displayed any signs of being able to shift, we couldn't be sure that she wouldn't pass the ability on to her own offspring—should she choose to create any.

I had hope that her mother's Seelie bloodline had diluted things enough to keep the dragon from returning for good, all the while knowing that anything was still possible.

I hoped, and I tried to let go. To remind myself that most things were not within my control.

Even so, the fear I'd long lived with still niggled now and then. I didn't doubt that it would linger for as long as I drew breath. But that hadn't been enough to stop me from saying yes to my wife when she'd expressed her desire for a babe.

At that moment, her body curled tight over mine as the sun had risen outside of our cottage, and the call of sleep doing its utmost to lure us to part with one another, I'd been shocked wide awake. I wasn't shocked she'd want to tempt fate in such a way—my mate hadn't any qualms when it came to that—but rather by how desperately I'd wanted one, too.

"They're pretty," Cherith chirped. "Besides, saying Mother gets boring, and I'm not allowed to call her Fia."

Fia laughed at that and continued creating her long chain of wildflowers. Herb and Spodge were hunting in the woods, but they always seemed to sense when she'd finished making them, and they would come running.

A rustle in the brush some feet away from the clearing of the cottage stole my daughter's attention, the paintbrush falling from her fingers. "Gilly," she sang and lowered to her knees as the woon came bounding over the grass.

Indeed, my wife had ended up with her much-wanted woon.

But although Gilly was friendly—most of the time—she didn't like living within any type of confinement. Even after being hand-reared, she'd taken to the woods and had refused to return when it was time to retire. It had broken Fia's heart, the sight and sickening energy of her sadness sending me into the woods to find the little rodent before she'd stopped me.

But her heart was soon mended when the ball of fuzz deemed a creature made it clear she would venture back to visit.

Mostly for food.

Gilly bounced into Cherith's arms, and I helped her sit up when she was knocked to the ground. Laughing, she didn't seem to mind. Like her mother, she had a heart that softened quicker for critters than it did her own ilk.

The woon twirled in circles over Cherith's legs and jumped at her chest, but she refused to give her up when I made to collect the creature to make her settle down—however that was possible. Woons were nothing but frantic energy with razor-sharp teeth. So I'd been quietly grateful when Gilly had chosen to leave—glad to no longer fear closing my eyes to sleep because something might nip and scratch at my toes.

Fia crawled over the grass, her cream, frilled blouse gaping at the chest and offering a tempting taste of her tits.

She smirked when she caught me looking but then offered Gilly one of the dried meats she often carried in her pant pockets. Although said pants resembled them—tonight's pair was a familiar silky gold in color—I couldn't remember the last time she'd worn true skirts.

I didn't mind. So long as she didn't mind needing many of them mended due to my impatient hands.

"Gilly," cried Vance, running through the trees from the direction of my study in the castle.

The little male of only four years was an expert at escaping his father, who would inevitably need to trail his scent through the halls to find him before his mother did.

Typically, he'd be found by the goblins first, too often chased from their kitchens.

Vance skidded to his knees on the grass beside Fia, plucking the woon who was still chewing a treat and squishing her to his chest. His unruly, rust-colored curls hadn't been tied back, that or he'd pulled them loose. Gilly snuffed and grunted, wriggling to be free of his arms and hair.

Fia smiled and petted the woon, which helped Gilly settle somewhat.

Jarron materialized beside me, cursing with his rough exhale of breath. "I swear, not a moment of fucking peace this entire week."

"He sleeps," I reminded him.

He guffawed. "Barely."

My uncle and friend liked to proclaim in jest that the moon goddess had gifted him a son intent on punishing him for his crimes against his mother.

Swiping a hand over his hair, which he now kept cropped close to his scalp because he also claimed to have too little time to groom himself, Jarron trudged over to his son to pry the woon from his grasp.

Persy wandered out from the trees, her crimson hair tied in a knot atop her head. "I thought you might soon need rescuing."

Fia eyed the bowl of chopped apple Persy carried. "And what did Orin have to say about that?"

"I didn't tell you?" she said, taking a seat beside Fia and pushing Gilly off her lap with a motion to wait as she fished a piece of apple from the bowl. "We're friends now."

Fia snorted, then paused, seemingly outraged when Persy didn't laugh. "You're serious?"

"No," Persy said, smiling then hissing when the woon bit her finger.

Vance laughed, squirming free of his father's hold and climbing down his legs to take some apple for himself.

"He's not even friends with his own mate," Fia said. "So I doubt you could pay him enough to be kind to you."

"Everyone has a price, but no." Persy gave the woon another piece of apple. "I simply ignored him, as per usual."

Fia frowned at Cherith, who'd taken a seat on her lap to help her with the flower chain. "He's nice to me."

Everyone laughed, but we soon sobered when she glared at us and insisted, "He is. I made him a picture."

That was news to us, and I lowered to the grass beside Fia, stealing our daughter with a tickle of her stomach. "My sweet little liar."

Cherith giggled, squirming, but when I ceased tormenting her, she sighed and said, "It's truly true."

"What was this picture?" Fia asked with enough eagerness to suggest she'd make him one herself.

"His famous strawberry pie, of course."

Persy snorted. "Of course."

After informing me that we'd received word of the hunt arriving next week, Jarron took his wife and son back inside.

He and Persy had chosen to remain and raise Vance at the castle. Some months after Fia and I were married, the pair had agreed to try to fix the mess they'd made of their connection one last time. In doing so, they'd finally accepted the bond—and that the mistakes of the past could not accompany them into the future.

Herb and Spodge returned. Gilly ran for the trees, preferring distance from the giant beasts, and Vance once again escaped his father to run to them.

Not knowing what to do with the younglings but sensing that they were to be careful with them, the two narlows often didn't know how to act when accosted by them.

Vance ran behind Spodge, hiding from his parents between his furry legs.

"Leave him," Fia said, smiling at Spodge. "We'll bring him inside with us soon."

Jarron didn't need to be told twice and all but ran from the clearing. His wife laughed as he dragged her with him.

Herb twisted when the tiny male ran between his legs next. Vance giggled and ducked out of sight every time the beast tried to get a look at him.

Cherith laughed, and my chest warmed at the feathery melody.

Then she rose from my lap and went to join them, the bowl of apples in hand.

I pulled Fia closer, her head falling to my shoulder and my fingers twining through her hair. The stars and moon watched the younglings and the narlows play hide-and-seek amongst the trees with us, Vance wearing the bowl as a hat.

Quiet chaos, this life we'd made for ourselves, yet I'd never felt more at peace.

Even the few encounters Regin stole with my wife each year at the meeting of the courts were not enough to worry me. Oh, they certainly irritated me, but he was no longer a pest I needed to erase from my mate's mind by squashing him between my teeth. He'd fumbled his chances with her numerous times, and she had never been his to possess in the first place.

And my wife had proven far beyond words that I consumed her as much as she did me.

So I tolerated it. They'd once been close friends, and although the male didn't deserve it, Fia had eventually decided to keep that friendship, but to a far smaller extent.

Later, as dawn kissed the sky, Fia murmured to my chest, her lips like a brush of silk everywhere they trailed, "We should take Cherry with us next time we travel with the hunt." I groaned when she sank lower, her lips tickling the hair beneath my navel. "It's safe enough if we remain in Gwythorn."

We'd traveled with my grandfather a handful of times before Cherith had come along, and I knew, although more than content within these small stone walls of the cottage, that Fia was eager to explore again.

"We'll speak to Gayle when he arrives," I said through my teeth when she clasped her soft hand around me and licked at the head of my shaft.

The hunt visited the castle grounds for a week each year, bringing the best of their findings to offer Olette. Which was how Fia had first decided she wanted to journey across the realms with them.

"He'll say yes," Fia said.

I chuckled, for she was likely right. Gayle had instantly taken to my ever so curious wife.

Then I hissed when she dipped her tongue down the length of me.

With the fire crackling, Cherith asleep in the rooms she shared with Vance inside the castle, Fia's mouth took as much of me as she could with a hunger that never seemed to cease.

Not for either of us.

I let her work me into a frenzy, the gleam brightening her violet eyes and her scent letting me know I was not alone in this mindless desperation. Then I ordered, "On your hands and knees, fire-breather," and almost exploded when she tore that perfect mouth from me and did exactly as she was told.

Not only did she do what she was told, but she arched her back and swung her head to the side, her eyes aglow with impatience and anticipation.

I trailed the soft curve of her spine right down to the glorious meat of her ass, only stopping when I found her wet and wanting. My finger slipped inside with spine-tingling ease, and we both moaned as I dipped it in and out.

Slow at first, I fucked her with my forefinger until her breaths became sound and her thighs widened to meet my thrusts. Then I dunked it faster and twisted, stroking her inner flesh and teasing her clit. She drenched my hand, releasing with a croaked cry at the third gentle gloss of my thumb.

I watched her head fall and hang, her thighs and feet quiver, and then I ceased torturing her and sucked what I'd earned from my fingers.

I sucked and licked with an approving groan while guiding her onto my cock with my hand at her hip. My spine locked as her wet heat welcomed me with a tight clench.

I didn't wait. I couldn't have even tried. Our skin slapped, and Fia panted as I pounded her deep and hard from behind—as I lost myself to the inescapable, incessant need to possess her in every way possible.

It hadn't lessened. It never would.

Fia fisted the bedding, cursing, all the while circling her hips in search of more pleasure.

I gathered her hair around my hand. "Beautiful creature." I tugged, and she rose with me as I leaned back onto my haunches. "Kiss me," I rasped, then groaned when her tongue dipped into my mouth, stroking over mine with the slower rhythm of my deeper thrusts.

"Going to fill you," I warned, knowing she was close to release. A grunted moan was torn from me when she pulled away to return to her hands and knees, and she reached climax again. Sliding on and off my cock, she milked me, making sure I followed with a rumbled bout of curses.

I shook so hard that I was unable to act quick enough to stop her when she unsheathed me to lay upon the bed. Then I grinned.

On her back, my heart and soul spread her legs for my eyes to feast.

"I've finally found you out, fire-breather." My chest heaved, but she evidently knew I was far from done.

Fia expelled a breathy, "Oh?"

Crawling closer, I toyed with my seed. Her thighs twitched as I stroked her swollen cunt, and a tiny mewl left her. "You cured me of one curse by giving me another."

Her laughter was rasped. "Is that so, dragon?"

"You've rendered me eternally insatiable," I said thickly and pushed her thighs wide. For it was always this way. Every evening or day—whenever we had time away from our daughter.

"Then we are still well matched indeed."

"We always will be." I pulled her over my thighs to impale her on my cock. She whimpered, the sensations too much but never so much that she would allow me to stop. "My greedy wife."

I rolled my neck. My blood roared louder by the second as I

eased her on and off me, as I watched her swallow me inside her drenched body, her hands gripping for purchase in the bedding.

When she began to shake, I pulled her up. I held her with an arm at her upper back and neck, my tongue lapping at her tits as I tilted my hips to make her break again. She unraveled in my arms, and I'd never seen or felt anything so fucking magical in my life.

Her moans grew louder. Her moon-washed hair clung to her sweat-misted skin. Her cunt squeezed harder when my teeth punctured her neck, and I drank her down like the elixir she was.

This mate of mine was not merely a cure, but pure poison.

One I'd not only hunted for but welcomed with relish into every facet of my life, every vein of my body. I'd never get enough, and if that was my punishment for taking her, for making her endlessly mine, then so be it.

I'd continue to be thankful when I woke starving anew each evening.

I laid her down upon the bed and licked at the blood still pooling above her clavicle, my thrusts slowing, deepening. "Had enough yet?"

A croaked, "Never," earned her a sharp rock of my hips, and she moaned. "I fear I'm incapable of such a thing, which sometimes worries me."

At that, all of me seized, and not in a good way. I lifted my head to stare down at her.

Fia smiled. Shifting some of my hair, of which she refused to let me cut, behind my ear, she traced my mouth. "A love like this cannot be normal, and you know it. No matter the connection."

I couldn't say she was wrong. We both knew of mated pairs who desired time alone, and some who had even separated and found other lovers.

Though the mere thought of not seeing Fia at least once an evening was not one I could entertain at all. It sickened me to so much as imagine it. "Then we are not normal," I said too gruffly. "And I do not want to be."

Fia stroked my cheek. "You're upset."

My nostrils twitched with a harsh exhale. "I will admit to feeling a little fucking anxious."

"There's no need to be. I just thought it might have lessened." A smile sparked in her eyes. "The intensity," she murmured. "After all this time."

I relaxed, but only as much as one could with a cock throbbing for movement inside his obsession's body. "What's wrong with the intensity?"

"Nothing," Fia whispered, her mouth rubbing at the corner of mine. "Everything." Her hands trailed down my back, and I shivered. "You are the breath in my chest, the reason for every changing beat of my heart."

I nudged my nose against hers, my own heart swelling. "I love you, too."

"This is not merely love, Colvin."

"Then please," I taunted. "Do tell me what it is."

But she didn't smile as I'd intended. Claiming each side of my face, she pulled my forehead to hers. "It's life or death. My existence is tied to yours, which is a very dangerous thing indeed, husband."

My exhale left me in a searing rush. I pressed my mouth to hers and whispered, "Then there's really only one thing for us to do."

"And what would that be?" she teased, though she already knew.

"To continue in this unquenchable surrender."

Her eyes immediately welled, and the sight was a knife to my heart.

I kissed her lashes, her nose and her mouth, then slid my arms underneath her. Slowly, I began to move inside her. With every touch of my mouth to her cheeks, her jaw, her neck, and her lips, I told her I loved her. That I was just fine with eternally yearning for her.

And that I would never wish to stop.

Fia twined her fingers in my hair, the arm at my shoulders curling tight. "Until every star burns out."

My lips grazed hers as I vowed, "And the moon ceases to hunt the sun."

ALSO BY
ELLA FIELDS

FANTASY ROMANCE:
A King So Cold
The Stray Prince
The Savage and the Swan

STANDALONES:
The Grump Who Stole Summer
Bloodstained Beauty
Serenading Heartbreak
Frayed Silk
Cyanide
Corrode
Evil Love

GRAY SPRINGS UNIVERSITY:
Suddenly Forbidden
Bittersweet Always
Pretty Venom

MAGNOLIA COVE:
Kiss and Break Up
Forever and Never
Hearts and Thorns

NEVER MISS A THING!

Follow on Instagram
www.instagram.com/ellafieldsauthor

Website
www.ellafields.net

Made in United States
Troutdale, OR
12/14/2023

15843066R00202